Sarah Bailey is a Melbourne-based writer with a background in advertising and communications. She has two children and is currently the Managing Director of advertising agency VMLY&R in Melbourne. Her internationally award-winning Gemma Woodstock trilogy includes *The Dark Lake*, published in 2017 and winner of the Ned Kelly Award for Best First Fiction and the Davitt Award for Best Debut, followed by *Into the Night* in 2018, and *Where the Dead Go* in 2019.

PRAISE FOR

THE HOUSEMATE

'With *The Housemate*, Sarah Bailey expertly plays with memory, guilt and grief to build a tension-filled, vivid world, where there are many ways to be haunted by the ghosts of our past. You'll be right there with the fascinating, flawed Oli Groves as her professional investigation of the Housemate Homicide increasingly veers toward personal obsession. Each new twist in the story skilfully balances bombshell revelations and believability, in a crime that feels achingly familiar, yet shocking at the same time. Much like Oli, I couldn't stop until I knew the truth, too.'

Jacqueline Bublitz, author of *Before You Knew My Name*

'The plot is brilliant, the pace is relentless . . . Oli Groves is a brilliant protagonist: brave and fragile, kick-arse and compassionate—and so very human. *The Housemate* is a book of great emotional power and depth—Bailey's best yet.'

Chris Hammer, author of *Scrublands*, *Silver* and *Trust*

'An enormously immersive story with Bailey's trademark gordian knot plotting, true to life characters and twists galore. This is Australian crime at its best and *The Housemate* is destined to summit the bestseller charts.'

J.P. Pomare, author of *Call Me Evie* and *The Last Guests*

'I'm as obsessed with Bailey's protagonist, Oli Groves, as Groves is with the story she is chasing. Clever, ambitious, prickly: she's the perfect journo to lead us through this clever and ambitious thriller. Loved the deep dive into the rotten underworld of secrets and corruption, and Bailey's wry take on the changing face of journalism. *The Housemate* is addictive reading in the very best of ways. Sarah Bailey knows her stuff.'

Kate Mildenhall, author of *The Mother Fault*

PRAISE FOR

WHERE THE DEAD GO

'Sarah Bailey has excelled herself . . . a well-written and exciting crime novel that builds to a taut and bloody conclusion.'

Canberra Weekly

'As riveting as the previous two, with a multilayered plot, compelling characters and vivid atmosphere . . . another addictive read from Bailey.'

Good Reading

'A tense, gripping end to a highly praised trilogy.'

Who

'Bailey always writes a killer thriller, and this is gritty and real.'

Readings

'[Gemma] is a well-rounded character, relatable in her frustrations and insecurities at work and at home but also an exemplar of the type of kickass female detective that Australian crime fiction writers are adept at creating.'

The Age

'A must-read for crime lovers.'

Better Homes and Gardens

'Next level crime fiction . . . police procedural at its finest . . . *Where the Dead Go* is compelling reading. Gritty, realistic, atmospheric and chilling. An absolute cracker of a read that I can't even begin to recommend highly enough.'

Theresa Smith Writes

PRAISE FOR

INTO THE NIGHT

'Melbourne's wintry streets come alive on the pages, keeping the dramatic tension high . . . Bailey's writing has grown stronger and more assured in this novel.'

Good Reading

'With its deft exploration of the intersection of public and private lives and a chance to peer more deeply into the mind and heart set of an engagingly flawed heroine, *Into the Night* seems set to be just as successful as *The Dark Lake*.'

Sydney Morning Herald

'*Into the Night* is a solid procedural, full of constant twists and reveals that keep the investigation fresh . . . with this expansion of her world, it feels like Gemma Woodstock might be with us for a while.'

Australian Crime Fiction

'Bailey's writing is stronger than ever, and the prickliness of her characters is a natural fit for the jarring confines of Melbourne's central business district . . . a bristling police procedural for fans of Emma Viskic and J.M. Green.'

Books + Publishing

'Every bit as addictive and suspenseful as *The Dark Lake* . . . Sarah Bailey's writing is both keenly insightful and wholly engrossing, weaving intriguing and multi-layered plots combined with complicated and compelling characters.'

The Booktopian

'Bailey's writing is sharp, her sense of place harrowing, and her mystery intriguing. A great read for anyone who likes complex characters and gritty crime.'

Glam Adelaide

PRAISE FOR

THE DARK LAKE

'*The Dark Lake* is a thrilling psychological police procedural as well as a leap into the mind of a woman engulfed with guilt.'

New York Journal of Books

'*The Dark Lake* hooked me from page one! Sarah Bailey combines the very best elements in this stunning debut thriller—a troubled detective still trying to find her way as a female investigator, a small town haunted by secrets both past and present, and a beautiful victim whose unsettling allure appears to be her biggest asset and largest downfall. With clever twists and all-too-human characters, this book will keep you racing toward the end.'

Lisa Gardner, #1 *New York Times* bestselling author of *Right Behind You* and *Find Her*

'This polished debut is a winner from the first page.'

Daily Telegraph

'I read *The Dark Lake* in one sitting, it's that good. A crime thriller that seizes you from the first page and slowly draws you into a web of deception and long buried secrets. Beautifully written, compulsively readable, and highly recommended.'

Douglas Preston, #1 *New York Times* bestselling author of *The Lost City of the Monkey God* and co-author of the bestselling Pendergast series

'Debut author Sarah Bailey depicts both the landscape and Gemma's state of mind vividly, bringing into focus the intensity of Gemma's physical and emotional pain and her increasing discontent. *The Dark Lake* adds to the trend of haunting, rural Australian crime fiction, and provides a welcome addition to the genre for those left bereft after finishing Jane Harper's *The Dry*.'

Books + Publishing

THE HOUSEMATE

THREE HOUSEMATES.
ONE DEAD. ONE MISSING.
AND ONE ACCUSED OF MURDER.

SARAH BAILEY

Srishti
Publishers & Distributors

Srishti Publishers & Distributors
A unit of AJR Publishing LLP
212A, Peacock Lane
Shahpur Jat, New Delhi – 110 049

editorial@srishtipublishers.com

First published in India by
Srishti Publishers & Distributors in 2023

First published by Allen & Unwin in
Australia and New Zealand in 2021

10 9 8 7 6 5 4 3 2 1

Printed and bound in India

For Sale in the Indian Subcontinent Only

FOR MY FRIENDS

(LUCKY ME)

SATURDAY, 3 OCTOBER 2005, EARLY

Through the dust and faded bird shit on the windscreen of her Mazda, Oli Groves watches the cops huddled next to the letterbox of 28 Paradise Street, St Kilda. The cop who just yelled at her, the bow-legged beanpole with the constellation of freckles and the permanent smirk, is talking animatedly and pointing a finger aggressively toward the house. His hot breath forms comical white clouds, but the faces of his colleagues remain solemn.

'Piss off!' he snapped when he encountered Oli standing on the bottom step of the porch, peering into the front door of the house.

Oli's pulse is racing, though she's not sure whether that's from his reprimand or the MDMA still coursing through her system. Before Beanpole blocked her view, she saw into the dark hallway: furniture on its side, the glint of glass on the worn floorboards. The curve of a female body lying there naked, a gaping wound in her abdomen. Half-open eyes staring blankly at the wall.

Oli squeezes her own eyes shut, then blinks a few times. Shakes her head and sniffs, adjusting the rear-view mirror to check her hastily applied make-up. With her fingers, she combs her long blonde hair, knotty with stale hairspray. The image of the dead body is fixed in her mind. *C'mon, c'mon. Keep it together, Oli. Clearly Jo was desperate, or she wouldn't have called you. She must know this is going to be big. What if it's a proper story, and you get to file it?*

Oli's gaze shifts to the police tape that Beanpole tied firmly to the wooden fence post after their exchange, before looking along the path, up the short flight of brick stairs to the concrete porch and open front door. The house itself appears innocent enough, though perhaps a tad neglected. The white weatherboards have a skirt of dirt, and the tiled roof is covered in lichen. The patchy lawn has been recently mowed, but the garden beds are thick with weeds. To the left of the front door sits a pair of terracotta pots with brightly coloured flowers spilling out in cheery puddles. A rainbow dreamcatcher dangles behind the glass of what Oli assumes is a bedroom window.

Movement draws her eyes back to the front door. Chief Inspector Gregory Bowman emerges from the house dressed in full scrubs, a young woman next to him. Oli gasps. The woman is covered in blood. A police-issue blanket hangs across her shoulders, her light brown hair is limp and her feet are encased in crime-scene booties. She's crying, tears smearing the blood on her cheeks. Bowman gestures for her to move along the porch where she is shielded by a hedge wall.

He speaks briefly to a woman who covers the speaker of her mobile phone to listen, their heads bent close. Bowman looks much older in real life than he does on TV; deep lines tunnel across his forehead, and his unusually thick hair has almost finished its transformation from dirty silver to crisp snow.

A trio of plain-clothes detectives arrive, all men. They duck under the police tape and march purposefully up the path, ignoring the cops—including, Oli notes with satisfaction, an eager-faced

Beanpole. There's no sign of Isabelle Yardley, and Oli's skin crawls with relief and a strange desire to sate her curiosity, to tug at a loose thread. To tempt fate.

It's bloody freezing. Her heart thumps as she rubs her hands together and cranks up both the heater and the radio. She begins to make notes in her book as the blood-soaked body flashes back into her mind. The ABC news bulletin reports that police have been called to a residence in St Kilda regarding the discovery of a body, but relays nothing more than Oli already knows.

More cops turn up and congregate on the lawn. It starts to drizzle and the muck on her windscreen morphs into ugly brown streaks. Oli's vision begins to blur just as a large hand raps sharply on the driver's window. She jerks in fright, throwing her weight against the car seat.

Then she winds down the window and thrusts her middle finger into Rob's laughing face.

'Want to get in?' Her deep voice is even huskier than usual.

'Nah, I'm good.' He squints at the house. He's wearing a T-shirt and jeans, and goose bumps prickle Oli's limbs. 'I can't believe Queen Jo isn't here.' Rob lights a cigarette. 'She loves a dead body.'

'She's at a wedding in the country.'

'How odd to think she has friends. But, hey, maybe you'll finally get a by-line.'

'Maybe.' Oli tips her head backwards trying to focus. 'I saw the body. It's lying in the hallway.'

Rob looks impressed. 'Excellent. I really hate getting out of bed this early just for grievous bodily harm.'

'And there's a girl on the porch behind the hedge, with blood all over her.'

Rob whistles. 'Ten bucks says they're prostitutes.'

'I don't have ten bucks. I'm broke till payday.'

'You can owe me.'

She rolls her eyes. 'Jo wants a hero shot of Bowman and whoever else ends up leading this thing.'

'Her wish is my pain in the arse.' Rob blows a smoke ring skyward.

Oli stares at a black stain on the sun visor, trying to work out what it could be.

Rob grins. 'Late night?'

'Not really.' She shimmies in the seat as she attempts to retrieve a tube of lip balm from her back pocket.

He laughs. 'That's not what your party-girl eyes tell me.'

'Whatever.' She smears the balm on her lips and pushes the visor against the ceiling. A wave of anxiety crashes over her. 'Jo should have sent TJ. No one's going to tell me anything.'

'Not with that attitude,' Rob agrees, yanking open her car door and winding up the window. 'Come on, we may as well get some mood pics while we wait for the gory details.'

A black Land Rover pulls up on the other side of the street. Melissa Warren from the *Herald Sun* is at the wheel, her dark bob hugging her sharp jawline. Rob pauses to photograph two people from the forensic unit coming out of the house, and Oli almost runs up the back of him.

The day seems reluctant to get started; the sky remains a murky grey, while the light rain has turned to a fine mist. Oli tucks her notebook inside her jacket, wedging it under her arm.

It's 6.39 am. Less than an hour since Jo first called, barking orders as Oli paid the taxi driver and fumbled for her keys in the badly lit entrance to her apartment block. She didn't even shower, just swapped her heels and dress for one of her sister's clean shirts and a pair of suit pants on the clotheshorse, spritzed perfume on her wrists and brushed her teeth. Now her tongue stings from the boiling coffee she bought at the McDonald's drive-through, and she can still taste the Bacon & Egg McMuffin she wolfed down. An alarming clamminess is creeping across her body, her hangover threatening to take hold.

Melissa Warren sidles up next to them, looking at Oli with undisguised contempt before casting her eyes skyward as if the gloomy weather is a personal insult. She brushes invisible lint from her tailored jacket and asks, 'Where's Jo?'

Oli squares her shoulders. 'Out of town.'

'Shame.' Melissa looks pleased. 'This is a juicy one.'

'How so?' Rob cracks his gum and appears bored.

'Well . . . Bowman was first on the scene, so it must be meaty, though of course the cops can hardly afford to dillydally at the moment.' Melissa lists the recent unsolved homicides, ticking them off on her manicured fingers. She clearly delights in holding court, and Oli finds her overt confidence both grotesque and magnetic.

Oli's entire cadetship has been a parade of people like Melissa, who sashay through life with an easy smile and answers at the ready. Oli hopes this characteristic will magically bestow itself upon her at some point—or that at the very least, she will get better at faking it.

'And,' Melissa adds, 'a female killer always has the public gagging.' She walks ahead, heels tapping assertively on the cracked path. 'Good luck, kids!' she calls over her shoulder.

'Reckons she's a bloody TV anchor,' Rob mutters, flaring his nostrils. 'Pity about her face.'

Oli gives him a look, even though she's certainly not about to defend Melissa.

More journalists arrive, their faces alive with the prospect of murder, walking briskly down the wide street flanked by scruffy cameramen. In stark contrast, neighbours emerge from nearby houses looking bewildered. A young couple watch the detectives on the lawn from the front yard of the house next door. Their toddler son, clad in a woollen jumper, nappy and gumboots, smacks a plastic spade against an upturned bucket. Four elderly ladies, one in a peach dressing-gown, stand in a huddle on their front porch, whispering to each other. A bald man with a neck tattoo rocks back and forth on his heels while holding a bored-looking tabby, and a middle-aged couple in gym gear are trying to wrangle three fluffy white dogs.

Words start to arrange themselves in Oli's mind. *Last night a house on Paradise Street, St Kilda, was the scene of a terrible tragedy. Neighbours were shocked to discover that a young woman had been killed, her body found in the early hours of Saturday morning . . .*

The noise punch of a backfiring car jerks Oli's thoughts to the present.

'Bowman's up.' Rob gestures to the house.

Her nerves skyrocket again. 'Right.'

'Hold this.' He hands her his camera and reties his straggly hair into a loose knot at the nape of his neck. 'What time do you need to file?'

'Jo said she wants something to review by nine.'

He takes the camera back. 'You'll be fine. And, bonus, it's stopped raining so I'll get some decent pics.'

Oli smiles at him gratefully and joins the throng of journos clambering to get to Bowman. Familiar faces jostle around her, sickly sweet perfume mixing with warm coffee breath. Phones ping with texts. The sun breaks through the clouds, and Oli squints, pen poised as questions rumble around her. 'Who lives at the property?' she calls out, adding to the chorus.

'Quiet, please.' Bowman's rich baritone demands attention. He pauses and looks slowly from left to right, a tired old cattle dog ready to round up the sheep. 'I'm going to make a brief statement about the circumstances we are dealing with here this morning, but there is minimal information at present, so I expect we'll hold a formal press conference at a later time. I won't be answering any questions this morning, understood?'

The mob nods, disappointed.

'A young woman is deceased, and we are treating her death as suspicious.' Bowman's tar-thick voice catches pleasantly on the tails of certain words.

Through the hedge, Oli glimpses the blood-stained woman wrapped in the police blanket.

A shiny blue Ford pulls up behind Oli's Mazda, blocking the end of a driveway. Detective Sergeant Isabelle Yardley emerges. Oli immediately finds it close to impossible to focus on what Bowman is saying. Her eyes are glued to Isabelle.

'We understand that the victim lived at the property with two other people.' Bowman pauses, acknowledging Yardley with a nod. 'They will both be questioned, but we believe a number of people were at the property last night, and we will be speaking to those individuals as soon as possible.'

Yardley ducks under the chequered tape and sails up the driveway. Her charcoal suit clings to her petite frame, and the fat curl at the end of her ponytail swings like a pendulum. She steps onto the front porch and turns, her laser-like stare landing on Oli.

Bowman's voice fades into a hum as Oli's legs wobble. Her heartbeat echoes in her head. Yardley refuses to break the stare, her face devoid of emotion. The emerging sunshine does nothing to quell the chattering of Oli's teeth. *Does she know? She must know. No, you're being paranoid. He would have told you.*

Oli's senses go into overdrive. Memories flood her system, and she feels both intense dread and the heady bliss of last night. She's acutely aware that Isabelle Yardley has the power to ruin it all, and that the loss would cripple her. For a horrible second, she thinks she'll be sick. She shudders through a deep anchoring breath.

'I'm not yet prepared to discuss how the young woman died,' Bowman says, 'but I can confirm that the scene in the house is quite confronting and we'll be allocating significant resources to get to the bottom of what happened as soon as possible.'

Bowman folds his arms, indicating he is finished. The media mob stirs and shouts questions again.

Yardley pauses briefly to speak to the other detectives on the front porch before stepping into a set of scrubs and disappearing into the house. Oli exhales.

A desperate screech cuts through the frenetic buzz. 'Get your hands off me!'

Heads whip around and cameras home in on an overweight, crying woman who is stumbling up the street. She tries to pull away from a man who's running after her and tugging on her handbag. Finally she breaks free and runs into the crime-scene tape, which slingshots her backwards. She crumples into a messy heap, hands pressed to the concrete path. 'My baby,' she cries, sobbing. 'Evelyn, no.'

The man shuffles over and squats next to the woman, placing his hands awkwardly on her shoulders.

'This is your fault,' she screams at him. '*Your fault!*' Still sobbing, she claws at his fingers and dislodges his grip.

Yardley reappears on the porch, where she zips open her scrubs and steps elegantly out of the white material. Her face is firm but her gaze sympathetic as she surveys the screaming woman and makes her way across the lawn.

Looking stricken, the young woman in the blanket emerges from behind the hedge. Several journalists gasp at the blood covering her face and hands.

Yardley pauses, glancing back and forth from the porch to the street.

'Alex!' The older woman scrambles to her feet, her eyes blazing. 'What happened? Where's Evelyn?'

Alex sinks to her knees, sobbing. 'I'm so sorry.' The blanket slips off her shoulders to reveal a pale-blue jumper stained with blood. 'I'm just so sorry.'

MYSTERY SURROUNDS HOUSEMATE HOMICIDE

Sunday, 4 October 2005

By Joanne Cardellini with Oli Groves

Mystery surrounds the death of a young Melbourne woman whose body was discovered in her St Kilda rental property in the early hours of Saturday morning. Homicide detectives say Evelyn Stanley, 21, was murdered in the house on Paradise Street. The cause of her death has not been confirmed.

Stanley, a University of Melbourne undergraduate arts student and aspiring actress, rented the property with two other women. Nicole Horrowitz, also 21, has not been seen since Friday evening. Police are appealing for anyone with information about the missing woman to come forward. It is believed a third housemate, 20-year-old Alexandra Riboni, called for an ambulance at around 3.30 am, though it's unknown if Ms Stanley was alive at the time. Ms Riboni was taken into custody yesterday morning, following a dramatic confrontation with Ms Stanley's parents, and continues to be questioned by police. Ms Riboni's partner, Melbourne University honours student Miles Wu, was a frequent visitor to the house and is also believed to be assisting police with their inquiries.

Neighbours have confirmed that the three women hosted a party at the St Kilda property on Friday evening and claim to have overheard several heated arguments in the backyard earlier in the night. Friends of the housemates say that tensions had been brewing between them for weeks, with one argument leading to a vehicle being vandalised with paint. It is understood that Ms Stanley's personal computer has been seized, along with other items from the house, including illegal drugs and a potential weapon.

Homicide detective Isabelle Yardley is leading the investigation and confirmed that she and her colleagues are in the process of interviewing everyone who was at the property on Friday evening, a group that allegedly includes a University of Melbourne professor. During a press conference on Saturday afternoon, DS Yardley said, 'A young woman is dead after what should have been a fun night with her friends, and another is missing. If anyone has any information pertinent to the case, we urge them to come forward.'

Ms Stanley's murder adds to the pressure that the Melbourne Homicide Squad is facing due to several unsolved cases, including the whereabouts of toddler Louise Carter, abducted from the bedroom of her Malvern home in June, and the murders of two prostitutes, brutally assaulted and dumped in St Kilda parkland two weeks ago.

CHAPTER ONE

TUESDAY, 8 SEPTEMBER 2015

THE SCREAM IS SHARP AND CLOSE. OLI IS DREAMING, A COMPLICATED narrative that is partly about a story she is working on, partly about hiding in her childhood bedroom. She can't summon a word she needs for the article. She's terrified she will just blurt it out when it comes to her but she doesn't want to be found. *Please don't let him find me,* she begs, clutching her sister as the scream reaches her ears and dismantles the dream. The scene twists and blurs into a messy whirlpool, then disappears. She blinks, confused, as her gaze settles on the dark bedroom. It's hot, her singlet and underpants sticking to her skin, and her long hair is damp with sweat. Dean has left the heater on again. Her heart thrums, and her fingers go to her wrist, the old childhood routine so ingrained it's become instinct. She counts to the beat of her pulse. *One, two, three, four. It's okay, just breathe.* She presses her fingers more firmly into her flesh. Feels calmer. *One, two, three, four.*

Shadows jostle across the white walls: it's still windy outside. She scans the closed wardrobe doors, the distinctive shape of the Eames chair near the window, the silhouette of the lamp in the corner.

Dean's breathing is steady and even, his mouth slightly open. One muscular arm hugs his stomach, the other reaches toward the bedhead. She watches him for a few moments, marvelling at the symmetry of his face. She's still not used to waking up next to him every day; a part of her refuses to believe it's real.

Another cry. *Amy.*

Oli pushes back the sheets and slips out of bed. Dean murmurs but doesn't wake; he rarely does. She stumbles on a shoe as she rounds the bed and steps into the hallway. Her fingers grope for the light switch. The empty corridor glows like a catwalk.

A strangled sob—not quite a cry this time, but still unnerving.

'Amy?' Oli's voice is shaky as it threads through the air.

There's no reply, and she's tempted to go back to bed—it's just past three, and she has to be in the office by eight. She pauses near the top of the staircase and grips the wooden rail, momentarily anxious she will fall into the dark abyss.

Her eyes follow the second hand of the grandfather clock illuminated in the moonlight. *If the second hand reaches the seven before Amy cries again, it means I won't be made redundant before Christmas. Dean won't be injured in a horrible accident.* She holds her breath as the black hand ticks on to the seven then proceeds to the eight. *Stop it,* she admonishes herself, *don't do that.*

She hears, no, *senses* movement in the house as she pads down the hallway past the cluster of framed photographs in between the two bedrooms. Her mind has transitioned fully from the dream and is now working its way steadily through the day ahead. It's clear she won't be getting any more sleep tonight.

The wooden sign hangs at eye level on the bedroom door: *Amy* in cursive font. Oli always feels funny about shutting their doors at night, locking two little girls in their princess cells, but Dean insists on it.

Oli places one hand on the door, the other on the handle. Turns and pushes. A line of light cuts across the creamy carpet. Gauzy curtains ripple in the breeze like a woman's long skirt. She falters. Did Dean leave the window open?

Her eyes go to the bed. Empty.

She steps forward, looking left then right and peering into the dark corners. Her legs weaken slightly. There's Amy.

But the relief is short-lived, goose pimples rising on the bare stretches of her limbs. Amy stares back at her from the mirror positioned on the dresser. She's sitting on the reupholstered piano stool. Dark hair swishes across the waistband of her lacy pyjama shorts.

'Amy?'

The little girl blinks. Once. Twice. Her lips begin moving, but there's no sound.

'Amy,' Oli repeats, walking across the room, 'come on, honey, you need to get back to bed.' She gently places a hand on Amy's shoulder. 'This way.'

The girl's skin is damp, her limbs obedient. She allows herself to be pulled upright and guided to bed. Oli pushes back the sheets and eases her in, smoothing the covers across her small frame.

Oli closes the window, locks it. Pulls the curtain across the glass. She watches Amy for a moment, then goes to her, thinking, as she often does, that those thick dark brows are jarring on such a young face. So *severe*.

'Go to sleep, Amy,' Oli whispers authoritatively, using her fingers to close the girl's left eye, which was still half open. Oli stares at Amy's sleeping face then pulls away, rubbing her eyes with her knuckles.

'Mummy.'

It's so faint that Oli wonders if she imagined it. She doesn't move. Doesn't blink.

Amy's breathing becomes as even as the tick of a clock. Adrenaline twitches through Oli's limbs as she backs away from the bed. Amy won't remember this; she never does.

Oli dashes along the hall, imaginary beasts biting at her heels. Dean is in the same position, his large feet exposed at the end of the bed. On the bedside table the clock ticks over to 3.27. Oli feels her way through a mound of clothes on the floor and pulls on one of Dean's sweatshirts. She plucks her pyjama pants from the end of the bed and collects her work satchel from the chair. As she heads downstairs, she avoids the second step, the only creaky one. Reaching the bottom, she quickly turns off the ground-floor security system and rushes through the silent dining room, her bare feet gliding across the floorboards, the shadowy furniture reminding her of an abandoned carnival. In the kitchen she flicks on all the lights and the kettle. The water boils as the wind rages outside, muted by the double-glazed windows.

She carries her tea into the lounge, her satchel bumping against her thigh. She feels a familiar frisson of energy, her fingers tingling with a desire to start typing. Laptop open, notes nearby and the steaming mug balanced on the armrest, she tries to forget about Amy, tries to forget about everything except her work.

Detective Isabelle Yardley watches from the mantelpiece as Oli starts to write.

CHAPTER TWO

THE WIND HAS DROPPED, AND TENTATIVE SUNLIGHT CREEPS INTO the kitchen. It's a huge room, easily as big as Oli's former apartment, with large glass doors running the length of the back wall, showcasing the tall fruit trees that border the neat backyard. Wisteria drips lilac from the eaves, and the blossom on the trees has the entire garden buzzing with insects. Appliances gleam from their positions around the room, an island bench cutting diagonally across the centre of the space, its waterfall of marble flowing into the bone-white tiles.

Dean's house is nestled in the heart of Camberwell, where the streets are wide grand affairs lined with spreading plane trees and manicured nature strips. The houses are not unlike their owners: classic structures that have been given new life with a few layers of paint or, more often than not, comprehensive renovations.

Despite the relative proximity, it feels like a world away from Oli's old place in Brunswick.

Amy and Kate sit at the round table in the corner, their chatter mixing with the rich timbre of Channel Nine's morning news anchor from the TV that hangs on the far wall.

'Shhhhh, girls.' Oli cranes her neck around the vase of white tulips on the bench.

The twins ignore her, so she finds the remote and turns up the volume, trying to piece together the story with what she can see of the news package while she adds chopped fruit and kale to the yoghurt in the blender. She gives up on listening and starts the blender, the deep buzz blocking out the girls' babble. On the TV, a female reporter is standing outside the Melbourne Town Hall. Oli turns off the blender and pours the green liquid into two glasses.

'Yes, that's right,' the reporter is saying, 'today we'll find out whether former Premier John O'Brien will face criminal charges in regard to the allegations made against him, which include awarding significant government contracts to associates, the sexual assault of two staff members, and threatening a junior staff member with violence and reputational damage as a means of coercing him into illegal activity.'

The news cuts to an edited sequence of the former premier in happier times, shaking hands and drinking beer at a charity event. His bald, slightly peanut-shaped head used to seem endearing to Oli, giving him a slightly goofy vibe, but she has now seen enough of him off camera and under pressure to know his temperament is anything but friendly.

The footage cuts back to the studio where an image is superimposed behind the anchor's left shoulder, a generic hospital scene with the words DANGEROUS DOCTORS layered over the top. 'At this stage it's unknown if . . .'

If what? Oli thinks, as Kate makes a strange shriek.

Sighing, Oli pops a blueberry in her mouth and carries the girls' scrambled eggs to the table.

Amy and Kate's thin frames are swamped by their stiff navy blazers. Their school logo is embroidered on the pockets with gold and red thread, their hair pulled back in neat ponytails. Their perfect ivory skin is plump and impossibly smooth. Oli finds it almost impossible to tell them apart, the only discrepancy the small mole on Kate's left cheek.

They are the spitting image of their dead mother.

'Eggs again,' moans Kate, as Amy ducks her head and bites directly into the yellow mound.

'Use your fork,' Oli says, just as Dean enters the kitchen. His hair is still wet from the shower, and he's wearing her favourite of his shirts, pale blue with a faint flicker of cobalt woven through the material. Just for a moment, she lets herself imagine that they're living together in her old apartment, cooking breakfast in the pokey kitchen after waking up in the sun-drenched loft. But it's a fantasy from ten years ago, before Kate and Amy were born. When everything was a million times more complicated and somehow so much simpler.

'Morning, my ladies!' Dean plants a kiss on each of the girls' foreheads, then on Oli's. His aftershave causes a pleasant wave of déjà vu to ripple through her.

She hands him the smoothie and drinks some of her own, blanching at the taste like she always does.

'You've really nailed this now, babe, it's perfect.' He looks at his half-empty glass with wonder.

'Thanks! There're eggs too if you want some. I need to jump in the shower. I've got to get going.'

Dean looks guilty as she hands him a plate. 'I was hoping you'd take the girls today. Some of the info we prepped last night has fallen through, and the press conference is at nine.'

Dean runs a PR firm that represents several high-profile individuals and organisations. He used to work in communications at the premier's office but now makes a lot more money running his own show.

'I don't think I can,' replies Oli, her short but peaceful commute evaporating before her eyes. 'I've got to file a piece by midday, and I might need to jump in and help TJ on the O'Brien coverage.'

A tiny crease forms between Dean's brows as he serves himself eggs on toast. 'Shit.' He closes his eyes.

Amy looks delighted. 'Daddy! You're not supposed to say that.'

'Surely a pro like TJ will be fine without you?' The slightest hint of irritation has crept into Dean's voice, and Oli reminds herself of her promise to make more of an effort with the girls.

'It's okay, I can do it. I've been up for hours and got a lot of my piece done already. And you're right, TJ will be fine. But I'll need to drop them early—I can't miss the editorial meeting or Dawn will kill me.'

Dean tips his head quizzically but looks relieved. 'You sure, Ol? I don't want to muck up your morning.' He starts eating.

'It's okay. I just won't wash my hair. It's no big deal.'

'Your hair looks perfect.' His eyes linger on her cleavage. 'Seriously, you're a lifesaver. You can take them to before care, so you should still get to the office by eight if you leave in the next thirty.'

She mentally adds the inconvenient detour to her morning schedule.

'Hang on, you've been up for hours?' He looks at her with concern. 'You couldn't sleep again?'

She glances at Amy, who is now pushing her food around her plate.

'Just insomnia,' Oli mutters, quelling a flash of resentment. Dean has no trouble sleeping despite the horror that must sometimes try to push into his thoughts. She once hoped they might share it, the clutch trauma can have in the early hours of the morning. But so far there haven't been any bonding opportunities in the middle of the night. He sleeps like the dead.

'You should take those pills I got you,' he says.

She shrugs. 'Maybe.'

He shrugs back, then starts eating.

She loves the way his hair curls at the nape of his neck, almost hiding the cluster of tiny moles behind his left earlobe. For the first time, she notices a few strands are grey.

'You work too hard,' he says in between mouthfuls, 'and you know you don't have to—not anymore. You should think seriously about going freelance. Write that book you used to talk about.'

She riffles through rubber bands and takeaway menus in the junk drawer, looking for a pen. She senses his eyes on her, but she doesn't want to have this conversation again. Ever since she moved in three months earlier, he's been like a dog with a bone about her working less, encouraging her to slow down. And even though writing for pleasure has an appeal, the ease with which he can grant her lifelong wish feels wrong. He's older than her and earns a lot more money. Plus, the girls' future is more than taken care of.

'Bingo.' She locates one of her black felt-tips; they always go missing in this house.

'Are you still going to make that appointment?' he asks, voice low and gruff.

'I think so,' she replies breezily, 'but I haven't booked it in yet.'

His expression is impossible to read. 'We should talk about this, Oli. Properly.' He glances at the girls and sighs. 'It's a big deal and . . .'

'And what?'

'It's just different to what you were saying last year.' He puts the plate down and moves closer, adding in a whisper, 'You know that if it happens, it happens. I thought the girls were enough. I thought *I* was.'

Oli tilts her head. Takes a step backwards. 'Am I not allowed to change my mind?'

He gives her a look and clears his throat. 'Let's talk later.'

She instantly regrets being deliberately obtuse. Echoes of her eruption a fortnight ago ring in her ears; for some reason, all the thoughts and feelings she'd been ignoring for months finally bubbled over. Playing mother to the twins isn't enough—it hasn't sated her maternal desire as she'd hoped it would. She and Dean had been curled around each other in bed talking about Christmas plans, then out of nowhere she found herself rushing off to sob in the ensuite. As she tried to explain, Dean hovered around her and wiped tears from her cheeks, but she saw the surprise in his eyes. 'I didn't think you wanted a baby this much?' he murmured uncertainly.

'I'm probably too old anyway,' Oli said. 'I'm almost forty.'

'The youngest, hottest almost-forty-year-old I've ever known.'

She raised the idea of going to see a fertility specialist and Dean listened and nodded, then kissed her eyelids and ran her a bath, gently washing every inch of her, drying her and carrying her back to bed, holding her until she fell asleep.

They haven't spoken about it until now, although she has sensed Dean has wanted to. She feels ashamed, ungrateful. She isn't exactly sure what she wants to say, isn't really sure what she *wants*, and it feels easier just to let days slide by. To say nothing.

Dean knocks back the last of his smoothie. Tickles his daughters and ruffles their hair. Then, in an obvious attempt to make peace, he grabs Oli from behind, briefly pressing his body against hers. He curls a hand around each wrist, pinning her to the bench, his hot breath snaking into her ear. 'You make me so crazy. I can't wait to be in bed with you tonight.' He pulls her hands together and places his left one over them both, then kisses his way up her neck.

She hates when he does this in front of the girls, but in spite of herself heat zaps through her. For a minute it's like how it used to be, when they would meet in dark bars to have drinks and dinner over candlelight, their limbs tangled in a dimly lit corner. When their nights were full of exquisite delayed gratification.

Kate shrieks again, shattering Oli's reverie. She wriggles out of Dean's hold and hastily wipes the bench with a cloth. The newsreader drones on in the background.

—

Oli pulls into the waiting bay at the McDonald's on Spencer Street, two blocks from the office. Rolls all the windows down and blows a neat line of cigarette smoke skyward, her phone pressed to her ear. She has tried to quit many times since taking it up in her late teens but has never been entirely successful, because she finds it incredibly anchoring. She's pretty sure Dean knows she smokes, but he never mentions it, and she goes through the motions of hiding the paraphernalia, eating mints and dousing herself in perfume before she comes home. Occasionally at the dinner table he'll quote some shocking statistic about smoking-related diseases or talk about how some guy from the office is quitting. Oli just murmurs generically while the girls declare their outright hatred for all smokers.

'Your car smells like fire,' Kate said earlier, climbing into the back seat of the Audi and wrinkling her tiny nose.

'Hmmm, it does a bit, how strange,' Oli replied vaguely, before launching into a one-sided Q&A about the school day ahead.

Now she mutters, 'Come on, come on,' eyes on the fast-food restaurant window. The piano music on her call comes to an end and a jaunty violin track begins. As she and the girls left the house, one of the researchers at the paper texted through the phone number of a business where a young woman Oli has been trying to track down allegedly works. The piece Oli's been putting together, on abuse in the prostitution industry, has been dying a slow death over the past few weeks, but if she can find this woman and get her to go on the record, she might be able to revive it. After a promising chat with the girl's manager, she's been on hold for almost ten minutes.

Dawn McGill, Oli's editor, calls her for the second time since she's been on the phone. She flicks Dawn a text and gets a response barely a second later: *CALL ME ASAP.*

'Yeah, yeah,' she mutters. Dawn only has one mode: urgent.

Oli scrolls through Twitter while the violin plays. A new pollie sex scandal. A sick elephant at Sydney Zoo. More madness from Trump. Madness everywhere.

'Here you are!' chirps a cheerful teenager wearing a headset. She hands Oli her order and flashes a smile peppered with metal. 'Have a nice day!'

Oli extinguishes her cigarette on the corner of the car mirror and wedges the butt there. Taking a bite of the muffin, she relishes its salty flavour. She used to come here about three mornings a week; she loved nothing more than to park herself on one of the plastic tables upstairs at 6 am with a Bacon & Egg McMuffin and a steaming black coffee, and pound out the draft of a story. But it feels wrong to leave the house when Dean and the girls are still sleeping.

Holding the food in one hand, Oli noses back into the morning traffic. She'll be pushing it to make the editorial meeting, but she needed a moment to herself after dropping the girls off. Even after short stints alone with them, she feels untethered. She can't seem to relax in their company, her nerves screaming like cicadas. It takes all of her energy to play mother.

Fortunately, signing them in was quick this morning. Amy and Kate hung their bags on the hooks in the entrance and floated off, whispering to each other without giving Oli a backwards glance. Even though she finds their rare displays of affection uncomfortable, indifference is worse.

She hasn't spent much time with other kids—her sister has none and her small friendship group is largely childless—but even she can tell the girls are different from their peers. They are so insular, so serious. Is it just because they're twins, she wonders for the millionth time, or is it grief? She can't bring it up with Dean; she knows too well the way his muscles will stiffen and his jaw tense, and the odd tone that will creep into his voice. It's the reaction he has whenever she expresses an opinion about his daughters. As far as he's concerned, the four counselling sessions they had after Isabelle died did the trick. Case closed.

Oli wolfs down the rest of the muffin, demolishes the hash brown and drowns the lot with boiling coffee. The past twelve months have been a crash course in parenting, and she still hasn't adjusted to the constant weight of responsibility she now carries. It's relentless—and, if she's completely honest, an unwelcome addition to her life. Her thoughts are often split in two, her impulses dulled and wrestled into submission. An invisible anchor connects her to Dean and the girls, creating a sense that she shouldn't let her work come first, or that at the very least, she should feel bad if it does.

Your own child will be different. You will want to feel the constant attachment.

Oli registers the disloyal thought and hates herself for it.

The Christmas holidays will be a much-needed circuit-breaker: ten nights in Vietnam, babysitters for the girls. She can't wait. Just the thought of time with Dean, away from real life, makes her skin tingle. Although admittedly, the September school holidays are only a few days away and Dean and the twins are going away without her, and she's looking forward to the time alone this will grant her almost as much as the Vietnam trip. Possibly even more. She groans. Her head is all over the place. Maybe Dean's right—maybe she should take a step back at work, ease her foot off the pedal.

The food sits uncomfortably in her stomach. No wonder she can't get pregnant, she keeps stuffing her face with fast food and cigarettes. She presses her lips together, the violin music grating on her nerves. In fits and starts, she applies the last of her make-up. Red light, lipstick. Red light, mascara. Nothing can mask her lack of sleep.

Did she turn on the alarm system at the house? Dean is fastidious about it, but she always forgets. Did she? She just can't remember.

The call disconnects as she hastily finds a spot in the staff car park, and low electronic beeps replace the violin, pulsing through the car. 'Damn it.' She brushes ash from her skirt as she winds up the window. Her phone rings again: Dawn. She glances at the cigarette butt and the greasy rubbish she shoved in the door console, feeling as full of regret as she does of food. She'll clean the car later.

She dives into the lift, spritzing perfume all over herself. Her phone buzzes in her bag. 'Jesus, I'm coming,' she mutters. Notepad in hand and a mint in her mouth, she enters the stuffy editorial room right on eight, holding out her phone and smiling at her boss, who still has her own phone to her ear.

Dawn doesn't smile back. 'Where the fuck have you been, Oli?' Her densely freckled face is a mottled red.

TJ is sitting at the head of the narrow table. Pia taps away on her laptop at the other end, her phone wedged between her shoulder and her cheek. 'Right, right,' Pia is saying, 'yep, send it to me.' She glances briefly at Oli, but her expression doesn't change. 'No, I can't right now.'

The smile fades from Oli's face. Dawn has the same wild-eyed look she had when they made the staff cuts in June. Oli swallows. There have been rumours of redundancies for weeks, and she knows she's been off her game lately—all year, if she's honest—and Dawn has always liked TJ more than her.

'What's going on?' Oli hates how husky her voice sounds; at times like this, her distinctive baritone feels so inappropriate.

Dawn folds her arms and sticks out a hip. 'There's been a development in the Housemate Homicide case.' She pauses. 'They've found Nicole Horrowitz.'

SATURDAY, 3 OCTOBER 2005, LATE AFTERNOON

Alex tries to pinpoint the moment it all went wrong. Her life sprawls out behind her, a series of twists and turns, all leading to one horrible moment. Which decision was the one that upset the balance? Which choice hurtled her so unrelentingly toward chaos? Her mind latches on to scenes from faded memories, wispy half-forgotten conversations, and others so startlingly clear they feel artificially planted in her mind. Of course, she knows there was no one thing: hers was a gradual fall from grace.

Earlier, at the house, she felt calm. Even with the screams and the blood, the same questions over and over, she had a sweet sense of being stripped back to her most basic form. She was aware of her fingers, her toes. She traced her ribs and clutched her kneecaps. Things that usually hustled for her attention were gone, and nothing mattered except for the slow beat of her heart.

But now ripples of shock rake painfully over her body, each wave crushing another part of her. Lungs, liver, heart.

The detective said she'd only be a moment, but it feels like she's been gone for hours. Alex looks around the small room: plain walls that were once white but now carry a beige tinge, scuffed grey lino, a square table made of some nondescript substance, a mirrored rectangle along the wall in front of her. A bit like a cell. Maybe it's intentional, an attempt to ease occupants into the idea of gaol. Alex rubs her eyes and looks at her reflection. Presumably people are watching her from the other side like they do in the movies—talking about her, judging her, wondering how the nice-looking girl could have killed her best friend. Vomit surges in Alex's throat, and she grips the side of the table, swallowing desperately. The acid taste is putrid, and she sips water from the glass the detective gave her.

Despite her winter coat and boots, she's freezing. Cold from the inside out. Bones and heart of ice.

Maybe she should have stayed in the hospital—the young doctor with the kind eyes had encouraged it—but after being examined, her body scraped for evidence and photographed like a corpse, all Alex wanted was to get the police interview over and done with.

'Am I under arrest?' she asked the officer with her at the hospital, after she'd finally been allowed to shower. Her hair was wet and combed, her face scrubbed clean of make-up and blood.

The cop was young, probably not much older than Alex. His features were too sharp to be handsome, and a thin white scar from the corner of his mouth to the middle of his left cheek gave him the impression of a hooked fish that had put up a fight. Clearly, he was guarding her, hovering in the periphery as she was guided through various examinations, her body scoured for clues. 'Not at this stage,' he replied stiffly, avoiding eye contact.

A flutter of something stirred then, the oddness of the situation so intense that Alex wanted to laugh. To scream. To rot into the earth, all traces of her existence erased.

She looks at the door. A laminated piece of paper spruiks a reminder to turn off the lights. Evelyn was always yelling at

Alex and Nicole to switch the lights off; raging at them about waste and the environment, and the electricity bills. They rolled their eyes and laughed, flicking the lights on and off until eventually Evelyn laughed too, more exasperated than annoyed, declaring them a lost cause.

Alex sips more water, then crosses her arms and glances at the cheap-looking clock on the wall: almost 5 pm. She hasn't slept in close to forty hours.

A faint tapping precedes the door swinging open. The detective is back, and there's another person with her, an older man with silver hair. They take seats opposite Alex. Lace their fingers and lean forward, expressions solemn. The detective waits for Alex to make eye contact before saying, 'Alex, this is Chief Inspector Bowman. We're going to ask you some questions now, okay?'

Alex nods, swallowing furiously.

Bowman presses a button on a device sitting at the edge of the table; Alex hadn't noticed it was there. 'DS Yardley and CI Bowman interviewing Alexandra Michelle Riboni on Saturday, 3 October 2005 at 5.11 pm.'

Despite her masculine business suit, Detective Yardley reminds Alex of a ballerina. Her dark hair is pulled into a high bun, her thick brows perfectly symmetrical above her pale blue eyes. She blinks, slowly, deliberately. Alex recalls a porcelain doll she had as a little girl.

The chief inspector places a notebook on the table, plucks a pen from his pocket. His broad shoulders are almost double the width of Yardley's narrow frame, and his shirt buttons strain across his chest.

There's a rehearsed sense to their movements, and Alex assumes a plan has been hatched in the time since she was deposited in this room—a discussion about how to handle her, to get what they need.

'Alex, we're sorry about your friend.' Yardley's voice is soft, her body language friendly, but Alex feels anything but reassured. Something tells her Yardley will be quick to pounce at the first opportunity.

Alex doesn't move, just stares at her hands.

Yardley continues. 'I know it's been a long day, Alex, and you're upset, but we really need you to tell us what happened last night, so we can help you. Can you do that?'

'No,' she whispers, surprised to find her throat aches.

'We need you to try, Alex. We need to understand what happened. Earlier, you said you and Nicole left the house after everyone went home. Is that right?'

Alex closes her eyes. She is back in the house on Paradise Street. In the kitchen. Cooking. Talking to Miles. Talking to the girls. Drinking. It had started out like so many other nights, but there had been no denying the nasty undercurrent. 'Yes. We went for a walk.'

Yardley looks puzzled. 'Were you meeting someone?'

'No, ah, we were just walking.'

'Why?'

'We just were.'

Yardley tilts her head. 'Where did you go?'

Alex is running, running away from the house. 'Just around. Like, not very far.'

'Did Nicole return to the house with you?'

Alex has the feeling again, of wanting to go back in time, to undo all the things that have been done. But it's impossible, like trying to scratch an itch in the marrow of her bones.

'No. She ran off. After that I was on my own.'

Yardley blinks. 'Where did she go?'

'I don't know!' Alex is crying now.

No one speaks for a few moments.

'You don't know why she ran off,' says Yardley. 'That's okay. We can come back to that, see if there's more you can remember about it later.'

Bowman writes something in his notebook, and a shrill sound builds in Alex's brain.

The night air is on her cheeks, the salty breeze from the sea. Nicole walking next to her, talking on the phone. Alex feels worried, worried it's all about to fall apart.

'What about when you came back?' Yardley presses. 'We know you returned to the house at some point before 3 am. Can you tell us about that?'

Alex can feel the eyes of the chief inspector on her. Gazing with pity? Frustration? Disgust? She shakes her head vigorously, trying to block out the noise as it climbs, higher and higher, like a kettle boiling.

'Alex?'

She's lying on her side, arms and legs brick-heavy with booze and drugs. The dull ache of fading rage. She is sick of fighting, sick of everything. The front door is open, and it's cold; she feels the shudder of the floorboards. Footsteps. Soft and firm. Firm and soft. Voices.

'What about your housemate Evelyn? Did you see her? Talk to her?'

Alex blocks her ears with her palms, tears and snot dripping onto the table. She opens her eyes. The world is sideways, but she recognises the familiar hallway. Upturned furniture. Milk-pale skin. The knife in her hand.

'All I remember is the blood,' she whispers. 'There was just so much blood.'

CHAPTER THREE

TUESDAY, 8 SEPTEMBER 2015

THE ONLY SOUND IN THE ROOM IS PIA'S TYPING. THE BLOOD DRAINS from Oli's face, and she sinks into the nearest chair before her legs buckle. The name Nicole Horrowitz creates an instant file path in her brain to a slew of old images and news headlines. Nicole and her former housemates are in the same category as Azaria Chamberlain and the Beaumont Children; their case is an unsolved mystery firmly fixed in Australia's collective psyche, journalistic gum on the nation's shoe. Oli has worked enough stories to know that some just have the X factor, the perfect mix of ingredients, a plot and characters that keep people wanting more. Try as the media overlords might, they just can't orchestrate that desired alchemy—sometimes death simply falls flat. But the Housemate Homicide had been a newspaper editor's wet dream from the start, and despite Alexandra Riboni's swift conviction, there has always been something off about the whole thing. It lacks the neatness of a clear motive. It lacks closure.

'She was found this morning. By a jogger, apparently.' One of Dawn's bright-red nails is chipped, and Oli's eyes are drawn to the blemish as she waves her hands around.

While Oli is taller than average, Dawn is at least six foot and her extremely feminine wardrobe of colourful blouses and floral dresses jars with her broad frame.

'He spotted a woman's body hanging from a tree,' Dawn concludes, 'and called triple zero.'

'Jog ruined.' TJ's face is lit with the glow from his laptop screen.

Oli is struggling to get words out. 'Where?'

'Tiny little place called Crystalbrook, up in the Dandenongs.'

Oli swallows. 'And it was a suicide?'

'Looks like it.' Dawn shakes her head from side to side in what is likely an attempt at expressing empathy, but there's a savage glint in her eye.

A panicky feeling has taken over Oli, and the coffee lurches in her gut. She summons a visual of the house on Paradise Street. Remembers watching from her car as Isabelle escorted a blood-spattered Alex Riboni from the scene. Remembers Evelyn Stanley being carried out in the body bag. Can still hear Yardley's crisp address to the media the following day.

It feels like yesterday, but it was almost ten years ago.

'Nicole was alive the whole time?' Oli says stupidly.

'She was,' agrees Dawn, 'and now she's not again.'

'Alex didn't kill her,' Oli murmurs. Her eyes lock with Dawn's, then TJ's. This is huge. Oli swallows. 'Is it definitely her?'

Dawn leans across the table. 'It's not official yet, but it's what I'm hearing from my source. Apparently, they found her old ID on the scene. It looks like she's been hiding away up there for years.'

'Holy shit.'

'Yep.' Dawn steps back from the table, looking pleased. 'Holy shit.'

'How long ago was it called in?'

'We got word around twenty minutes ago. When I phoned you.'

Oli connects the dots. It's early days, but word will spread like a match hitting gas. 'Who else has it?'

Dawn's face darkens. 'We don't know. Nothing is live yet, aside from reports of the body, and the only reason that blew up was because the jogger's wife posted about it on social media. She's a fitness guru with an Instagram following, so one of the TV networks picked it up.' Dawn blows her fringe out of her eyes. 'I'd say everyone is fact checking. You know how it goes—if we have it, they have it.'

'When are we breaking it?'

'We're going live at 9 am. Basic speculation only. Then we'll do updates on the hour, get some old shots up until we have something new.'

Oli's eyes glaze over as she starts to draft the copy in her head. *One of the missing pieces in the Housemate Homicide puzzle turned up this morning. Nicole Horrowitz, presumed murdered, was found dead by suicide in the rural suburb of Crystalbrook. Her whereabouts for the past decade remains a mystery.*

'I want you on this, Oli, one hundred per cent,' Dawn says. 'I wanted you on your way there *now*, but you weren't answering your phone, which completely baffles me.'

Oli's face flushes. 'I—'

Dawn holds out a hand and closes her eyes as if Oli is a small child who has made an unholy mess. 'It baffles me, but I don't want to discuss it. I just want a dirty big deep dive into this whole thing. It's perfect timing with the ten-year anniversary looming, and I'm thinking we'll do a double-spread feature Saturday week, maybe a four-pager. Gwen can push on with the other feature we planned for the anniversary but ramp it up a bit, make it more of a tribute to Evelyn. I want you to cover the crime, the conviction and Alex's appeal. I want you to dig the whole mess back up and flog the living shit out of it. Drop that garbage you're writing about the prostitutes and get your arse up to the scene.' Dawn plucks a Post-it from her notebook and squints at it; her eyesight is appalling, but she refuses to admit it. 'Take Cooper Ng from Kylie's team with you. Apparently he's got an interview lined up with Alex Riboni for the true crime podcast we're doing. I don't know the details, but that interview is absolutely key now, so make sure you get him to lock it in with her asap, then you can take over. We need to turn it into an exclusive.'

'You want me to take him to the scene?' Oli says, confused.

'Apparently he's good with a camera, so it saves me finding a photographer to go with you.'

'Sorry, who is Cooper Ng?' Oli says, just as TJ says, 'We're doing a podcast?'

'Yes.' Dawn snorts. 'We're "diversifying our revenue streams", which may or may not be code for turning us into a radio station.' She rolls her eyes. 'Anyway, the kid is on level three with the digital team. Kylie tells me he's not a bad interviewer. Clearly the bar is getting lower and lower these days, but based on my conversation with him this morning I can confirm he has the gift of the gab, so maybe she's right.'

Oli has no idea who Cooper Ng is—there are lots of new faces upstairs, and she generally tries to avoid the digital department. But whoever he is, she's not happy about having to make small talk on a long car trip with some stranger. 'Can't I take Knowles?'

'Nope, he's on the trial,' Dawn says. 'Just get moving, Oli, I want something meaty online before the 6 pm news, and I want to run a secondary story online later as well, which we can push hard in print tomorrow. So get whatever you can. See if the cops will talk and if any locals knew her. TJ's obviously tied up with O'Brien, but Pia can do some background on the property for you and stay across the police reports and news coverage.'

Oli stands up, slinging her bag over her shoulder. She hesitates before saying, 'You know I covered the Housemate Homicide back then, when I was at *The Daily*?'

Dawn gives her a strange look. 'Yes, that's why I want you on it now.'

—

TJ is waiting for her outside the bathroom. 'Bloody good story,' he remarks.

'Sure is.'

He frowns. 'You okay?'

She nods. She and TJ have seen it all over the years: bosses have come and gone, they've moved papers and offices, they've navigated new media laws and the seemingly never-ending digital transformation. Both landed in crime early. TJ joined *The Daily* around two years before Oli, and she's been playing catch up ever since. Back then he was still Timothy Jack, a charming young man who tried, but regularly failed, to check his privilege. The silver spoon has left a permanent dint in his mouth, but at least he's aware of it. Despite their differences and inevitable competitiveness, they've always been firm friends, though Oli wonders if that's just because he has never seen her as a real threat.

Three years ago, Dawn promoted Oli to a senior role alongside TJ when the legendary Martin Boon retired. TJ still tends to get the bigger stories, but there are generally enough to go around. Oli has the sense that he enjoys their gentle rivalry; it keeps him on his toes without giving him a serious run for his money.

Her phone starts ringing: Dean. She switches it to silent.

TJ's gaze is unrelenting.

'I didn't sleep very well last night, but I'm fine.'

He cracks his knuckles. Crosses his arms. 'I wasn't asking how you slept, Ol.' His spotless white shirt looks brand new and hugs his chest and shoulders. He always seems so put together. In all the years they've known each other, Oli has rarely seen him lose his cool. He is as reliable as the paper, turning up day after day, dark-gold hair neat, ready with an easy smile and a wry quip. He and his wife Angela don't have children; they own two large dogs, and an apartment full of gadgets and designer furniture. They go skiing in New Zealand every August and are constantly training for a marathon.

'I'm fine, TJ,' Oli insists.

'Okay.' But he doesn't uncross his arms. His eyes dart left, then right, and he leans closer, 'I really thought there was going to be a sweep this week.'

'I figured when I saw Joosten in the office on Monday. I actually thought that's what Dawn was about to announce when I came in.'

'Yeah.' TJ grimaces. 'Joosten met with me yesterday. He seemed to be sussing out my thoughts on Dawn—you know, if she's cut out for the future shape of the business. I think he's considering another restructure.'

Oli's brain feels scrambled. This Nicole Horrowitz thing has really thrown her. Suddenly all she can think about is Isabelle. 'Joosten wanted to talk to you about Dawn?'

Oli usually gets along well with Alistair Joosten, the Sydney-based managing director. They have a shared interest in celebrity memoirs and cryptic crosswords. But he didn't give her so much as a second glance this visit. And Dawn? Surely she's not on the chopping block? She's not everyone's cup of tea, but she's tough and she works her arse off. Oli would rather work for her than have some new boss to impress; someone with an onslaught of ideas and a remit to cut costs.

'What did you say to him?' Oli asks.

TJ hesitates. 'I kept my cards pretty close to my chest. Said it was a tough market right now, what with social media leading the news and all the traditional networks investing so heavily in online platforms. I mean, it's no secret our advertising model is turning to shit. Blah, blah, blah. But I told him Dawn seems to be holding it together, all things considered.' TJ flashes his white teeth. 'I think Joosten is a bit scared of her.'

'He's not an idiot,' agrees Oli, wondering whether TJ is being completely straight with her. If he senses weakness in Dawn, will he pounce? Oli's also vaguely annoyed that Joosten didn't seek out her opinion.

'It's funny, you know,' TJ says, 'but even though I know the headlines, I can't for the life of me remember the details of the Housemate story. I guess I was up to my ears in the Carter kidnapping and just never touched it.' A little smile plays on his lips. 'I do remember good old Jo riding your arse something chronic, though. God, she was a slavedriver.'

Oli is keen to change the subject. 'Do you reckon O'Brien will get off today?'

TJ makes a face. 'Probably. The guy's a piece of shit, but he's a clever piece of shit. He covered his tracks pretty well, and there're still a lot of people barracking for him.'

Oli sighs. 'God, it's depressing. Dean reckons he was always a total creep.'

'I know. No matter what the ruling is, I'm hoping his wife will still talk to me. I've been working her for weeks, and I think she's ready. She's been staying at a hotel since July, you know. I doubt she'll stand by him now, not after yesterday's statements. It's too humiliating.' He grins. 'Getting her on the record will be pure gold. She might offer up stuff that hasn't come out yet.'

A feeling flares in Oli, the kind she occasionally gets when she talks to TJ. The sense that she'll never be as good as he is because she lacks the wiring that makes him the ultimate journalist: the ability to shut off all emotion, to work a story like a robot.

Dawn barrels out of her office and stalks toward the news desk.

'I better go.' Oli shuffles out of her boss's line of sight. 'I need to find this Cooper kid. Hopefully he can actually take a decent photo.'

TJ laughs. 'It sounds like he's a slight upgrade from a work experience intern.' He runs his hand through his hair.

She steps past him. 'Well, good luck out there.' It's what they always say to each other.

'You too.' He narrows his eyes. 'Hey, didn't Dean's wife lead the Housemate Homicide case? I'm sure she did.'

Oli remembers the haughty flick of Isabelle's ponytail, the burn of her gaze. The younger version of herself kissing Dean outside her apartment in a taxi and stumbling around the city trying to crack a story. So desperate to prove herself.

She lifts her shoulders as casually as possible, relieved TJ can't see the flush creeping up the front of her neck. 'Yes, I think she might have.'

Three Christmases ago, the newspaper's digital department moved from the ground floor to level three, joining the sales department while leapfrogging news and editorial on level two.

'This is a bad sign,' TJ had predicted at the time, as they watched the surprisingly large stream of people make their way up the open stairwell, carrying Apple laptops and portable speakers. 'It's a physical depiction of the pecking order, Oli. We'll be in the basement by 2020.' Oli had thought he was being overly dramatic and told him so, but then the research team switched with finance a year later and now sit in what is virtually an oversized cupboard next to the ground-floor toilets. Plus, when the editorial team's fridge broke last month and Oli ventured up to the third floor for some milk, she discovered a cafe-grade coffee machine and a cupboard full of herbal tea.

Apparently TJ was right: in this new era of journalism, digital is clearly closer to heaven.

Oli reaches level three and finds Kylie Archer, who points out Cooper Ng. Kylie has been with the paper for over fifteen years, dodging the multiple waves of redundancies and embracing the increasingly digital world with her trademark gusto. She's the kind of person you can't picture ever being a little girl, sporting the same spiky bleached blonde hair the entire time Oli has known her. She has a penchant for themed jewellery, and today bright-yellow daffodils dangle from her earlobes. 'Cooper's good, Oli. Annoying, definitely, but he's good.'

'Right.'

Kylie squeezes Oli's arm, her bracelet jangling. 'God, this Housemate Homicide thing is fab, isn't it? Dawn gave me the heads-up so we can pull together a layout, you know, a round-up of all the people at the house that night.' She points to a skinny redhead arranging images on a giant computer screen, dragging them into place with a pen that glides over what might be a type of iPad. The three housemates smile out from the centre, looking like sisters. They're surrounded by a montage of young faces, hairstyles ten years out of date.

'Well, it was a good story then,' Oli says. 'I guess it's still a good story now.'

'It's a cracker,' Kylie declares. 'I gotta say, I thought Nicole Horrowitz was dead. I really thought that Alex killed them both.'

Oli is reminded of how polarising the case was, how divided Australia had been about Alex's involvement in Evelyn's death and Nicole's disappearance.

'First we need confirmation the body is Nicole,' Oli reminds her. 'Nothing's official yet.'

'I reckon it's her,' Kylie says firmly.

Oli fights to keep the irritation out of her voice. 'We'll see, I guess.'

Unfazed, Kylie pats Oli's shoulder maternally. 'I hope you get some good stuff out there today. I'll look forward to reading it.' She pauses long enough to take a few noisy gulps of water from a bright-blue canister before wiping the back of her hand along her mouth and yelling, 'John!' Oli startles. 'John!' Kylie repeats, taking off to chase him down.

Oli approaches the rear of the giant computer screen Kylie pointed out. On the other side she finds a scrawny-looking Asian kid wearing giant purple headphones. He stops mid-bop and yanks them off, springing to his feet. 'Olive Groves! *Great* to meet you. A real honour.' He grins and pumps her hand with unexpected strength. 'I'm Cooper. Cooper Ng. Some of my mates call me CNN. My middle name is Nicholas, but I'm down with whatever suits you. Coop, Coops? I really don't mind.'

Cooper's short black hair has been corralled into one giant peak slightly to the left of his crown, and he has three silver studs in his left ear. He wears glasses with thick black frames, his short-sleeved shirt skims his thighs, and his jeans bring new meaning to the term pipe-cleaner. He stuffs his headphones—and about a million other electronic devices and cords—into a backpack.

'Are you cool with me calling you "Oli"? I notice your by-line is always Oli. Olive Groves is a downright cracker of a name, though. Total gold! Your parents must have had a sense of humour.' Oli opens her mouth to speak, but he hurtles on. 'Are you going to change your name when you get married? I figure you won't, but people can surprise you sometimes. You know how there are some chicks who are total feminists but then they overlook something really basic like taking a dude's name? It's the worst.'

She blinks. 'Are you ready to go?'

'Um, let me see.' He pats himself up and down, appearing to run through some mental checklist. 'It's still cold outside, right?'

'Yes.'

'Well, it's lucky I have this piece of quality goodness then, isn't it?' He yanks a multicoloured ski jacket from the back of his chair, wrestles it into a small bundle and wedges it under his elbow. 'Ready!'

'Great.' Oli's back teeth grind together.

'Let's go, then, shall we?' He swings his backpack on. 'Bye, Chelsea!' he calls out. 'See you, Graham!'

His colleagues fail to respond, earplugs in, eyes fixed zombie-like to their screens. Cooper charges off toward the lift, and Oli trails behind, plucking an apple from the brimming fruit bowl.

In the lift, Cooper keeps talking. 'This whole thing is crazy, huh? I never get sent on stories, but it's just such a coincidence that I've got Alex coming up on the pod.' He flicks his finger up and down his phone at an alarming speed. 'I've got alerts on all of the Housemate Homicide chat groups and keywords. The second this thing hits, I'll give you the vibe. There's going to be, like, a *billion* conspiracy theories doing the rounds as soon as people hear about Nicole Horrowitz turning up dead.'

The lift pings, and the doors open.

'I know where you park,' he says cheerfully. 'I have this thing about matching cars to their owners. You're the white Audi.' He points to the car. 'Very fancy.'

The faint flutter of irritation that has been simmering in Oli threatens to boil and spill over. She has no doubt her new car was the talk of the office for weeks, but Dean insisted she needed a decent car to help with the girls, and her old Mazda hardly seemed worth defending.

'Do you come down here and spy on everyone?' she asks.

Cooper reaches inside his jacket, then holds out an old-fashioned cigarette case, silver and engraved with an intricate floral pattern. He taps it conspiratorially. 'I smoke. You notice lots of things when you smoke. Hear lots of conversations. James Gilchrist told me that, when I did work experience at Channel Seven. Gilly's such a legend—I mean, you probably know him, right? Anyway, smoking has led me to discover many interesting things.'

After reaching the car they stand on either side, looking at each other over the roof.

'You smoke?' Oli says sceptically.

'I know, I know,' Cooper says guiltily. 'I'm a traitor to my tribe, a rare breed of millennial. I don't use Snapchat either. I like my digital footprint curated and permanent. I'm actually kind of old-fashioned,' he adds earnestly. 'I have no interest in getting a tattoo. And I'm not sold on Uber—their disregard for paying tax bothers me.'

'Get in,' Oli says curtly. 'It'll take us an hour to get there.' She beeps the car open and slides onto the dark leather seat, surreptitiously shifting the rubbish from the door and shoving it under the seat.

Cooper hoists himself into the passenger seat. He sniffs deeply several times and turns to her, looking delighted. 'You smoke too!'

'Not when I'm on the clock.' She starts the car.

He pulls on his seatbelt then gasps, his index finger pointed skyward as if to indicate a bright idea.

'What is it?'

'I forgot the camera!' He swings the door open and runs back to the lift. 'Don't go without me!' he cries as the doors swallow him up.

CHAPTER FOUR

OLI'S KNUCKLES ARE WHITE, CURLED LIKE CLAWS AROUND THE steering wheel. Cooper continues chatting away. In the fifteen minutes since they left the office, Oli has been treated to a blow-by-blow account of his resumé, starting with the holiday job he had at the local video store when he was fifteen. Now he's five minutes into a detailed review of the sleep-monitoring app he's recently started using. The stop-start rhythm of the traffic is amplifying her tension, and as they slow for yet another red light she breathes out through pursed lips and inhales deeply through her nostrils.

Eventually they escape the bustle of the city via the tollway and arrive in suburbia. Skirts and suits are replaced with active-wear, and rows of taxis have morphed into mums with prams, but Oli barely registers their surrounds. Her brain is stuck on a loop of old faces: Nicole, Evelyn, Alex. Isabelle.

This bloody story was always going to come back to haunt her, she thinks grimly, tuning out Cooper's babble. Despite the undeniable surprise, there's a sense of inevitability in Nicole turning up. Secrets tend to come out eventually, whether they are forced into the light kicking and screaming, or simply float slowly to the surface. The pulsing momentum of unfinished business can be strong. This story was certainly the anomaly in her own resumé, the loose tooth that her mind often felt compelled to probe. She produced pages and pages of copy, spent weeks immersed in the world of the housemates, trying to make something interesting out of the ordinary, all the while arguing the toss with Jo, the whole saga culminating in their popular coverage of Alex's trial. But in the end, it amounted to very little. The story turned out to be a dud, a nationwide let-down that left everyone feeling cheated, Oli included.

She can still picture the corner of the newsroom back at *The Daily*: the wall of photos, the piles of paperwork; a dynamic mural of the murder, Alex's arrest and, ultimately, her trial. The shrine had remained in the office for weeks, almost as if Jo thought that by leaving it there, someone might work out what had really happened—anything to avoid the sustained feeling that the point had been missed. Oli knew her own fascination with the occupants of 28 Paradise Street had bordered on unhealthy, and Isabelle Yardley's involvement had only compounded her obsession. To be fair, she was hardly alone: the entire country was swept up in the story.

She recalls feeling unsettled by the unchecked judgement that spewed forth from every armchair detective in Australia, all convinced they had the answers. Talkback radio exploded, and the brave new world of online blogs hyperventilated over the saga, flooding the internet with think pieces about the dangers of drugs and female promiscuity, cautionary tales that suggested no one should be surprised that when young women play with fire, they will likely get burned.

Nicole was always considered the key to the whole thing, the missing girl with the missing details. FIND NICOLE, FIND THE ANSWERS, screamed the headlines. HOMICIDE DETECTIVES DESPERATE TO FIND NICOLE HORROWITZ. Dubbed the popular one of the three, Nicole was the nice girl from the nice family with a history of good grades and impressive sporting achievements. Classmates went on the record declaring her charming and charitable. There were rumours, of course—there were rumours about all the girls—but Nicole's documented warmth and generosity saved her from the most vicious scrutiny. In contrast, Alex was the foster kid with no alibi, fingerprints on the murder weapon and blood on her hands. Her emotional reaction at the house, widely interpreted as a confession, turned into a stubborn silence, and there was little faith in her claim that Nicole had disappeared in the middle of their mysterious night walk without her phone and wallet. And then there was poor Evelyn, the centre of the whole thing, who, despite being stabbed four times in the back and chest, lost a good deal of her posthumous sympathy when it was revealed she'd had a cocktail of illicit drugs charging through her bloodstream and a great deal more hidden in her bedroom.

Cooper is still nattering away, while Oli is now firmly lost in the past. The old frustration returns as she remembers dead end after dead end, the inconsistent story arcs and the nonsensical clues. If Nicole really has turned up in the middle of nowhere, does that mean Alex was telling the truth? Or does it mean something else entirely?

Oli knows the case all but broke Isabelle. Jo even wrote a piece speculating about the strain it had put on the young detective. Dean never went so far as to admit that Isabelle was struggling—not to Oli, anyway—but you could see it on her face plain as day every time she fronted up to the press. Cracks appeared in her usually perfect exterior, and Oli hates to admit she experienced some joy in witnessing Isabelle's weakness. Back then, the whole police force was under fire, and the media delighted in fuelling the flames: crime statistics splashed across the front pages alongside questions about dead prostitutes, the ongoing gangland wars and the lack of leads in the Carter abduction. After Evelyn was killed, the cops were scrambling, desperate for a conviction.

They got one in Alex Riboni, but Isabelle and Bowman copped a lot of heat for the way the case had been built around convenient forensics and circumstantial evidence. Accusations of incompetence hung in the air, the lack of motive compounding the issue. Alternate possibilities continued to circulate, and by the time Alex was sentenced Oli could almost feel the tide turning, the universal shift that tipped the party-girl orphan from guilty to innocent. Alex was sent to gaol under a maelstrom of doubt.

Guilt bubbles up as she remembers lying to Jo about being sick that evening so she could sneak off with Dean. Poor Jo, dead from cancer in 2010. She was a horrible boss, but she didn't deserve to waste away like that.

Despite the conviction and sentencing, Alex's legal team refused to give up, relentlessly appealing her case. Evelyn's toxicology was scrutinised, comparable cases unpacked, experts wheeled in to claim she had likely struck out in a violent episode—her emotional outbursts were well documented. Alex's powerhouse of a lawyer presented a compelling appeal that Alex was the victim and Evelyn the out-of-control monster. Alex had been dragged from her bed in the middle of the night by crazy, naked Evelyn, who threatened and attacked her; she was left with no option but to fight back. The evidence that had put Alex away was flipped and twisted. It was self-defence, her lawyer cried, and after three years she was out of gaol and in a rehabilitation centre.

Nicole's disappearance was reframed too: Evelyn must have driven her to suicide, or potentially even killed her.

Chief Inspector Bowman's carefully worded statement delivered outside court, moments after Alex's release, was deemed unsatisfying by the media, and Evelyn's alcoholic father made a spectacle of himself when the salivating journos requested a comment. Mitchell Stanley called Bowman a useless cunt and Isabelle Yardley a stupid slut, before tripping over. His pixelated bum crack appeared in every news bulletin, accompanied by an edited version of his rant.

Despite the sunshine, cool sweat beads in Oli's armpits, and she shifts uncomfortably in the leather seat. This morning feels like too much too soon. She wants to reacquaint herself with each piece of the story, to feel her way back into the narrative, word by word.

'How did you arrange the interview with Alex Riboni?' Oli asks Cooper, interrupting his monologue about computer software he's recently purchased.

He attempts a low whistle, but it comes out more like a squeak. 'We've been avoiding the big chat this whole time, haven't we? You know, the reason we were brought together today.' He rubs his hands and tips his neck from side to side. 'I have to say, it was all pretty cool, you know, tracking her down like that. And I've been working with one of the guys at the office who is a musician on the side, and he's developed this cool sting for the podcast intro, it's so ominous, like, super moody, and—'

'Cooper!'

He shifts gears easily. 'Right, back to Alex, sure. Well, someone in one of the Facebook groups said she worked with her cousin at an environmental consultancy. You know, one of those places that encourages businesses and schools to put more sustainable practices in place—recycle more, stuff like that.'

'What does she do there?'

He shrugs. 'Project management, I think. Anyway, I messaged the Facebook person and found out the company is called Everyday Green. I tried a few times to get in contact with her, but they wouldn't put me through. I even sent a letter, but I didn't hear back, so in the end I tracked her down on social media.'

'She has a public account?' Oli asks, surprised.

'Only Twitter. And it wasn't easy—she goes under Al_R_85. But I had a hunch it was her. She kept retweeting links to victim advocate sites and stories about legal loopholes and mistreatment by cops. And environment stuff. I sent her a DM, and we messaged back and forth a few times. I think it took her a little while to believe I was legit.'

'And then you just asked her to do an interview?'

He dips his head up and down. 'Pretty much!'

'When was this?'

'About three weeks ago. The digital team is planning to launch the podcast series with the Alex interview at the end of this month, but we have a ton of other interviews lined up.'

'Right.' Oli is unconvinced. 'And was this all your idea?'

'No, it came straight from the big man himself. Joosten gets we need to diversify—you know, evolve or die.'

Oli makes a dismissive sound, masking the betrayal she feels. 'What we really need to do is invest in quality journalism.'

'Podcasting *is* quality journalism. I've heard *The Australian* is working on one, and they've invested a massive portion of their budget in it.'

'Podcasts clearly have their place,' Oli says, pragmatically, 'but a newspaper isn't a broadcaster, and I don't really think jumping on the shiny bandwagon is the way to go when we could be building on what we already have and what we're known for. You know they cut half the subeditors last year?'

Cooper lifts his skinny shoulders, clearly happy to disagree. 'Don't worry, my mum doesn't get it either. She thinks I'm just dicking around on my phone.'

'Yes, well.' A cramp is forming in Oli's left calf. 'Your mum sounds smart. When is the interview with Alex scheduled?'

'Sunday morning at the office, but we spoke last week.'

'You already spoke to her?' Oli can't believe what a wasted opportunity this is—the kid is sitting on exclusive content about the one person that everyone will sell their soul to speak to.

Cooper looks confused. 'Of course. I had to plan out my interview questions and get a feel for the tone of the show.'

She laughs in spite of herself. 'It's a true crime interview, isn't it? I would have thought the tone is pretty set.'

Cooper reddens. 'I just want to make sure she feels comfortable with me. She seemed to appreciate it.'

Perhaps Oli's being too harsh. 'It's always a good idea to put the subject at ease,' she offers.

'Yes,' he says, brightening. 'Exactly.'

'Hang on. You said you're doing the interview at the office? Have you thought about where?'

'In the studio.'

'What studio?' she asks, veering off the highway and stopping at a red light.

'I turned one of the empty meeting rooms into a studio. It's got proper soundproofing and everything.' He pauses to throw a stick of gum into his mouth. 'I looked up how to do it on the net—a combo of old carpet and egg cartons—and got one of the IT guys to help me. It's come up a treat, you'll love it.'

Oli doesn't comment. For some reason, the thought of Cooper hammering carpet onto walls at the office makes her want to punch something.

'Anyway,' she prompts.

'Anyway, what?' He looks at her.

'What did Alex say?!'

'Oh, right,' he drawls.

Oli wrestles with her exasperation. He's like a puppy you have to yank back onto the path every couple of steps.

'She seems great, actually. Shy at first, but she warmed up. I got the sense she's really angry under all the grief. I guess you would be if you were sent to gaol for something you didn't do. I think she's totally ready to tell her story.'

'So she's still claiming she didn't do it?'

His forehead wrinkles. 'Of course.'

'What did she say?'

'Well, we didn't exactly get into specifics. I want to save the detail for the real interview, so that it feels genuine. But we discussed the key things I want to cover, and I asked her if anything was off limits. She said she was ready to talk about everything.'

Oli lifts an eyebrow but doesn't say anything.

Sensing her judgement, he juts out his bottom lip. 'She seems genuine.'

'Maybe, but she's also had ten years to get her story straight.'

'I think she's just ready to talk,' he says earnestly. 'I was only a kid back then, so I didn't remember the story very well, but I've watched a stack of old footage over the past few weeks, and Alex seems really different from how she was back then.' He pauses. 'She said she's started to remember stuff from that night. New stuff.'

Oli's nerves go on alert. It seems Alex was days away from coming forward with new information about her friend's decade-old murder, when Nicole suddenly turned up dead. Had the women been in touch? Oli tries to feel out the angles. If Nicole knew that Alex was claiming to remember details that might implicate her in Evelyn's murder, could that have provoked her enough to die by suicide even though she was in hiding?

Oli's pulse starts to race again. The more she thinks about it, the more she finds the idea of listening to Alex Riboni giving her account of what happened all those years ago incredibly appealing. What will she sound like? Will she be defiant or confident, soft or loud? Will she really reveal the truth about what happened that night?

Even though part of Oli is still furious about the idea of the paper investing so much effort in this podcast when her team have been told they can't have new laptops, she starts to plan out the interview, feel her way through the cadence of the conversation.

'What's the format of the podcast?' she asks Cooper. 'The structure, I mean.'

'Well, Alex will be the first guest, so I'm still figuring it out. I see myself playing the role of narrator, you know, setting the scene and doing all the background stuff, but then interspersing it with Alex's comments. And I want to get her to talk about everything she remembers from the night Evelyn died. And I want to track down some of the other people who were there, get their perspectives as well. My vision is to stitch the whole thing together like one of those old radio plays. I've done a few trial runs, and it works.'

Oli is still sceptical that something so ambitious should be left to a kid, but she simply says, 'Have you got interviews with their friends and family lined up?'

He puffs out his cheeks. 'No,' he says sheepishly. 'Not yet, but I will.'

'Evelyn's mother will probably speak to you,' Oli surprises herself by saying. 'She was always desperate to share information about her daughter.'

'That would be cool. She reckoned her ex-husband was involved, right?'

An adjacent car changes lanes unexpectedly, and Oli brakes sharply, cursing under her breath. 'Yeah, Mitchell Stanley, an ex-footy player. He used to play for Essendon, I think, before he injured himself and transitioned into coaching. After he stopped playing football, he got heavily into drugs and gambling, and lost all his money. And he screwed around a lot.' Oli scrunches her nose, locating memories stored in far corners of her brain. 'I don't think anything suggested he was linked to what happened—Geraldine Stanley just hated him. They were going through a nasty divorce, and she blamed him for Evelyn wanting to move out of home at such a young age.'

'That TV interview Geraldine did was so sad,' Cooper says earnestly. 'I watched it twice last week.'

'I do remember that Evelyn and her father had dinner together the night before she died.'

Cooper is typing notes into his phone at an impressive pace, muttering to himself.

'God, I can still remember Geraldine turning up at the house that morning.' Oli shivers. 'It was awful.'

'How did she know what had happened?'

Oli shrugs. 'No idea. But when she turned up and saw the cops, she lost it.'

'The poor woman.'

'Yeah.' Geraldine's screams echo through Oli's mind, making her skin crawl.

'I've got an idea,' Cooper exclaims.

'What?' She's following the GPS on her phone, which starts to glitch, reloading their route.

'You should come on the podcast! For starters, your voice is incredible, but mainly because you were there at the scene. You can give the journo perspective.'

'I don't think so.' She tries to soften her deep timbre.

'Come on, it would be great!' Cooper is palpably working himself into a frenzy. 'It's perfect, actually. I bet there are heaps of other crimes you've covered over the years, and we can work our way through all of them.'

'I . . .' Oli is saved by the phone ringing, and she answers via Bluetooth. 'Lily, hi. You're on speaker,' she adds quickly, although knowing Lily, it won't bother her either way.

A lead? Cooper mouths at her eagerly.

'My sister,' she hisses.

He cups his ears knowingly to indicate he won't eavesdrop.

'Jesus,' she mutters.

'What, Ol?' Lily sounds annoyed. 'You're driving, aren't you? I hate talking to you while you're driving.'

'Sorry.' Oli tries to tell whether Lily's words carry the slur that suggests she's been drinking.

Lately it has become apparent to Oli that she enjoys the thought of talking to Lily a lot more than she enjoys actually talking to her. The closeness they shared as little girls and young women has shifted, but Oli's muscle memory still responds with a feeling of intimacy in anticipation of every conversation with her sister, only to be disappointed as she reorients herself to the reality of their polite chatter. They teeter on the edges of each other's worlds, trying to make sense of them.

'Did you see the news?' Lily says. 'Sorry, stupid question, of course you did. Is it true, Ol? God, I remember that story. It was bloody everywhere, huh. I even remember the name of the brothel everyone was saying she worked at. Calamity Jane's, wasn't it? And remember how you wore my shirt to work that morning, and I found out because I saw you on the news later that night. Remember, Ol? I went ballistic.'

Oli rakes her fingers through her hair. 'I remember.'

Cooper smothers a smirk, then makes a show of looking out the window.

Oli turns down the volume as Lily's voice tinkles through the car. 'How was that ten years ago? Fuck we're getting old.'

'Yep.' Oli's knuckles are white.

'Are you at work? What are you doing?'

'I am, and I need to get going soon—I'm on a deadline.'

'You're always on a deadline,' Lily says scornfully. 'Mum and I thought you might slow down now you have the girls. And Dean.'

'Lily, not now,' Oli says firmly. 'Do you need something?'

'Not really.' She sighs loudly. 'I just want to complain about Rebecca.'

There's the slightest tension on Oli's foot as they hit an incline, and the car shifts into a lower gear. The road becomes slightly rougher, with cat's eyes running along the dividing line in the middle. The houses start to thin out, replaced by long stretches of ferns and native grass.

'What's Rebecca done now?' Oli surveys the intersection ahead.

Lily groans. 'She's like a ghost popping up all the bloody time—a money-grubbing, evil bitch ghost who has no pride and no morals. Basically she's just doing her standard bullshit. Anyway, don't worry, I can complain later. Can I call you tonight?'

'Maybe.' Oli is now pretty sure that Lily has been drinking. 'I don't know how late I'll be.'

'Seriously, Ol, isn't Dean loaded? Surely you can stop busting your balls?' Lily sighs. 'Anyway, you're lucky Isabelle's dead, that's all I can say. I wouldn't wish an alive ex-wife on anyone. Also, Mum wants you to call her.'

Lily hangs up. The white noise in the car amplifies, and Oli clears her throat in an attempt to banish the awkwardness.

'My mum's always at me to call her,' Cooper says after a few moments. 'And I still live at home!'

Oli reaches past him and pulls open the dashboard compartment, retrieving the packet of cigarettes from under the car-care manual. She hits the button to wind down her window.

His Adam's apple protrudes awkwardly. 'I thought you didn't smoke at work?'

She eases a cigarette into her mouth straight from the packet and flicks her lighter, leaning toward the flame. 'I do today.'

CHAPTER FIVE

ABOUT HALFWAY UP THE MOUNTAIN, THE GPS ON OLI'S PHONE REALLY starts to lose it. The guiding arrow on the screen goes haywire, swinging wildly from left to right. Dawn is texting her, wanting updates, and Oli impatiently flicks the alerts off the screen with her left thumb, while trying to keep a grip on the cigarette in her right hand. 'Come on, come on,' she mutters, using her knees to steady the steering wheel.

'Here,' Cooper offers, clearly alarmed, as he loads Google Maps on his phone. 'I'm with Telstra.'

'So?'

'They have the best network coverage.' He relaxes into his seat. 'So, back to my idea about you co-hosting the pod. What do you think?'

Oli groans inwardly. This kid is relentless. 'I'm a print journalist, Cooper.'

'So far. But who knows what might happen next! You could switch to TV, radio, or something completely unrelated to journalism. Did you know that on average these days people will have up to four different careers?'

'Print suits me,' Oli snaps. 'I have no interest in working in another field. Plus, it's all I know, and I don't think I'm at a stage in my life where I can just transition to something else.' This isn't dissimilar to the dialogue she's been having with Dean lately, and the same heat rises in her cheeks.

Cooper laughs. 'You're not that old!'

'I'm old enough to know that I like the job I have.'

'We'll see.' He seems immune to her irritation.

Bushland completely surrounds them now, layer upon layer of green.

Cooper adjusts the cuffs on both legs of his skinny jeans. 'So, who do you think did it?'

'You mean, who killed Evelyn Stanley?'

'You must have a theory.' He spreads in his fingers in a dramatic flourish and stares at her expectantly.

'I always thought Alex did it. I thought there was a good chance she killed Nicole too, but I guess I was wrong.'

'Really?' He looks disappointed.

'Yes. I wasn't sure whether it was premeditated, self-defence or something in between, but that's what all the evidence pointed to.'

'But why?'

'Jealousy and betrayal, probably. The usual Shakespearean stuff.'

He makes a face. 'Do you really think she would kill her friend because she was jealous?'

Oli laughs. 'Yes, especially if she was off her face on drugs and booze.'

'There were heaps of other people at the house that night,' he says defensively.

'Sure, but only Alex's DNA and bloody fingerprints were on the knife and Evelyn's body.'

He frowns. 'I guess. It just seems way too obvious.'

Oli hides a smile. Cooper's interactions with Alex have clearly got in the way of his objectivity. She remembers feeling like that—getting defensive of someone just because they agreed to an interview or gave her a lead.

'Well, mate, we are an example of why this story captured the hearts and minds of the nation. Let's just pray we finally get some answers today. Hopefully Nicole left a suicide note.'

'I hadn't thought about that,' he says, his eyes shining. 'That would be kind of amazing . . . for the story, I mean.'

'Yes, it would.'

'Still, no matter what, I think the older guy being at the house that night is suss.'

'Julian McCrae, the professor?'

'Yeah. I mean, our uni teachers wouldn't have gone to one of our parties. Way too risky.'

'Things have changed a lot in ten years,' Oli points out. 'I'm not sure people would have been as attuned to that kind of thing back then. But, yes, the timing was unfortunate for McCrae. He was cleared pretty quickly, though—of the murder, anyway. His wife gave a statement confirming he came home early that night. All of the other party guests had alibis too. The couple Tanya and Roy, another girl Amber. They all went home well before Evelyn was murdered.'

'McCrae's wife could easily have lied. Maybe she didn't want to admit that her husband was fooling around with his students.'

'But the others all confirmed he left.'

'I still want to talk to him,' Cooper huffs. 'Get his side of the story.'

'Have you tried to contact him?'

'Yeah. I messaged him on LinkedIn a few weeks ago, but he never replied. He's still teaching, though, so he won't be too hard to find.'

'When you spoke to Alex, did she say anything about where she went that night?'

Cooper shakes his head. 'No, I didn't ask about that. Like I said, I wanted to save the main points for the interview. She did say she was comfortable with talking about Evelyn, though. You know, like the moments after she died, and when Alex called the ambulance.'

Oli remembers the statement Alex made in court, her face white and her voice shaking: *I remember thinking that maybe the bath had somehow overflowed into the hallway, and that's how the water got all over the floor. But it wasn't water. It was blood.*

'Maybe you can get Bowman to talk to you as well.' The thought comes out of nowhere. 'He'll be a great juxtaposition to Alex, and it's a nice angle, the case he built that was overturned. I'd say it still pisses him off—his strike rate is almost perfect.'

'Sure, I like the idea of interviewing him,' Cooper says, sounding terrified. 'Do you think he'd do it? Heaps of cops in the States do podcast interviews, but things are pretty different over there, aren't they? Do you reckon you could speak to him? It would definitely be better coming from you.' He pauses for breath just as his phone connection drops out. 'Hey, no way!' he exclaims.

They approach a roundabout with no signs and, not knowing which way to go, Oli pulls over. Cooper grabs the phone from the holder and prods the screen. After a few moments, a shiny black BMW tears past. Oli accelerates in pursuit. 'It's fine, Cooper. I know where we're going.'

He raises his eyebrows cartoonishly. 'How?'

Oli gestures to the BMW. 'I don't think Melissa Warren is heading to a midweek mountain picnic.'

Mercifully, the impromptu car chase lulls Cooper into silence. Oli follows Melissa's BMW up the winding curves of the mountain for a few hundred metres, until the road turns almost one hundred and eighty degrees onto a steep dirt incline. Oli jerks the car to the right, and Cooper's arm flies out to brace against the dashboard.

Up ahead, the serene bushland has been invaded by emergency vehicles. A small cluster of people wearing jeans, boxy blazers and sunglasses are talking into their phones: homicide detectives. The second cluster is more eclectic. An attractive woman in a tailored skirt. Two scruffy men in jeans with cameras propped on their shoulders.

'Shit.' Oli parks precariously on the edge of a bend, wedged between two cars, the arse of the Audi sticking out onto the road. It's definitely not legal, but she figures it's unlikely anyone will be handing out parking tickets.

'Wow.' Cooper surveys the scene, and Oli feels a jab of irritation at his naked awe.

A steady stream of vehicles continues to appear, comically navigating the narrow road. A few metres away, Melissa is already setting up for a piece-to-camera in front of a blooming wattle tree, her frozen forehead giving her a slightly shocked look that will probably work well for this particular story. She's been unbearable since she switched to television six years ago, and her recent make-up endorsement deal has served to make her more so. Her long-suffering cameraman is ready to capture every move, a hairbrush and make-up bag jammed under his armpit.

Oli flicks off the ignition and exits the car, blinking into the glare as more cars push their way into the crowded space. She hasn't seen the media swarm like this in a while, but then again, not many cold cases suddenly catch on fire like this. So much for having the scoop.

Melissa spots Oli and scowls.

'Got the camera?' Oli snaps at Cooper. 'You should get a photo to Dawn as soon as you can, even if it's just a holding shot.'

'I sure do,' he replies cheerfully, sliding on a pair of ridiculous-looking sunglasses. But then he hesitates. 'Um, where to?'

Oli gestures at the police cars before walking toward them, and he falls into step behind her. The sun feels hollow; its light isn't translating into heat. She shivers, her insides somersaulting. The red and blue lights that pulse from the police vehicles are half-hearted in the sunshine. On the other side of the cars, a line of cops creates a human shield in front of a narrow dirt driveway that runs for a few metres before disappearing into thick bush. A wonky letterbox sticks out of some shrubbery to the left of the clear space; a faded number nine sits above the rusted slot, and someone has written No Junk Mail neatly across the bottom in black paint.

'Take a shot,' Oli hisses at Cooper.

He obliges, capturing a few angles before looking at her uncertainly.

'Send them to Dawn. I'll just be around here.'

He scampers off, and Oli breathes a sigh of relief.

She's surprised to see Constable Rusty Frost arrive. She hasn't seen him for well over a month; he's been on leave. She saw photos of South America on Facebook, shots of him and a mate in Vegas. She sidles up to him, notices his hair is shorter. 'Rusty, hey. Welcome back. What can you tell me?'

A soft-pink blush spreads from his cheeks toward his ginger hairline. 'Hey, Oli.'

'Good break?'

'Great break.'

'I'm glad to hear it. What can you tell me about this?'

He shakes his head and groans quietly. 'Sorry, Ol. Not today.'

'Come on, Rusty. Can you confirm if it was a suicide? Please?'

He keeps his mouth closed, little muscles in his jaw clenching.

She drops her voice. 'But it's definitely Nicole Horrowitz? That's what I'm hearing.'

'Jesus, I haven't even been inside.' He straightens his shoulders assertively, then seems to get flustered again. He still won't look her in the eye. 'That's what I've heard, okay?' His voice is almost a whisper.

Oli's heart begins to hammer. 'And she hung herself, is that right?'

'*Oli, enough.*'

Angry voices erupt behind them: more media have arrived. Someone is standing in someone else's shot, and everyone's complaining about the reception. Half of them are on the phone, the other half madly texting. Modern journalism at its best, Oli thinks wryly.

'*Bowman's coming.*' The rumour spreads through the crowd like a virus. But after a few moments, everyone breathes out. False alarm. There's no sign of the chief inspector.

Cooper returns and looks at Rusty then back at Oli in a way that suggests he somehow knows about their romantic past.

'Hello.' He sticks out his hand without introducing himself.

Oli rolls her eyes. 'Rusty, this is Cooper Ng. He works with me at *Melbourne Today*. Cooper, this is Senior Constable Frost.'

'Nice to meet you, Cooper,' Rusty says, shaking his hand.

'You too.' Cooper pulls a business card from his pocket and hands it to Rusty before darting off again, snapping shots like a tourist.

Rusty raises his eyebrows and shoves the card in his pocket. Mildly embarrassed, Oli smiles up at Rusty. 'He's very green,' she says. A female cop is now standing in earshot and gives her a dirty look. 'I'll come find you later,' Oli says, while Rusty studiously ignores her.

She cuts across the front of the crowd to find Cooper, discovering him about twenty metres along the property's wire fence, standing in dense shrubbery.

'What are you doing?' She ducks to avoid a stick scraping her face.

'I was hoping there might be a line of sight to the house, but there isn't. I got a couple of good pics of the police before, though. They were talking ominously.'

'Ominously?'

'Yeah.' He steps toward the road, lifts the camera, and takes a few covert snaps of Rusty and his colleagues through the tree leaves. 'You know, like serious cop chat. They're good shots. The uniforms look great against the bush.'

Fighting the urge to roll her eyes again, Oli pulls up an aerial view of the property on Google Earth. Number 9 Laker Drive looks to be about half a hectare. A stream cuts across the rear-right corner, and there's a small square of grass at the back of the house. But aside from that, the block is thick with trees.

'That's the house?' Cooper peers over her shoulder.

She zooms in, peering at the rickety roof. 'I guess so. It looks more like a cottage.'

'Weird to think Nicole was hiding out here, huh? I wonder if she's been here the whole time?'

'I doubt it.' Oli kicks the ground and loosens some stones from the dirt. 'How many years was Alex in gaol for? Three, right?'

'Just over. She got out in April 2009, and she was sentenced in January 2006. I still can't believe you were at the house that morning,' he says whimsically. 'And now we're here. That's some full circle stuff, huh. I mean, there's no way you would have thought you'd be covering the same case all over again a decade later.'

There's no way Oli could have foreseen any part of her current life ten years ago. 'I guess you just never know which stories have more to give.'

'It's actually just dawning on me how crazy it is that I have the interview lined up with Alex on Sunday. Everyone's going to be gunning to talk to her now.'

'No shit,' Oli mutters, looking again from the image on the phone to the trees in front of her.

'We might even be able to get advertisers in a bidding war to sponsor the first episode.'

'The guy who found Nicole was jogging,' Oli says, ignoring Cooper as she scans the borders of the property. 'But I doubt he was jogging through this.' She indicates the thick bracken surrounding them.

'Maybe he was running on the road. Or up the driveway?'

Oli scrolls back over the map. 'No,' she says, straining her neck to look further up the road. 'Come on.'

Cooper glances back at the crowd. 'Everyone else seems to be staying over there.'

'Exactly.' She stomps through the long grass, hoping it's too cold for snakes. As she follows the thin wire fence through the trees, she steps between tufts of native grass. An old memory settles over her. Dry grass scratching her plump legs as she scrambles to follow Lily and her father. They were bushwalking somewhere on their grandmother's farm before she died.

'Come on, girls, keep up!'

Lily bounds ahead, disappearing over a ridge. Oli is exhausted, her muscles aching, arms covered in welts. She sits on a rock. Adjusts her sock so her blister doesn't rub against her sneaker. Pulls a biscuit out of her pocket and starts to eat it. She is always so hungry.

'You okay, kiddo?' Her father appears, his face ruddy as he swats flies away. 'Want me to carry you back to the house? Maybe your mum will be awake by now.'

'No.' Oli quickly gets to her feet, the blisters on her soft skin stinging as she rushes past her father to catch up with Lily, praying he won't pick her up.

Behind her, Cooper's panting breaths drive the memory away, leaving her feeling empty. Ravenous. Her stomach rolls.

She pushes past a sapling, and it slingshots back, hitting Cooper in the face. 'Ow!'

'Sorry.'

They've reached a fence corner. There's a narrow gap between the post and another fence corner, which Oli assumes marks the border of the next property. A thin dirt path cuts into the ground between them.

'He must have been running along here,' she says. 'Unless there's a path on the other side as well.'

A bird lets out a low call that seems to soak into the ground before whipping back to the sky. They walk down the narrow corridor, the smell of eucalyptus thick in the air, trees stretching toward the clouds. It's pretty, but for the first time today Oli's glad of Cooper's company. The thought of being out here alone is unsettling.

He mirrors her thoughts. 'I reckon it could get pretty creepy out here.'

'I'm not much of a nature fan,' she admits. 'With the exception of indoor plants.'

'I have a virtual pet. Two, actually.'

She focuses on picking up scraps of information, little details that will allow her to describe the place where Nicole Horrowitz chose to die. Then, still scanning the scene, Oli comes to an abrupt halt. Through the trees she spies the distinctive blue-and-white chequered police tape and, beyond that, a cluster of people. Two cops in uniform and two male detectives in suits and winter coats stand a little further along.

'Bowman.' Cooper points to the right of the group, where Gregory Bowman's white hair glows through the trees.

Oli's pulse picks up again. She ducks down and creeps further along the fence.

'Where are you going?' Cooper whispers.

She doesn't reply but keeps moving parallel to Bowman. He's homing in on something. She starts to jog, still bent at the middle. Not far from Bowman there's a blur of white: forensic technicians clad in body suits. She trips on a tree root and stumbles against the flimsy wire fence.

Bowman has stopped. Two of the techs are on their hands and knees a few metres from him, crouched over a synthetic sheet, but his face is fixed skyward. Oli knows what she is about to see.

She closes her eyes. Opens them. Allows her gaze to scan up.

A woman hangs in midair. Rope loops around her neck and over the lowest branch of a giant gum. The cord twists slightly in the wind and makes a faint creak.

Cooper stops short next to Oli and draws a sharp breath. 'Holy shit.'

Oli's own neck feels tight, sore, as she tries to swallow past the lump that has formed in her throat.

Cooper's hands shake as he lifts the camera.

MARCH 2006

Hundreds of people call her name. This must be what it's like to be a movie star, Alex thinks, taking in the swarm of faces. Mouths open and shut like squawking birds, and words blur into an indecipherable mass of noise. Alex flinches as something large and black is shoved in her face. A microphone. Hundreds of circles glint in the crowd, the shine from the camera lenses catching in the sun. Alex keeps her head down, looks at her feet. Black boots, no scuff marks, cheap but new. Her eyes drift to a reporter standing to the side of the courthouse, and the one next to her.

Alex imagines being at home on the couch with Evelyn and Nicole, speculating about the girl on the news.

She looks guilty, Evelyn would say.

One hundred per cent, Alex would agree.

Ugly outfit, Nicole would add.

'This way, head down, good girl.'

Alex's lawyer, Ruby Yeoh, is a tiny but terrifying woman with a fringe as straight as a builder's level. Alex has spent a significant portion of the past few months looking at Ruby's face, which is generally twisted with disappointment. 'You don't make my job easy, Alex Riboni,' Ruby says often, shaking her head.

But they both know that Ruby loves the cut and thrust of the law, the drama of court. She has been on a high this past week, counting down the days until she can perform on stage. Alex is her reluctant co-star, incapable of learning her lines no matter how many times they go over them.

'Almost there,' Ruby barks, as she pushes Alex along, reassuring in an aggressive way.

They break through the crowd and step into the revolving door at the front of the courthouse. Alex is herded through security, holding up her scrawny arms as she's scanned for weapons.

The fuzziness lifts for the first time since that night at the house. This is it, she thinks. Funny, when it all comes down to it, that what goes on record in a court of law is simply a version of reality just like everything else. Alex wonders how many people lie on the stand. A quarter? Half?

She looks around as Ruby tugs her toward a large wooden door. It will be over in no more than a fortnight, maybe less. An overwhelming sense of relief slams through her, and she trips, stumbling to the floor. Ruby's tiny mouth turns down at the edges as she grabs her shoulders, holding them for a second as if some sanity can be passed on.

'Sorry,' Alex mutters.

'Just keep it together,' Ruby hisses. '*Please.*'

The security guard shuffles his feet. High heels click on the tiled floor behind Alex. Someone coughs. She can't stop noticing every tiny detail. All she wants is for it all to stop. To sleep through the rest of her life and be born into a new one. To go back in time and choose the other path.

'Ready?'

She looks at Ruby blankly. All she can see is Evelyn on the hallway floor. Her twisted left leg. Evelyn had told her she broke that leg as a teenager when she fell off her horse. Evelyn's poor leg looked broken all over again, but Alex never found out if it was. No one cares about a broken bone when you are dead.

Alex hears panting, then a desperate sound of panic. If only they could take it all back.

She is back in the hallway again. Everything is tinted red with Evelyn's blood.

'Alex?' Ruby grabs her shoulders, shakes her. 'Alex?'

It's her making the terrible noise, panting like a wounded animal, just like she did at the house that night.

Ruby shakes her again. 'Alex, come on. It's time to go in.'

CHAPTER SIX

TUESDAY, 8 SEPTEMBER 2015

BOWMAN SEEMS TO LOOK DIRECTLY AT THEM.

'Down,' Oli hisses, pulling Cooper to the ground by the tail of his shirt.

Even though she's crouching, she feels dizzy, catapulted back in time to the moment that will always be seared onto her brain. The body hanging from the tree has caused the old panic to flood back. The heightened state of awareness returns, the painful intensity. The feeling, the *knowing*, what is at stake and not wanting to think consciously about what she's doing, just needing to do it. *Don't think, just fix this. Breathe in, breathe out. Breathe, please breathe.* The bushland blurs into the pale, upturned face of her mother. Dry lips, glassy eyes. Oli barely registers the empty pill bottle on the floor, just presses her hands against the bony chest, hands sliding in sweat and vomit. *Please, Mum, breathe. Please.*

'What do we do now?' Cooper whispers, oblivious to Oli's turmoil.

'What?' The greens and browns of the bush comes back into focus, the old scene slipping away. 'We just stay here,' she murmurs, peering around the rows of tree trunks.

Bowman is still there. The forensic team are wielding a ladder and a stretcher. A large black bag. He gestures to the tree, and they all look up at the body. Oli does the same, properly this time. Long brown hair. Army-green Converses. Small white hands. Bloated face.

Bowman speaks to the group for a few moments, gesturing to the right before he walks back the way he came, phone to his ear.

The forensic team approach the gum tree with a ladder, their faces set in hard lines.

'Come on.' Oli's legs are jelly as she stands again.

They walk back along the track in silence.

'Was it her?' Cooper asks as they reach the turn. Then, 'It was her, wasn't it?'

Oli mentally sifts through the three photos of Nicole Horrowitz that ran in the news coverage. 'I think so. She used to have shorter hair, lighter. That . . .' Oli pauses. 'That woman had long hair.'

'I guess it grew.' He clicks on the image. Zooms in. 'I don't know why I took this,' he says. 'I'm not going to do anything with it.'

'I know.' During the first year Oli worked at the paper, she took an earring from a crime scene. She knew it belonged to the victim; it must have fallen on the ground and been kicked across the hotel car park amid the attack. The woman died in hospital two days later. Oli kept the earring in her wallet for years, would occasionally get it out, look at it. 'I get it,' she adds.

He gives her a grateful glance.

They make their way back to the driveway. The crowd is bigger now, and Oli recognises several journos from competitor papers and news sites. 'We need to find out if she was living here with someone.' Oli ignores a pointed look from Melissa Warren, who is applying a hideous shade of coral lipstick.

'How are we going to do that?'

'We meet the neighbours.' Oli's eyes land on the letterbox. 'We go to the local shops, maybe the post office.'

Pia calls, but the connection cuts in and out, and Oli hangs up in frustration. Then Pia texts her. 'It looks like the house belongs to a couple who live in Tasmania,' Oli tells Cooper. 'It was left to them four years ago when their elderly uncle who lived here passed away. There's no apparent link to Nicole Horrowitz, but Pia's trying to contact the owners.'

'Maybe she was renting it from them?' Cooper offers.

'Maybe.' Oli thinks about the small strip of shops they passed through earlier, the huge blocks of land. It's so isolated out here. Residents would certainly notice a new face, but they probably wouldn't question a long-lost niece or distant cousin. Nicole could have pretended to be anyone and slipped fairly quickly into anonymity—forged a new life, or stolen someone else's. But why? Was she so scared of Alex that she fled, or did guilt drive her away?

'I read about this person once who was renting a house from someone who died, and they just kept living there for years,' Cooper says. 'All the relatives just assumed she was paying, but no one was tracking the money. That was somewhere in the States, though.'

'Shhhhh.'

Bowman is walking down the driveway toward the media pack, his stocky body moving in calm, even strides. He stops just as the sun emerges from behind a cloud, and hands shield faces from the glare, giving the impression of a collective salute to the chief inspector.

Oli spies Rusty up the back behind an ABC cameraman. Even from here she can see a little tic pulsing under his left eye. She edges around the crowd, reaching him just as the press officer calls for attention. 'Quiet, please.'

Cameras are adjusted on shoulders, or fitted and locked into place on tripods, their lenses aimed at Bowman like guns.

'Any updates?' Oli murmurs to Rusty.

'Oli,' he moans under his breath. 'Stop.'

Cooper is climbing onto the raised earth behind them, trying to capture an image of Bowman on the dirt stage looking out at the desperate swarm. It will be a great shot, Oli thinks begrudgingly. Perfect for tomorrow's front page.

'I appreciate that there is a lot of interest in our presence here today,' Bowman begins, 'but I am not in a position to share many details at this stage. There are family members who need to be informed.'

About seven people shout questions, all variations on a familiar theme: is Nicole Horrowitz dead? It's been asked on and off for the past ten years.

Bowman waits for the noise to die down, rocking gently from his heels to the balls of his feet. 'I can confirm there is a deceased person on the property, and we are in the process of determining the sequence of events. We are not yet in a position to confirm the cause of death or the identity.'

Oli slides her gaze toward Rusty. He's staring at her. She flashes him a smile, but his expression remains resolutely neutral as she looks away.

She finds it hard to imagine a future with Rusty now, but not that long ago she thought they might end up together—marriage, kids, the whole thing. He was like a big kid himself, always joking around despite his serious job. Their relationship was chaotic and unpredictable, but it was fun. His shift work and her unorthodox hours led to unexpected late nights out, and his sense of adventure had them exploring her home town like it was a foreign city. She felt safe with him, while acknowledging that their default mode was friendship as opposed to the unchecked, limb-weakening passion she had with Dean.

It was all going well, fun and easy. And then out of the blue Isabelle died, and almost instantly her feelings for Rusty officially shifted. Their relationship suddenly seemed childish, something to tolerate but not to nurture.

Dean had called her as she was leaving the office after working late one night. It was eighteen months since Isabelle died, eighteen months of her daring to hope that a future with Dean might one day be possible. She was in the middle of texting Rusty, asking if he wanted her to pick up some takeaway, when her phone rang, a private number. Thinking it was a tip-off, she answered. 'Hello.'

A male voice. Him. 'God, your voice still drives me mad.'

She couldn't speak.

'I saw you today. You were walking down Flinders Lane, and now I can't stop thinking about you. I called your front desk and tracked down your phone number. Meet me.'

The years slid away. She ended things with Rusty less than three weeks later, claiming a lack of compatibility, an absence of connection, something that suddenly seemed critically important.

Rusty moves next to her, shifting his weight. The soft musk of his aftershave stirs dormant memories. But then he's gone, marching off to stand on his own on the other side of the crowd. The wind shakes the trees, and the minty tang of eucalyptus replaces the artificial scent. A minute later, her phone buzzes. *You didn't hear this from me, but apparently one of the guys found a note near her body. Not a suicide note, a death threat.*

CHAPTER SEVEN

A WATTLEBIRD SHITS ON MANNY CHO'S BALD HEAD, AND EVERYONE loses their minds. But Oli barely notices the ribbing that breaks out as the esteemed reporter cleans the mess off with a tissue. She's too busy rereading Rusty's text message over and over.

A death threat changes everything. A death threat suggests someone knew Nicole was here. Was being found enough to push her over the edge? Or was she so scared for her life that she wanted to beat someone to it? The possibilities writhe like snakes through Oli's brain.

Bowman is heading back up the driveway, and Oli steps away from the crowd and walks along the dirt road. She'd meant what she said to Cooper earlier: she'd always assumed that for whatever reason, Alex killed Evelyn. Her thoughts on the fate of Nicole were less clear. She believed it was most likely that Alex killed her too—on their late-night walk, when Alex could have disposed of the body—but Oli also thought there was a chance Alex had threatened her, caused her to flee or die by suicide. Of course, there was a theory that Nicole and Alex had killed Evelyn together, but why would Alex take the blame? Whatever really happened, Nicole being alive presented a risk to anyone who didn't want the truth to come out.

Oli grimaces, knowing the most likely person to threaten Nicole is Alex Riboni. And if she's a suspect in Nicole's death, the podcast interview is going to be at risk.

Tiny wrens dance in the nearby branches, and a pair of rosellas fly low, almost skimming the roof of Oli's car.

The three girls had been close from the moment they met, that was the one thing everyone agreed on. Close in a way that some of their peers described as unusual. Beneath the anger and grief, it was clear their loved ones were scared, aware the girls' formerly innocent friendship had somehow turned dangerous.

Nicole's dead body appears in Oli's thoughts. Maybe it still is.

Cooper runs to catch up with her. 'Where are we going?'

'I need food.' She gets in the car and pulls the door shut.

'Food,' he repeats, clambering into the passenger seat. He looks at the media pack. 'Like lunch, you mean?'

'Nothing else is going to happen here.' She inches the Audi backwards, nudging the car behind her. She narrowly misses the tail-light of the one in front as she executes a tight three-point turn and leaves the makeshift car park in a cloud of dust. 'And as I said, we need to talk to people who might actually know something about Nicole living here. Not cops.'

Oli considers telling Cooper about Rusty's text but decides against it. It's not like she's obliged to share anything with him, and he'll just drive her crazy with bogus theories.

He digs around in his backpack, pulling out various cords and connecting the camera to his laptop while sporadically hitting buttons on his phone screen.

'Happy with what you got?'

'Yeah.' He flicks through the images. 'I mean, I'm not the best photographer in the world but I'm okay. I've done a few courses.' He keeps scrolling. 'Bowman looks about a hundred years old.'

'He must be close to retirement.' She turns off the dirt road and back onto the uneven bitumen. 'I remember thinking he was ancient when I first started out.'

Cooper zooms in on one of the images. 'Yeah, he's retiring in March.'

She frowns. 'Where did you hear that?'

'Um, I'm not sure.' Cooper's eyes are fixed to his screen. 'I think Joosten mentioned it.'

'You're in regular contact, are you?' she asks, bristling.

Cooper finally turns to face her. 'I was up in Sydney last month meeting with the exec team. It's like I said, Joosten's been heavily involved in getting the podcast off the ground. He's keen to make sure it has national appeal. I think the Bowman thing came up then.'

'Well, it certainly sounds like your project is getting a lot of support from the business.'

'It really is.' Cooper chews his lip thoughtfully. '*Serial* has really paved the way—it had, like, *millions* of people downloading episodes the second they dropped. The stuff they've ended up finding out is amazing. Plus, podcasts are more user-friendly than print. People can consume them while they're out and about, which is cool.'

Irritation rolls up and down Oli's body. Trust the exec team to throw money at something new rather than invest in their flagship product. Plus, if podcasts are going to be a major part of the media landscape, they need to be done properly, with rigour, and led by someone with the experience to craft the right narrative. The last thing the industry needs is hundreds of kids like Cooper running around with their smartphones, broadcasting god knows what to anyone who will listen. She tries to convey her point without being completely dismissive. 'I'm sure for some stories podcasts are great, but they're not trustworthy like print.'

He scrunches up his nose. 'Maybe not yet, but they're getting there.'

'And they don't get published regularly enough,' she adds. 'Not like the paper which is delivered every day, no matter what.'

'They could be if we changed the business model. Plus, do you ever wonder what the benefit is of people knowing stuff as it happens? I mean, they didn't used to, and it's not like the general public *do* anything with most of the information we publish.'

Her eyes bulge incredulously. 'We need to present the facts and get the information into the public sphere as quickly and accurately as possible. It's the most important logistics job in the world.'

'Agree to disagree!' Cooper singsongs just as his laptop pings. 'Sent!' He grins and cracks his knuckles. 'I can relax now.'

Oli raises an eyebrow and tries to calm down—this kid is really pushing her buttons. 'Hardly. We're just getting started.' They reach the shopping strip, and she steers the car in a wide arc, parking in front of a bright-red Australia Post letterbox. 'You can wait here, if you like?' She grabs her wallet and swings the door open.

'Are you kidding me?' He shoves his array of equipment into his backpack and scrambles after her.

The supermarket is tiny, more akin to a milk bar, with three aisles of packaged goods and a modest but fecund fruit and vegetable section. Jaunty music plays from a dusty speaker on the wall. The front counter features two small stacks of newspapers, and on the front cover of *Melbourne Today* is a shot of John O'Brien's arrest back in March, with TJ's by-line visible under the headline: 'GUILTY,' SAYS FORMER COLLEAGUE.

Oli plucks a chocolate Big M from the fridge and a packet of chips from the sparse rack near the door. She gives Cooper a look, and he reluctantly selects an apple. They deposit their goods on the narrow check-out counter. An older woman stands next to an ancient cash register. Her thick brown curls are pulled back from her face with tortoiseshell combs, and she wears a soft lilac jumper with small pearls sewn into the collar. On a cord around her neck hangs a pair of glasses that she slides onto her nose.

'Is this your shop?' Oli asks her.

She beams. 'Yes, it is. My husband and I own it. Have done for over thirty years now.'

'It's lovely.'

'Thank you, dear, we like it.' The lady looks around the shop as if she hasn't noticed it in a while.

'Crystalbrook is such a beautiful place,' gushes Oli. 'It must be wonderful being right in the middle of nature. You must know everyone in town.'

Cooper stands next to her, stiff as a board, and Oli hopes the woman doesn't think he is her boyfriend.

'Well, yes, we probably do.' The woman nods proudly. 'Now, do you need a bag, dear? That will be seven eighty-five.'

'No, thanks,' Oli replies cheerfully, handing over ten dollars. She takes a punt that the lady hasn't listened to the news today. 'I have an old schoolfriend who lives around here, but I'm not exactly sure where. I think it's on Laker Drive, does that sound right? About halfway along. She mentioned in an email that it's a real bush property, almost a cottage.'

'I know Laker Drive!' the lady exclaims as if it's a quiz.

'My friend has long dark hair?'

'You must be talking about Natalie Maslan,' says the woman knowingly. 'She's around your age, I think.'

'Yes, Natalie!' Adrenaline pumps through Oli's system.

'They're in here now and then. She's a pretty young thing, but far too skinny if you ask me.' She looks approvingly at Oli's ample hips.

'Well, thanks.' Oli backs toward the door. 'I've misplaced her phone number, but we might head over there now to see if she's home. It's been ten years since I've seen her!'

The woman beams. 'I'm not sure what she does exactly, but I think she works from home. They've only been here a few years. She's very . . . What's that word everyone uses these days? Introverted. She's very introverted. Although I'm sure she'll be thrilled to see an old friend.'

Oli pauses, one hand on the door. 'You said "they". Does Natalie have a partner?'

The woman brushes some lint from her sleeve and gives Oli a puzzled look. 'I'm not sure about that, dear, but she does have a little girl. Evie. She's an absolute doll. Didn't Natalie mention her to you?'

—

Oli hustles Cooper down the side of the supermarket into a worn dirt lane. Clusters of weeds sprout from the base of an old rubbish skip, and a large crow eyes them curiously from its perch on a nearby rooftop. She pulls out a cigarette and fumbles in her bag.

'Here.' He produces a neon-pink lighter and flicks his thumb, and the flame flares in the white sunlight.

'Thanks,' she mumbles. She bends forward, sucking in air until the tip catches. 'Want one?'

'Nah, I'm too wired.' He paces on the spot and rakes his hand through his hair-spike before combing it back the other way. 'Nicole Horrowitz had a kid,' he says, stating the bleeding obvious.

Oli smokes hard and fast, calmed somewhat as the nicotine hits the depths of her lungs. 'Looks like it.' She bats the tip of the cigarette against the brick wall. 'And she named the kid *Evie*? Jesus Christ.' Oli is angry but can't work out exactly why. It's almost as if she feels fooled by Nicole Horrowitz. It does seem as though the missing woman is giving the whole country a giant, posthumous up yours.

After dropping this bombshell, the supermarket owner had told them she thought the child was about ten. 'Shy little thing,' she'd said fondly. 'Just like her mother.'

Oli kicks her heel against the building. 'Christ, what the fuck is going on?'

Cooper eyes her uneasily. 'If that woman is right and this kid is ten, then it's possible Nicole was pregnant that night. Maybe she witnessed whatever happened between Alex and Evelyn, saw her friend die. Maybe she wanted to protect her baby, and that's why she ran off?'

'Or,' Oli counters, 'Nicole told Alex she was pregnant when they left the house together on their walk. Maybe they argued about it, had an altercation, then Nicole ran off and didn't want anyone to know she was pregnant. Maybe that's why she stayed away this whole time.'

'Why would they argue about that?'

'I don't know.' Oli tries to think. 'The father was probably someone they knew?'

'Miles Wu?'

'Maybe.' Oli kneads her temples as if this will help clarify her thoughts. 'What if Alex came home from her walk with Nicole and told Evelyn that Nicole was pregnant with Miles's baby. Evelyn might have taken Nicole's side, causing Alex to flip.'

Oli tries to summon details about Miles. Tall. Shaved head. Fit and lean. Studious. He didn't seem like the type of guy who would sleep with his girlfriend's best friends, but Oli is well aware that people don't tend to print that kind of thing on a T-shirt.

Cooper looks confused. 'Maybe Nicole only meant to hide out for a little while and wait for things to settle down, but when they didn't she decided to have her baby away from the spotlight and made a fresh start somewhere.'

Oli tries to picture it. 'Alex always maintained that Nicole wasn't there when Evelyn died. And the DNA supported that. If Nicole felt guilty about something I don't think it was Evelyn's murder.'

Cooper squirms, twisting his arms in front of his body.

'What?'

'Well, when we spoke on the phone the second time, Alex told me that part of what she could remember was waking up in the hallway after Evelyn was dead. She said she could hear someone in the house.'

'Are you serious?'

He nods. 'That's what she said.'

'We need to speak to Alex as soon as possible. We can't wait until Sunday.' She gestures at Cooper. 'You need to call her now. Quickly.'

'I can't,' he cries. 'She wouldn't give me her number.'

'*What?*' Oli is in danger of exploding. 'What do you mean?'

'She said she wasn't comfortable giving me her phone number. The two times we spoke she called me, and her settings were on private.'

'Well, how the fuck are you going to contact her?'

'Twitter.' He looks offended. 'That's the only way she said she was happy to communicate.'

Oli closes her eyes. Breathes. 'Well, do it now.'

The slightest hint of smugness seizes his features. 'I messaged her before we left the office. I asked her to call me.'

'But she hasn't,' Oli says flatly.

'No.' His expression drops as he glances at his phone, looks nervously at Oli then back at the screen. 'She hasn't read my message yet.'

'Okay.' Oli sounds a lot less frantic than she feels. 'The second you hear from her, you need to tell her the interview has to happen as soon as possible. *Before* Sunday. We can talk to her in the middle of the night if she wants, I don't care. We need to get her on the record before she changes her mind or is dragged back into custody.'

Cooper blanches and steps away from Oli, squaring his bony shoulders. 'Like I said, it's been pretty hard to get her to agree to the whole thing. I don't want to freak her out. She trusts me at the moment, and I want to keep it that way.'

'Well, you'll have to reconcile wanting to make a new friend with wanting to be a journalist.'

His nostrils flare, and he opens his mouth but then changes tack. Oli can hear him counting under his breath. 'When she calls me,' he says evenly, 'I will ask if she wants to do the interview earlier, but it's up to her.'

'Cooper, you do realise there's a possibility Alex has something to do with what happened to Nicole, right? They might have been in touch.'

'I'm keeping an open mind until we do the interview.'

'You'll need to keep an open mind way beyond that, my friend.' She's aware of how patronising she sounds, but someone needs to teach him how real journalism works. 'It's not your job to judge. It doesn't matter what you think. We deliver a point of view and make sure we balance anything Alex tells us with the known facts. You're not her lawyer.'

'Surely I can have an opinion.'

'Of course you can. You just have to keep it to your goddamn self. Either that, or you go and work at the *Sun*.'

She frees the straw on her Big M and breaks the silver seal, gulping down the sweet milk. She notices that his fists are clenched again, and she hides a smirk. Good, let him get worked up, he's obviously had an easy run so far, what with jaunts to Sydney and the exec team falling all over itself to get his podcast off the ground.

Time for him to have a taste of the real deal, the ninety-nine per cent of the job where things don't go the way you want them to. She pulls open the chips and munches them noisily.

'Don't you think there's a chance it was Nicole all along? That she killed Evelyn?' Cooper speaks with an urgency that tells Oli this is his theory; this is what he's secretly hoping Alex's interview will prove.

Oli sighs. Sating her appetite has made her tired. 'The DNA says no. Alex was there, covered in blood. Alex's prints were on the knife and on Evelyn. Alex admitted to doing it. She even said Nicole wasn't there.'

Cooper pouts. 'You said in the car that it was probably jealousy. And maybe you're right, but maybe it wasn't jealousy over a guy.'

'Sure,' Oli says diplomatically. 'The green-eyed monster comes in many forms.'

'The day before she died, Evelyn auditioned for a role in a movie. Did you know that?'

Oli is momentarily floored. Had she known that? She crosses her arms and looks at him expectantly. 'So?'

'So, she got the part. She was going to move to Sydney in the new year.' He lowers his voice as if someone might overhear. 'I bet she told the girls that night. Nicole always wanted to be an actress. Maybe she was jealous.'

'That hardly means she killed her friend.'

'I'm just trying to keep an open mind,' he says sarcastically. 'It could have been anything—revenge, a psychotic episode.'

'Drugs, or shame. Shame is big with young women. Maybe Evelyn was about to reveal some big dark secret about Alex to the world, and she lashed out.'

'Maybe they had ties to the Mafia.'

Oli rolls her eyes. 'I said an open mind, not fantasy land.'

'And then, ten years later, the guilt finally got to Nicole,' Cooper continues dreamily. 'She tried her best to make a new life for herself, but ultimately she just couldn't get away from what she did. It ate her up inside until *bang*, she ended it all.'

Oli has a sudden thought: what if Alex tracked Nicole down somehow? What if she came to the house on Laker Drive and took Evie? Maybe that's why Alex hasn't called Cooper yet—she might be halfway across the country with a kid in tow.

But then the suicide wouldn't make sense. Surely Nicole would stop at nothing to get her child back if someone took her. Oli considers a different possibility: maybe it was all too much for Nicole and she decided to end her life and take her daughter with her. She might be dead on the property somewhere.

Oli glances at her watch. 'I need to file something soon.' She scratches the side of her face—something is making her skin itch. She looks up at the trees accusingly.

Cooper is bouncing around as if he needs to piss. He cranes his neck back toward the main street. 'There's a cafe over there. We can grab a coffee, and you can write up your piece? I mean, I don't really know how you usually work, but I'm happy to do whatever you want.'

Oli closes her eyes, trying to think. The trouble with this job is that there's no roadmap telling you what to do next; there's just deadline after deadline, and angry editors yelling and texting from the office.

She scans what she can see of the main street. Dawn's intel suggests that the jogger spotted Nicole's body early this morning, and from what Oli saw of her corpse, she hasn't been dead longer than a day. Oli feels a surge of hope. If Nicole planned her suicide, there's a chance she also made plans to protect her daughter. Perhaps she entrusted the little girl to someone she knew would look after her and keep things as normal as possible.

Oli rams the empty milk carton into the chip packet and starts back toward the car. She wants to believe the child is alive. 'Come on!' she yells over her shoulder.

'Where are we going?'

'To the school.'

'School?'

'Yep.' She fires up the car, revs the engine, then activates the GPS app, which thankfully has decided to start working again. Once Cooper is in too, Oli reverses onto the road. Her heartbeat is racing ahead of her brain. 'We need to find Nicole Horrowitz's daughter.'

CHAPTER EIGHT

CRYSTALBROOK PRIMARY SCHOOL IS ALMOST ENTIRELY CAMOUFLAGED by gums. The twists and turns of the unwieldy building seem to accommodate the tree trunks and native shrubbery rather than the other way around. There are only four cars parked out front: two Toyotas, a Ford ute and a tired-looking Holden, hardly the fancy specimens always parked in front of Amy and Kate's school. No cops, which might just mean they're slow to move—or, thinks Oli grimly, it might mean they already know Nicole's little girl is dead.

Oli pulls open the heavy front door and strides confidently toward the reception area, tossing her long blonde hair over her shoulder as she looks past the worn partition. Cooper stands to her left, repeatedly lacing his fingers. A young woman in jeans and a lemon-coloured jumper is rustling through a filing cabinet, humming loudly to an Usher song on the radio.

'Hello. My name is Sarah Finlayson.' Oli speaks loudly, using her trusty old fake name. 'From the Education Department.'

The girl startles and promptly drops two folders. Her fringe is set in a thick curve above her wideset eyes, giving her a distinctly churchy look. 'Oh!' She looks at Oli and looks at the folders. 'Um.' She bites her lip.

'You can get those.'

The girl squats to pick them up, her face flushed. 'I'm Hayley. Did you say you're from the Education Department?'

'Yes, that's right,' Oli says primly. 'We're here to inquire about a student. Evie Maslan.' Oli speaks briskly and flits her eyes impatiently around the room.

'Evie Maslan?' Hayley's face lights up, then drops. 'Why, what's happened?'

'Evie is ten, correct?'

Hayley looks from Cooper to Oli. 'Ah, yes, ten or eleven.'

'Must be her,' Oli murmurs, letting her gaze rest on the wall before whipping her eyes back to Hayley, who straightens her shoulders in response. 'Is Evie in class right now?'

Hayley shakes her head. 'She doesn't go to school here.'

Cooper flips out his iPad and starts typing. 'Do you know which school she attends?' His voice is several notes deeper than normal. 'I'm Clark Wayne,' he adds, clearing his throat.

'Her mother homeschools her, but she's linked to our community so attends our events occasionally. Please, can you tell me what's happened?'

'I'm sorry,' Oli says, 'we really can't discuss it. Have you met her parents?'

Hayley's hand goes to fiddle with her necklace. 'I met Natalie a few times. She's nice.'

'Mmmmm.' Cooper acts as if this piece of information is fascinating.

Oli gives him a sharp look, and he busies himself with clearing his throat again.

'Should I get the principal?' Hayley squeaks. 'I can call him?'

'No, that won't be necessary.' Oli holds out her hand. 'Thank you for your help.' In situations like this, she finds it's best to keep people talking, moving and thinking. The more their senses are occupied, the less likely they are to remember details. 'Like I said, our investigation is confidential, so we'd appreciate it if you kept this exchange to yourself, Ms . . . ?'

'Oh, ah, Thurston. Hayley Thurston.'

Oli smiles stiffly. 'Thank you, Ms Thurston.'

'Of course. As long as Evie's okay.' Hayley pulls on the locket around her neck. 'She is okay, isn't she?'

'Have a good afternoon, Hayley.' Oli sets her lips in a line and heads to the door.

Cooper gives Hayley an awkward wave and follows.

'Clark Wayne?' Oli says as she gets in the car.

Cooper's dark eyes shine. 'Yeah, well, I was trying to think of an alias, but I knew if I said Bruce Wayne it might be kind of obvious, so I figured I'd combine Clark Kent *and* Bruce Wayne.'

'Genius.'

Cooper looks pleased.

Before starting the car, Oli calls Dawn and fills her in.

'This kid stuff is incredible, Oli, but I'm not running with it until you've got more.'

Oli bites her lip and puts the keys in the ignition. 'We'll push the cops, see if they'll talk once we tell them what we've got.'

'Good. We need to get some new info up as soon as possible to go with the shots.' Multiple phones trill in the background, and a male voice dips in and out of range. 'Can you get us copy in an hour?'

'I'll try.'

'It looks like O'Brien's going to get off, so TJ's lining up some interviews. But no matter what, we'll have to juggle both stories for the next twenty-four hours.'

'Okay.' Oli presses her lips together. 'Makes sense.'

'When are you speaking to Alex Riboni?'

'The interview is supposed to be on Sunday, but we're pushing to speak to her earlier.'

'Good,' Dawn purrs. 'That will show the slugs at the *Sun*. There's a lot riding on it, Oli, so make sure that kid knows what he's doing.'

Oli hangs up and starts the car. 'Damn it.'

'Everything okay?' Cooper says.

'Just deadlines.' She exhales slowly. 'It's fine.'

He checks his phone. 'Still nothing from Alex.'

Oli is starting to think that there won't be an interview with Alex at all.

—

Thick bushland blurs as they drive past, heading to the cafe on the main strip.

'Do you do that kind of thing all the time?' Cooper asks, a tentative note in his voice.

'What kind of thing?' Oli yanks down the visor.

'Pretend to be someone else?'

She shrugs. 'Sometimes, it just depends. Often it's the easiest way to get information, especially before a story breaks and people refuse to talk to you.'

'Don't you feel bad lying like that? I mean, she seemed nice.'

'No,' Oli replies. 'I know what I'm using the information for, I know my intentions are good. As long as that's always clear in my head, I don't feel bad.'

He stares straight ahead.

'What, you don't like that answer?' She glances at his profile, sees his jaw set at a stubborn tilt.

'I thought only cops went undercover,' he says after a few moments.

'Cops conduct extensive undercover operations. I just throw a fake name around now and then in exchange for information. Sometimes making yourself part of the story is the best way to get the facts.'

When Oli first met Dean eleven years ago, she was going by Sarah Finlayson. She had parked herself at a bar, eyes ringed with dark liner, tight white singlet exposing her tanned cleavage, when Dean came to her rescue. He firmly removed the sweaty arm of a man she'd been talking to who had started to blatantly grope her.

Oli was after the scoop on some high-flying lawyers allegedly involved in wide-reaching fraud that involved one of the big four banks, and she knew that two of the key players frequented this bar every Friday. So, she had tarted herself up three weeks in a row, but all she'd learned so far was that rich professional men could be just as creepy as poor uni students, and that drinking too many lemon, lime and bitters gave her mouth ulcers.

Dean Yardley was different. 'I'm sorry that dickhead was harassing you. Guys like that give men a bad name.' Dean proceeded to study her face so intently, she felt like she was being examined under white light. 'Do you want me to sit with you while you wait for whoever it is you're waiting for?' His wedding ring glinted, and his cologne filled her nostrils, reminding her of crafted wooden furniture and old movies. She could tell he was older than she was, but he was very good-looking—of course, he was also very married.

'It's just me,' she said. 'But I'm fine, thanks.'

His hand on the small of her bare back felt protective, not predatory. She didn't want him to stop touching her. 'I'm sure you know this,' he said, 'but you have the most incredible voice.'

'Thank you,' she said simply.

He smiled. 'I'm Dean.'

'I'm Sarah.'

'And how do I contact you, Sarah?'

'You don't.'

He pinched the skin between his eyes as if he couldn't believe what was happening. 'Fair enough.'

She discreetly pulled in her stomach, stuck out her chest.

'Well, even if I never see you again, I'm not sure it's safe for you here alone. You might get hassled by another creep.' His tone was loaded, but he didn't try anything on. He told her later that although he wanted to kiss her right there in the bar, he thought it was important that if anything happened between them it was on her terms.

'Honestly, I'm fine.' She smiled at him, and he smiled back, his eyes glued to her lips. 'And surely you have to get back to your friends?'

'Boring businessmen.' He laughed. 'From out of town. Believe me, I'd rather hang with you.'

He offered to buy her a drink before he returned to his table. She acquiesced and spent the next half an hour sipping the elaborate cocktail, her nerves on fire every time his gaze shifted her way.

The dodgy lawyers never showed up, and Oli left, even though she wanted to stay. Dean tipped his beer and winked at her as she weaved through the crowd to the exit. She smiled back and elbowed off unwanted attention until she was safely in a cab.

On the following two Fridays, she returned to the bar. She finally scored a lead on the lawyers, but Dean didn't show again.

He appeared two months later, outside court, while she was jostling with her peers, shouting questions at the premier about infrastructure overspend. Dean, outrageously handsome in a suit, was standing with the communications team. His eyebrows shot into the air. 'Sarah,' he mouthed. She shrugged and winked, a move that was completely out of character, but he made her feel light. Playful.

She sometimes wonders how things would have turned out if she had pretended not to recognise him, had turned down his offer of a drink later that evening.

'I don't do it as much as I used to,' she muses to Cooper. 'I guess it's different these days—so much information is on social media.'

'So where to now?' he asks.

'We need to find the kid. Dawn's not keen to run with it until we can be sure.'

He swallows. 'Do you think Evie could be at the house?'

'I think it's possible. Or Nicole might have taken her somewhere safe.' Oli pauses, daring to say what they're surely both thinking. 'Or it could be a murder–suicide.'

'Yeah, I figured that too.' Cooper looks out the window, his jaw tensing again.

'But,' she reasons, 'if they found another body at the house, I think Rusty would have told me. Assuming he knew.'

Cooper brightens. 'So maybe Evie is with someone else. A friend or something.'

'Maybe.'

'Maybe she's with a neighbour?'

'I hope so but realistically there's every chance she's dead too, so we should be prepared for that.'

'That's pretty negative,' Cooper says prissily.

Oli looks at him, eyebrow arched. 'When you've been doing this as long as I have, you tend to assume the worst.'

He shrugs like he thinks this is a bad strategy. 'Nicole might have had a partner, so maybe Evie is with them.'

'Sure,' Oli says sarcastically, 'in which case I'd really like to, first, know who he is and, second, see what he has to say about the whole situation.'

Cooper looks confused. 'She might have had a female partner.'

Oli forces herself to stay calm. 'Sure, whatever. Male or female, the point is that partners are problematic. They're the most likely to kill you, and your kids.'

'You saw her,' Cooper whispers. 'Did it look like she'd been murdered to you?'

'No,' says Oli, scratching at her chin, her nose, 'but we don't know what happened yet. Maybe he did something to Evie, and it drove Nicole to take her own life. Statistically, if you're murdered it's most likely at the hand of your partner, ex-partner, kid or parents. In that order.'

'I know the stats.' Cooper turns his head to look out the window. 'I'm not an idiot.'

Oli sails through the roundabout, easing them back into the main street of Crystalbrook. 'Had you ever seen a dead body before?'

'Not in real life,' he mumbles.

'Well, if you're going to be a crime journalist you need to get used to it. It's not as bad as being a paramedic or a cop, but it's still pretty bleak sometimes.' She meets her own gaze in the rear-view mirror, hating how naive her round blue eyes make her look. 'Though I have to say, that scene today was pretty bad.'

Cooper nods, looking stricken.

She hopes he isn't about to fall in a heap. 'Anyway, that's enough Journalism 101 from me for today. I need to get some copy to Dawn.' Oli indicates the cafe on the other side of the road adorned with old-fashioned lampposts and cast-iron trimmings. 'You can start making some calls.' She holds up her hand as he opens his mouth to speak. 'We need to start lining up other interviews—with family members, Miles Wu, everyone at the party that night who will talk to us.'

'Okay, sure.' Cooper wipes his palms on his jeans. 'I can do that.'

'And I want to go through your questions for Alex. God, I hope she gets in touch soon.'

Without warning, the road shudders beneath them. A fire engine screams past at breakneck speed, heading in the direction of Laker Drive. Less than thirty seconds later, another does the same. Cooper's mouth pulls into an O.

'Shit,' Oli says.

He looks at her. 'You said nothing else was going to happen at the—'

'Shut up, Cooper.' Oli puts her foot to the floor.

CHAPTER NINE

A NEAT CLOUD OF SMOKE BILLOWS ABOVE THE TREES. OLI AND Cooper are silent, both lost in their own scrambled thoughts. Oli's entire body is like a coiled spring as she sifts through the possibilities. Maybe Evie was locked in a storage shed and set it on fire in an escape attempt?

Oli grits her teeth and pulls over at the Laker Drive turn-off, her stomach in knots. She turns to Cooper. 'Take the car and see if you can get higher. We can always pick up the aerial footage from the TV networks, but if you can find a lookout you might get a decent shot of whatever is going on.'

'Where are you going?'

'To find someone who can tell me what the hell is happening.' Without waiting for his reply, she heads off on foot, thankful again she's wearing her boots. The cool air is already hazy with smoke, but there are no sirens now. The only sounds are the swish of the trees and the erratic orchestra of birdlife. She starts to jog, her legs protesting immediately. She used to swim three times a week, pushing her body through the water while she turned stories over in her head. When was the last time she went to the pool? March?

She rounds the bend and is greeted with chaos. Cops are hustling people away, trying to direct the traffic along the narrow road. Wisps of smoke dance past, latching on to clothes and hair. A Channel Nine cameraman she knows a little approaches her. Everyone calls him Mud; she has no idea what his real name is.

'What happened?' she asks.

'Dunno. I was packing my gear, and there was a sound, sort of like a shot. Then everyone started shouting that there was a fire, and the cops asked us to stay back.'

'Is the fire at the house?'

'I reckon. That's where the fireys went, right up the driveway. A bloody nightmare getting them through all the journos. And the cops had only just navigated the body coming out. You know what this mob is like—people were hell-bent on getting a good shot rather than helping the cops. It wasn't pretty.' He sniffs unattractively and swallows whatever he manages to dislodge from his sinuses. 'My lady's in there now, hobbling around on her high heels trying to get the lowdown.'

Oli knows the reporter he's usually paired with, a tiny blonde with a big smile who wears brightly coloured jackets. Tamara? Tammy? She recently graduated from fluff pieces to headlines but has failed to tone down the outfits.

'I heard a couple of cops were in the place when it went up,' Mud adds.

Oli thinks of Rusty, feels a pull in her gut. 'Any casualties?'

Mud shrugs. 'Not as far as I know.'

She relaxes slightly.

'Might have just been something was left on, an oven or stove, but I dunno, maybe it's suss.'

It's what Oli is thinking too, but could someone have snuck onto the property with cops everywhere?

'Are you heading back?' she asks Mud.

'Yeah.' He scratches his crotch and squints into the smoky sun. 'My lady has her own wheels. I need to get back to the office and start sorting out this shit.' He gestures to the camera slung over his shoulder, then looks skyward again. 'You need a lift back to the city?'

'Um, no, thanks. I drove.' Oli says goodbye to Mud and makes her way to the front gate.

Cooper texts her a bunch of photos he's taken from further up the mountain. The dark-grey nest of smoke looks like a mistake in the middle of the greenery. A chopper shot would be better, but they're not bad, and she writes back that he should send them in.

She reaches the end of the driveway, where the smoke is slightly thicker. There are fewer people around than before, many of them in uniform. A handful of reporters mill about, gunning for interviews and doing their grabs, but she guesses most have headed back to the city. The firefighters are packing up as well.

Bowman is sitting on the back step of an ambulance, looking furious. His coughs evolve into a splutter, but he waves away a paramedic's offer of a water bottle. A few metres away, Rusty talks into his phone, a dirty smudge on his face. He winces at the paramedic applying a bandage to his hand.

'Rusty!' Oli calls out.

He lifts his gaze, indicates that he's fine with a swift gesture.

She slides her eyes back to Bowman, who has stopped coughing and is getting to his feet. He looks so vulnerable that she feels embarrassed—it's almost like seeing him naked.

'Excuse me, Chief Inspector,' she says, approaching him. 'Were you in the house when the fire started? Are you injured?'

'I'm not injured,' he replies firmly.

'Can you tell me what happened?'

He doesn't reply but stares at her. Up close she can see grime in his pores. She remembers his shattered expression at Isabelle's funeral as he delivered an emotional tribute, standing next to a large photo of the slain detective. Not for the first time, Oli wonders how close they were, whether she confided in him.

Bowman pulls his gaze away and starts walking, heavy-footed but at a surprisingly fast pace.

Oli rushes to keep up. 'Has the fire destroyed the house?'

He holds a hand out as if to silence her. 'We'll give a statement once we have more information.'

'I know she had a kid,' Oli blurts. 'A little girl.'

He grimaces. 'Are you running with that?'

His stare is cool, and goose bumps break out on Oli's arms. 'We plan to. I have enough to speculate.'

'Right.' He turns from her and keeps walking.

'Will you give a comment? There must have been evidence of a child in the house.'

He doesn't reply.

She stops following him, frustrated. 'Did you process the scene before the fire?'

'No comment,' he replies robotically, without turning around.

'Are you sure she wasn't on the property?'

'Not today, Ms Groves. We'll talk another time.'

'Tomorrow?' she yells. 'I can meet you whenever suits.'

The wind gusts, stirring up more smoke. Bowman joins a small group of men and women in uniform.

'All clear!' a firey shouts to his colleagues, before he mutters something into a walkie-talkie.

Oli sidles up next to him. 'How did the fire start?' she asks, her face pulled into gossipy worry. 'I've just come from next door.'

A benefit of not being on TV is that no one recognises her, and she doesn't look groomed enough to arouse suspicion.

Jolly old Oli, her father's voice taunts in her head.

'We're not sure yet.' The firey sniffs a few times and wipes his face. 'Apparently there was an explosion inside. There's a big old fireplace in the main room, so maybe something was still burning in there—or it could have been dodgy wiring. Lots of houses around here aren't maintained that well.'

'Could it have been a bomb?' Oli wonders aloud.

He scoffs. 'Nah, doubt it, but I wasn't first on the scene. Good thing no one was inside—it was wiped out in no time. A tiny old place. Must have been freezing in winter.'

'How many bedrooms?'

The firey withdraws. Narrows his eyes. 'You're a journo?'

'Yep,' she replies without hesitation.

'Well, probably best we stop talking, then.'

'Two bedrooms?'

He throws her an exasperated look.

Oli tries to find Rusty, but he's disappeared and doesn't answer his phone. She heads back down Laker Drive and calls Dawn.

'This is unbelievable!' She sounds like she's won the lotto. 'The pictures the kid sent are great. Absolutely fab. We're posting them in a minute.'

'It will take me an hour to get you copy now.' Oli narrowly avoids stumbling in a pothole.

'Don't worry, Pia's drafted something that will be fine until yours comes through. It's all pretty soft at this stage, but we're in a good place. The reader stats on the 2005 recap and photo gallery we pushed live are going absolutely bananas. Like, fucking nuts. There are already over five hundred comments.'

'Cooper told me there are several Housemate Homicide Facebook groups,' Oli adds. 'Some pro Alex, some anti.'

'Check them out. Get Cooper to talk to the most opinionated members and get some quotes.'

Oli isn't sure that adding fuel to that particular fire is necessarily the best idea, but she's hardly about to argue when Dawn's in full flight.

'We're hearing that the *Sun* is going to run a poll on whether Alex was the killer. Can you believe it? God, they're tacky.'

Oli makes a sympathetic sound as she reaches the end of the road, wondering where Cooper is with her car.

'I haven't seen anything come through confirming the cause of death,' Dawn says. 'Did they say anything at the scene?'

'She definitely hung herself.'

'Okay, good. We'll stick with speculation for the time being, but lay it on thick. You can allude to the child too, I checked with legal—but no details, not even gender, okay?'

'No problem,' Oli says, before adding, 'Bowman and another cop were near the house when it went up in flames. They weren't injured. I spoke to Bowman afterwards, and he didn't deny that Horrowitz has a child.'

Dawn emits a controlled scream. 'Christ, this is too good. We might run a few different pieces, see what grabs.'

The Audi appears just as Dawn starts reeling off plans for tomorrow's edition. Oli shifts Cooper's backpack from the passenger seat onto the floor and awkwardly arranges her long legs around it. 'Let's go,' she mouths, and Cooper nods, tearing off down the road.

Dawn chews on something as she talks, and the sporadic swallowing sounds make Oli feel nauseous. Or perhaps it's Cooper's driving; he flips between the stop-start style of her nervous mother and the speeding of her overconfident sister.

'Now about the feature,' Dawn says, 'what are you thinking?'

Oli pictures Nicole's body hanging from the tree. 'Well, until we know whether the kid is alive or dead it's hard to say, but I think I'll start with today and work backwards. Focus on the tragedy of two young women ending up dead, a decade apart. I obviously want to find out what Nicole Horrowitz has been doing these past ten years, speak to anyone who knew her, and identify the kid's father.' Oli watches the trees whip past. 'I'm also thinking we profile the Paradise Street house. How it was the epicentre of the friendship group, and the social hub for the girls the summer before Evelyn died.'

'And you'll speak to the other party-goers, right? The old boyfriend?'

'Yep, we'll start working on quotes. See if they'll agree to interviews.'

'Okay, good. I think this will come together well, Oli. I'll want your roughs by Sunday. I assume that's doable?'

Anxiety settles across her chest. 'Should be fine.'

'Great, Sunday morning. Gotta go, Joosten's right up my arse today. Hey, tell the digi kid that his photo's up on the site. It looks good.' Dawn hangs up.

Oli glances across at Cooper, who looks ridiculous driving her car.

'Evie wasn't in the house?' he asks.

'I don't think so.'

'That's good.'

She pulls out her laptop and starts typing. The motion of the car reminds her of when she first worked in news and wrote on the bus to and from work. 'Your photo is online,' she says.

'Really? That's cool.'

'Yeah.'

'I still haven't heard from Alex. She hasn't read my message.' He combs at his hair with his fingers. 'Do you think she's going to get back to me?'

'It's not a good sign,' Oli says.

'I feel stressed.'

'Welcome to journalism,' she replies, typing furiously.

—

Dean calls when they're about halfway down the mountain. Oli has so far refrained from making comments about Cooper's driving, which seems to be getting worse.

'I'm sorry I never called you back,' she begins, switching off the car's Bluetooth. 'Crazy day.'

'No worries,' Dean replies. 'You're out on the road?'

'Um, yes. I'm in the car but I'm not driving.'

'I'm guessing that means there's no chance you can pick the girls up tonight? Nina's sick, and I really need to be in a meeting at four pm.'

'Um, sorry, I can't.' Oli mentally curses Nina the babysitter, who is much more likely to be hungover than sick. 'We're on our way back now, but we're probably still forty-five minutes from town. Plus, I've got to file my piece, which I've only just started.'

'Are you with TJ?'

Oli glances at Cooper. 'No, I'm with another colleague.'

'Right.'

She wedges the phone against her ear and keeps typing, determined not to be the one to fill the silence.

'I guess I can ask Toni to pick up the girls,' Dean says. 'I'm sure she won't mind.'

Oli rolls her eyes. 'I'm sure she won't.' Toni is their next-door neighbour and was good friends with Isabelle.

'Hang on, I'll text her now.' There're a few moments of muffled sounds. 'Alright, done, cross your fingers.'

'Crossed.'

'What are you working on?' Dean's voice is light; he's clearly keen to change the subject.

'Nicole Horrowitz has turned up dead. A suicide, but there're some weird circumstances. As you can imagine, it's been a crazy day.'

He inhales sharply. 'Jesus, wow. I saw something earlier about a death in the hills, but I didn't know it was her.'

Oli wonders if he's thinking back to that time when both she and Isabelle were doggedly obsessed with the housemates. Both of them seeing Dean.

'So,' he says, 'I'm guessing that means you'll be home pretty late?'

'I'm really not sure yet. I've also got a feature to write.'

'That's great, Oli,' he says sincerely. 'I know how much you love them.'

'Yes,' she says, feeling a ripple of pride. 'It's a lot to do in not a lot of time.'

'You'll be great. I just don't want you to work too hard.'

'Likewise,' she counters. She thinks she hears him sigh.

'Also, I want to check you haven't forgotten about taking the girls to the swimming carnival on Thursday night?'

Shit. She thought the carnival was weeks away. 'Of course not. I'm looking forward to it.'

'Okay, great. I really want one of us to be there. Anyway, I better go. I'll sort dinner so you can eat something decent when you get home. Good luck with your story, I'm sure it will be great.'

Dean and dinner, she thinks as the call disconnects. Before she was with him, all her meals were sporadic and varied. She ate so frequently that meals themselves seemed unnecessary; regular sit-down dinners just weren't part of her schedule. She ate at her desk, often late at night, usually something salty straight out of a box. On nights off, she and Rusty became takeaway connoisseurs. But Dean believes in the power of a home-cooked meal. He likes the routine of dinner and feels strongly that the family unit should revolve around it.

Oli stares out the window and wonders if he's finding it hard to adjust to a life with her. Saying yes to his proposal felt hasty but right, an inevitable step forward in their renewed romance. It was her thirty-ninth birthday, and they'll be married within the year. The synchronicity appealed almost as much as the diamond-studded band he presented to her.

She and Cooper have hit suburbia again, the tapestry of green on either side of the road replaced by large double-storey houses with several cars clogging the driveways. Faded play equipment sits on front lawns beside dirty wading pools full of leaves. Oli thinks about the house on Paradise Street: the knobbly rosebushes in the front yard, the row of shoes next to the door. Evelyn's bloody body in the hallway.

Oli gets back to work on her laptop, the screen filling with words as she describes the scene at Laker Drive, implies suicide, and briefly recaps the events from ten years ago before finishing with the suggestion that a child might have been in Nicole's care at the time of her death. Oli skims the piece from start to finish, editing as she reads under her breath. It's good, punchy, with reveals in all the right places.

'You do have your licence?' Oli inquires politely, after Cooper drifts into the left lane before dramatically overcorrecting.

'I was a late bloomer driving-wise,' he admits happily, 'but I got my licence when I was twenty-one.'

She grits her teeth. Surely he can't be much older than twenty-one now.

'I think driving this car is making me nervous,' he explains. 'My family aren't really car people, but this is pretty amazing.'

'Eyes on the road,' she says pointedly.

The moment they hit the city, they're greeted by gridlock. She gives her copy one more cursory check before tethering to her phone and sending it to Dawn. Oli's mind flashes to the image of Nicole's body hanging from the tree, and she wonders where the little girl is. She remembers the creek running along the rear of the property and thinks grim thoughts.

'So we're going back to the office, yeah?' Cooper says, flicking the windscreen-wipers on instead of the indicator. 'I need to get a few things sorted for the podcast. Plus, my bike's there. Do you ride? It's the best. Really good for fitness—and the environment, obviously.'

'No, I don't. I'm going to work offsite for a few hours and get a jump on my feature, but I'm happy to swing past the office first to drop you off.' She's itching to get away from him and have some time to herself.

'Sure,' he says amiably. 'Hey, so if Alex gets back to me, I'll let you know straight away.'

'Yes.' Oli puts her phone down. 'Day or night, if you hear from her, you call me.'

'I really hope she does.' His brow furrows as he turns into the car park. He stops too far from the security checkpoint, and Oli pretends not to notice as he unbuckles his seatbelt and hangs halfway out the window to wave her pass against the scanner. At least he doesn't have trouble parking. 'Here we are.' He turns off the car and rolls his shoulders.

She hands him his backpack and gets out, then goes around to the driver's side with her hands on her hips.

A text from Dawn arrives. *We're running your piece now. Good work. Keep me across the Alex interview.*

Despite her exhaustion, Oli feels the rush. It never gets old, her words in print.

Cooper springs out of the driver's seat. 'So unless I call you in the middle of the night to conduct a covert interview with Alex, should we meet here first thing? Your desk?'

Oli is already a million miles away, deciding where to go for food. She's starving.

'Oli?'

'Sorry, what?'

'Tomorrow morning. Should we meet at eight? You're usually in pretty early and, like you said, we need to go over my interview questions.'

'I'm sorry, Cooper, but I'm more of a solo worker. Why don't you just send them to me to look over?'

'Deal.' He sticks out his hand; she looks at it, then shakes it. 'Thanks, Oli, this was great. A real memory-bank day. I'd better get filing!' He scampers off, clutching the camera, the tails of several cords hanging out the top of his half-open backpack.

CHAPTER TEN

THE AUTOMATIC GATES CLOSE SILENTLY, BLOCKING OFF THE TREE-lined street. A few beats later, the garage door starts its descent, sealing Oli safely inside. Home. Dean's Land Rover is already here, and she sits in the dark for a few moments, trying to decompress before she heads inside.

After she dropped Cooper off at the office, she drove to her favourite pub in Richmond for a beer and a bowl of chips, which she devoured in between mapping out the framework of her feature, all the while checking for updates from the cops. They still haven't confirmed the identity of the body, even though the majority of news outlets are running with Nicole's name while dredging up photos of the housemates and images from Alex Riboni's trial. The police must be struggling to get on to Nicole's family, and no doubt the fire has made processing the scene more challenging. Oli tried a few searches to determine if the Horrowitzes still live in Melbourne but couldn't find any personal details. A missing daughter turning up dead is bad enough, but the fact she was alive for so long then died by suicide will surely carry extra pain. And if it turns out they have a granddaughter, they'll have to come to terms with that as well.

Sitting in the garage, Oli texts Rusty's personal phone to ask if he's okay, hoping he might offer more intel. She's tempted to message Cooper and double-check if he's heard from Alex, but she doesn't want to encourage dialogue. Plus, she thinks wryly, Cooper will call, email *and* text if he has even the slightest update. She closes her eyes briefly. Babysitting him was exhausting—though admittedly he turned out to be a good photographer, and taking the shot of Nicole showed some unexpected spunk. It helped that Oli enjoyed being out of the office and working a big story.

She thinks back over some of their conversations. Alistair Joosten's apparent involvement in the podcast surprises her. She'll talk to TJ about it; they're in the same boat, after all, battle-weary soldiers in an increasingly crowded and high-tech field.

She knows she should head upstairs, but she's enjoying the quiet of the garage. The dry air gives it a cosy feel. Cans of paint line the shelves on the left wall, and an impressive array of tools hang on the back. Who knew you could own so many things? When she moved out of her rented apartment, there was nothing to pack from the single-car garage except an old tent and a tatty broom.

Dean knows his way around the corporate ladder, but he's rather fond of the other kind as well. He collects skills like a Cub Scout, always embarking on some kind of learning adventure and encouraging the girls to do the same. Last year his mother told Oli that he's always been like that. *Desperate to compete with his brothers,* was her theory. Dean has two older brothers born a year apart, but there's an eight-year age gap between Patrick and Dean. Patrick and John are doctors, athletic and amiable, so it stands to reason that Dean would feel the need to prove himself. He's constantly mastering something: pruning the fruit trees, building a bird feeder, learning a language. Conversely, he's forever wanting Oli to outsource tasks, to slow down and do less.

Most people would kill for a life like this, to have someone like Dean. Ten years ago, *she* would have killed for it. And maybe that's the problem. It feels too good to be true, like it might be taken away as quickly as it arrived. Her thoughts splinter, shards of glass hovering in space. She tosses her head, and the pieces retreat to the edges of her mind.

She can't sit in the garage all night.

The snappy scent of garlic fills her nostrils as she steps into the stairwell. Kate is playing the piano, a haunting classical melody that weaves through the house. Oli stops short on the landing. A tinkle of female laughter. It must be Toni; she remembers Dean saying he would ask her to pick up the kids. Toni lives next door in a stunning light-filled house with a lap pool and a rooftop balcony. Her husband is a financial expert who spends a lot of his time in Dubai and New York. Toni and Isabelle used to go on holidays together with the children when their husbands were stuck at work. A few months ago Toni invited Dean and Oli for dinner, and in the kitchen she noticed a photo of Isabelle and Toni on a pin board, drinking cocktails. Isabelle looked happy and relaxed, nothing like the serious detective Oli had observed at crime scenes and press conferences.

Kate finishes her piano piece and starts a new one.

Oli wants nothing more than to go straight upstairs and have a shower, crawl into bed and fall into a long dreamless sleep. For a minute she craves her pokey old apartment with its double bed and worn flannel sheets.

Laughter flares again, followed by Dean's low-pitched chuckle. Oli has a strange sense of being an intruder in her own house. She makes her way quietly down the corridor, her fingers tracing the photo frames on the wall. Dean and the girls; the girls on their own. Dean and Oli, taken on the night Dean proposed. On a side table is a small frame with a photo of Isabelle holding Kate when she was a baby.

Oli stops in front of the picture. Isabelle's fingers curl around Kate's plump legs. Her eyes exactly match the sky-blue of her shirt. She was petite, but Oli saw first-hand her quiet power. It's hard to believe that in the end she was wiped out so cruelly. Oli has never said anything to Dean about the photo, or commented on the one in the lounge room—it would be a petty thing to raise—but all of a sudden she wonders how he would react if photos of her ex were on display in their house. But this is different, of course: the tragedy of Isabelle's death means the normal rules don't apply. Grief trumps insecurity.

Underneath the tinkling piano, Oli detects a male voice that doesn't belong to Dean. *Who is that?* She corrects her posture and fluffs out her hair. As she enters the kitchen, she arranges her face into a pleasant expression. Nathan Farrow, Dean's main university client, is seated next to Toni at the island bench, and Dean stands opposite them both. Amy is at the kitchen table, sitting bolt upright while she types away on her laptop.

Toni spots her first, her expression dipping a little before resetting. 'Olive! Hi.'

'Hi, Toni.' Oli waves awkwardly, depositing her satchel on the spotless bench. 'Hi, Nathan.'

Oli's only met him once before, at a fancy lunch Dean's business hosted a few months ago. He's in his fifties, tall and trim, and seems to be experimenting, unsuccessfully, with facial hair. From their brief conversation Oli remembers thinking he seemed surprised to find himself in such a senior position. He has relied on Dean like a prosthetic limb ever since the uni was embroiled in a sex scandal three months ago. A male student claims he was assaulted by a male teacher on campus after hours; the teacher denies it. The student has mental health issues. For the sake of her relationship with Dean, Oli was happy to see the story go to TJ.

'It's nice to see you again, Oli,' Nathan says. 'I'm sorry I'm always monopolising your husband.'

The word 'husband' hangs in the air, but no one corrects him.

'Hey, babe.' Dean puts down his beer and ambles over, kisses Oli on the lips. 'Nath tagged along with me. We've got some more work to do tonight, unfortunately. Want a drink?'

'No, thanks.'

Toni throws back the remaining contents of her glass and rakes a hand through her curly black hair. 'I was just telling Dean that there have been some break-ins in the neighbourhood, over in Grant Street and one on Nolan.'

'That's no good,' Oli says.

'Yeah. Jewellery and electronics. Some cash.' Toni ticks the items off on her fingers. 'Definitely worth being extra careful.'

'Absolutely.' Oli has found that despite their expensive security systems and overblown insurance policies, people in this area are much more worried about being burgled than those in her old suburb.

Toni slides off the chair and straightens her fitted T-shirt. 'I should be off. I'm sure the boys haven't done a scrap of homework, and god knows what state the house is in.'

'Thanks for helping out, Tones,' Dean says. 'You're a lifesaver.'

'Oh, no problem! Any time. It's always nice to hang out with the girls. Such a pleasant change to my stinky boys, god love them.' Toni gives Amy a tight hug. 'Good to see you, hon. Let me know how you go with your project, okay?'

Amy nods, smiling up at her.

'It was nice to meet you, Nathan.' Toni shakes his hand.

'Absolutely.' He nods and grips her hand. 'Very nice.'

Oli exchanges a smile with Dean. Clearly Nathan is taken with Toni.

'I'll just duck in and say bye to Kate.' Toni waves at Oli and kisses Dean on the cheek. 'You guys have a great week! Might catch you on the weekend.' She exits the kitchen, an attractive ball of energy.

'Want some dinner, Oli?' Dean clears his throat, plucking Toni's empty glass from the bench before rinsing it out. His face is flushed; he's clearly had more than one drink, which is unusual.

Despite the chips she ate earlier, Oli is still starving. 'Sure. What is it?'

'Salmon. Toni whipped it up.'

'It's very good,' Nathan says.

Oli wrinkles her nose. She'd kill for a steak or maybe some pasta.

Dean arranges the food on a large white plate. He opens his mouth as if to speak, then seems to change his mind. He pours himself a glass of water.

'Thanks.' Oli sits on the chair Toni vacated. It's still warm. 'How are you, Nathan?'

He presses his lips together, nods. 'Oh, you know, not bad. Dean is keeping me on my toes. No doubt I'd be in a hopeless mess without him.'

'Nathan did a great job today.' Dean sips his water as he watches Oli shake soy sauce onto her meal. 'Go easy on that, Ol, it's full of salt.'

She puts the bottle down and avoids eye contact with him. Dean puts it back in the cupboard.

'Hey, Ames, time to get ready for bed, please.' Dean's tone doesn't invite argument. 'Tell your sister.'

Amy closes the laptop abruptly. 'Goodnight,' she says.

'Night, Amy,' chime Oli and Nathan.

She leaves the room. A minute later, the piano stops.

'Night, Kate!' Dean calls out.

Her little voice reaches the kitchen. 'Goodnight.'

'How's the world of journalism going, Oli?' Nathan asks.

'Good, thanks. Busy.'

Dean tips his head sideways and looks at her with affection. 'Media is going through the same transformation as education. People want their news in snack format. That's why the PR game has become such a nightmare—it's just headlines, no one reads the bloody detail anymore.'

Oli feels defensive. 'Our numbers are still pretty good.'

Yawning, he circles his shoulders in their sockets. 'Journalism is no safer from automation than any other industry.'

'I'm not sure that's true,' says Oli, thinking back to her conversation with Cooper.

'I saw O'Brien got off today,' Nathan says tentatively, looking between the two of them.

Oli nods. 'Yeah. Good lawyers, I guess. And lots of practice dodging the truth.'

'His career is still ruined, though,' Dean says.

'I'm sure a generous board position will come his way in the not-too-distant future,' Oli says.

Nathan nods and takes an awkward sip of beer. 'That does seem to be the way the cookie crumbles.'

'Maybe, maybe not,' Dean says. 'The court of public conviction is gaining strength, as you know all too well, Nath.' Dean is in a strange mood, Oli thinks. He makes a half-hearted attempt to clean the spotless bench, then fusses with the dishes drying in the rack before he brings his hands together in a silent clap. 'Nath, we should knuckle down. We've got a fair bit to cover.'

'Yes, absolutely yes,' Nathan says, and points to the lounge. 'Should we set up in there?'

'Yes, mate, you go ahead. Feel free to commandeer the dining table. Read through the prop I sent you, and I'll be in shortly.'

Nathan picks up his bag. 'No worries. Well, goodnight, Oli. Thanks for putting up with this.'

'Not a problem.'

Now that Kate isn't playing the piano, the kitchen feels hollow. Oli tunes in to the steady tick of the grandfather clock.

Dean comes around the bench to massage her shoulders. 'You okay?'

She nods. 'It was just a long day.'

'I hope it's okay that Nath's here. I meant to text you.'

'It's totally fine.'

Dean's fingers probe her tense muscles, and she starts to relax. 'Has that Horrowitz girl really been holed up in the sticks the entire time?'

'We don't know.' Oli's thoughts return to the events of the day. 'Someone else was definitely living there until a few years ago so I doubt it. But at this point I suppose anything is possible.'

'It all seems very bizarre.'

'I know. And we think she was living there with her daughter.'

He looks puzzled. 'She had a kid?'

'We're pretty sure.'

'Who's we?'

'I got buddied up with this kid from the digital department and had to play babysitter all day. He's a total pain in the arse, actually.'

'I bet.' Dean's gaze drops to the floor.

'What?'

'Nothing.'

'Dean?'

'I'm sorry, it's just Isabelle worked on that case, you know.'

Oli tilts her head, trying to read his body language. 'Yes, I covered the story. Don't you remember?'

He ignores her question. 'It really broke her.'

Oli goes to the sink and pours a glass of water. Gulps it down thirstily before saying, 'That was a long time ago.'

'She was under a lot of pressure. I was really worried about her.' He reaches for Oli's hand. 'I worry about you too.' Little sparks of electricity run through her as he strokes her palm, traces his finger up her wrist. There's something oddly pleasurable about being compared to Isabelle, having Dean pair them in this way.

'I'm not a cop, Dean,' she says gently. 'It's totally different. Plus, I don't even know if the case will be officially reopened. It might be a dead end.'

He dips his head and gives a small nod, then nudges her legs open, standing between them. Her limbs give way, and he presses his pelvis into hers. 'I know, I know. It's just . . . Look, don't take this the wrong way, but sometimes this feels like a second chance. I can be a better husband than I was back then.' He stares into her eyes. 'A better person. You know what I mean.'

Oli casts her mind back to their secret dates, their secret emails and texts. The primal intensity of it all. She was obsessed with him. She hung on to any suggestion that his marriage wouldn't last. She spent half her waking life waiting for him to call. Every text triggered a mild panic attack. Even though she'd expected it, the emotional gut-punch when he told her he couldn't see her anymore was brutal. She barely ate, barely slept, and walked around in a haze for months, unable to purge herself of him. Disoriented and broken, she wondered if she might not survive.

And now, impossibly, she has unfettered access to him. She's living her own fantasy.

His voice cracks. 'I'd be lost without you, Oli, and so would the girls. You're so important to me.' His fingers massage the back of her scalp as he kisses her gently.

She closes her eyes and tries to let herself melt into him, conscious of Nathan in the other room.

Dean's lips nuzzle at her ear. 'Now you're finally mine,' he whispers, 'I can't lose you.'

'I'm not going anywhere,' she says, staring at her reflection over his shoulder in the mirrored splashback.

—

Oli slips past the twins' closed doors and down the hallway, clutching her old laptop to her chest, a shoebox under her arm. Her skin is clammy and flushed from sex, her limbs loosened by endorphins, but she's more alert than she has been all day. Nathan didn't leave until almost eleven, and she was asleep when Dean came upstairs. He was gentle but determined; he is always so physical, so intense. Afterwards, he fell asleep immediately, his arm resting across her abdomen. But she lay there, the image of Nicole's dead body playing on her mind.

Oli opens the door at the end of the passage and flicks on the light. Isabelle's room. The built-in wardrobe runs the length of the wall opposite and goes all the way to the ceiling. On the cream sofa bed are several folded blankets, alongside a trio of case-less pillows. A piano keyboard stands in the corner, some sheet music propped on its ledge. The curtains are partly open, and the window behind the uncluttered oak desk looks down onto Survey Drive.

She eases the door shut and gazes out from behind the glass. After a few moments, a red car slowly sails past. There's a flurry of movement near the front fence—a possum darting up a tree, or perhaps an adventurous cat. Pulling away, she sets her laptop on the small side table that faces the door, and plugs her charger into the wall. Her old machine whirs to life, making faint electronic noises.

She places the shoebox on the oak desk. Smooths her hand across the glossy grain.

Isabelle used to love this room. Dean said she fed the twins in here when they were babies. Later, it became her study.

Another car screeches into the street, and its headlights sweep across the front gate, lighting up the driveway. Its motor is revved obnoxiously as it passes the house, then the night settles into silence again. Oli sits, her feet tucked under her legs in the leather office chair, and tugs off the cardboard lid. Six notebooks and dozens of memory sticks. All have labels: little white pieces of paper sealed with sticky tape to protect the names she wrote on them. When she left *The Daily*, she spent an entire weekend saving all of her old pieces, research notes and contact lists, wondering if it would prove to be a complete waste of time. Clearly not.

She flicks through one of the notebooks. Her messy shorthand fills every page, and so many words are underlined that any attempt at emphasis has clearly failed. It's both familiar and foreign. Her writing has evolved over the years; it's less round these days, more clipped and impatient.

Facedown under the notebooks there's a photo frame, the one she used to keep on her desk at work: her and Lily at their mother's wedding, arms around each other with their tongues poking out. Both tall with matching wheat-coloured hair parted harshly in the middle, skin tinted tan, blue eyes ringed with black liner. Lily's dark-brown spray of freckles charming as always, Oli's plumper face completely unmarked. Their dad always delighted in telling the story of a toddler-aged Oli trying to wipe the dirty spots off Lily's face when she was sleeping. The photo had been taken a few years before Oli met Dean. She had deferred from her arts degree and was waitressing at a hotel bar in the city; she made more from tips than from her hourly wage, wrote the occasional magazine article, and worked on short stories when she couldn't sleep. Lily was employed at the art gallery and dating a revolving door of attractive men.

Oli looks at the photo again. Both girls are flushed, full of champagne and broadly happy for their mother, if only because they were relieved that she was finally someone else's problem.

Eleven years before the girls posed at their mother's wedding, Bradley Groves had gambled away the last of the family savings and taken off in their only car, never to be seen again, leaving their mother with a mound of debt and no obvious way to pay it back. Seven years after that, Oli had scraped her unconscious mother off her bedroom floor, still picking up the mess he had left behind.

Pretty Lily and jolly Oli.

Oli's jaw starts to ache, and she swallows determinedly. Why does this photo make her so sad? Lily seems happy enough now; Shaun adores her, and they've bonded over their mutual hatred of his ex-wife. Oli has Dean. And the girls. Their lives are a version of what they used to talk about when they speculated about their futures. In many ways, it's all turned out better than they ever thought it would.

But Oli feels guilt when she looks at this photo, like she's somehow betrayed this former version of herself.

She puts the notebook back and digs around in the box, looking for the one she used during the Housemate Homicide story: A4 with a plain beige cover, filled with hundreds of pages of notes, phone numbers and questions. She runs her hand over the textured surface, remembers holding it as she watched Isabelle at the press conference the day after Evelyn's body was found. Jo stood next to Oli and bitched about the incompetence of the police, having rushed back from the country wedding. Oli, on the other hand, was mesmerised by Isabelle. The young detective spoke clearly, her voice feminine but powerful. She confirmed that Evelyn Stanley had been murdered, stabbed with a kitchen knife and left to die in the hallway. Her housemate Alexandra Riboni had been arrested. She'd confessed to the crime. Nicole was missing, presumed harmed.

Oli rubs her eyes, looks around the room. A framed map of Italy hangs on the far wall. A sleek silver pencil holder sits on the desk. Books on the bookshelf. Isabelle's things. Dean understandably wants to retain keepsakes for the girls, but surely this entire room doesn't need to be closed off, treated like a minimalist shrine. Oli sighs. It's difficult to separate Dean from his past. So many things compete for his attention. Funny how it seemed simple when they first met: only one obstacle. Now, over a decade later, she has what she wished for. Isabelle is gone.

The heater has switched off, and a light chill runs across Oli's shoulders. She pulls her dressing-gown tighter, then unfolds herself and stands up, her knees cracking. Walking over to the shelf on the other side of the room, she rubs the small of her back. Picks up a glass vase. Runs her finger along the ornaments. Isabelle may be gone, but Oli's curiosity is as ravenous as ever.

She pauses before she slides open the left wardrobe door. It's jam-packed with boxes and bags. A pair of high heels stands on the wooden floor; she squats to pick them up. They're small, size seven. Black velvet with diamantes studded along the straps. Her feet are two sizes bigger.

As she stands, her head brushes against something soft. From the wardrobe's silver rod hang a few clothing bags, grey and shapeless, their tails tucked behind a stack of boxes.

Her hands shake as she unzips the first bag, loud against the quiet of the house. She freezes. A police uniform, out of date, perhaps twenty years old. Her heartbeat thrums in her neck. She tugs the zip shut and pushes the bag to the left, exposing the throat of the next bag. Inside, two dresses share a hanger: one is cherry-red, the other black and beaded. Both look expensive, the material finely woven. In the final bag is a snow-white wedding dress of sleek satin. Oli detects a faint floral fragrance.

She pushes the bags hard against the wall, her heart pounding. Her eyes shift higher. There are two tiers of boxes on the shelves above the clothing. More of Isabelle's things.

She pulls off the lid of the nearest box. It's stuffed with glossy gift cards wishing Dean and Isabelle well on their wedding day. Oli traces the embossed patterns, glides her fingers along the embossed font. Some are from people she knows, most from people she's never heard of. All express their certainty that Dean and Isabelle are a perfect match, a pair of soulmates lucky to have found each other.

Oli wrestles with unwelcome images of Dean and Isabelle, some messages from the cards worming their way into her brain. If the couple were so perfect for each other, why did Dean seek Oli out five years later? Why did he risk what he had with Isabelle? Oli lifts the box onto the floor and opens the one beneath. Cards, photo frames. Pieces of paper. Notepads. A driver's licence that features a surprisingly unflattering photo of Isabelle. Oli sifts through a few handwritten recipes, then more photos of Dean and Isabelle with dates scrawled on the back. There's a note from Isabelle to Dean: *I just want to say how much I love you!* A narrow love heart before the scrawl of her name. Valentine's Day, 2004. A year before Oli met Dean.

There's a loud creak in the hallway, and she startles, dropping the note back into the shoebox and jumping to her feet. Spins around. Nothing.

For a few moments, she stands completely still. The house is silent except for the steady tick of the grandfather clock downstairs bouncing off the walls. The light from the alarm system glows green in the corner. After the twins were born, Isabelle had panic buttons fitted in every room as well as a state-of-the-art security system. When Oli asked Dean about it, he mentioned Isabelle was worried someone might break in and hurt her or hurt the girls. Constant fear was the price she paid for being a homicide detective.

Spooked, Oli returns the boxes and slides the cupboard door closed. She goes to the desk and quickly logs on to her old computer. Finds the memory stick labelled HH06.07, the ink blurring under the clear tape. She fumbles as she inserts it into the side of the outdated machine. Drags and drops the files one after the other. Hours of work. She connects to the wi-fi and signs in to her Gmail, attaches the little icons and sends them to herself.

The grandfather clock chimes, its familiar melody rolling through the house. One o'clock.

Oli shuts the laptop, unplugs the power cord. She takes the beige notebook and puts the rest of her things back in the box and jams it in the cupboard underneath Isabelle's old clothes and next to her beautiful shoes, then rushes down the hallway back to bed.

FEBRUARY 2006

Being hated by so many people is strange. It feels like pressure, an invisible weight bearing down on her. Most days Alex wakes up suffocating under it.

But as hurtful as it is, as gut-wrenchingly awful, she doesn't want to block it out. She deserves it.

She pesters Ruby for updates, devours every article. It's like reading about strangers or characters in a book. Their lives appear to be somehow both more and less than what they were. Mysterious. Like three young women who didn't know how good they had it. Who didn't know how bad things were about to get.

Being hated is better than being dead.

Being hated is better than being gone.

At least, Alex assumes it is. It's not like she can compare notes with the others.

Not only is she hated, she's famous. Infamous. Her face is everywhere.

She traces the photos in the newspapers Ruby brings her until her fingers are dark with ink.

From her spot in the communal hall at mealtimes, Alex watches her face flash up on the nightly news. The media alternates between using the photo of the three of them at Ren and Matt's New Year's Eve party and the one of Alex at her high school graduation. In the group shot, Evelyn pouts prettily, her head tipped to the side. Alex is laughing. Nicole, the tallest, stands in the middle, staring down the barrel of the lens as if the photographer has just challenged her to something. In the early days, a few news articles mistook them for sisters, and it's not hard to see why.

In both pictures Alex's light brown hair is flowing and glossy, her smile friendly and open. She looks so happy, so full of promise.

Those photos don't belong to her anymore. They have become the property of the media, sublet by the nation. Never in a million years did she imagine that her face would be beamed into people's homes, her little life published in papers all around the country.

Who took the photo at the party? She tries to remember, but comes up with nothing. Her brain does that a lot lately; thoughts start to form, then fade away.

She says please and thank you to the staff, but her voice sounds distant. The only person she really speaks to is Ruby, and even that is vague, only one layer deep. Alex can't risk going any further.

At night when she can't sleep, she imagines talking to Nicole and Evelyn. Imagines telling them about this new adventure and its cast of characters: the girl who always sits in the corner after dinner narrating TV shows and the curly-haired chef in the canteen with the tattoo of Dumbo on her forearm.

And then the grief arrives. Alex lies in the dark struggling to breathe, holding the edges of the narrow bed, eyes fixed on the ceiling. As she hovers on the edge of sleep, she pictures her life like a huge spider web. Starting with the knot of her childhood, bouncing from foster family to foster family, primary school, then secondary school, each a chance for a fresh start. A new web formed when she met Evelyn and Nicole: more deliberate, stronger. For the first time in her life, Alex felt in control. Felt like she was going somewhere.

Felt like she had a real family.

But you were wrong, so wrong, chants her wounded brain.

Alex misses them. Misses the intimacy. Misses the sense of being part of something.

She mourns them, she really does. But a part of her is relieved too. Relieved to be free.

CHAPTER ELEVEN

WEDNESDAY, 9 SEPTEMBER 2015

'OLI?' DEAN'S FRESHLY SHAVEN FACE APPEARS IN FRONT OF HER. He looks worried. She blinks several times. Her head is foggy, eyelids heavy. The feeling of being caught in a lie hits her in an instant. Isabelle's dresses, the boxes of cards and notebooks, are like a pulsing clue in the corner of the room. She jerks forward, pulling herself up.

But she's not in Isabelle's room. She's in bed. Her laptop is cool against her forearm, and the cord of her dressing-gown is twisted around her body.

'Oh, sorry.' Her deep voice is extra thick and woolly. 'I must have fallen asleep working.'

She vaguely remembers coming back to bed, not being able to sleep. Checking and replying to emails while Dean snored softly next to her, the well wishes in the wedding cards playing on her mind.

Lines appear on Dean's forehead, and he gestures to her phone on the bedside table. 'You slept through your alarm. Are you sick?'

'No, I'm fine,' she says, although she does feel clammy. 'Any news on the Horrowitz case?'

Shaking his head, he grimaces slightly. 'There was nothing on the bulletin before.'

She relaxes back against the pillow.

He straightens and puts his hands in his pockets. Oli feels grimy in contrast to his iron-pressed neatness. 'I have to go in a minute.'

'What time is it?'

'It's just gone seven.' He looks around the room. 'You should take those pills if you can't sleep. You shouldn't be getting up in the middle of the night to work.'

'I know, I only meant to do some reading. I don't even remember falling asleep.'

Dean smooths her hair aside and kisses her gently on the lips. He looks into her eyes, his fingers tangling in the golden strands. 'I'm driving the girls to school now, and I'll pick them up tonight and take them to Mary's for dinner. You just relax, okay? Maybe work from home today if you're not feeling well—it's not like you haven't put in the hours.'

'I'll see,' Oli murmurs.

Mary is Isabelle's mother. Oli's met her twice, and both times were incredibly awkward. Oli has no interest in going to her house for dinner but doesn't like not being invited either. The thought of being compared to Isabelle by her mother is unbearable, although Oli assumes at some point she'll have to get used to it. After spending the past two Christmases interstate with her other daughters, Mary is planning to stay in Melbourne this year.

Dean's irises glow golden-brown as he bends to kiss her on the forehead. 'Love you.' He straightens. Smiles.

'Same,' Oli says.

His footsteps trail down the hall, then the stairs. His muffled voice calls out, 'Amy! Kate!'

There's the buzz of their responses, a flurry of domestic sounds. The slight vibration of the garage door opening and closing, followed by the low rumble of Dean's car.

Oli lies in the dark for a few minutes, her head spinning with snippets from her old articles, the long-forgotten case details dusted off and fresh in her mind. She'd forgotten the strangeness of the girls' friendship, all of the loose threads leading nowhere. She wonders whether any evidence from the scene suggested Nicole was pregnant. She's never heard a whisper of it, but it's something the cops might have kept quiet. She could ask Rusty—or, even better, she could pitch it to Bowman, see if he bites.

Her mind jumps to Isabelle's dresses, the beautiful shoes. She shouldn't have gone through her things like that, but now all she wants to do is spend the day rummaging in the other boxes. Sifting through every single detail about the life that Isabelle and Dean had together. But it's not healthy, and Oli knows all too well what can happen when someone goes digging, finds things they shouldn't.

Her phone bleats, forcing her mind back to the case.

A text from Cooper: *Alex still hasn't read my message, but let's meet anyway? I'd really like your help with the podcast. Have you read my interview notes yet?*

The kid is nothing if not persistent. Doesn't he realise there might not be a podcast without Alex?

Oli is mid eye roll when TJ texts her. *O'Brien's wife topped herself.*

—

Oli throws herself in the shower, washing her hair like it's an Olympic sport. She drips water all over the carpet while she stands in the bedroom wrapped in a towel, trying to find something to wear. She pulls on a woollen dress and applies foundation and mascara at breakneck speed. She puts her old notebook in her satchel next to her current one and drags a brush through her wet hair as she runs down the stairs, then grabs her coat and a scarf from the hatstand in the hallway and sets the alarm. Yesterday was big, but today is going to be insane. The two stories will perform a public boxing match, fighting it out on the front pages for the next few days, their popularity dependent on the unpredictable nature of the people involved and the quality of the info that the police breadcrumb to the media.

Oli scrolls through her emails as the garage door cranks skyward. Media alerts are pouring in. The editorial meeting has been pushed back to nine because O'Brien's lawyers are doing a presser at eight, and even though all of the media outlets are reporting it, the cops still haven't provided any further information about the scene in Crystalbrook. Oli considers what the silence means. They might have found Evie Maslan already. Oli's mind conjures a little girl lost in the bush, huddling against a tree overnight in the freezing weather—or dead, her small body buried in a shallow grave.

'Fuck,' Oli murmurs.

She drives to work in a daze. At the lights she loads the *Melbourne Today* website, glancing from the road to the screen while praying there are no cops around. Her piece is still the first article on the home page, but it's been edited. She skims it quickly, noting the details that have changed. The reference to Nicole having a child is gone, some of the language softened. What the hell?

Furious, she clicks back to the home page, which has already been updated. A thumbnail of Julie O'Brien's smiling face is now above an old picture of Evelyn Stanley. TRAGIC END TO DAY IN COURT, reads TJ's headline. Julie is all elegance and good breeding, pearls at her throat, coral lipstick and straight white teeth. The lights change, and Oli accelerates, still glancing at the screen. Evelyn is thin in comparison to Julie, her light-brown hair limp at the roots, head tipped to the side, heavily made-up eyes relaxed in a sardonic smile. Oli's seen the picture a thousand times; they used it back in 2005. The other shots they dug up didn't work as well with the story, whereas the skimpy outfit and dark eyeliner gave the murdered young woman an edge, playing into the trope that all three housemates were caught up in something untoward.

Julie O'Brien and Evelyn Stanley: two strangers brought together by the news cycle.

Oli briefly ponders what Julie O'Brien was doing back in 2005. Probably watching the news with her husband, quietly judging the trio of housemates and reassuring herself that her perfect family would never be embroiled in a scandal like that.

In the car park, Oli smokes a cigarette while she speedreads Twitter. The armchair detectives have rallied and are firing opinions into cyberspace, using hashtags to formalise their uninformed views.

She crushes her smoke against a concrete pillar before it burns halfway. Finds a mint and shakes out her damp hair into what she hopes will pass as a stylish tousled look rather than an ungroomed mess.

The office is chaos. Almost everyone is talking into a phone. As Oli rounds the corner to her desk, a camera crew hustles past, threatening to bowl her over. She enters Dawn's office tentatively and pulls her scarf off, almost choking herself in the process. Sits.

Dawn's tall frame is clad in a blue dress dotted with daisies. 'I don't care, I don't give a *fuck*. Get me the shots *now*.' She drops her mobile onto her desk and gulps back an entire glass of water, her eyes darting around manically. A droplet trails from the left side of her mouth. 'Good, you're here. Get into the boardroom. Bronwyn's in there already. I'll find Pia, and we'll work out what we're going to run pre-lunch. The *Sun*'s got an O'Brien exclusive, apparently.'

'Why did you remove the reference to the child in my article?' Oli asks.

'The exec team advised that we pull it.'

'Joosten?'

'Yes, him and others.'

'Well, I'm not okay with it,' Oli says. 'It was an exclusive, and now other sites are running with it.'

'Yes, well, apparently the *Sun* also got their mitts on O'Brien's sister-in-law this morning, so you and TJ can commiserate together.'

Pia stumbles into Dawn's office, shoves a bunch of papers at Dawn and starts talking into her phone.

Oli says, 'I still think—'

'Not now, Oli. For the love of god, let's get moving.'

Gwen and Brent appear in the doorway, wide-eyed. They trip over each other comically as they push inside.

Dawn rakes a freckled hand through her hair and looks up at the ceiling. 'Fine, let's meet in here.' She starts to pace the rug that runs along the side of her desk. 'O'Brien's presser is on in five, so we'll have that copy live in less than an hour along with the video and a montage of the dead wife. Oli, what's going on with the cops? Why are they keeping so quiet on Horrowitz? I'm hearing nothing.'

'Me neither,' Oli admits. 'I'm guessing they'll do a media call this morning. Maybe there's a problem locating the parents.'

'Well, we can only stretch the suicide out for a few days unless there's new info, but the kid angle will last much longer if we can lock it down.'

'That's why it should have stayed in my piece,' Oli says evenly.

'I explained that, Oli,' Dawn says. 'You get something concrete, and we'll run a whole cover on it, and we can allude to you breaking it first, okay?'

Oli nods; she can't be bothered arguing anymore.

'We can do all the background copy from here—you just feed us anything new, okay?'

Oli nods again.

'And chase down the Riboni interview. We need it.' Dawn looks her straight in the eye. 'I'd like to pull your feature forward a day or so. Doable?'

'I doubt it,' Oli replies quickly. 'I won't be able to speak to enough people by then, and like you said, it needs new news. We'll have to corroborate anything Alex says. I'm also going to try to get a comment from Bowman.'

Dawn folds her arms. 'Okay, fine.' She pouts, thinking. 'Today let's just make sure we're first with every update. I want to run maps of the area, speculation from locals. I want a timeline. Pia, can you brief the art department on some graphics? I want to brand this thing, get it looking really slick—what we did yesterday looked like shit. Reuse the photos that Cooper kid took, they're pretty good.'

Oli's stomach growls.

Dawn skims the printouts Pia gave her earlier. 'Just remember to use your brains—we sure as shit don't have the time or money for a lawsuit right now.'

Oli turns to Pia. 'Did you track down the property owners?'

'Yep, Tasmanians Rachel and Will Tiernan.' Pia doesn't look up. 'I spoke to them about half an hour ago. Nice people. They're horrified someone died there, even though they've never actually set foot on the property. Basically, they're no help, they had no idea someone was living there, and they were planning on selling when they got around to it. I get the feeling that money is not in short supply.'

'And they have no links to Nicole or the other girls?'

'Not that they know of.' Pia's fingers dance across her phone.

Oli arches her back. 'If Nicole started living in Crystalbrook four years ago, where the hell was she before that? And why hide out? Alex never suggested that Nicole killed Evelyn, and once Alex was in prison surely it was safe for her to come home?'

'Is there any chance she was in witness protection?' Brent says. 'Maybe that's why the cops are being so slow to confirm the details.'

'As much as I love your Nancy Drew role-play, I'd appreciate it if you get out of my office and find somewhere else to have this conversation.' Dawn is reading something on her phone, her right eyebrow jerking toward the ceiling.

They exchange glances as they file out of her office.

'Apparently Melissa Warren's landed an exclusive with Nicole's parents,' Dawn calls after them, her voice now eerily calm, 'so just make the fuck sure no one gets to Alex Riboni before we do.'

—

Cooper is sitting at Oli's desk watching something on his laptop. The left heel of his huge white sneaker taps against the floor, purple headphones fixed on his ears.

'Can I help you?' Oli says sarcastically, placing her computer next to his. She reaches past him to grab her coffee mug. She is plotting out what she needs to do, who she needs to contact. The story is fragmenting in her head, and she needs to pull it into focus, corral it into something more manageable. It doesn't help that Crystalbrook is so far away—the last thing she needs is another two-hour round trip. Nor does it help that she's been ordered to secure an interview that wasn't hers in the first place.

'Oh, hey, Groves!' Cooper pulls off his headphones and looks up at her before cracking his knuckles and slurping something unidentifiable from a glass bottle. STICK IT TO THE (HU)MAN runs across his T-shirt in huge black font. 'You ready?'

'I'm not ready for anything except a giant coffee. Maybe no one told you, but it's another big news day, so I don't have time to sit and chat.'

'But we need to run through my interview questions.' He blinks at her dolefully.

'Fuck's sake, Cooper,' Oli hisses. 'At this rate there won't be an interview! You haven't even heard from Alex.' A thought emerges. 'Are you sure it was Alex you were talking to?'

He looks offended. 'Of course.'

'How?'

'Well, for starters, her voice is the same. And she knows all about what happened back then.'

'That would be easy enough to fake,' Oli retorts. Jesus, she thinks, what a waste of time all the podcast hype will have been if it turns out Cooper's been duped by some looney. 'Either way, our interview chances are looking shakier by the minute, so we better get moving on a backup plan, seeing as this podcast is so important to everyone.'

'We?' Cooper says hopefully.

'You,' she corrects. 'I've got shit to do.'

'Okay,' he says, looking glum.

Oli clenches her jaw. She'd happily take Dawn's unpredictable fireworks over Cooper's adolescent moodiness. 'We can speak later. And if you do hear from Alex, the same rules apply—drop everything and contact me.' She heads to the kitchen, phone in hand as she googles hospitals and GPs in Crystalbrook and the surrounding suburbs.

Cooper trails after her, carrying his laptop. 'Kylie suggested that I think about changing the podcast anyway. Turn it into more of a real-time investigation to match your coverage. Do you think that might work? It gives us an out if Alex doesn't come through.'

Oli shoots him a sharp look while she fills the kettle, scrolling through the search results with her free hand. 'Later, Cooper,' she says firmly.

'It makes sense.' He looks thoughtful. 'People can follow along and get up to speed when new info drops. It really could be the next *Serial*.'

'Nothing wrong with aiming high,' Oli mutters, taking screenshots of the contact details for the three medical clinics that service the area around Crystalbrook. The kettle boils, and she pours the steaming water into her mug, dissolving the coffee granules. Adds milk.

'I was thinking it could work in with your piece, and we could cross promo them. You know, like mutual shout-outs. The sales guys will love it.' Cooper's face is flushed with excitement.

'Always my top priority.' She sips her coffee. It tastes funny. She looks for a spoon but can't find one, stirs the brown liquid with a knife.

Cooper kicks the skirting board under the bench. 'I just figure it might be cool to keep teaming up.'

She sighs. 'Look, Cooper, I don't want to be rude, but I really work better solo. If it happens, I'll help with the interview, and I'm happy to look at a revised structure and share quotes with you, but podcasts really aren't my thing. I—' Oli stops short as Dawn approaches.

'Oh good, you're both here. Change of plans. Well, actually, there's just extra plans.' Dawn turns to Cooper. 'I just spoke to Joosten about your email, and we agree there might be merit in pairing you up to work on the feature and the podcast together. We're getting word that the *Sun* might be launching a podcast series in the wake of O'Brien's case, "giving a voice to victims".' Dawn manages to look both impressed and disgusted. 'But I think the Housemate story might give us an edge. It will rate better with a younger audience, and that's what we need right now.'

Oli looks at Cooper. He sweeps up some crumbs on the bench with his fingers, depositing them in the sink, and studiously avoids her stare.

Dawn continues, 'We're going to run a promo online this afternoon for both the podcast and the print coverage, and there's a chance we might do a run of TV ads too. We'll be promising exclusive interviews, plural, so make sure you get them.'

Cooper emits an excited squeak.

'Oli,' Dawn barks.

Oli tries not to gag as she takes another sip of coffee. The texture is ominously thick, and the milk has curdled on the surface. She tips it down the sink and watches as white clumps gather in the plughole. 'Yes?'

'You'll need to play editor on this whole thing, make sure it all comes together. I'll speak to the sales guys. We need to explore subscriptions.' She claps, and Cooper and Oli both jump. 'I mean, do you think people will pay for this kind of thing?'

'I absolutely would,' Cooper says. 'But I listen to, like, *heaps* of podcasts. I've probably listened to hundreds. I have them on all the time, when I ride into work and when I play squash. Even when I'm in the bath.'

Dawn looks at him as if he's gum on her shoe. 'That was a rhetorical question, but thanks for the insight. Just don't fuck this up, okay?'

Oli jumps in. 'We're on it, Dawn.'

Dawn's phone starts to ring, and she stalks off.

Pia joins them, dumps a dirty plate in the sink. 'Apparently Bowman's doing a presser at police HQ about Nicole Horrowitz, at two.'

'Thanks.' Oli feels completely bamboozled.

'No dramas. Oh, and also, don't use anything in the fridge. The thermostat is broken, and everything in there has gone to shit. Someone should have put up a sign.'

—

'Sorry about that.' Cooper follows a fuming Oli back to her desk. But he's not sorry at all; the little shit looks downright smug.

'That was not okay,' she snaps. 'I don't appreciate you pitching ideas that involve me behind my back. This is my *job*, Cooper. Not some game.'

'I'm sorry,' he says, more contrite. 'But it's good that Dawn's happy with the idea, right?'

Oli squeezes her eyes shut. She already felt defeated by the day, and now she has to manage Cooper while trying to navigate the biggest feature she's written in months. And launch a podcast. And juggle Dean and the girls.

Cooper starts rambling again, something about sound effects, and Oli holds up a hand. 'Just get everything you've got on the podcast so far and meet me at Breakers in twenty minutes.'

He darts off, and she quickly checks her email alerts: still nothing new on Nicole or the child. She glances at the TV screens. The networks show rolling coverage of detectives coming and going from the O'Brien residence in Albert Park; solemn-looking reporters speak earnestly to camera.

She grabs her things and heads outside. As she walks around the building to Breakers cafe, she tries two of the Crystalbrook medical clinics, doing her best Sarah Finlayson doctor impersonation. Unsurprisingly, neither will confirm whether they have a patient named Evie Maslan on their books, though Oli can tell they both check their records. She thinks it's likely that Nicole avoided taking the little girl to the GP, but it's worth a shot. She wonders if Nicole's been calling herself Natalie Maslan the whole time and what kind of identification she has. Of course, it's always possible for paperwork to be faked and for loopholes to be found. Last year Oli worked on a story about stolen identities; it happens more often than people think.

She kicks through a pile of leaves. Maybe Evie isn't Nicole's daughter—she could be a niece or a cousin or something. But then why was she living with Nicole? Oli sighs. No matter who the little girl belongs to, it's not a good sign that she hasn't turned up yet.

Oli enters Breakers, nabs her favourite table and nods hello to Col, who starts making her a coffee. She begins to make a mental list of people to contact for her feature. Miles Wu. Evelyn's father Mitchell Stanley. The couple, Tanya and Roy. Evelyn's friend Amber.

Col brings her coffee over. 'It's like Christmas for you lot this week, isn't it?' He gestures to the front page of the newspaper on the table next to Oli.

'Something like that,' she replies.

'I've always hated that O'Brien prick.' Col throws a tea towel over his shoulder. 'He's a creep no matter what the court says. But I can't believe that girl turned up after all those years.' He shakes his head. 'The mystery solved after all that time, huh?'

If only that were the case, thinks Oli, looking at her old notebook. The story seems more convoluted than ever. She wonders where Cooper is, although she's happy to have some peace and quiet. For a few minutes she focuses on her notes.

The door swings open, and a large group file in. A few minutes later there's still no sign of Cooper, but she'll be damned if she's going to call him. She thinks of more people to contact: Nicole's family, McCrae, Ren and Matt from the house next door to the housemate murder property, Bowman.

One of the wait staff drops cutlery in the kitchen, and the crash halts all conversation. Slowly chatter builds again and blends with the whir of the coffee grinder, the pleasant buzz of the milk frothing. Normally Oli loves working in noisy environments—something about it forces her mind to focus—but not today. Every sound stabs at her brain.

More people enter the cafe. Still no Cooper. It's been almost thirty minutes.

'This is ridiculous.' She gathers her things and gets to her feet, just as he bursts in.

He makes a beeline to her, eyes wild.

'Can't you tell the time?' she says crossly.

His chest rises and falls, and he combs his fingers through his hair. 'It's not Nicole.'

She looks at him blankly. Someone squeezes past her, trying to get to their table, and she stumbles and holds on to the chair to steady herself. Her phone starts buzzing on the table. 'What do you mean?'

'The dead woman,' Cooper huffs. 'It's not Nicole. It's Alex.'

CHAPTER TWELVE

CARS AND TRAMS SAIL BY, AND SPARROWS FLIT BETWEEN THE GUTTER and the footpath, searching for crumbs under the watchful gaze of a mangy crow. Oli stands outside Breakers, feeling numb. Her brain is struggling to process this new information.

Cooper paces in front of her, increasingly distressed. 'I messaged Alex this morning, even though she still hadn't read the other one. I just figured that maybe if she heard it come through, it might prompt her to respond, but she was dead the whole time!' His face loses the last of its colour. 'I mean, holy shit, Oli. She's dead.'

'Has it been confirmed?'

He nods. 'Yep, it just hit the newsdesk, and I ran straight here. Alex's lawyer posted it on Twitter after she ID'd the body. She's the next of kin—how sad is that? Look, it's legit.'

Oli glances at his screen, quickly reads the message and recognises Ruby Yeoh, the lawyer from Alex's trial. 'Okay.' Oli squints into the sky, trying to quell her intense feeling of being overwhelmed. 'Where's your camera?'

'Huh?' Cooper looks at her blankly.

'The camera from yesterday. I want to look at that photo.'

'I deleted it off the camera,' he mumbles. 'But I sent it to myself.' He swipes at his phone screen a few times and hands it to her.

Oli enlarges the image, each zoom amplifying her dread. Just like she saw Nicole yesterday, she now sees Alex. All three girls were so similar: same build, same height. The kind of hair that was easily dyed and restyled. In her mind's eye, Alex and Nicole merge into one. 'Fucking hell.' Oli hands the camera back to Cooper.

A horn blares, and they both jump. A little girl starts to cry and is promptly whisked onto her father's shoulders; she gleefully wipes her lollipop across his bald head.

Cooper swallows, clearly desperate for some direction. 'What do we do now?'

'Let me try Rusty.'

'The cop from yesterday?'

She nods, ignores a missed call from Dawn and dials Rusty. 'Jesus,' Oli says when he picks up, 'what the fuck is going on?'

He keeps his voice low. 'It's the other girl. Alex Riboni. I think they realised when they brought her in last night, but they had to wait for her lawyer to come in this morning. It's a nightmare 'cause we already contacted Nicole's parents. Understandably, they're a mess. Anyway, the autopsy is happening now, but I don't think there're going to be any surprises. We think she caught the bus up there the day before we found her.'

'But it was Nicole's house?'

'We think so. A woman who looks like Nicole was definitely living there with a kid. It wasn't Alex—she lives in the city.'

'So she went to Crystalbrook to see Nicole?'

'No idea, but I assume so. Bowman was pissed about your article, by the way. I think he called someone at your paper.'

'Yeah, well, that was a bullshit move. It was a legitimate lead.'

'I'm just the messenger, Ol.'

'What about the fire?'

'I haven't heard anything more. The word yesterday was that the fire in the main room caught and hit the gas supply, but a team's out there today so we should know more later.'

In the background are voices that fade as Rusty starts walking away from whomever is talking.

Oli asks, 'Were Alex and Nicole in contact this whole time?'

'I don't know. I doubt we're going to know much more until we find Nicole.'

Oli suddenly feels an overwhelming wave of frustration. 'What the fuck happened yesterday, Rusty? Why was everyone so sure that it was Nicole up there?'

'It was a total fuck-up,' he admits. 'They didn't get the body down for a few hours due to some error with the coroner call-out, and Nicole Horrowitz's old ID was found at the scene, which was obviously what leaked. There was no reason to think she was someone else—they look similar, and no one had sighted her for years.'

Oli glances at Cooper and says more quietly, 'What about the other thing you mentioned? The letter.'

'I shouldn't have said anything to you about that, Ol. You can't run with it, okay? I've heard nothing since.'

'Was it for Alex or Nicole?'

Cooper isn't even pretending not to listen now.

'*Oli*. Be fair.' Rusty has clearly reached his limit.

'Okay, okay,' she says. 'Jesus, Rusty, this is big.'

'It's pretty crazy,' he agrees, calming again. 'Talking of death threats, this O'Brien situation is really blowing up too. We'll have to provide him with security. People are out for blood because of his wife.'

'Sounds like a great use of resources,' Oli says sarcastically.

'I know. What an arsehole.'

Rusty joined the force full of optimistic passion to right wrongs, and she knows he worries that he's now further away from achieving this than he ever was as a civilian.

'Thanks, Rusty,' Oli says, meaning it. 'Thanks for talking to me.'

'It's nothing. All going to be in the presser today, anyway.' His tone is deliberately casual, but it doesn't mask his emotions, and Oli feels bad for calling him even though she'd be crazy not to milk him as a source.

'Honestly,' she adds, 'I really appreciate it. We're going pretty hard at this.'

'I have no doubt.' He hangs up.

She shoves her phone in her pocket, newly energised.

Cooper seems to have recovered from the shock of Alex's death, his eyes shining with something akin to excitement. 'I didn't mention this before, but I have something that might help.'

Oli hugs her laptop to her chest. 'What?'

'I spoke to Alex twice on the phone. Last week and the one before.'

'Yes, you told me already.' Oli starts walking to the office, gesturing for him to follow.

He lopes awkwardly along beside her. 'The first time we spoke was really brief. Just a quick chat.'

'Right.' Oli is only half-listening. She can't stop thinking about Alex being the body they saw hanging from the tree yesterday.

They sidestep a pair of sausage dogs wearing tweed coats.

'But the second time we spoke was more like a practice interview. Alex wanted to know what I was going to ask her. And I was keen to get my bearings, seeing as I'd never done anything like this before.'

'And?'

'And I might have recorded it.'

Oli stops walking. Looks at him.

He smiles tentatively.

'I could kiss you,' she says.

—

Oli and Cooper enter the office via the fire escape and take the stairs two at a time. They're going to Cooper's studio, and it's unspoken that they want to avoid their peers.

'Why didn't you tell me yesterday?' she asks him.

'I didn't know Alex was dead, and I didn't exactly ask her permission to record the call.'

'Didn't exactly?' Oli echoes.

'Didn't at all.' He pulls ahead, and Oli's breathing intensifies as they hit the fourth floor. 'Come on,' he calls out to her unhelpfully.

When they reach level five, he pushes through the heavy door and holds it open for Oli. The walls are completely barren, the threadbare carpet spotless.

'What's up here apart from the studio?' she asks, puffing as she follows him along the corridor toward the rear of the building. Her phone is going bananas, vibrating continuously in her bag.

'Nothing. We shouldn't even be up here. There were plans to move everyone here, a while ago, but there was a dispute about the refurb fees so now the landlords are trying to find other companies to move in.'

'Why would we move up here?' Oli asks, confused.

'It's cheaper than downstairs, and the paper is losing money. We were going to sublet the lower floors to another business.' He stops in front of a closed door, swings off his backpack and sticks a hand inside, feeling around for a few moments before pulling out a set of keys. 'You know there's going to be a sale?'

'There've been rumours of a sale for as long as I've been here,' Oli says dismissively as he unlocks the door. 'They've always amounted to nothing.'

The room is small, and every surface is covered in black carpet. An Apple Mac sits on the desk against the wall alongside several speakers and other sleek devices. A scratched round table with two chairs sits in the centre of the room, two microphones positioned in the middle. Cooper pulls out his laptop and plugs cords into its side.

'Wow,' she says, 'this is quite the production.'

'Yep.' He straightens, hands on hips as he surveys the room. 'It's not bad considering we threw it together so quickly. The sound quality is surprisingly good.' With the door shut, his black hair and clothing blend into the walls. His pale face floats in the darkness. 'I'll pull the files up. It will take a few minutes to download.'

Oli sits at the table and opens her laptop. The clack of her typing is dulled by the padded room, and there's something comforting about being sealed off from the mayhem of the newsdesk.

'I come up here a lot to work,' Cooper says, after a few minutes. 'One of the IT guys helped me set up this spare computer, but I had to organise a different wi-fi network. It's not exactly kosher, but it works. The password's CoopsScoops100, capital letters at the start of each word, with a hashtag at the end.'

'Of course it is,' Oli says wryly, reading back over her draft. It's good enough for holding copy, so she connects to the wi-fi and sends it to Dawn.

'Okay, you ready?' Cooper asks, straightening as he looks at Oli.

She closes her laptop. 'Sure.'

He guides the mouse to a file on the giant screen, double-clicks then hits the space bar. The low hum of white noise fills the room. A series of muffled sounds is followed by Cooper's voice, more serious and stilted than in real life: 'Today is just a warm-up, so we both feel comfortable when we do the real interview. Okay?'

Oli can only hear soft breathing.

'Right.' Nerves creep into Cooper's recorded voice. 'So I'll just walk you through the kinds of questions I'll ask when we do the real thing. Please let me know if there's anything you don't feel comfortable answering.' The rasp of a page turning. 'So, Alex, to start with, I'll be asking you why you've decided to share your story now.'

There's a sharp intake of breath, then Alex Riboni's voice fills the room.

—

Oli badly needs the bathroom, but she doesn't move, transfixed by Alex's tentative account of the night her life was ruined and she became a pariah. Her voice is calm, confident. She sounds completely different to the terrified young woman thrust into the spotlight and metaphorically strung up to be stoned almost ten years ago.

'I'm tired of not having a voice.' A short silence. 'Things are different now.'

'How?'

'I'm older. And I'm not scared anymore, I have nothing to lose.' Another pause. 'I've started to remember things about the night my friend died.'

'And you're ready to tell people what you remember?'

'Yes, I am.'

Cooper's interview style is surprisingly polished. He's polite and respectful, gently coaxing. There's nothing of the unbridled child in his careful questions. 'Despite your acquittal, a lot of Australians still think you killed Evelyn Stanley. There are Facebook groups full of people convinced that you got away with murder. If you tell your story now, are you worried about reviving the speculation?'

'I can't help what people think, but I do know I didn't want my friend to die.'

Oli's mind drifts to Alex at the trial. The image of the woman hanging from the tree yesterday slices unpleasantly into her thoughts.

'Alex, what do you think happened to Nicole Horrowitz?'

'I think she ran away.'

'In the middle of night, leaving all of her things?'

Alex seems to hesitate. 'Yes.'

'What do you think she ran away from?'

'From everything.'

Oli looks at Cooper. 'What does that mean?'

'Don't know, she didn't elaborate. It's something I would have pushed in the real interview.'

His recorded voice says, 'The three of you were obviously very close, but a lot of people who knew you back then said things had started to go wrong before the party that night. Can you tell me about that?'

Alex's breathing becomes more audible, tiny wheezing noises that fill the room. 'We just . . . Things were complicated. We were very young, and I was scared of losing them. And then,' she swallows past a sob, 'and then I lost them anyway.'

'Have you seen Nicole since that night at the house? Do you know where she is?'

There's a pause, a silence so long that Oli thinks something is wrong with the tape.

'No, I haven't seen Nicole since that night.'

Oli and Cooper lock eyes.

'She didn't really answer the second part of that question, did she?' he says.

'No, she didn't.'

—

Oli leaves Cooper in the studio transcribing the phone call with Alex. They've forged a hasty plan to divide and conquer. He gave her a set of keys to the studio, and she gave him the keys to the Audi so he can drive back to Crystalbrook and try to find out more about the woman calling herself Natalie Maslan. Oli is going to stay in the city and attempt to make contact with family and friends of Alex and Nicole before Bowman's press conference.

She scrawled Rusty's number in the front page of Cooper's notebook. 'Call him if you get yourself into a pickle,' she said.

'What kind of pickle?' he asked nervously.

'A journalistic pickle.'

Now Oli rushes down the corridor, the weight of the story sitting right on top of her chest. She presses her fingers in between her collarbones, trying to relieve the pressure. Thoughts roll around in her head. Why did Alex agree to speak to Cooper, and what exactly was she planning to reveal? His recording is by no means explosive, but there's grit in Alex's tone, a quiet power. Oli has done enough interviews to recognise someone on the brink of letting loose, sensing the freedom that will come with telling their truth. This momentum jars with Alex suiciding less than four days later. What happened to have her sink so quickly to such a desperate place?

Oli careens around the corner and heads to the lift. She pauses as she hears its doors open. Dawn steps out, followed by TJ. Oli ducks into an alcove, but they don't even glance in her direction. They head up the hallway toward the empty offices, heads bent close, indecipherable murmurs bouncing off the bare walls. Oli reaches the empty lift just as the doors are shutting; she steps inside and jabs the button to close the doors, her eyes on their retreating figures.

TJ was talking to Joosten about Dawn, and now Dawn and TJ are having secret meetings?

But Oli can't think about that now—she needs to focus on the story. Her impatience flares. She wants all of the information immediately, for there to be a magic code allowing her total access, but the years have taught her that instead this will be a slog. Phone calls, emails. Chasing people down. Waiting. The heart and soul of journalism remain the same no matter how much technology you wrap around them.

An electronic beep announces her arrival on level one, and she steps out of the lift hoping to find Pia and Brent. All the TVs are playing news footage of Bowman in Crystalbrook yesterday, and Oli glimpses Rusty's red hair in one of the shots.

Pia and Brent are in the meeting room next to the boardroom. 'Anything more on Nicole Horrowitz?' Oli says in greeting.

Several sheets of paper are scattered on the table in front of them, devices lined up like weapons.

'We're not sure,' Brent says. 'There are a few social media accounts in her name and variations of it, but we're pretty sure they're not her.'

'What about Natalie Maslan? Or Evie Maslan?'

Brent stifles a burp and takes a swig from his water bottle. Nods. 'We think this might be them.' He holds out a piece of paper. It's a copy of a newspaper article, a story in a local rag about an environmental program the local council set up. CRYSTALBROOK PLEDGES TO HELP THE CLIMATE, reads the headline. In one photo, several parents are tying newly planted native trees to wooden stakes. No names are listed, but Oli thinks one of the women might be Nicole Horrowitz: a sunhat casts a shadow across her heart-shaped face, but the eyes—the eyes are hers. Oli is sure of it. There's a photo of some students too. *Evie, Rosie and Max all love working in the garden*. Oli looks at the grainy photo of the smiling little girl.

'Guys, this is great.' She checks the publication date. 'Hang on. This ran three weeks ago?'

Brent and Pia nod.

The timing must mean something. She remembers Cooper saying that Alex worked for an environmental company, something to do with sustainability programs. Maybe she stumbled upon this photo. She could even have been involved in setting up the initiative.

'We're also seeing if Duffy can run some facial recognition on Facebook and Google Images,' Brent says. 'But I'm not sure it's that reliable, and all the photos of Nicole are obviously ten years out of date.'

'Find out where Alex worked,' Oli says. 'She might have been in Crystalbrook for a job. Keep me posted. I'm going to hit the road and try for some interviews.'

Pia calls after her, 'Will you go to the presser, or do you want me to?'

'I'll go.' Oli grabs a half-finished packet of M&M's from her top drawer and pulls the beige notebook out of her bag. She thumbs through it, scanning her decade-old handwriting until she finds the list of mobile numbers and addresses. She eats another chocolate and runs her finger down the familiar names. She tries the number she had for Miles Wu but is greeted with an automated message informing her that it's disconnected. There's no point contacting Nicole's parents—from what Rusty said, they'll still be with the police.

Oli calls the landline number next to Geraldine Stanley's name, but it rings out, no answering machine. It's already past eleven; she's running out of time. She scans the last few names.

Cara Horrowitz, Nicole's sister. Oli types the number into her phone and calls.

CHAPTER THIRTEEN

THE TWENTY-MINUTE TRIP TO BRUNSWICK STREET FEELS LIKE IT takes a lot longer. The cab reeks of smoke, and the reggae music blasting through the speakers does little to hide the sharp ticking the taxi makes when it idles.

Cara answered Oli's call, guarded but willing to talk. Oli offered to come to her house, but Cara declined, suggesting a cafe. Oli ticks off what she knows about Cara, which isn't much. Adopted three years before Nicole was born. The girls were close as children and teenagers, but drifted apart after Nicole moved out. Cara never went to uni and was working in retail when her sister went missing. Unlike Nicole, she stayed in the family home well into her twenties.

'There!' Oli points to the cafe as they sail past. The cab driver launches into a rant about city traffic conditions, but Oli doesn't engage, just pays and waits for the receipt.

After she enters the cafe, it takes a moment for her eyes to adjust. Potted succulents take up precious real estate on the tiny tables. A few solo customers sip lattes, laptops open in front of them. In the middle of the room a young woman tries to control three toddlers, her voice rising as strands of hair fall from her messy bun; a babycino tumbles across the table, milk froth spraying in an impressive arc.

A dark-skinned woman sits in the back corner watching Oli. Cara.

Oli lifts her head in acknowledgement and approaches. Cara's head is wrapped in a colourful silk scarf. There's a faint hole in her left nostril, and gold hoops hang from her ears. She has the most perfectly sculpted eyebrows Oli has ever seen.

'I hate reporters,' Cara announces, after they shake hands.

Oli removes her satchel and drops into the chair opposite Cara. 'I'm liking them less and less myself,' she says diplomatically.

Cara watches blank-faced as one of the toddlers descends into a tantrum. 'I need a coffee before we talk.' She yawns, squaring her broad shoulders. 'Sorry, I'm knackered. My kid is only six months old, and he still hasn't mastered the art of sleep. I can barely function unless I have caffeine these days.'

'I have twin stepdaughters,' says Oli in an attempt to build rapport, but she immediately feels awkward referring to Amy and Kate that way. She smiles, keen to move the conversation on. 'Is your son with your partner this morning?'

Cara stiffens. 'It's just me. No partner.' She clearly has no intention of making this easy.

Oli presses on. 'Right, what coffee would you like?'

At the counter she orders two short blacks and hands over her credit card. She glances back at the table. Cara is hunched forward looking at her phone, forehead furrowed. Oli never spoke to her during the initial investigation, but she remembers that Jo did. Back then Cara was twenty-four. She's only a few years younger than Oli. Jo deemed her a miserable bitch, but that doesn't mean much—Jo didn't really like anyone.

'So, why call me?' Cara says when Oli returns to the table. 'I'm hardly the epicentre of this thing.'

'I found your number in my old notebook,' Oli replies truthfully.

'I worked on the story back in 2005 when I was at a different newspaper.'

'And you figured my parents will be tied up with the police today?'

Oli smiles. 'The thought did cross my mind.'

The coffees arrive. Cara knocks hers back in three short gulps. Dabs her lips with a napkin and applies some tinted lip balm. 'My sister did always demand a lot of my parents' attention.'

'In what way?' Oli asks, taking a sip of her drink.

'In every way. Nicole is the kind of person who takes up a lot of time and energy. A real force of nature, I guess you'd say. My parents doted on her.'

Oli blinks, surprised at the bitterness in Cara's voice. 'That must have been hard.'

'I got used to it. Plus, it wasn't just them. Everyone loved her. I think . . .' Cara pauses. Pivots. 'So, do the cops have any idea where she is? Is that why you want to talk to me?'

'I don't know. The police haven't released any new information yet, but that doesn't mean they don't know where she is. There's a press conference later today, so they might say more then.'

'Why did everyone think it was Nicole up at that house yesterday?' Cara asks. 'My folks are beside themselves.'

'Some evidence at the scene led them to assume it was her. It's awful, but it happens.'

'Pretty shit for the families,' mutters Cara.

'I know this is all very difficult,' Oli says, 'but I do think your sister was living in that house. I think that's why Alex Riboni was there.'

'I wouldn't know,' Cara says churlishly.

'You never heard from Nicole after she went missing?'

'Nope.' Cara scrunches up her serviette. 'I thought she was dead. Are you sure the dead woman is Alex? Maybe the cops got it wrong again.'

'They wouldn't release the name unless they were sure.'

'Pretty shitty to spend all that time in gaol, then just top yourself.' Cara speaks like she's spoiling for a fight.

'Yes. My paper was actually about to interview Alex. Apparently she wanted to go on the record with some new information.'

'Bummer,' Cara says flatly.

Oli chooses to ignore her sarcasm. 'You didn't want to be with your parents today?'

'No, I didn't.'

Oli doesn't reply, just looks at Cara and waits a few seconds.

'Yesterday was the first time we've spoken since Titus was born,' she elaborates.

'You're not close?'

'We have the occasional phone call, and I see them at Christmas,' she replies breezily. 'But it always makes me feel like shit, so . . .' She shrugs and wipes her sleeve across her nose. 'I see my biological dad a bit these days. My mum's dead, though. Heroin.'

'I'm sorry,' Oli says.

'It's fine. I never knew her.' Cara taps her teaspoon lightly on the table. 'And now Nicole's disappeared all over again, huh?' She slumps back in her chair. 'God, it never ends.'

'Have you spoken to her?' Oli asks casually.

Cara passes the salt shaker back and forth between her hands and says in a dramatic movie-trailer voice, 'Not since that fateful day in 2005.'

Oli tries to hide her frustration. Cara is hard to read, and her sarcasm is like a toxic poison infiltrating what Oli assumes is an interesting and vibrant personality.

Cara sighs. 'Like I said on the phone, I really doubt I'll be much use to you.'

'And yet here we are.' Oli looks at her expectantly.

'Huh?'

'You didn't say no to the idea of talking to me. That tells me you want to say something.'

Cara crosses her arms. Rolls her eyes. 'I was curious.'

'Curious?' Oli says sceptically.

'What, everyone else is allowed to salivate over this bullshit and I'm not?'

'Cara, I'm not trying to upset you.'

She mutters under her breath, and for a few moments Oli thinks she might cry. But instead she throws her hands up in the air. 'What do you want from me? Childhood anecdotes? A sibling-rivalry subplot?'

Oli's cheeks ache, tingle with heat. Cara is starting to annoy her. 'What do I want? I want to know what happened that night. Young women don't go around stabbing each other for no reason. And I don't like stories that don't make sense. I think Evelyn Stanley knew something or threatened someone or did something. I think Alex stabbed her, but I think there's more to it. And your sister is the key to the whole thing, I'm sure of it.' She pauses to breathe.

Cara's dark eyes shine. 'Even if you're right, I can't help you. I don't know shit.'

'You were close.' Oli softens her voice. 'You and Nicole shared a room until she moved out, and you stayed in touch. You were at the house the day Evelyn died. Maybe you don't realise what you know.'

Cara's bravado visibly fades, and she seems less certain. Her long fingers worry the large wooden beads that hang around her neck. 'I wasn't at the party. I wasn't invited.'

Oli ignores her jealousy and presses on. 'I know, but I remember you were at the house in the morning, right? Back then everyone spoke to the parents. But parents only see what they *want* their kids to be—siblings see the real picture. Tell me what the girls were really like. What Nicole was really like.'

'It's true that we were close, growing up.' Cara looks at Oli as if daring her to object. 'Really close. But I don't think anyone ever knew Nicole.'

'What do you mean?'

Cara's gaze fixes on the wall, and her pupils dilate. 'Nicole was different. It's hard to explain. She was very extroverted and always had heaps of friends, but at the same time she didn't really let anyone in. She could be very selfish.'

'Wasn't she a volunteer?' Oli asks, cocking her head. 'I remember something about her working with disabled kids.'

'Yeah, yeah,' mutters Cara. 'A couple of shifts here and there, a few charitable donations, a passionate speech at a school assembly, and she was a saint.'

Oli holds up her hands. 'I never met Nicole and I have no point of view. I just want your version of her.'

Cara unfolds her arms and grips either side of the table. 'Okay, look, I loved my sister, but that doesn't mean I always liked her. She was incredibly self-centred. Extremely manipulative. And even though we didn't have much money, my parents spoiled the living shit out of her.' Cara blinks several times, clearly trying to ward off tears, then grimaces. 'Nicole was their princess. It was gross, and yes,' she rolls her eyes, 'I was jealous, of course I was. I mean, come on, I'm adopted, then three years later the baby they've always dreamed of shows up. It was never going to be a good situation, but it didn't help that Nicole was born the way she was.'

'Which was how?'

'Just, like, I don't know. Like she could turn water into wine. She was lucky, but it was more than that.' Cara suddenly looks confused. 'You would always find yourself doing things for her, even when you didn't want to. Like you knew it was a bad idea, but you just couldn't help it. She got her own way without being obvious.'

'She was resourceful?' Oli suggests.

'Yes, and charming—she could always see a way. She knew what made people tick, and she drew them in, made them feel good. She listened to them, and they appreciated that. People felt indebted to her.' Cara pushes her fingers into her eye sockets; her nostrils pinch, then flare. 'We weren't well-off, not at all, but you wouldn't have known it to look at her. I don't know what she was doing to get her hands on some of her clothes after she moved out. Maybe her friends gave her things, I don't know. She certainly didn't pay for them with her babysitting money.'

'Do you think she was involved in something illegal?'

Cara's left eyebrow jerks skyward. 'Maybe. I really don't know what she got up to after she left home.' She sighs. 'After school finished, she relied on me less and found new people to do things for her. She told us uni was a fresh start, then seemed to kind of forget about us. Her attitude really hurt my parents even though they wouldn't admit it. She treated them like shit and left me to pick up the pieces.'

Cara reminds Oli of a scorned ex, one who can see her partner's flaws but would still rather be in a toxic relationship than have them be with someone else.

'You remember that show *Family Ties*?' Cara says abruptly. Oli nods. 'She was like that Michael J Fox character. She had money-making schemes for days. Even when she was a little kid, she always had a plan. She would negotiate deals with our parents. Friends. Even teachers.'

'She wanted to be rich?' Oli probes.

'She didn't like having to wait for anything, so I think she wanted the freedom of wealth.'

'And you? Did she try to negotiate with you?'

Cara meets her gaze and makes a noncommittal sound. 'I wasn't immune to her. Plus, she was my sister. It was just the two of us.'

'Tell me about Alex Riboni and Evelyn Stanley.'

Cara shrugs. 'They were nice. I met them a bunch of times, and they were all really friendly—or they were to begin with.' Her brows pull together. 'I remember being surprised that Nicole seemed to have made such genuine friends. But after a while, something went down between them. The last time I saw them, Evelyn was a flat-out cow, moody and rude.'

'But you have no idea what the issue was?'

'Nope. I went over to the house just before lunchtime to drop off Mum's fondue set that Nicole wanted to borrow. The three of them were arguing when I got there—I could hear shouting when I knocked on the door.'

'So it was just Evelyn who was angry?'

Cara's face relaxes as she casts her mind back; her eyes drift to the ceiling. 'It was mainly Evelyn, but Nicole seemed annoyed, and the tension was crazy. I remember feeling really awkward standing in the kitchen.' Her brow furrows. 'It was something about a computer.'

Oli feels a prick of interest. 'A computer?'

'Yeah, I think so . . . I'm sure Evelyn said something about a computer.' She bites her lip and shakes her head. 'I'm not sure about the details, but that is definitely something I remember.'

'What about Miles Wu?' Oli tries to hide her frustration. 'Tell me about him.'

'Miles? He was a complete puppy dog. You should have seen the way he mooned around after Alex. It was kind of pathetic. But he genuinely seemed like a nice guy. A bit nerdy and book smart, you know? I couldn't believe it when people were saying he was fucking Evelyn.'

'That would explain the tension, though, right? If Miles was into Evelyn?'

'Sure. But it was Evelyn who was angry, and Nicole too. Not Alex, though—she was kind of quiet. And I really didn't get the feeling they were arguing about Miles.'

'What do you mean?'

'It just didn't feel like they were busting up over a guy. Nicole was worried, like she could tell something bad was going to happen. She was covering her bases, trying to mediate and smooth things over.' Cara's bottom lip juts out slightly, and her chin tilts toward the ceiling.

Oli mirrors her expression and matches her body language without being obvious. It's an interview tactic that rarely fails her.

'Honestly,' Cara says after a moment, 'if you'd seen them together you would understand what I'm saying. I don't think Miles was the issue.'

'Okay.' Oli discards the line of questioning. 'What do you think happened at the house that night?'

Cara directs her dark gaze at Oli and crosses her arms. 'Science doesn't lie. Alex's DNA was all over the weapon.' Cara shrugs. 'Case closed. I don't think my sister's a killer.'

'But you have no idea why she would disappear into thin air?'

She taps a fingernail on her empty coffee glass, then juts forward with sudden urgency. 'Something was going on in that house. I could feel it. I think they all got tangled up in something they couldn't handle. Which is weird, because I always thought Nicole could handle pretty much anything.'

CHAPTER FOURTEEN

OLI WATCHES CARA SAUNTER OFF DOWN THE STREET, HER HEADSCARF glinting in the sun. Her assessment of her sister rings true, her conflicting emotions seem authentic, and the argument she claims to have overheard feels important. There are a few witness reports of disagreements between the housemates in the lead-up to Evelyn's death, but there has never been an explanation, only speculation. And no particular mention of a computer that Oli can recall from the trial, although the girls' devices were all removed from the house. During the trial, Alex admitted to arguments with both housemates but remained vague, attributing the tension to stress about their study.

Oli stands on the wet footpath, thinking it over. Alex's recorded voice keeps echoing through her mind. *I've started to remember things about the night my friend died.*

Digging around in her bag for her sunglasses, Oli makes her way toward a bench adjacent to a tiny square of parkland. A little girl peddles past slowly on a tricycle, her helmet so low it almost covers her eyes.

'This way, sweetheart, this way.' An older woman in jeans and a hoodie jogs awkwardly behind the trike, holding out her hands as if this will prevent the girl from pedalling into danger.

Had Alex really started to remember things, or had she simply grown tired of hiding the truth? Apart from her emotional confession hours after the murder, Alex had never spoken publicly about Evelyn's death, claiming there was a gap in her memory. Until the interview.

Oli suddenly feels very alone. She tries to call Dean; no answer. Lily never called back, and Oli considers calling her now but decides she doesn't have the energy for that conversation.

In the end, she calls Dawn.

'Oli, holy shit, we've got it!'

'What?'

'TJ struck gold with the O'Briens' neighbour. She's gone on the record with a whole load of stuff that Julie O'Brien confided in her about. It sounds like that bastard was worse than anyone knew—drugs, hookers, possibly underage.'

'What?' Oli's stomach clenches involuntarily as she steels herself against old memories threatening to invade her thoughts. 'Are you sure?'

'Apparently that was the last straw for Julie,' Dawn says excitedly. 'One of the prostitutes is allegedly threatening to publish photos from back when she was seventeen.'

'Jesus,' murmurs Oli. 'That's awful.'

'I know. Thank fuck we landed it, though. We're going live with it shortly, and it's going to shit all over whatever the *Sun* has.'

Oli feels a twinge of jealousy. 'That's great.'

'It is. Now, tell me, where are you on the Housemate story? I still can't believe the cops fucked up like that.'

Oli fills her in on the conversation with Cara.

'What does she think was on the computer?' Dawn asks. 'Nudes?'

'Or maybe evidence of a motive. I'll dig around and see if anyone else knows anything about it.'

'It would be great if one of the girls was getting her gear off,' Dawn says, 'but until you have proof, ideally photographic evidence, it doesn't sound like there's much we can run with.'

'Not really,' Oli admits, her heart sinking. 'But it's good context for my feature. If Cara's right and the girls were mixed up in something, people might be more willing to come forward now than they were ten years ago. And maybe I can press the cops, see if anything was found at the Paradise Street house that they're keen to go over again now.'

'Worth a shot,' Dawn says distractedly.

Oli pauses, working out whether to reveal what Rusty mentioned to her in Crystalbrook. She decides to ask in case Dawn has heard something too. 'Did your source say anything about a letter at the house where the body was found?'

'You mean a suicide note?'

'No, some kind of threat?'

'I didn't hear anything about that. Why, what else do you have?'

'Nothing yet.'

Oli knows Dawn is annoyed because she does the laboured breathing that TJ always imitates when he's recounting his interactions with her. 'Just make sure you get aggressive out there. If you need to kick down some doors to get something new, then fucking kick them down.'

'It's not easy,' Oli says feebly. 'My contacts are all old.'

'Well, get some new ones,' Dawn grunts. 'And I want an update on the new plan for the podcast as soon as possible. We're trying to secure an advertiser, and they want an overview of the first episode before they sign.'

After Dawn hangs up, Oli closes her eyes, leaning back into the park bench. Advertisers are not an audience she typically needs to worry about.

Without warning, she thinks about all the boxes in Isabelle's room. She can understand Dean wanting to keep some memorabilia for the girls, but it's really getting to her that he has barely got rid of any of his dead wife's things.

Oli feels the familiar pinch of guilt. Who is she to judge how Dean grieves? She's never lost a partner, let alone a husband. Plus she's still here, she's with Dean, and Isabelle is far from being any kind of threat. So why then does she feel so uneasy? Is it because, deep down, she's worried that karma is yet to play out? She sighs. Navigating the ghost of Isabelle isn't getting any easier. The shock of her death is still raw. Even now when Oli thinks about it, her muscles tense and her pulse quickens.

That morning, Oli woke up at Rusty's. They both had the weekend off and were planning lazy brunches and maybe a movie. She stumbled into the shower, while he stayed in bed watching sport on his laptop. Eventually he joined her, singing loudly and off key, and she swatted at him with a face washer and got soap in her eye. Wrapped awkwardly in one of his cheap towels, she was looking into the foggy mirror, pulling gently at the corner of her throbbing eye, when the story came on the radio.

'It is believed that the detective was heading home from a local gym when she was struck down just after six this morning. The driver failed to stop at the scene, and the body of the detective was discovered by a local resident who called for an ambulance.'

Oli knew it was Isabelle. She just knew. She ran into the lounge, clutching at her eye and rifling through the cushions on the couch in a desperate search for the remote. She cried out impatiently as she jabbed at the buttons until she found the 24/7 news channel. They were running footage of a suburban road dotted with witch's hats. Images of Isabelle flashed onto the screen.

Oli sank to the floor just as Rusty walked in, still singing. His gaze bounced from Oli's face to the screen. 'Jesus, what the fuck?'

She didn't reply. She didn't even blink, just stared at the TV for what felt like hours. Footage came and went of Isabelle at press conferences, even a photo of her with Dean and the girls. Her name ran along the bottom of the screen, and Oli pictured the crash scene so many times, could see Isabelle's broken body lying on the road so clearly, that she wondered if it was possible she'd done it in her sleep.

While Rusty fielded calls from shocked colleagues, all Oli could think about was Dean: how he was coping, and whether there was now a chance they could be together. Rusty had no idea about her history with Dean, and she wonders how he felt when he found out she and Dean were together a few months after they eventually split.

'Oh, you silly thing,' the older lady exclaims as the little girl steers her trike off the path.

As Oli watches the lady get it back on track, she fishes in her bag for a muesli bar. She chews on it, thinking about the conversation with Cara, her mention of the argument over a computer. What could it have been about? Maybe one of the girls discovered an incriminating email—Miles cheating on Alex with Evelyn? Nicole might have found out and told Alex, who retaliated in the worst possible way. Nicole felt guilty enough to panic and go into hiding. Or what if one of the girls stumbled across evidence of McCrae being in a relationship with a student, and they were blackmailing him? But they weren't in high school—would it really have been that scandalous?

Oli needs to speak to Miles. And the neighbours, Matt and Ren. And Professor McCrae. The other guests.

She starts with Tanya and Roy. Their Facebook profiles reveal they are no longer together, although both now live overseas. Their accounts are set to private. She shoots them each a quick generic message asking for a quick chat. Amber doesn't come up in the search and she's not on LinkedIn either.

Next Oli calls the mobile numbers she has for Matt and Ren, but neither connects. She searches on Facebook, and Matt's page loads, an out-of-date profile with dozens of condolence messages on its wall. He died in an accident a few years ago; the unexpected news is sobering as Oli scrolls through his friends list. She finds Ren, but he hasn't used Facebook in years; his profile photo is a shot of a border collie. She sends him a quick message, then realises she has a landline number scribbled in her old notebook below his mobile number. She calls. It goes straight to voicemail with no recorded message, so she identifies herself and asks that he call her back.

She plugs Miles's name into Facebook, but gets too many results to sort through easily. She switches to Google and adds 'Melbourne' to the search. Hundreds of news articles come up, as well as a LinkedIn profile with his picture. She recognises him easily: serious face, short black hair. Assuming his profile is up to date, he's currently an accountant at a firm called Stawell & Finch. She googles the company and finds a number for reception.

When Oli and Jo spoke to Miles back in 2005, he was awkward and a little standoffish. But in fairness, not many people are prepared to be thrust viciously into the spotlight, to suddenly see their own face splashed across the front pages of the paper. To have their girlfriend of two years accused of murder.

Oli calls the number and speaks to a pleasant woman called Bridie with a strong British accent. 'Miles is very popular today!' she trills. 'But he's not in. Can I get him to call you back?'

'Do you think he'll be in tomorrow?' Oli asks casually.

'I'd say so. He's unwell, but I don't think it's serious. Where did you say you were from?'

'It's Sarah Finlayson from the tax office.'

Bridie takes her number. 'I'll have him call you as soon as possible,' she says earnestly.

'Great, thank you!'

Oli strongly suspects Miles's sickie is related to his past hurtling so abruptly into his present, but hopefully Bridie's right and he'll be in tomorrow. Oli needs to find an edge to this case, something beyond the old facts.

There's no phone number for McCrae in her old notes, just an email address. She searches online for current information about the psychology professor but again can only find an email address and she is pretty sure she won't get a reply if she sends him a message. Maybe Dean can help her get in touch with him, via his contacts at the university, though she suspects he won't like to be asked.

She quickly checks Twitter. It doesn't seem like anything new has surfaced since she left the office, but Channel Seven has started promoting their interview with Geraldine Stanley. Dawn will be spitting chips.

Oli launches Facebook on her phone again. There's an account for Mitchell Stanley. She enlarges the profile image, which is obviously very old, from his football days. He looks tanned and healthy, with white teeth and sparkling aqua eyes, a far cry from the clammy drunk who made such a scene outside Alex Riboni's appeal. Oli sends a message explaining who she is and asking that he call her.

It seems none of the other party guests have online profiles. Oli finds Cara Horrowitz's Instagram account, but it's set to private. The profile picture shows her holding a baby.

Oli searches the Housemate Homicide groups that Cooper mentioned, her eyes widening as she scrolls through the swathes of comments. It would be easy to get lost in this world for hours: the pages and pages of speculation, the baseless arguments about what happened. She takes screenshots of some of the more impassioned posts, wondering whether she and Cooper can weave the commentary into the podcast. On Twitter, a handful of people are proclaiming sympathy for Alex, but the majority ascribe her suicide to guilt. Between the Housemate Homicide resurgence and the O'Brien saga, new tweets are loading faster than Oli can read.

Who were the other people Jo hustled to speak with back then? Parents, friends. University staff. Before long, their faces blur into one another in Oli's mind.

She wanders back to Lygon Street and buys a Krispy Kreme doughnut from the 7-Eleven on the corner and takes a seat on the bench out the front. She eats as she reads her emails, feeling increasingly restless. Still ninety minutes until the press conference. She calls Cooper.

'Oli, hi. Hang on.' A scuffling sound. 'I've just put you on speaker. Hello, can you hear me? Shit, Oli, driving this car is incredible, by the way. I think we understand each other now.'

She smiles in spite of herself. 'I'm glad you're enjoying it. Just be mindful you're not on my insurance policy. I spoke to Cara Horrowitz, Nicole's sister.'

'You did? That's great! How did you manage that?'

'She still has the same phone number. I called her, and she agreed to meet.'

'Oh.'

'Mm,' Cooper says after she has relayed her meeting with Cara. 'I'm obviously no expert, being an only child, but couldn't her vibe just be good old-fashioned sibling jealousy? With Cara being adopted, that must have created a strange dynamic.'

Oli stuffs the last of the doughnut into her mouth, vaguely annoyed by his assessment. 'I think a few things she said are worth pursuing, especially if Nicole wasn't as perfect as everyone made her out to be.'

'I guess.'

'Anyway, it's the comment she made about the computer that really has me interested. I don't remember that coming up before, and if Cara's right about the argument she overheard, it might mean something.'

'Yeah, that part doesn't sound like something she would make up.'

'Hopefully we can get on to Miles and see what he knows.'

'Do you think Cara would go on the podcast?'

'She said she hates journalists, although she did end up being happy to talk. It's like she's still trying to figure Nicole out.'

'I'll speak to her. Send me her number?'

Oli ignores him. 'We need to look into a possible link between Alex's job and Crystalbrook.' She explains the article Brent and Pia found. 'What about you? Any luck out there?'

'I think so.' Controlled excitement creeps into Cooper's voice. 'There were cops everywhere, so I was, like, trying to be discreet, but I found a guy who was happy to talk to me. He works at the petrol station. Benny. He says he knows Nicole, but he said she looks really different now, which fits with what the supermarket lady told us. And Benny told me he's always known Nicole as Nat.'

'Any idea how she was supporting herself?'

'He wasn't sure. Said she seemed arty, like a hippy.'

'Helpful.'

'He actually was,' Cooper says earnestly. 'Nicole filled up her car on Monday night.'

'Model?' Oli barks.

'A 2011 Subaru Forester. Teal.' He doesn't hide the pride in his voice, and Oli navigates a strange cocktail of anticipation and irritation that he has such a good lead.

'What about a kid?'

'Yes,' Cooper breathes. 'He said she pretty much always has Evie with her. The kid was with her on Monday. Apparently, Nicole told Benny she'd broken up with her boyfriend and was planning on leaving Crystalbrook.'

CHAPTER FIFTEEN

OLI OPENS HER LAPTOP RIGHT THERE ON THE PARK BENCH AND starts typing: HOUSEMATE HOMICIDE, HORROWITZ ON THE RUN. She puts it all in: Evie, Cooper's conversation with Benny, the description of the car and the possibility of a recent break-up. She even alludes to an incriminating letter being found at the scene. At the last minute she adds Cooper's name to her by-line before shooting it off to Dawn.

She calls Cooper back. 'You should stay in Crystalbrook. See who else will talk to you. And try to find out who the boyfriend was—if he exists.'

'I'm already on it,' he says, sounding pleased. 'I'm asking lots of questions and most people seem happy to talk to me.'

'Good. And try to talk to the cops. If they think you have new information, they might be willing to do an exchange.'

'Okay, talk to the cops. No problem.' Cooper sounds less confident.

'We need to discuss the podcast too. I'm thinking the first episode can be a detailed overview of what we know about that night on Paradise Street. I can describe what it was like to be at the house the morning Evelyn's body was found, so we don't need to sort out any interviews. It will buy us some time.'

'I like that. Yes, that's good.' Cooper's voice brims with excitement.

'And we need to speak to the legal team about using grabs from your phone call with Alex. If we can include her voice in the promos, I don't think we'll need to worry about getting an advertiser.'

'Shit, are you serious?'

'Of course. We're sitting on pure gold, but we need to cross our t's, dot the i's.'

'Okay, I'll call them.'

'Chat later.' Oli shuts her laptop. A strong wind has come out of nowhere, and it matches her mood. Leaves swirl in mini-tornadoes while tree branches buck dangerously at parked cars. She hails a cab that deposits her back in the city, and she ducks across William Street just as it starts to drizzle. A woman in a tight pencil skirt hobbles past, yelling into her phone, her suit jacket shielding her hair from the rain.

Oli flattens herself against the wall so she's under the laneway awning. Her phone beeps with a Facebook message from Mitchell Stanley. *I will call u 2morrow.*

'Yes,' she whispers. Finally some traction.

She fires a message back. *Great, thank you. I look forward to hearing what you have to say. Happy to meet in person if you like.*

She calls Dean.

'I can't believe the news about Julie O'Brien,' he breathes. 'I mean, I know John's a prick but, still, it's awful.'

'Yeah, it's pretty sad.'

'Anyway, how are you feeling? You didn't take my advice and work from home?'

'No. How do you know that?'

'You're not the only investigative journalist in the house,' he teases. 'I can hear you're outside, and it doesn't sound like the noise our garden makes.'

Oli looks around; the laneway is shielded from the hubbub of the city. 'There's too much to do. I had to come into the office.'

'I caught the news before. I can't believe it was the other girl up in Crystalbrook. It's crazy.'

'It's been pretty hectic. I'm about to go to the press conference.'

'You're at police HQ?'

'Yep.'

'I'm just around the corner.' He drops his voice. 'Shame I can't sneak out to meet you. Like old times.'

Her stomach flips gently. He rarely refers to their past, the strange sixteen months when they met in secret, in the middle of the day, at night. When he would come to her apartment early in the morning, stay for a blissful hour, then go, leaving her giddy but also unsure if she would ever see him again.

After he made contact eighteen months ago, their previous intimacy allowed them to accelerate into a familiar rhythm. But the removal of all restraint, the complete lack of caution, meant it felt new. Oli could see him whenever she wanted. Call him. Touch him. There was such freedom to it, such abandon. But since she moved in, it's been different. Dean has been different.

She catches her reflection in a tinted car window, sees the line of worry etched between her brows. 'I'd like that,' she says, tears welling in her eyes.

'I'm trying not to think about it,' he adds huskily. 'I have too much to do today, and I can't afford to be distracted.'

'Dean, do you think there's a chance you can put me in touch with Julian McCrae?' she blurts, knowing she has sabotaged the moment but too desperate for information to care.

'Julian McCrae?'

'Yes. He was the professor at the Housemate Homicide party, and he works at Melbourne uni. I really want to talk to him.'

'I know who he is, Ol, but I'd really prefer you don't chase him down. He's highly respected, and I don't want the uni embroiled in another scandal. One's enough for now, and Nath would lose it if something else blew up. He's anxious enough as it is.'

'I'm not accusing McCrae of anything, I just want to ask him some questions.'

'Sorry, Ol. If you really need to talk to him, you'll have to figure it out, but I wish you'd just leave it alone. He was cleared back then, so I don't see the point in rehashing it now. Look, I've got to go. Don't work too hard, okay?'

Stung, she stands there for a few moments before calling Pia and asking her to track down McCrae's home phone number. 'I'm guessing he won't be listed, so perhaps try his wife,' Oli suggests.

Ignoring the pointed stare of a barista, she sneaks into the bathroom in the cafe next to the police station. She uses the toilet then washes and dries her hands, runs a brush through her hair, reapplies her make-up. In the stuffy police foyer, she joins the growing line to go through security. As she pushes her way through the media pack, she scores an elbow to the ear and one to the ribs. Someone hisses her name, and she looks around but fails to locate the source. She finds a spot about ten metres from the media wall behind the TV journos and their cloud of hairspray. A *Melbourne Today* photographer is up the back: Zach with the neck tattoos. Oli waves, and he gives her a thumbs-up.

Rusty is up the front, facing the crowd. Oli tries to get his attention, but he is deep in conversation with another cop.

A few people gather on stage. A greyhound-thin woman in a sleek pantsuit clutches at a clipboard and stabs her phone with a manicured finger, glancing repeatedly at the audience. A sound guy checks the microphone, and a woman with hearing aids and a long braid stands in front of the Victoria Police pull-up banner.

Bowman appears and walks straight to the raised platform. He looks annoyed, as if he's been dragged away from the last ten minutes of a sports match. He taps the microphone and nods at the PR woman, who responds with a frantic series of head bobs.

'Okay, ladies and gentlemen,' Bowman booms. 'Let's get this show on the road.'

The woman with the braid starts signing in Auslan, and the room settles into the modern white noise of whirring devices and clicking cameras.

'By now I'm sure you are all aware that the deceased woman discovered on a property in Crystalbrook yesterday was Alexandra Riboni,' Bowman says. 'We released this information earlier today. I can now confirm that, based on the autopsy findings, her death is *not* suspicious.'

A reaction ripples through the audience, and a woman from the ABC calls out something about Nicole Horrowitz.

'We believe Ms Riboni was suffering from a mental illness,' Bowman continues, 'and we are currently investigating her final movements and the circumstances around the fire that occurred at the property after her body was found. We believe it was deliberate and possibly intended to cause harm to emergency services personnel following Ms Riboni's death.'

He pauses as a Mexican wave of chatter passes through the room.

'I am well aware that there is significant speculation about the resident of the property in question, and we are exploring all avenues at this early stage. I would encourage you all to ensure you are doing due diligence when it comes to any form of publication about this case. Regardless of the identity of the woman who was living there, we suspect we are dealing with a vulnerable person who may have mental health issues of her own. At this stage, we would simply like to talk to her and confirm that she is safe.'

The PR greyhound steps forward self-importantly. 'The chief inspector will take no more than three questions, then that will be all for today.'

The pack surges forward, arms in the air like schoolchildren.

'Yes, Melissa.'

Oli rolls her eyes. Bloody Melissa Warren.

'There are reports that the resident of the house was Nicole Horrowitz and that she was living there with a little girl named Evie.' She splays a taloned hand in the air, clearly annoyed she's referencing a lead broken by Oli's paper. 'One can only assume Alex Riboni went there to confront her, or interact with her in some other way. Did you know the women were still in touch?'

'One can assume lots of things, Melissa, but my department is only concerned with facts. No comment and next question.'

Oli smirks. She catches Rusty's eye, and he smiles before directing his gaze at his feet. He knows how much she hates Melissa.

Hands shoot up in the air again.

'Stacey.'

'Are you saying, Chief Inspector, that you believe Ms Riboni set a bomb to go off in the house following her death?' asks Rachael Brown from the ABC.

'We're still investigating, but it does seem a device was in the house and set to go off, yes.'

Oli looks at Rusty again, but he's staring straight ahead.

'Bill.'

Bill Ferguson from Channel Ten nods. 'Chief Inspector, when did you become aware that Nicole Horrowitz is still alive, and have police been tracking her whereabouts?'

Bowman's lips form a thin line. 'That's two questions, Bill. My team investigated the death of Evelyn Stanley ten years ago to the best of our ability. We made a conviction, and despite that ruling being overturned, I believe our original investigation was sound and accurate.'

'With all due respect, that doesn't answer—'

'Ms Horrowitz wasn't under investigation then, and she isn't now,' Bowman says firmly. 'If she is located, we would welcome the chance to talk to her.' He trains his intense stare on Bill Ferguson, who shuffles his feet slightly. 'I appreciate that doesn't answer either of your questions, but there you have it.'

Greyhound returns to the mic, looking flustered. 'Thanks, everyone, that's it. Please direct all inquiries to our media team. We'll provide updates as necessary.'

A dissatisfied rumble breaks out as Bowman leaves the room.

Oli doesn't quite know what to make of the presser. Clearly a fair dose of pride in the original investigation is tangled up in all this for Bowman, and perhaps he even feels a responsibility to honour Isabelle's memory. But to just dismiss Nicole Horrowitz as a suspect doesn't really make sense—unless he knows something that hasn't been made public yet.

As the crowd disbands, Oli keeps track of Rusty's head bobbing along the side of the room. His auburn hair is unruly; he's forgotten to put wax in it.

She shoots him a text. *Time for a quick chat? I want to talk to you about the fire.*

He retrieves his phone from his pocket, looks at it, then sweeps his gaze across the sea of people until he sees her and shakes his head. He pockets his phone and takes off down the hall.

Irritated, Oli waves goodbye to Zach, who gives her another thumbs-up. She nods hello to a few journos as she makes her way to one of the stiff lounges near the security checkpoint. She loosens her shoe and rubs at her ankle, looking around the large space. The station is only a few years old, a step up from the premises on St Kilda Road where the Homicide Squad used to be based. Isabelle only worked here for two months before she was killed.

Oli remembers the panic that followed her murder, the fear that settled over the entire force. It seemed someone was targeting cops, literally running them down on the street. But then, three weeks later, the arrest came, bringing with it a collective sigh of relief. Theo Bouris was on parole after serving six years in gaol for manslaughter, a charge he denied. Isabelle's statement had put him away; she was first on the scene and pulled him off the dying victim. He held a grudge—more than that, he hated Isabelle. He had already reoffended on parole, robbing a retailer at knifepoint while claiming he had no money to support his family. He knew his freedom was limited, so he made the most of his last few weeks, hiring a car and hunting Isabelle down like an animal, destroying her life like he believed she had destroyed his.

Shaking off these dark thoughts, Oli messages Pia to ask that her piece be updated with key quotes from Bowman's presser. For a few minutes she watches the TV reporters set up outside the building, patient cameramen waiting while lipstick is reapplied. Melissa Warren has scored the prime position under the glowing Victoria Police sign and looks solemn as she's filmed, her dark bob immune to the wind's havoc. Once their grabs are in the can, the toothy smiles are replaced by scowls as they cross their arms and curse the weather. They totter off to do their edits and wrap for the day.

Oli sighs. She loves print, but the cookie-cutter neatness of TV does appeal sometimes, especially the hours.

She flicks through the main news sites. No one has anything new. Jan Swee, who writes for *The Guardian*, has managed to speak to a couple who lived near the girls on Paradise Street, but the quotes are bland and the piece is fairly weak.

Meanwhile, TJ's front-page piece on O'Brien is red-hot. Oli reads it with admiration and envy. When TJ looks good, she looks bad, or at least less good. Their perceived success is based on comparison rather than a specific goal, and the only reassurance is that the news cycle ensures their podium finish is in constant rotation.

Oli stretches out her legs and checks Twitter. Outrage has erupted about something Donald Trump said at a campaign event. She scrolls through the comments thread for a few minutes before admitting to herself that she is stalling for time.

Back in the cafe next door, she orders a coffee from the same kid who evil-eyed her earlier and tips him fifty cents as a peace offering. She works on her feature, trying to build up some layers, but despite a few good sentences here and there, it feels hollow. She switches to drafting a podcast script and gets into a better rhythm.

Her phone rings, still on silent, the screen lighting up with a number she doesn't recognise.

'Olive Groves.'

'Did you see the press conference?' She can't place the voice: male, angry. 'What complete bullshit.'

'I'm sorry, who is this?'

'Mitch Stanley. You're the journo who contacted me, right? God, I can't believe this shit is still happening.'

'Mr Stanley, yes. I wasn't expecting to hear from you today.'

'Yeah, well, I watched Bowman serve up his standard crap just now and figured I'd call.'

Faint electronic sounds make their way down the line, and Oli tenses. Is he calling her from the pokies? Memories of her dad calling her mum to say he'd be home late enter into her thoughts.

'I'm glad you called,' she says, opening her notebook, pen poised. 'I'm not convinced that the cops disclosed all the information they have, both now and back then.'

'They didn't do shit back then,' he says bluntly. 'Just like they're not gonna do shit now.'

'I remember you were quite vocal about the appeal back then,' Oli says tentatively, sounding out how far she can push him. 'How do you feel about Alex Riboni's suicide?'

'Frankly I couldn't give a shit about her. She stabbed my baby girl—I would have killed her myself if I had half the chance.' His voice wavers unevenly. 'Losing your kid like that, it screws you up. It completely fucked up my whole life. And her mother's.'

'I honestly can't imagine.'

'Yeah, well.' He sniffles. 'Can't do much about it now.'

The staff at the counter break into hysterical laughter, and Oli folds herself into the corner of the booth, shielding her phone from the noise. 'Can you tell me a bit more about why you're so angry at the police?'

'They're just a pack of useless morons. Raked me over the coals, accusing me of all kinds of things, but I would never have hurt my little girl. The whole thing was just a total waste of time. I told them what was going on! But they did nothing about it. And what happens? They build a bullshit case against Alex Riboni, and she sails out of gaol a few years later. What a joke.'

Oli stops taking notes, trying to follow his logic. 'Mitchell, help me understand. You said you think Alex Riboni murdered your daughter, is that right?'

'Yes.'

'Right. So does Alex being dead bring some closure for you?'

'Not in the slightest. I think she was paid to kill my daughter, and I want to know why.'

CHAPTER SIXTEEN

OLI'S BRAIN BUZZES. DID SHE HEAR MITCHELL CORRECTLY? HE thinks Alex was paid to kill Evelyn? She chews her lip, remembering his erratic behaviour a decade ago. 'Let me make sure I'm clear,' she says slowly. 'You believe that someone *paid* Alex to kill your daughter?'

'Yep.' Mitchell sniffs loudly. 'You saw her in court, pretending she didn't remember what happened. What a load of shit—she knew exactly what happened. She killed Evelyn and pocketed a whole lot of money.'

'Do you have any proof of this?' Oli keeps her voice free of judgement, measured and even. 'For starters, she was in gaol for several years.'

'Well, they gave it to her when she got out, then. Probably they paid to get her out of gaol, so you should look into that too.'

Oli's excitement drops a notch. 'Mr Stanley, perhaps we can talk in person? I'd prefer it, and what you have to say is obviously very important.'

'Can't,' he says. 'I'm in the hospital for a few days.'

'Oh, I'm sorry to hear that,' she says, while her doubt intensifies.

'Yeah. My whole bloody system is packing it in. Doctors reckon I can't drink anymore, which is not going to work too well.' His laugh comes out as a snort. 'I'm in and out of hospital like a bloody jack-in-a-box.'

Oli murmurs sympathetically, trying to quell her attitude toward him; she knows it's mainly because he reminds her of her father. She takes a deep breath. 'Well, I'm listening now, and I want to know what you think happened.'

'It was Evelyn who told me.'

'What?'

'She did,' he says defiantly.

'Your daughter told you Alex was paid to kill her?' Oli's forehead rumples as she tries to keep up. 'I'm sorry, I don't understand.'

'I borrowed a lot of money off her.'

'From Evelyn?'

'Yeah. I'd got myself into a bit of a mess, gambling and the like. Pissing away our savings. Anyway, in the autumn I told Evelyn how bad things were, asked her not to mention it to her mother. I wondered if she could loan me some money, just until I got sorted. It's not like I expected her to say yes, but she said she could.'

Oli flips to a new page. 'How much money are we talking?'

'She gave me five thousand dollars.'

Oli's eyebrows shoot up. 'Five thousand dollars.' She writes the figure down with a flourish.

'Cash.'

'That's a lot of money for a student living out of home.'

'Exactly,' he says triumphantly. 'She wasn't earning that kind of dough babysitting, that's for sure.'

Drugs, Oli thinks. *Or perhaps prostitution.* But all she says to Mitchell is, 'You didn't ask about it?'

'No. I should've, obviously, but I needed the cash. I promised to pay her back, and that was that. Look, I knew it was suss, but I didn't want to get into all that.'

'Where did you think she was getting the money from?'

He sniffs and mutters, 'Drugs.'

'What made you think that?'

'Evelyn was different that year. She pulled back from me a fair bit. From Gerry too. It broke her heart, even though she was too proud to admit it. But something was up. A few times when I saw Evelyn, I knew she was coming down from drugs but I didn't say anything. Not my place.' He sighs. 'I only saw her two more times after she gave me the money. I was trying to get the dollars together to pay her back, but things just weren't going right for me.'

In his voice Oli detects a sense of his struggle with himself, a desire to be a better person only to be continually thwarted by his own poor decisions.

'We had dinner the night before she died, but I'm sure you know that. For some reason, everyone always thought that was a big deal. Anyway, when I saw her that night she wasn't doing so well.'

'Physically?'

'She wasn't looking her best, but that's not what I mean. She was always so pretty—well, you've seen photos, obviously—but she was run-down. Gotten herself really skinny too.'

'Did she mention money that night?' Oli presses. 'Or say anything about Alex and Nicole?'

'She was upset. I told her things were still bad for me, and she said that she wished she could help me out again but that things had changed and she was running low on cash. She wanted me to pay her back, and I said I would as soon as I could. I asked her if everything was okay, and she started crying. I asked her if it was something to do with a bloke, but she said it wasn't that.'

'Did she give you any idea what she was upset about?'

'She said things were bad at the house. I got the feeling she was fighting with the girls.'

Oli's impatience bubbles to the surface. 'I need to be clear, Mr Stanley. At any point did your daughter say anything about Alex Riboni threatening her or being paid to harm her?'

'Not in so many words,' he admits. 'But I'm telling you, she was on edge. She was scared of those girls, and I'm not just saying that 'cause of what happened.'

'But she didn't say why?'

'You sound like the cops,' he mutters. 'Look, she didn't spell it out, but I knew my daughter, and something was up with her.'

'Did she say anything about the party they were having the following night?'

'She mentioned it. She told me Nicole invited that professor. Someone should be looking at him—I've heard he's not short of a bob. Maybe he was giving her money.'

Oli presses her fingers to her temples. 'So, in your opinion, why did they have people over when they were arguing?'

'I don't know, do I.' Mitchell is clearly losing his patience too. 'I guess they were trying to patch things up.'

'Okay, okay.' She tries to think. 'There have been some reports of Evelyn earning money at a brothel. I know she told you she was short of money, but did she mention anything about what she was doing for work?'

'My daughter wasn't a slut. She barely even had boyfriends. That Calamity Jane story was a load of shit.'

'Of course,' Oli murmurs, thinking that a father is never going to react well to the possibility his daughter was getting paid for sex.

'She was going to focus on her acting. She got a role in Sydney she was considering, and I had the feeling she planned to drop out of uni. I told Gerry, and she went ballistic. She always wanted Evelyn to get a degree above anything else.'

'You told your wife about your conversation with Evelyn?'

'Uh-huh. Called her the next day, the Friday. Like I said, I was worried. She wasn't herself.'

'Was Geraldine worried too?'

'I think she thought I was exaggerating. We were going through a rough patch.'

Oli recalls Geraldine's anguished cries, Mitchell grabbing her as she lurched along Paradise Street toward her dead daughter.

'She blamed me for everything.' He doesn't sound bitter, just resigned.

'Did you tell her about Evelyn lending you money?'

'Of course, but I don't know if she believed me. Maybe she just didn't want to think badly of Evelyn. She knew she shouldn't have five grand to loan out.'

'And you told the cops everything you've told me?'

'Yep, but they didn't give a shit. They had their suspect, they weren't interested. They just wanted it all sorted so they could move on to something else. But as far as I'm concerned, the lazy fuckers only got half a killer. I loved my daughter, but she wasn't perfect. She got a whole lot of cash from somewhere, and I think the same person paid Alex to hurt her.'

A woman starts talking in the background—a nurse asking him a question? He mutters a response.

Oli looks at her page of shorthand, her head spinning. 'Thank you for speaking to me, Mr Stanley. Can we talk again?'

'I'll talk to you every bloody day if you can get the pigs to do their job,' he says before abruptly hanging up.

Oli sits there feeling numb. If he's telling the truth, then Evelyn must have been involved in something sinister. But what? No one else is likely to come forward if that involves a risk of being implicated in illegal activity.

First things first: if Oli can confirm Mitchell mentioned the money to the cops, it would show some consistency in his claims. Maybe Rusty can validate it for her. She quickly shoots a message to the number he called her from, asking that he doesn't speak to anyone else in the media. Knocking back the last of her cold coffee, she tries to stitch all the disparate pieces of information together in her mind.

She stands up to go just as Bowman steps into her line of sight outside the cafe. The coffee cup rattles across the table as she pushes her chair back and bolts toward him. 'Chief Inspector!'

He freezes. Turns. Scans her up and down. He says something to the man in the suit next to him before ambling over, his expression impossible to read. His blue eyes are watery, his papery skin riddled with sunspots and broken veins.

She musters some confidence. 'I want to talk to you about the Housemate case.'

'Tell me, Ms Groves, how are the twins?'

'Oh.' Oli is completely thrown, anxiety rolling across her body. 'They're fine, thank you.'

He nods. Digs his hands into his pockets. 'I'm glad to hear it.'

Still nervous, she says, 'I want to include some quotes from you in a feature I'm writing.'

Bowman says curtly, 'You ran with the child story.'

'I did.' She lifts her chin, trying to convey a bravery she doesn't feel.

His expression doesn't change, but a different energy runs through his eyes. 'That didn't impress me much. Nor did your paper's coverage of the O'Brien saga today.'

'Well, your press conference just now didn't impress *me* much.'

He surprises her by laughing. 'I guess we're even.'

'I have some new information,' she says, feeling emboldened. 'And some questions for you.'

Something skitters across his face: irritation, or grudging respect? 'I'm happy to hear your theories, but as I said earlier at my underwhelming press conference, this might be a fairly straightforward case in the end. Not everything is a story.'

She ignores the subtle dig. 'Can we talk now? I want to know if you found a computer at the Paradise Street house. There might have been something relevant to the case on it.'

He pulls at his nostrils. Clears his throat. 'Like what?'

'I'm hoping you will tell me.'

He glances at his watch, an old-fashioned timepiece with a few clock faces sitting inside the larger one. 'We found two computers at the house. But there wasn't anything on them that I think would be of interest to you.'

Undeterred, she ploughs on. 'I just spoke to Mitchell Stanley, who had some interesting things to say about his daughter and her friends. Things I'm not sure your team ever looked into.'

Bowman snorts softly and looks at his watch again. 'I have an event to get to shortly, and I can't be late as I'm the keynote speaker. Tomorrow night should be fine, assuming everyone behaves themselves. The Lion & Ox on Exhibition. I'll be there by five-thirty.'

'I can't tomorrow night,' she manages, cursing the twins' end of term swimming carnival. 'What about Friday?'

He nods, looking amused. 'Clearly this important conversation can wait until then.'

'I'd rather speak with you now. I'll keep it brief.'

'Not possible, I'm afraid.' He loops his thumbs into the belt holes of his trench coat, checks his phone and frowns. 'Friday it is.'

'Thank you, Chief Inspector,' she breathes.

But Bowman is already walking away, his broad shoulders hunched.

Oli heads slowly in the opposite direction, her heartbeat dropping back to a normal rhythm. She isn't sure how well that went, but a meeting's a meeting. Her phone rings again: Cooper. 'Any luck out there?' she asks.

'Oli.' His voice is subdued, missing its usual perkiness.

'What? What is it?'

'I've spoken to heaps of people, but right now I'm with a bunch of cops up here, and they've just got a call about a Subaru turning up in Warrandyte.'

'Has it been dumped?'

'It's at the bottom of the Yarra River.'

CHAPTER SEVENTEEN

EVERYONE IS WELL ON THEIR WAY TO DRUNK WHEN OLI ARRIVES back at the office. TJ is sitting on top of Brent's desk sans tie, looking extremely pleased with himself as he regales the small group with the ins and outs of his interview with O'Brien's old neighbour, who revealed she frequently saw young prostitutes coming to the former premier's house when his wife was away. Oli is offered a beer but turns it down, half-heartedly joining the chatter. She feels disconnected from her co-workers, skirting around the action and sticking to small talk. Once critical mass has been achieved, with more people drinking than working, someone suggests the pub, and everyone eagerly pulls on jackets and gathers their belongings. Oli politely declines a few invites and heads back to her desk.

Pia bounces over, colour in her cheeks, and hands her a sticky note. 'I couldn't find Julian McCrae's mobile number, but this might be his landline. His wife listed it on a website she used to run selling pottery. It's in East Melbourne, and I matched it to the ABN registered under her name. I rang earlier—the voicemail message doesn't mention their names, but it sounds like an older woman. Worst-case scenario, you can go to the uni campus and track him down, though I get that probably isn't your preference.'

'No. I'd much rather harass him on the phone,' Oli jokes.

'Your specialty,' Pia says, smiling.

'Thanks, Pia,' Oli says gratefully. 'You're a legend.'

'No worries,' she replies. 'I'm off to be a drunk legend.'

'Have fun.'

'You're not coming?'

'No, I have a few things to tie up here.'

Pia shrugs; she knows Oli isn't a big drinker. 'See you tomorrow.'

Oli buys a packet of chips from the vending machine and munches away, going over her notes. Almost two hours later, Cooper walks in and gives her an update from the car crash scene in Warrandyte just as it starts to hit the TV reports. No one was inside the submerged Subaru, but divers are still searching the area, unwilling to rule out that there are bodies in the lake. Oli watches the dark footage of the Channel Nine reporter who gestures to the river behind her.

Cooper looks drawn, uncertain. 'I heard one of the divers say that the doors were open. I'm not sure what that means.'

Oli offers him a chip, and he takes a small handful. The machinery in the office hums, the bank of TVs flickering as they jump from story to story. She can tell he's rattled.

'Jeepers, it was intense out there,' says Cooper. 'I kept thinking I didn't know what I would do if they pulled a kid out of the water.'

'You would have done your job,' Oli says.

'I guess.'

'You would have,' she insists. 'Like yesterday. You just kicked into gear and kept going.'

He nods but seems unconvinced.

'Do you think it's worth you going back to Warrandyte tomorrow?'

He is clearly surprised to be asked. 'Maybe. But I don't get the feeling Nicole's connected to the area. And it's a lot of time in the car that I could be putting to better use.'

He looks to Oli for confirmation and she nods and then tells him about her conversation with Mitchell Stanley.

'Evelyn was selling drugs?' he says when she's done.

'I'd say that's most likely.'

'Do you think they were all dealing?'

Oli imagines the rhythm of the share house, the girls living on top of each other, borrowing each other's clothes, doing each other's make-up. 'We know they were all taking drugs. It's not much of a stretch.'

He doesn't comment. His usual perkiness has definitely been tested by the events of the day.

'Why don't you sort out your photos?' Oli says authoritatively. 'I'll write up some copy to go with them. If we get everything through by 8 pm, we'll make the morning print edition.'

They work in silence. 'This is the best one,' Cooper says finally.

She looks at the image: the Subaru being winched out of the river, a group of emergency workers in high-vis gathered on the banks. She nods. 'Send it to me.'

After filing the piece along with the photo, she stretches her hands above her head and breaks into a yawn. Wonders where the fuck Nicole Horrowitz is.

'I'm wiped too,' says Cooper, catching her yawn. 'So, what now? Home time?'

She thinks about going home to Dean's empty house, and the temptation to trawl through Isabelle's things surges in her core. 'Do you have plans?' she blurts.

'What, right now?' Cooper looks startled. 'Ah, no. Mum's got dinner for me, she always cooks a curry on Wednesday, but I guess I could—'

Oli stands and pulls on her coat. 'Let's go to Paradise Street.'

—

They creep along St Kilda Road. Clouds clog the sky, hiding the stars and blocking the glow of the moon, which is trying to show off its full orb. Cooper's bike is strapped to the back of the car, secured with a fluorescent-green cord. Oli can see the silhouette of the handlebars through the rear window.

'Did you always want to be a journalist?' asks Cooper. He's texting someone, his messages filled with gifs, and Oli wonders if he has a partner. They must have the patience of a saint.

'Pretty much. I always liked to write, but I didn't get into it straight away. I went overseas for three years after high school. I didn't go to uni until my early twenties.'

'How come?'

'I wanted to get away.'

'From what?' He looks at her with interest.

'I just . . . It's hard to explain.'

Even Cooper seems to understand that it's not up for discussion. 'Fair enough. What did you do when you were over there? I've only ever been to Asia, and only for a couple of weeks. Mum took me to meet all my relatives in Singapore. I can't imagine being away from Australia for three years—I'm a real homebody.'

'I thought all millennials want to take off overseas?'

'Not this one,' he says cheerfully. 'I want to make my career in Melbourne. I mean, it's a great city, why not?'

Oli casts her mind back to that time, when she was working in bars and pubs. Waitressing. Writing snippets here and there, documenting the people she met, the things she saw. It was a dreamy, wonderful few years of anonymity, the perfect antithesis to everything she'd left behind and the drama yet to come. She kept to herself, alone in crowds of people. She started dabbling in drugs, weed, pills, and enjoyed dancing for hours with strangers then going home on her own.

'You should think about it,' she says. 'Take a gap year or something. I loved it. I worked in bars mainly, but I wrote as well, travel pieces and articles about being an Aussie in Europe. A lot of them got picked up here and in the UK. It helped me get a job when I finished my degree.'

'You studied journalism?'

'Arts. I started doing law, but I switched out after a year. I wanted to write. But journalism has changed a lot since then. Maybe these days I would make a different choice.'

'Half my uni subjects covered the impact of social media on journalism.'

'Yeah, there's that, and just the overall sense you're always just scraping the surface now. The news cycle is a lot faster than it used to be.' She laughs, self-conscious. 'That probably makes me sound really old.'

With a nod, he looks out the window.

She rolls her eyes. 'Anyway,' she says lightly, 'that's why a story like this is interesting. It's not just about the reporting—there's the chance to dig a bit, push people to talk. It's not over in a day. It has some depth.'

They stop for a red light. Nearby, a young woman, her thin legs pale and bare under a fluffy tan coat, leans back against an old Telstra phone box, her heavily made-up eyes half closed. A white ute pulls up next to her, and she stands to attention, smiling and leaning into the passenger window.

'I thought street prostitutes were illegal?'

Cooper's tone is so naive that Oli has to stifle a laugh. 'I think the cops pick their battles. Like the rest of us.'

He nods wordlessly, watching as the girl swings herself into the ute.

The pub on the corner of Grey Street is lit up like a Christmas tree. A trio of backpackers sit smoking cigarettes in the gutter out the front, and the line to get in snakes around the corner. Oli takes a right into Barkly Street, passing wine bars and restaurants, beautiful old houses nestled between run-down apartment buildings.

'Where do you live?' she asks him, navigating the backstreets.

He interprets her question as an invitation to narrate his entire family history. 'We live in Box Hill. Dad's brother is there too, just a few streets over from us.'

'Nice.'

'I'm an only child.'

'You mentioned that.'

'Heaps of cousins, though.'

'Right.'

'I always wanted a cat, but my mum's allergic.'

Oli doesn't reply.

The street reaches a dogleg, marking the start of Paradise Street.

'This is it,' Oli says, interrupting Cooper as he describes his mother's allergies.

He angles his body forward, the seatbelt straining against his scrawny chest. 'Number twenty-eight, right?'

Oli nods. The streetlights create dull yellow circles every few metres, and while some of the houses have their porches lit, most are dark. 'It's further down.' She keeps the car at a low hum. 'There.' Bringing it to a stop, she flicks off the headlights. A For Lease sign is nailed to the front fence, black graffiti scrawled across it.

A jolt of déjà vu charges through her. Aside from a new garden bed on the left side of the lawn and a row of rosebushes along the front fence, it looks almost exactly the same.

'I *totally* remember the moment the news broke,' Cooper whispers. 'I was in the den watching cartoons, eating Weet-Bix—or maybe it was Coco Pops—anyway, I could hear the radio from the kitchen, that news music they used to have, and a newsreader said a woman had been killed in St Kilda, and we'd been to Luna Park the weekend before. And so I just completely freaked out. I snuck into the lounge that night to watch the news from behind the couch. My mum and dad were talking about it—you know, like playing detective. Mum said the girls sounded like trouble, but she's pretty conservative.'

'I was right here,' Oli says. 'In a much less expensive car than this one.' She feels a stab of affection for her old Mazda; she loved that car.

Cooper bounces back against his chair. 'It's such a spin out!'

Oli is starting to regret bringing him here. Now that she has seen the house again, coming here feels kind of foolish. What did she expect, a lightning strike of inspiration? A clue?

'Seriously,' he says, 'it's like you're retracing your steps, uncovering new leads.'

She notices fresh flowers piled up beside the front gate: some roses and a sheaf of daisies. Alex's death has stirred up the old grief. People don't know where to put their symbols of sadness, so they return to the scene of the original crime.

'Imagine living in a place where someone died like that.' Cooper makes a face. 'Gross.'

'Well, maybe that's why it's for lease. Murder isn't exactly a selling point.'

He grabs his phone and starts prodding at the screen. 'Wow, I don't think it's sold since Evelyn died. I guess the owners just figured it was easiest to keep renting it out.'

'We should go,' Oli says. Pressure is building in her chest. 'I'll drop you home.'

'It's kind of out of your way.'

'It's fine.'

'Well, sure, that would be great.' He stretches his legs. 'The longer I can spend in this car the better. I got a BMW one of the few times I've ordered an Uber. That was cool. It's maybe the best car I've ever been in, but it was only a ten-minute trip.'

Oli pulls away from the kerb. They pass the block of land where a prostitute was found beaten to death a few weeks before Evelyn died. Jo didn't invite Oli to the scene that morning; she took TJ instead.

Those weeks were frenzied: the second prostitute murder, the Carter child snatched from her bedroom, Oli's secret dates with Dean. She was deliciously exhausted, running on empty but high from the constant stimulation, the anticipation of Dean, the roller-coaster of the news cycle.

Cooper seems intent on getting his inner monologue out. 'Another big day tomorrow, huh? I really hope I can sleep tonight—sometimes I have trouble going to sleep, but once I'm out, I'm out. So the trick is getting relaxed enough to trick myself into just nodding off. I told you about that app I'm using, didn't I?'

Circling her fingers around the volume knob on the stereo, Oli turns it to the right, unsubtly drowning him out. As she drives, the Paradise Street house looms fresh in her mind, and Mitchell Stanley's accusation echoes through her thoughts. *Those lazy fuckers only got half a killer.*

CHAPTER EIGHTEEN

OLI ALL BUT BOOTS COOPER OUT OF THE CAR, THEN WATCHES HIM in the rear-view mirror as he wrestles the bike off the tow bar. She can't quite make out his house in the dark but sees a large lemon tree in the front yard. A soft light is angled from one of the eaves into the garden, revealing a statue next to the bottom step.

Once Cooper disappears through the front gate, she drives. Smokes a cigarette while completing aimless laps of suburban streets. Winds the windows down, drawing cold air into her lungs, happy to be lost. She pulls over at a 7-Eleven and buys a Cherry Ripe. She's aware that she is avoiding going home but chooses not to analyse it. Plus, she reasons, swallowing the last of the chocolate bar, she thinks better when she drives.

Just as she decides to head home, Lily rings. 'Are you working?'

'Hi, Lily,' replies Oli, turning back onto the highway. 'How are you?'

'Shaun's stuck in Sydney, and I'm bored.'

Oli hesitates. 'Well, as fate would have it, I'm actually about five minutes from your place.'

'That's weird.'

'Very. Do you want me to come over?'

'Are you spying on me or something?'

'Do you want me to come or not, Lily?'

'Of course. Beats drinking alone.'

Her sister hangs up, and tension settles across her shoulders. 'Probably not a great idea,' she mutters.

Lily and Shaun live in a sprawling Californian bungalow that's in desperate need of work. It has four bedrooms, three of which were physical markers of the former Mrs Monroe's fertility failures. These empty rooms became such a problem that Shaun ended up putting locks on the doors and sealing them off.

'I mean, it's not his fault she couldn't have kids,' Lily says, leading Oli down the wood-panelled hallway a few minutes later. They lift their legs high to step over a collection of paint tins and rollers. 'Wine?' Lily is already holding a bottle.

'Just the one.'

Oli looks around the kitchen. Despite the wear and tear, the appliances are modern. A Thermomix takes pride of place on the bench; Lily regularly boasts that she uses it to make everything from cocktails to muesli. Photos plaster the fridge—Lily and Shaun in all kinds of exotic locations, shots of Lily and some women Oli doesn't know dressed up at the races.

Lily hands her a generous glass of wine, and she looks at it doubtfully before taking a sip.

'You're not pregnant, then?' Lily folds her arms disapprovingly.

Oli blinks, then looks back at the glass in her hand. 'What? No. Jesus, Lily.'

'Well, you better not wait too long, Ol. You're not young, and you'll want to get Dean on board while he's still besotted with you enough to consider it.'

'The twins are a lot already.' Oli squeezes the glass so hard she worries it might break. 'I don't think you realise.'

Lily rips open a box of crackers, spilling them all over the bench. 'I mean it's true, I'm a childless ignoramus.'

'Come on, Lily. I didn't mean it like that.'

'Well, that's how it sounds,' she grumbles. 'But seriously, take it from someone who knows, if it's important to you then make sure you get on with it. I figured Shaun would come around to the idea of a baby, but I had no idea how scarred he was from the whole fertility rollercoaster with Rebecca. He's just not interested now.' Lily speaks bluntly, her sleek blonde hair swinging around her pretty face, but Oli detects the disorientation beneath, the sense that she took her eye off the ball and misread the play, stuffing up an easy catch.

'I'm not sure it's that important to me,' Oli says quietly. 'Or to Dean.'

Lily swallows a giant gulp of wine and looks hard at Oli. 'That's not what you said at my bachelorette party.'

Oli cringes. What a disaster that night was. It ended with her vomiting repeatedly after consuming what felt like gallons of vodka punch. She had felt so disingenuous, the heralded sister who barely knew Lily anymore. Meeting stranger after stranger who told her Lily was a dream friend. Desperate to fit in, Oli uncharacteristically threw back glass after glass. She remembers laughing with Lily's friends at a local bar, then being deeply engrossed in conversations in Lily's kitchen and later in the lounge. The night culminated with a handful of women standing around a hastily made fire in the backyard at dawn, writing down their dreams and yelling them into the sky before throwing them in the flames, which was apparently a karmic wishing well.

'Things change,' Oli says dismissively.

Lily arches an eyebrow. 'That was less than a year ago.'

Oli's cheeks flush. 'Well, if I remember correctly, once children were off the table, you were going to sell this place and live overseas.'

Lily fixes her gaze on the bench. She doesn't speak, and Oli worries that she is about to cry. 'I'd still like to live in Europe at some point,' she says, 'but Shaun's work is going great guns so we're staying put for now. I guess that's what marriage is all about, right? Compromise.' It's impossible to miss the irony in her tone.

'Lil . . .'

'It's fine. I'm honest with myself about where I stand. Shaun and I talk about it. We're getting a puppy. And a cat.'

'Okay. That sounds good.'

'Come on, talk to me. I know you want to have a baby. Is it Dean? He doesn't want more kids?'

Oli closes her eyes and pictures the twins, their faces so much like their mother's. 'It's not that. It's complicated. The girls have been through a lot, and we're all still getting used to each other. It's not easy slotting into their lives.'

Lily snorts. 'Nothing is easy, Ol.' She eats another biscuit. 'Mum's worried about you. She thinks you're shutting her out.'

'Jesus,' Oli mutters. 'I'm just busy.'

'She's a nightmare, I know, but I would appreciate it if you'd call her—or, even better, take the girls over there and let her pretend she has grandchildren for a few hours. Get her off my arse.'

'I'll call her.'

'My therapist says that it makes sense you gravitated toward an instant family.'

'What?' Oli rolls her eyes impatiently. 'Why is your therapist talking about me?'

'Sometimes we talk about you when I'm avoiding my own issues.'

'I really wish you wouldn't do that.'

Lily shrugs. 'You can go to therapy and talk about me.'

'Fuck off, Lily.'

'Hey.' She puts her hands in the air. 'You should go to therapy, and you know it. You never unpacked everything that happened with dad. Nor did you work through why you ditched Rusty and rushed into things with Dean.'

'Dad has nothing to do with Dean!'

Lily folds her arms across her chest, causing her collarbones to flex above her white singlet top.

Oli is tempted to slap her across the face. 'I did go to therapy. Several times. I just didn't feel the need to talk about it.' She remembers the awkward hours spent in the psychologist's room.

Lily splashes more wine into her glass. Her wrist is so fine, her fingers long and thin. The bigger Oli gets, the smaller Lily gets. Her father's old chant rings in her mind: *Pretty Lily, jolly Oli.* He sensed a weakness in her, something that didn't exist in Lily. Is it still there? Is she walking around inviting people to take advantage of her?

Sipping her wine, Lily cocks her head. Little lines form around her lips, making her look alarmingly like their mother. 'How is your work going, anyway?'

Oli looks at her, surprised.

'I read your articles, you know. All of them.'

'It's fine, it's busy.'

'I wonder where she is. The housemate, I mean. Nicole Horrowitz.'

'I don't know. Doing what she does best, it seems—running away.'

'Maybe someone is helping her hide. There's probably plenty of sickos out there who'd get a thrill out of harbouring a fugitive. People looking for some excitement in their lives.'

'Maybe you should ease up on the therapy.'

'I'm serious! You reckon she has a kid now, right? Maybe they're holed up with the father. Or she could have blackmailed him to help her, threatened the life of the kid if he refuses—I mean, she's clearly a total psycho.'

'Lily, you have no idea what you're talking about. Did you see the news tonight? They might both be dead at the bottom of the Yarra!'

'Nah, the car was a ploy. And she's as guilty as sin, I've always thought it.'

Oli rinses her wineglass, puts it in the sink. 'Unfortunately, I'm only interested in facts.'

'Well, that's your issue right there.' Her sister laughs. Her voice is nowhere near as deep as Oli's, but her laugh has always been throaty, nice to listen to. 'But, seriously, something was obviously going on with those girls.'

Sensing her sister is about to launch into amateur-detective mode again, Oli says, 'I have to go, Lil. Thanks for the drink.'

They walk back down the hallway in silence. Lily opens the door and rests her head against it. 'I don't want to fight with you, Oli. I just wish you would talk to me.'

'We just spent an hour talking!'

Lily crosses her arms, pursing her lips.

'I'm absolutely fine.' Oli smiles broadly and steps forward to hug Lily. She smells familiar, like rain and roses. 'Honestly.'

They pull apart. Lily looks sad. 'Night, Oli.'

—

Oli eases the front door closed and slips off her shoes. She washes her face in the downstairs bathroom, then makes her way upstairs.

'You're late.' Dean's voice floats out from the dark, not a hint of sleep in it.

'Sorry to wake you.' She undresses, slips into bed.

'I wasn't asleep. I was waiting.'

She turns to face him. The light catches the outline of his face, the shimmer of his eye. 'You didn't call.'

'I figured you were working. I didn't want to hassle you, I know you don't like that.' He kisses her, setting off little sparks all over her bare skin. 'Were you just at the office tonight?'

For a moment she considers telling him she saw Lily, but she doesn't want to recap their conversation. 'Yeah. It's been a long day.'

'I bet.' He's annoyed. 'Were you working alone or with the pain-in-the-arse colleague?'

She flips over and arches her back against his body. 'Alone.'

Although he traces down the upper side of her arm, his body remains rigid.

'How are the girls?' Oli asks.

'They're fine. We had a nice dinner.'

'That's good.' She feels a clench of jealousy at the thought of their night at Mary's. No doubt it churned up memories of Isabelle.

Clasping his arm around her waist, he pulls her close, then hooks his leg between hers and pins her against the mattress.

'I have to leave early in the morning,' she says lightly. 'It's going to be another crazy day.'

He tenses again. 'But what about the swimming carnival? You know I'm presenting at the board meeting with Nathan.'

Oli's head begins to pound. 'That's why I'm starting early, so I can leave the office early without any hassle.'

'I wish you had more time for us.' He presses hard into her. Grabs her breasts.

Her breath catches in her throat. She wants him so badly, just her and him like it used to be. 'I know, but there's a lot of pressure lately at work. I want to do a good job.'

Pushing her onto her back, he climbs on top of her. He cups her chin in his hand and strokes her hair, caressing her scalp. She is wide awake now, her mind racing, the events of the day charging into her brain. She ignores them all. She just wants this.

'I just don't like it when you're not here, Oli,' he says. 'I want you all to myself.'

CHAPTER NINETEEN

THURSDAY, 10 SEPTEMBER 2015

THERE'S AN UNIDENTIFIABLE CORD IN THE CAR CONSOLE. OLI examines it while she waits for the garage door to open. It's definitely not hers, so it must be one of Cooper's. He seems to have at least ten on him at all times. She sends a photo of it to Cooper. *Hopefully this one isn't critical?*

Pulsing dots appear on the screen. *Nah, I've got tons of spares.*

She reverses onto the quiet street, flicks on the headlights and heads toward the office. The grey sky churns, making rain. It's only just gone six, so Cooper is up early. When Oli was starting out as a journalist, the pre-dawn hours almost killed her. She recalls struggling to stay awake in editorial meetings and falling asleep on the couch at night watching TV. Cooper is clearly a different breed of young person, one of those spring-out-of-bed types. Plus, he probably isn't partying as hard as Oli used to; he seems more likely to be in bed early with a cup of tea.

Up ahead, the light turns red and she slows. There's not a car in sight, so she just sits there staring at the road. Lily tapped into a truth last night, one that Oli has been ignoring for months. The rational part of her brain knows that because she put Dean on a pedestal for so long and yearned for his affection so much, his sudden availability in itself was intoxicating. When Isabelle died, being with him suddenly became a possibility, and Oli grew obsessed with the idea. Even though she didn't actually pursue him, the eight years of progress she made in the quest to get over him was instantly null and void, her feelings for Rusty collateral damage.

Oli breathes out, barely daring to acknowledge the nasty little thought clawing at the edges of her mind. *It isn't what you thought it would be.*

And that's just it. She hurtled into her fantasy future at an alarming speed, going from her simple carefree life to one of pressure and predictability. Dean is so intent on being a unit, desperate to avoid repeating his mistakes. But it also feels like he believes the only one of them who needs to compromise is Oli. She probably should appreciate his wealthy lifestyle, but instead she feels trapped in the stupidly large house and frustrated that her career seems suddenly expected to take a back seat. Kate and Amy bring out an awkwardness in her, an oafishness that makes her feel not only completely inadequate but also hopelessly inferior to her predecessor. Isabelle.

Her presence lingers in the house like the fragrance of a secret lover, her death still as shocking as a slap. If Isabelle was alive, she and Dean would be together. Everyone must think it, but it's not something Oli can talk to him about. Expressing her feelings about being runner-up to a ghost is impossible.

She massages her temples. And what about her? Would she still be with Rusty? Sweet, simple Rusty, who happily ate cereal for breakfast, lunch and dinner. Rusty, who read his star sign every day and drove around on an empty tank of petrol as though it was a masculinity test. Unlike Dean, he wasn't prepared for every circumstance, but he was sweet. Patient. His problem-solving approach was gung-ho but cheerful. He gave her space and knew her job came first. He just didn't make her crazy, not in a good or a bad way.

When she glances in the mirror, she looks surprisingly alert considering her lack of sleep. This story has unlocked some of her old energy, a charged sensation that has her limbs buzzing and her mind alive.

She puts her foot on the accelerator. A few hundred metres along the road a large truck blocks the road in front of her, and a short, stocky woman in high-vis tilts a stop sign, directing Oli to turn right down a side street. Cursing, she weaves the car along unfamiliar roads, following the detour signs. She comes to a T-intersection on Myer Street and quickly reorients herself, turning right toward the city. She passes a primary school and a community centre. A magpie swoops low, almost hitting the windscreen, and she ducks involuntarily. Her foot goes to the floor, and the car skids to a halt.

A realisation hits Oli like a ton of bricks. Isabelle died here. Just up from a petrol station, a few metres from the community centre. Struck down and killed on her way back from the gym, where she had submitted her lithe body to sixty minutes of cardio before embarking on the four-kilometre jog home. Her sharp mind would have been alive with endorphins, a day of family activities ahead, her latest case no doubt still pervading her thoughts. Oli has trouble enough switching off, finding a place to put the darkness, but it's surely nowhere near as bad for her as it is for those on the front line of crime like Isabelle was. Oli often marvelled at Rusty's ability to seal the evil off, lock away the horrible scenes and conversations in a section of his brain. But Oli gets the feeling that Isabelle was more like her—that the things she saw, the cruelty she witnessed, had her questioning the entire human race, had her wondering if she could trust anyone.

And she was right to question it: the darkness had got her in the end. One moment Isabelle Yardley was running along, full of life; the next, her body was flying skyward like a plastic bag in the wind. The tragedy of it hits Oli all over again. Isabelle was such a force, so impressive and accomplished. Oli spent so long idolising her, obsessing over her, that her sudden death still fails to compute.

Dean and the girls were sound asleep at home when Isabelle was killed, about to wake up to a Saturday morning of pancakes and swimming lessons. Oli's hands start shaking. She stares at the stretch of nature strip she saw on the news that morning. It's easy to imagine Isabelle running along the quiet road, clad in sleek gym clothes, her long dark hair tied back from her face.

Did she see the car coming? In that split second, did she know she was going to die?

Oli has never asked Dean about that morning, but in her mind's eye she sees him opening the front door to grim-faced cops who proceed to shatter his world into pieces. Did he tell Kate and Amy straight away, or did he let them live in the bubble for a few hours longer? Did he come here and see Isabelle dead on the side of the road? Did he break down when he identified her broken body in the morgue?

Was he in love with her when she died?

And how did Theo Bouris know she would be here? In court he said he'd been watching her for days. A chill runs through Oli. Even though he's in prison, she doesn't like the idea of him knowing where the house is.

She becomes aware of a white ute indicating and overtaking her; the tradesman gives her a curious look as he passes. After scanning the stretch of road one more time, she sets her jaw and drives toward the office, refusing to look in the rear-view mirror.

—

Cooper is at her desk again. Oli tenses, expecting to feel annoyed but instead feels relieved. She's sick of her own thoughts anyway, and Cooper is nothing if not a distraction.

'Morning!' he trills, removing his purple headphones as she approaches.

'You're in early.'

He looks around as if he's just realised no one else is in. 'I've always been an early bird, actually, even when I was a teenager. Some mornings I'd get up to edit videos at, like, five, and I would—'

She holds up her hand to stop him. 'Any news on Nicole?'

'Zilch. I just texted the cop I met yesterday—he's a really cool guy. The divers worked into the night but turned up nothing. They'll go again today, but my guy doesn't think they're going to find anything. Apparently they're checking CCTV for footage of the car but, again, nothing has turned up so far.'

'Impressive that you have such a solid source already.'

Cooper shrugs. 'I told him we might interview him for the podcast sometime—you know, get the perspective of a millennial cop.'

'Well played,' she says begrudgingly.

Cooper glows with pride. 'Anyway, no Nicole.'

'Christ, this woman is like Houdini.' Oli thinks about what Lily said. 'Maybe she lied to Benny at the servo and she has a partner who is helping her and Evie hide.'

'Could be,' he says. 'Hey, so I've been thinking about the first episode. Your suggestion makes sense, and if we're going to focus on the house party and the fallout the day after, there's nothing stopping us from getting started.'

'Okay.' Her nerves flare at the thought of recording.

'The fridge down here is still dodgy, but I checked level three and it's sweet up there if you need milk for your coffee.'

She drops her bag on the floor near his shoe, a ridiculous rainbow slab of leather and rubber with velcro instead of laces. 'I have an idea.' She has quickly reached her early-morning Cooper quota. 'Why don't you go and get us some nice takeaway coffee from next door while I map out my notes for the podcast?'

'Can do.' He stands up, pulling on his backpack, then bites his lip and looks around the desk. 'Where's your KeepCup? Mine's in here.' He pats his bag.

Oli glares at him, but he just holds her gaze, blinking like Bambi. She plucks her wallet from her bag and hands him her credit card. 'I left it at home, so how about you buy me one with our coffee?'

Cooper eyes the card before taking it gingerly and sliding it carefully into his own wallet.

When he's gone, Oli types up an overview of the first two days of the Housemate Homicide story. People start to fill the office, but Oli is lost in the past, the words flowing directly from her brain to her fingertips. A few times she hears O'Brien's name muttered, everyone thrilled with the reaction to TJ's exclusive.

Cooper returns in triumph with her coffee cup. 'Here,' he crows, placing it in front of her.

'Thanks.' She takes a sip, eyes him warily. 'What?'

He squares his skinny chest. 'I got an email from Miles Wu. Alex contacted him last week and told him about her interview with me and now he wants to talk.'

—

When Dawn thrusts a piece of paper at Pia, all the ruffles on her fuchsia blouse jiggle. 'Get this up online as soon as possible. And see if this man or anyone he knows will talk.'

Oli steps out of Dawn's office doorway so Pia can get past. 'What's going on?'

'It's breaking now.' Dawn points at the screen. 'TJ just called me about it.'

Oli glances behind her. The newsroom is unusually quiet. Cooper is still at her desk, his hands frozen over his keyboard, eyes fixed to the bank of TVs. A twenty-seven-year-old man has come forward claiming that John O'Brien molested him when he was a teenager. Oli eases her boss's door shut and watches the TV on the edge of Dawn's desk. A swarm of journalists accost a jowly lawyer as he clambers out of a taxi on Collins Street. Looking flustered, he pauses on the pavement and confirms the key points of his client's claim. Now a tradesman with a family of his own, the accuser says he was thirteen when he helped his father complete some landscaping work at O'Brien's house during his school summer holidays. He was just doing basic things, the lawyer stresses, like fetching nails and weeding. Sweeping. There was a pool on the property, and after they knocked off for the day O'Brien insisted the boy have a swim. O'Brien lent the boy some board shorts that used to belong to his son, and it was when he was in the bathroom getting changed back into his clothes that the sexual assault allegedly occurred. The boy's father was outside having a beer with his employees, none the wiser. Afterwards, O'Brien told the boy that if he ever said anything, his father's business would be ruined. Not yet in politics, O'Brien was working as a senior consultant at a high-profile corporate firm at the time.

Oli baulks every time the lawyer uses the word 'molestation'. She focuses on the dark-purple skin tag that wobbles on his fleshy jawline.

TJ is there, right in the thick of the scrum, his blond head towering above the flowing blow-waves as the pack moves like a support crew alongside the lawyer, who has stopped talking and is trying to make his way to his office.

'Where are we with the podcast?' Dawn says suddenly, spinning around. 'And don't forget, tomorrow I want you to write a piece for the paper introducing the first episode with some background about why we're doing it and what people can expect next.'

Oli blanches. 'You didn't mention a launch piece. Do you really think it's necessary?'

'Yes,' Dawn barks. 'Content fuels content. Come on, Oli. Surely you've noticed that people just want to consume the same thing over and over, then rake it over the coals until there is literally no part of it they have not chewed, swallowed, spat up and eaten again. They watch shows and then watch shows about the shows they've just watched.' Dawn snorts derisively. 'The more we can milk each story the better.'

Through the glass panel they observe an intern sticking up a glossy poster on the communal pin board near Oli's desk. She stands back to reveal the contestants on the new season of *The Bachelor*: cosmetically enhanced women arranged in a layout reminiscent of a horseracing form guide. The intern carefully draws a cross through one of the faces with a Sharpie.

'Jesus Christ,' Dawn mutters. She spreads out her fingers and presses them around her skull as if trying to make the stupid stop.

Oli tries to take advantage of this vulnerable moment. 'Do you really think I should write the launch piece? Maybe it should come from someone else—it would be more objective.'

'No, it has to be you. Your readership is decent, and this way it all ties together.'

Crossing her arms, Oli looks at the floor. 'Fine.' It's hard to know if her involvement in the podcast will appear like a promotion or the beginning of a phase-out.

'And you need to get moving,' Dawn says. 'I need this thing up and running so the exec team can find something else to masturbate over.'

'We're recording the first episode this morning, and we're already working on the narrative for episode two.'

Dawn seems to calm a little. 'What else?'

'We have a few interviews lined up.' Oli refrains from mentioning names; all of a sudden it feels safer to remain vague. 'It's all under control.'

'Alright, alright.' Dawn's eyes are back on the TV.

'And Bowman agreed to meet with me tomorrow night.'

Dawn's head jerks up. 'He did?'

'Yes.' Oli's deep voice cracks.

Dawn gives her a look, seems about to say something, then shakes her head.

Oli self-consciously runs her tongue along her teeth. 'What?'

'Oli, I've always thought you were a good journalist.'

She feels the room tilt slightly.

'It's not going to get any easier around here,' Dawn continues matter-of-factly. 'Surely I don't need to tell you that.'

'No,' Oli says, uncertain.

'The old way just won't cut it anymore.' A hint of defensiveness in her voice. 'Different things are being prioritised. The podcast is a good example—Joosten thinks that part of the business might end up being more profitable than the paper.'

Oli makes a face. 'I want it to do well, of course, but I think that might be a little ambitious.'

Dawn pumps lotion from a bottle next to her keyboard and applies it aggressively to her bejewelled hands. 'The exec team have plans for several podcasts, Oli. Honestly, I feel like I'm drowning in them. You're lucky to have a shot at it first up.' Dawn gives Oli a pointed look, then brushes lint off her skirt and yanks open the door. 'It's time for the editorial meeting.'

Oli remains standing as the others file into the small space, uncertain whether she's just been given a warning or a pep talk.

Dawn runs her tongue along the front of her oversized teeth. 'Are you coming in or not?' She directs her laser-like glare at Cooper, who is hovering in the doorway.

As Dawn paces behind her desk, assigning tasks and making snide comments about the competition, Oli barely listens.

'That was my first editorial meeting,' Cooper stage whispers thirty minutes later, as he and Oli walk back to her desk. 'God, it's so cool how she arranges the news like that.'

'Yeah.' Oli glances back at Dawn, who is on the phone, moisturised fingers tangled in her wavy hair.

'Um.' Cooper looks at Dawn too, then back at Oli. 'So I guess we—'

'Let's record this bloody thing.'

—

'You're sounding *great*.' Cooper removes his headphones. 'Your voice is totally made for this. It's so low and husky, which obviously works for the genre.'

Oli pulls off her headphones. She is raw with nostalgia, disoriented from her journey back in time. The apprehension feels fresh, the sense of being overwhelmed, desperate, while lurching from theory to theory. Trying to corral words into a logical sequence.

'Seriously, I think it's really strong.' Cooper gets up to turn on the computer behind him, then spins back around. 'It's like I'm right there with you, rocking up to the house at day break. Being yelled at by the cop and seeing Evelyn's body in the hall. It's such great detail.'

'I was high as a kite on ecstasy.'

'What?'

She starts to laugh. 'It's true. I was in a cab home from a massive night when my editor called me and said I needed to go to the scene.'

He blinks several times. 'Really? It sounds like you were so together.'

'Back then I was quite good at pulling up at work after an all-nighter.' She yawns. 'Not like these days. Now I can barely make it to midday after a full night's sleep.'

'I've always been too scared to take drugs. Plus, there's no weight on me, so even one beer goes straight to my head.'

'Well, it's not exactly something I partake in these days.' She looks around the little studio. It's starting to feel familiar; despite the material covering the walls, it doesn't seem claustrophobic. She notices a whole bunch of movie postcards Blu-Tacked to the backboard of the desk.

'Film club.' Cooper looks at them fondly. 'Once a week we go to the cinema and discuss the movie afterwards. You should come, it's really fun.'

'Maybe,' she says, thinking that she would actually quite like to be part of a film club. 'Hey, so you told Miles you'd meet him at 11.30 am, right?'

'Yep. I should probably get going.'

She hands the headphones to Cooper. 'I think I should go.'

He hesitates. 'Sure, okay. Do you want to drive, or should we get a cab?'

'No.' She starts packing her things. 'I think *I* should do the interview with Miles.'

'Alone?'

She nods. Meets his gaze.

Cooper physically deflates. 'But he knew that Alex had been in contact with *me*. That's why he got in touch.'

Oli stands up. 'I know, but you have work to do here, and this is important. We need Miles to tell us something new. We can't risk it going wrong.' She thinks about her strange conversation with Dawn earlier. 'There's a lot riding on it, and I have a lot more experience with this kind of thing.'

Cooper busies himself with the microphone, swivelling it around. 'Okay, I'll get this all edited. Cut in some of Alex's comments, and grabs from the news the night Evelyn was found.'

'That would be great. Keep working your cop contact from yesterday too and try to find out if Nicole was telling the truth about splitting with a boyfriend. Pia will let us know if anything official comes through. I'm going to try to set up a time to talk to McCrae on my way to see Miles. I'll be out of action for a few hours this afternoon, but you can just text if you need anything.'

'Cool,' Cooper says glumly.

She pauses at the door, watching him. Disappointment is written all over his face. 'Once we have the podcast sorted,' she says, 'we can prep for tomorrow.'

'Tomorrow?' He lifts an eyebrow quizzically.

'My meeting with Bowman. You should come.'

She leaves Cooper in the studio struggling with his mixed emotions, and takes the lift down to the car park. Just when she reaches the Audi, TJ calls out to her.

She waits by the open car door as he jogs over. He's wearing his outfit from this morning's TV footage; he looks polished, trustworthy. He really should have ditched print and gone into TV—he would have made a fortune. Last year he was a panellist on a news show, and after it aired bunches of flowers with women's phone numbers attached to them arrived at the office.

'Nice work on O'Brien's neighbour,' Oli offers. 'It clearly prompted the other guy to come forward.'

'Thanks! I'm paying for it today, but it came together well. The claims are pretty damning.' TJ doesn't look like he's paying for it: he's clear-eyed and clean-shaven, the Ken-doll version of a journalist.

'They are.' Oli senses he hasn't sought her out for a casual chat. 'I'm just on my way out to speak with Alex Riboni's ex.'

He nods, impressed. 'Good get.'

'Thanks.' She moves to hop into the car. She's not really in the mood to talk to TJ.

'Oli, something is going on.'

She whips her head around. 'What do you mean?'

'Here.' He lifts his hands, gesturing to the building. 'I think they're going to sell, for real this time. To one of the TV networks, probably. This podcast stuff is only the beginning. You can forget real news, we'll just be serving up a kind of reality TV.'

Oli narrows her eyes. Is TJ pissed she's so involved in Joosten's pet project? 'I think the podcast will actually work out okay. I've put an investigative bent on it.' As she says this, she realises it's true. What she recorded with Cooper is good, and she's excited about their plan for the next episode. Making a podcast is not that dissimilar from writing a feature; the storytelling elements are the same.

TJ shrugs impatiently. 'This is serious, Oli.'

'How do you know all this?'

'I just do.'

'Did Dawn tell you? Or was it Joosten?'

TJ doesn't say anything for a few moments. 'Oli, I'm not sure Dawn can be trusted.'

'Really?' She crosses her arms. 'Because the other day you told me you thought she was doing a good job.'

He looks annoyed. 'It's not exactly an easy environment to navigate. But there are a few things that have me worried.'

'Like what?'

Pressing his lips together, he doesn't reply.

'TJ, I—'

She startles when he grips her shoulders. 'It doesn't matter. Listen, I reckon we should think about getting in front of it. Go out on our own, maybe. Do it our way. Stop having our stuff edited by people with an agenda.'

Oli shifts out of his grasp. 'Are you talking about Dawn?'

'I'm talking about everyone.' He rubs his eyes. 'It's going to turn into a land grab around here, and I'm not sure where people like us will end up. Even though we get paid shit, we're still considered expensive.'

'You're the one having secret meetings with management,' Oli says stiffly. 'I just want to keep my head down and do my job. I'm not interested in the politics.'

'Jesus, I'm not—' He puffs out his cheeks and walks in a frustrated semicircle. 'Look, you should consider what I'm saying. Things are different for you now, right? Dean will support you. Having a safety net will allow us a few months to find our feet, try a few things and work out the type of content we want to focus on.'

Heat floods her face. 'That's a bullshit thing to say. You have no idea what my personal circumstances are.'

His eyes dart to the Audi then back to her. 'I'm just being practical. I've spoken to Angela. We have some money put aside that we can fall back on for a while. I just think you and I have a chance to say up yours to the fat cats and take a crack at creating something really special before we get swept up in a situation neither of us wants to be a part of—or before we're screwed over.'

Charisma radiates off him, and Oli feels herself relenting. But then doubt flickers in her core. She's seen him do this a thousand times: coaxing out a connection and getting the outcome he wants. She has a sinking feeling that she's being played. Tested. That if she articulates her lack of commitment to the paper, it will somehow be used against her.

'I appreciate the heads-up, TJ, but I'm sure everything will be fine. I'm not worried—it's business as usual for me. I've got a great feature to write, and I'm determined to make this podcast as good as it can be.'

His expression loses some of its easy charm. 'We should stay tight, is all I'm saying. I'm sorry if this isn't coming out right.'

She gets into the car. 'I'm not going behind your back, if that's what you're worried about. I can assure you that no one is having secret meetings with me.'

'Cool, Oli, I get it,' TJ says, backing away in defeat. 'Just remember you can't opt out of the politics. At some point you're not going to have a choice.'

'I'll talk to you later, okay?' She starts the car. Stares straight ahead.

TJ lifts his hand in a half-hearted wave as she exits the car park. What the hell is going on? First Dawn, now TJ. Tears of frustration well in her eyes. She'll be devastated if the paper is sold. It's her touchstone, important in a way that's hard to define. No matter what is happening in the world or in her life, the paper ticks along.

She turns onto Flinders Street, blinking the tears away. Breathes. She calls the number Pia tracked down for McCrae.

A woman answers on the second ring. 'Hello, Diana speaking.'

'Diana McCrae?'

'Yes, who is this?' Her tone is light, friendly.

'My name is Oli Groves. I would like to speak to your husband if he's available, please.'

A long beat of silence. 'In relation to what?'

'I'm a journalist working on a story about the recent suicide of Alexandra Riboni. I know Professor McCrae taught her many years ago, and there are a few things I want to run by him. I think there's more to Evelyn Stanley's death than was revealed in Alex's trial. I'd like his point of view.'

'How *dare* you.' The warmth evaporates from Diana's voice.

'I'm sorry,' Oli says patiently. 'I don't mean to upset you, I just want to speak with Professor McCrae. Can you please ask him if he will speak with me?'

'No, he will not!' Diana sounds furious. 'He doesn't want anything to do with those girls.'

The phone slams down hard in Oli's ear—the benefit of having a landline.

CHAPTER TWENTY

OLI NOSES THE CAR IN FRONT OF A MERCEDES, GIVING THE DRIVER a half-hearted wave. This is what she hates about being a journalist, the feeling that permeates after a run-in like the one she just had with Diana McCrae. She hates people assuming the worst of her, speaking to her as if she has no empathy. Her desperate need for a narrative pound of flesh makes her seem like an enemy. What TJ said is right: journalism has become blurry, far less heroic, and even people like Oli are seen as shameless, willing to destroy lives and invade privacy for the sake of a by-line.

It's not like she hasn't been hung up on before, verbally abused and even shoved out of the way, but for some reason she's deeply unsettled. Hopefully Miles will be more receptive than Diana, even though he's expecting Cooper.

A horn blares as Oli veers across two lanes, spotting the sign for Stawell & Finch Accountants. She parks in a visitor bay and makes a dash for the reception. 'Hi, hi,' she announces on arrival, trying not to puff.

A bored man in a headset keeps typing. 'Yes?'

'I'm here from *Melbourne Today* to see Miles Wu. He's expecting me.'

His eyes flit to the screen, then to Oli. 'You're Cooper Ng?'

'Yes.' She meets his gaze. Tilts her chin.

'Okay, sure,' he drawls. 'Whatever. Wait over there, please.' He points at two chairs covered in rust-coloured fabric and a coffee table that looks like a spaceship.

Oli hovers, distractedly flicking through a copy of the *Sun*.

A *ding* announces the arrival of an elevator, and Miles Wu steps out. Oli recognises him straight away, even though his body has morphed into that of a swimmer, broad shoulders thinning to a triangular waist. He scans the reception area, sees only Oli and hesitates. She approaches him with her hand out. 'Hello, Miles. I'm Oli Groves from *Melbourne Today*.'

He doesn't offer his hand. 'I think there's been a mistake.'

'No mistake. Cooper couldn't make it, but I'm the senior journalist he reports to. I actually covered the Housemate story in 2005. I was at Paradise Street the morning Evelyn died.'

Miles shakes his head. 'Alex agreed to talk to Cooper. That's why I called him.'

'I understand, but he and I are like partners. We work closely together.'

'Do you have ID?' Miles crosses his arms and glances at the receptionist, who is clearly listening.

'Sure.' Oli retrieves her *Melbourne Today* credentials from her wallet and holds them up.

'Okay.' He brings his hands together at his mouth, exhales and nods. 'Let's do this, I guess.'

The automatic doors slide open, and Cooper rushes in. 'Sorry, I'm late! I caught a taxi here and underestimated how long it would take.'

Creases dent Miles's forehead.

'Miles, hello. I'm Cooper. Genuine apologies for my tardiness.'

Miles looks between the two of them. 'I thought you weren't coming?'

'Change of plan,' Cooper trills. 'I moved a few things around so I could make it because I really appreciated you reaching out to speak with *me*.'

Oli barely refrains from elbowing him in the ribs. 'Shall we find somewhere to talk, Miles?'

'Yes. Um, upstairs. We have an in-house cafe. It's not fancy, but it's okay. It has whatever kind of milk you want—almond, soy, whatever . . .' Miles is babbling.

Oli smiles reassuringly. 'Sounds great.'

Cooper and Oli follow Miles up the open curved staircase. Oli shoots Cooper daggers while he comments enthusiastically on the ugly décor and asks Miles inane questions about his job. The cafe consists of a dozen tables and chairs, a mismatched collection of fake pot plants arranged around a coffee machine, and a chirpy-looking waitress. A line of people are waiting for takeaway coffees, eyes glued to their phones, and a few groups of people in suits are having meetings, but there are some empty tables on the other side of the room.

'Cooper, why don't you grab us some drinks?' Oli says loudly. 'I'll have a short black, please. Miles, what would you like?'

'Oh, ah, green tea, please.'

'Thanks, Cooper.' Oli doesn't wait for his reply; she simply steers Miles to an empty table furthest from the counter and sits opposite him.

She knows he's thirty-one, but he looks younger, with smooth, unblemished skin and dark hair without a hint of grey. He wears a cardigan and a pen in his shirt pocket that might or might not be ironic. He shifts nervously, putting pressure on his forearms then off again.

'Are you okay, Miles?'

'Yeah.' He lurches forward and looks at her earnestly. Looks away. 'Sort of. It's just, I've spent ten years trying to forget all this, and now it's . . . back.' He laughs bitterly.

'I imagine that's quite hard.'

'I have a wife and a kid, and someone with a camera was waiting outside our house this morning. My wife completely freaked out. She's not used to it like I am—or like I was, anyway.'

'I don't think this will be like last time. Stories die more quickly these days.'

Miles nods. 'I hope so. I don't think I can go through that again.'

Cooper rejoins them, sitting next to Miles and ignoring Oli. 'Drinks are on their way.'

'Thanks,' murmurs Miles. His hands drift to his cheeks, where he holds them for a second.

'So, Miles,' Oli prompts.

'Christ,' he mutters, squeezing his eyes shut. 'Alright. The thing is, I didn't exactly tell the truth back then.'

As Oli watches him, anticipation fires in her belly. The waitress arrives at their table, and they exist through a few excruciating moments while she extracts the drinks from her grip and arranges them.

'What do you mean, Miles?' presses Oli, once they're alone again.

'There were things I saw . . . there's stuff I know.' His jaw wobbles. 'Things that happened that I didn't tell anyone about.' Flecks of dandruff are visible in his sharply combed part, which Oli has a prime view of now that he has dropped his face into his hands.

She waits for him to talk, sensing this conversation is ten years in the making. She glances at Cooper, whose lips are wrapped around the straw of a drink that looks revolting, some kind of brown goop. 'We're not here to judge,' he says. 'We're here to listen.'

It's a corny line, but it seems to work. Miles looks back up and lets out a strange little laugh. His eyes have a slightly hysterical glint, unable to focus on any one thing. He toys with the salt shaker, picking it up and putting it down. 'I don't even know why I'm talking to you.' He laughs again. 'I really don't. But my wife said I should get it off my chest, and I guess I feel like I owe it to Alex.' He leans forward, and says to Cooper, 'I told you, she called me. Last week.'

Oli leans forward too. 'You spoke to her?'

He nods. 'I was at work, and she called me out of the blue.'

'How long had it been since you last spoke to her?' Oli asks.

'I hadn't spoken to her since that night at the house.'

'The night Evelyn died?' presses Oli.

He nods, his face pinched with guilt. 'I wanted to talk to her—so many times I thought about it, but I don't know, it's hard to explain. It was all so weird. That part of my life seems like it happened to someone else. I mean, you see stuff on the news and you process it, but you just don't think about the people being real. And then suddenly it was happening to me, my face was on the news and it was just insane. My parents totally freaked out, and I just didn't know what to say to Alex. And I didn't know what she would say to me. I think part of me just wanted to shut the whole thing out, shut her out.'

Oli holds his gaze until his eyes pull away. 'Did it work?'

'No, not really. I don't sleep very well.' She nods sympathetically, and he sighs. 'Something like that happens, and you just start questioning everything. I lost all faith in my ability to judge people. Looking back, I'm not sure I really knew Alex at all.'

'But you feel like you owe something to her now?' Oli asks.

Regret ripples across his face, and he nods slightly. 'Sort of.'

'Tell us about your conversation last week,' Oli says.

'Alex said she wanted to go public with new information, but that she wanted to talk to me first. We were going to meet up today.' He fumbles with the sugar. Messages and emails cause his phone to vibrate across the table; he picks it up and frowns before placing it firmly facedown.

'But why now?' Oli wonders. 'Why would Alex come to you now?'

'She said she'd started to remember what really happened that night, and she wanted to talk.' He takes a sip of his tea and wipes his mouth. 'She said she was going on the record with your paper so that the cops couldn't shut her down.' Miles looks across at Cooper. 'She said she spoke to you and that she was going to record an interview. I think she liked the idea of speaking for herself, being able to say it in her own words and not having it get twisted in print. But she never would have gone on TV, she was too shy for something like that.' His gaze is still on Cooper. 'I think she trusted you. That's why I called. After what happened to her, I figure it's probably what she would have wanted.'

Chills settle over Oli's body. Alex's suicide is making less and less sense. If she had gone on the record and provided more information about her role in Evelyn's death, then perhaps Oli could understand: the purging of information might have been too much. But Alex never made it that far. What happened to her between when she called Miles last week and her decision to take her secrets to the grave? And why go to Crystalbrook? Was she lured there by Nicole?

'Did Alex tell you what she remembered?' Oli asks.

Miles shakes his head. 'Not really, just that she wanted to tell the truth. She said she didn't care if people hated her more than they already did, that it was time to come clean. She was really wired. To be honest, I think she might have been high.' He shrugs. 'Maybe she was—I mean, I guess it's obvious now that she was pretty unstable.'

Oli wants to prevent him from tumbling into a guilt spiral. If he goes there, this is likely to turn into a counselling session, and there's no time for that. 'Miles, I was at the trial. I sat through every minute. I know there was a lot of speculation about what happened, about whether Alex killed Evelyn and why—whether it was premeditated or happened in the heat of the moment.'

Miles's face twists in pain.

'I never doubted it was Alex,' Oli continues. 'That's what all the evidence suggested. The self-defence ruling a few years later didn't change the fact that Alex took responsibility for being the one who ended Evelyn's life.'

'I know,' Miles says quietly.

'I remember thinking it was pretty bloody lucky, from your perspective, that you hauled your stoned arse to the house next door and decided to get even more wasted with your mates.'

Miles keeps his head hanging forward.

'Were you really with them for the rest of the night?' Oli asks.

'Yes.' His voice is firm. 'That's true. I left the girls' house after a fight with Alex. The guys and I went down to the shops then back to their place, and I stayed there the whole night. We had no idea anything had happened until we saw all the cops and reporters in the street the next morning.'

'You were at the scene?'

'Not until Alex was being taken away.' Miles looks sheepish. 'We'd done a lot of drugs, and there were still drugs in the house. There were cops everywhere.' He looks down at his hands. 'We didn't know what to do, so we just cleaned up as best we could, and Matt snuck out the back to get rid of everything.'

'Weren't you worried about your girlfriend?'

'In between trying not to puke my guts up, yeah, of course. I was in a total panic, imagining the worst. I called Alex a bunch of times, and I called Evelyn and Nic, but no one answered. I finally went out the front and saw Alex coming out of the house with a blanket over her, covered in blood. And then a detective started explaining to me that Alex was being taken in for questioning because Evelyn was dead. They asked me to come to the station too. I think I was in shock for a long time.'

Cooper's leg starts to jiggle in Oli's peripheral vision. His glass of sludge is empty; he's completely transfixed by Miles. She becomes aware of the conversations around them: budgets, growth pipelines, weekend plans. Plates and cutlery are being cleared from nearby tables, and a pop song dances around the corners of it all.

She takes a deep breath and runs her tongue along her teeth, chalky with coffee remnants. 'Miles.'

He jumps.

'What did you want to tell us?'

He exhales shakily. 'God, I can't even explain it. The whole night was pretty weird from the start. The girls had been acting strangely for weeks, and I think Nic organised the dinner as a bit of a circuit-breaker, but it didn't work. The guys from next door, Ren and Matt, turned up half cut, and two of our other friends, Tanya and Roy, came too. I remember they were talking to each other in Spanish because they were about to go on some holiday, and they'd been at a language class that afternoon. It was pretty annoying after a while. And some other girl was there too—Amber, some new friend of Evelyn's, I think—but she was only there for a bit. It all went downhill pretty quick. Ren dropped a bottle of wine on the kitchen floor before we had dinner. There was glass and wine everywhere, and Evelyn seemed really pissed off. Then that professor guy showed up, and he was so awkward and nervous. I could tell Evelyn was annoyed he was there.'

'Julian McCrae,' Cooper offers.

'Yeah.'

'Do you know who invited him?' Oli asks.

'Not sure,' Miles says uncertainly. 'I know all the girls liked him—they talked about him sometimes. It used to annoy me when Alex brought him up, but I think it was Nicole who was the closest to him. She was really into psychology, which is what he taught. But for whatever reason, Evelyn clearly didn't want him there that night. Even Alex and Nicole seemed a bit freaked out by it.' Miles pauses. 'Like I said, the whole night had a weird vibe. Matt and Ren seemed really pissed about him being there too. I think they figured it meant we couldn't, you know, do drugs in case he went to the cops.' Miles laughs nervously. 'It was shaping up to be a pretty shit party.'

'Did you get the feeling McCrae had been to the house before?' Oli asks.

Miles's eyes narrow in thought. 'I don't think so. Like I said, he seemed really awkward. It was as if he felt obliged to be there. I know there were a lot of rumours about him being a creep, but he didn't seem sleazy. He was more like someone's dad. He brought two bottles of fancy wine like he was trying to impress everyone.'

'What did Alex say about him being there?'

'We didn't really talk about it. We kind of weren't really talking by then.'

'We'll come back to that,' Oli says quickly, not wanting him to lose momentum. 'What happened after dinner?'

'Everyone went out into the yard. Or, I think they did. Maybe Tan and Roy were still inside—Nic as well? I'm not sure, I was pretty drunk already. But that's definitely when the fight broke out between Alex and Evelyn.'

Oli knows all this from the trial and is itching for him to give her something new. 'But you always said you didn't know what they were fighting about,' she says. 'Is that true?'

'I have no idea!' He sounds defensive. 'They'd been at each other for weeks. Lots of sniping and moody silences. This seemed like more of the same, but because they were both drunk it was pretty heated.'

'Any chance they were fighting over you?'

'No, no way. But Alex was really scatty, going off at me over every little thing. Every time I asked her what was wrong, she shut down.' Emotion flickers across Miles' face. 'It was really frustrating. I was pretty close to breaking up with her. She'd turned into a different person—they all had. They were so secretive and aloof.'

'So the two girls were fighting outside,' Oli says, coaxing him back to the facts.

'Yeah. They were down in the corner of the yard yelling at each other, calling each other selfish. They were being pretty nasty.'

'Nicole wasn't there?'

Miles scrunches up his face. 'I can't remember her being there, but Ren was going back and forth to his house to smoke, and there was another party in the house behind the girls', which was really noisy. I remember Tan and Roy came outside to have a cigarette, but I think Nicole and the professor were inside.'

Alarm bells go off in Oli's head. No one mentioned this at the trial. 'McCrae was alone with Nicole?'

'I think so. Or maybe he'd gone by then.' Miles looks up, clearly struggling to download the memories from some far-flung corner of his brain. 'Actually, no. No, he was still there later when Tanya was trying to get everyone to drink her punch. I remember because he went on about being allergic to strawberries and said he couldn't drink it. He was acting really weird. And I remember Matt making some joke about him. He left straight after that—I didn't see him again, anyway.'

'What happened next?' Cooper is literally on the edge of his seat.

'Alex stormed off inside, leaving Evelyn in the backyard. I tried to talk to her, but she brushed me off. She was upset. Everyone went inside to listen to records and play a stupid charades game that Tanya made up. But I wanted to have a smoke. I was kind of pissed off.'

Oli nods encouragingly. 'So you stayed outside?'

'Yeah. I got my cigarettes from inside, then I went around the side of the house. A bunch of old crates were stacked up there, and I sat on one and had a smoke. I think Evelyn went back inside. I don't know if anyone knew where I was, but I could hear them all laughing and talking through the laundry window.'

'Including Alex?'

'I think she'd had some weed at some point. It always used to make her crazy, and she was acting like an idiot.' He looks guilty. 'I just figured we both needed some space.'

'Okay, so you're around the side of the house,' prompts Oli.

Miles swallows, panic returning to his eyes. 'First I heard Nicole talking to someone in the laundry. I don't know who it was. It was too noisy to hear properly, but I could hear Nicole's voice. Then she came out the back.'

'Nicole came outside?' Oli clarifies.

Miles nods. 'She didn't see me.'

Oli's lips part. This is new, as far as she knows. He never spoke about this at the trial.

'I could tell she was angry. She was sort of pacing around near the back fence. She climbed onto the bottom of it and looked into the neighbours' yard, the ones having the party. Then I think she texted someone.' His eyes go back and forth between his hands and Oli. 'That's what it looked like from where I was sitting, but I was probably about ten metres away. And then she . . .' His voice wobbles as he draws himself up and squares his shoulders. 'God,' he mutters before the words tumble out of his mouth. 'She went over to the shed in the corner of the yard, and she got Billy out. I could see her standing there in the dark, holding him, and then she,' Miles emits a soft bleat, his breath coming out in little huffs, 'she got this weird look in her eyes, then she just threw him. She threw him against the fence.'

Miles scratches at his wrist, his fingers pushing under the metal watchband until he tugs it off with a dramatic flourish and itches the dented skin for so long that Oli has to glance away.

At the next table, the waitress flirts with an older man who looks delighted, his rich laugh reverberating around the room.

Cooper is staring at Miles, stricken.

'I didn't do anything,' Miles says after a moment. 'I just stayed hidden around the side of the house like a fucking pussy.'

'Miles, who was Billy?' Oli hears her voice waver slightly.

'Evelyn's rabbit. She bloody loved him. Let him free in her bedroom half the time.'

'And it died?' Oli swallows, picturing the scene Miles just described. 'It died after Nicole threw it at the fence?'

He nods vigorously. 'The sound, I'd never heard anything like it. Even with the music playing . . .' He puffs out his cheeks. 'Yeah, it died.'

The waitress sidles up to their table. 'Anyone after anything else?'

'No, thanks,' whispers Cooper, and Miles shakes his head vigorously.

'Righto.' She clears the cups, walks away.

'What happened after that?' Oli asks.

Miles is deflated after his big confession. 'Nicole didn't even look at Billy,' he says flatly. 'She just went back inside. I remember I started shaking all over. It's hard to explain, but it was like seeing your mum snort drugs or hit someone. It seemed so out of character and just so totally bizarre. Plus, I was wasted.' He laughs ruefully.

'A part of me thought I'd made it up, but when I went back around the house I could see Billy on the ground.'

'Did you say anything to the others?'

'No. Ren and Matt went to their place to get more drugs, which they brought back to the girls' place because McCrae had finally gone home. The girls were all dancing in the lounge room. Including Nicole.' Miles hesitates. 'They weren't fighting anymore, but it all felt a bit off. There was still a lot of tension. The other girl, Evelyn's friend, had gone by then, and I just sat on the couch with Tan and Roy pretending everything was fine. I tried to talk to Alex, but she told me to fuck off.' Miles grips one hand in the other. 'After a while, Tan and Roy left. Nicole and Evelyn were still dancing, and Alex was getting pretty messy, so I tried to get her to lie down on the couch with me.'

'Did she?' Oli asks.

'Sort of. She sat down for a bit, but she wouldn't really talk to me. And then Matt said he wanted to go to the shops for more cigarettes, and I said I'd go with him. I just wanted to get out of the house. I didn't want to think about Evelyn going outside and finding Billy.' He coughs. 'I know that makes me sound like a total prick, but I knew she would lose it, and I didn't want to be there to see it.'

Oli pictures a younger version of Miles on the stand, pulling on his tie as he told the court about the late-night hunt for cigarettes. 'At the trial you said you went to the shops with Matt and Ren, and that you didn't go back to number twenty-eight after that. Is that true?'

'Yeah. We walked up to the 7-Eleven on Fitzroy Street and bought smokes and chips, then we dicked around outside for a bit. A guy was sitting on the street bench playing guitar, and Ren asked him if he could play. I texted Alex, but she never wrote back. Then we went to Matt and Ren's place. We smoked more dope, and I passed out on the floor in front of the TV.'

Oli purses her lips as she considers her next question.

Miles rushes to add, 'I think I blocked out what I saw in the yard. I didn't want to have seen it.' He runs his fingers through his hair like he's still trying to comb the memory away. 'And then the next morning, when we found out what happened, all I could think about was Alex and whether she really had killed Evelyn. I felt like I'd slipped into a parallel universe. My girlfriend was on trial for murder. It just,' he looks between Oli and Cooper, 'it was so surreal. I didn't know what to do or what to think.'

'Did you think Alex was guilty?' Oli asks bluntly.

He reels back, his weight against the chair. 'I guess I did. It's like you said before, the evidence was so damning. I couldn't see another explanation, and all the girls were acting so oddly that I thought anything was possible. My parents definitely thought she did it—they were beside themselves. The shame almost killed my grandma.' He chews his lip. 'I think in the end it did.'

'But now?' Oli presses. 'What do you think now?'

Miles straightens. Speaks with a new urgency. 'I'm not sure, but something was going on with the girls. Something wasn't right.'

'Explain what you mean.'

'They were always close, but in those last few months it was like they joined a cult or something. They would stop talking when I came over. Alex had never been moody, but all of a sudden she started lashing out at me. She also got really needy, wanting constant reassurance that I cared about her. She had all these grand plans, things she had never mentioned before. They all did.' Miles's dark eyes flick to Oli's. 'And they started buying really nice things. One time, maybe two or three weeks before Evelyn died, Alex and I were going out for dinner when I saw her take money from the drawer in her bedside table. I checked the next morning when she was in the shower, and at least two thousand dollars were in there—a big pile of fifty-dollar notes.'

Momentarily forgetting their feud, Oli and Cooper exchange a glance. This echoes what Mitchell Stanley said about his daughter.

'Her savings?' suggests Oli.

Miles shrugs. 'Maybe, but I don't think so. She was on Centrelink and babysat on weekends. It didn't really add up. Plus, all three of them were suddenly throwing money around. They bought new clothes and talked about going overseas. When I asked Alex about it, she got angry and brushed me off.'

Oli thinks quickly. This is good stuff, the kind of detail that will keep the story in orbit for a few more days. 'Are you willing to go on the record?'

'I just want this to be done.' Looking stricken, he grabs his phone and shoves it in his pocket without glancing at it, his dark eyes wild. 'It's been ten bloody years of wondering. My wife thinks I need closure, and I was hoping Alex would provide it. I'm happy to talk if you think it will help.'

Oli gives him her business card and explains the likely next steps. It goes into his pocket with his phone.

'You've already got my details,' says Cooper.

Oli ignores him. 'Miles, one last thing. Did Alex have a laptop?'

He nods. 'And a shared computer at the house that they all used for uni. I think it was Nicole's, brought with her from home. That was another weird thing, actually.'

'What was?' Oli asks.

'They got the internet disconnected at the house, maybe a year before this all happened.'

'Disconnected?' Oli says. 'Why?'

'I don't know. I remember thinking it was weird. I mean, it was obviously different back then—a lot of people didn't have internet at home, especially in a rental. People were only really using email.'

Oli feels wired as her brain races ahead. 'Did they say anything about it?'

'Nicole just said it was always cutting out, and when I asked Alex she said they wanted to save money by using the uni internet. But she definitely had enough money to pay for it, so there must have been some other reason.'

DAY THREE OF THE TRIAL, 2006

Alex flips an imaginary coin and bets on what Miles is going to do. Heads he'll talk; tails he won't. But even in her mind's eye, she can't quite see which side of the coin is facing up. Decisiveness feels out of reach these days.

She knows Miles had been suspicious of her behaviour. Always asking questions about money, why she was spending so much and where it was coming from. He'd asked about her relationship with Nicole and Evelyn too. She's not exactly sure what she told him that night, she has a vague memory of arguing with him. Of admitting she was in over her head with something. She's seen him twice since the night of the party. The next morning, briefly, when she was sitting in the detective's car out the front of the house, wrapped in a blanket, Miles emerged from Ren and Matt's place dressed in his clothes from the night before. He looked at her with the strangest expression. He didn't try to talk to her, just stood on the street watching as Evelyn's body was carried away.

Alex saw him again the next day when she was charged. Or, she thinks she did. His face in the crowd, among the other faces. His mouth completely still. All the other mouths were twisted into ugly cries, screaming her name, but he just stared as she was pulled and picked over like a piece of meat.

Actually, she saw him a third time: on the news just over a week later. He went to Evelyn's funeral and stood up the front with her family.

Even though they're survivors of the same tragedy, the others gone or lost, it hasn't brought them together.

Miles has an alibi. Alex is a killer.

Miles is innocent. Alex is guilty.

He is free to go on and have a normal life. Her future is ruined no matter what happens.

And all Miles ever wanted was a normal life. He craves average, yearns for contentment. Not like Alex, who got greedy and dared to dream for more. Dared to seize an opportunity.

He never understood her restlessness. Didn't understand how she could be so dissatisfied, want so much more than she had. But that's because he doesn't know what it's like to have so little.

When they started going out, she marvelled at the way he always put people at ease. How thoughtful he was. But even his kindness ran thin. The further the house had slipped into darkness, the more it jarred with his goodness. Alex worried that he could see what she had become, that he was judging her. She pushed him away. Better he be mad with her than disappointed, shocked. She imagined trying to explain it to him, just how far she had fallen, but that was impossible. What they had done was impossible.

Miles has principles. He probably won't lie outright, but he might feel he can't explain it either, the strangeness that settled over the house. The quiet evil that took hold of his girlfriend. He might give her the benefit of the doubt. Alex can hardly blame him—she doesn't know how to explain it either.

Funny how everyone just wants her to remember. All she wants is to forget.

CHAPTER TWENTY-ONE

OLI SQUINTS INTO THE ENDLESS STREAM OF CARS AS SHE WAITS to turn onto the main road. She wants to discuss what Miles told them, unpack what he claims Nicole did to Evelyn's pet rabbit, but there's no way she's letting Cooper think the way he acted is acceptable. Her rage is back, and she wants him to speak first, to acknowledge his audacity. Instead he sits in sulky, defiant silence. Oli guns the car and jerks through a gap in the traffic. After a few minutes of driving, she relents. 'Want to tell me what the fuck that was about?'

He doesn't reply, just stares stubbornly out the window.

She flicks off the heater, which is about ten times more effective than the one in her old Mazda. She's sweaty, her shirt sticking to her back. How dare Cooper be so insolent? Jo would have killed her if she'd behaved like this. 'I told you *I* would talk to Miles. You should have stayed at the office and worked on the podcast. Even parking the fact you completely ignored me, it made us look unprofessional.'

Cooper's chest rises and falls in quick succession. 'It was *my* interview. Miles called *me*.'

Oli hits her fist on the steering wheel. 'You're the one who orchestrated us working together! It wasn't my idea, but if you want to work with me I need to be able to trust you—and that childish performance didn't help.'

His lips bulge into a pout. 'I can't trust you if you steal my leads.'

'Look,' she says, pressing her fingers into her temples at the lights, 'I get you're new to all this, so maybe you don't understand how it works, but I've been doing it for a long time. If we're going to work on this story and make this bloody podcast happen, we need to act like a team.'

Cooper turns to stare at her, his gaze burning into the side of her face. 'No shit.' He puts on his headphones and looks the other way.

—

Brent's water bottle collapses noisily as he sucks liquid out of it, his eyes never leaving the TV screen on the wall of the newsroom. The bottle crackles as the plastic reverts to its former shape.

On screen, John O'Brien wears dark sunglasses and holds a newspaper like a shield. The disgraced premier weaves his way through a throng of people, escorted into a dark car outside his Albert Park home. 'No comment,' he says.

'You bloody pervert!' someone screams off camera.

O'Brien pauses. His suited handler also stops. 'I reject all of the claims made against me and will be fighting them through our justice system, which I respect wholeheartedly. Unfortunately, this is a case of "He said, she said", or in this instance "He said, he said", and I have complete faith that the truth will win out. And now, if you'll excuse me, I'd like to continue grieving for my wife.'

A wad of paper hits the screen amid a series of groans.

Oli hasn't seen Cooper since they arrived back at the office. He got out of the car without a word and disappeared into the stairwell. 'I'm still meeting with Bowman tomorrow,' she called after him, her voice bouncing off the concrete walls. 'By myself,' she added unnecessarily, annoyed that he was bringing out her pettiness.

No doubt he's in the studio finishing off the podcast. In spite of everything, Oli feels a rush of excitement. Her distinctive voice has always made her wary of doing any kind of radio—she even hates leaving voicemail messages—but she enjoyed the recording a lot more than she expected and has a feeling it will sound pretty compelling. Hopefully Cooper's irritation won't affect the finished product.

She looks down at her notes. Roy hasn't responded to her at all, and Tanya wrote back explaining she has nothing further to add to the statement she made after Evelyn's death. It's frustrating, although admittedly Oli doesn't hold out much hope that either of them know anything that will move the story along—their appearances in court were vague and unhelpful, and indicated a superficial friendship with the housemates. There's still no news on Nicole or the child, nor any suggestion of a widespread search. The cops issued a release that suggests they're worried for the welfare of the missing duo, but there are no specific details.

For almost an hour Oli steadily works on the podcast launch piece, easing the words into shape, deftly connecting the ten-year-old murder of Evelyn Stanley with the fresh death of Alex Riboni, and explaining what the podcast will explore. It's bizarre to write in the first person, but there's something cathartic about it. She's in the zone, her fingers flying across the keyboard, when her phone rings. 'Oli Groves.'

'You called looking for my son.' A brash voice, unmodulated.

Oli holds the phone slightly away from her head, looks at the number. 'Mrs Neroli?'

'That's right. Name's Marion.' Despite the volume, she sounds pleasant. Friendly. 'You're from the paper, is that right?'

'Yes, I'm a journalist. I'm working on a story about the Paradise Street murder. I really want to speak with Ren. Is he there?'

Marion makes an excited screech, forcing Oli to hold the phone away from her ear again. 'I'm always telling my friends that Ren knew the Housemate Homicide girls. He used to be at their place *all* the time. And now the other one's dead! I met the one who's still missing, you know. Just briefly, but we spoke. Going back ten years ago now, of course. She seemed like a nice girl. And they were all so pretty, weren't they? I gave Ren grief about them, but he always said nothing was going on.'

Oli thinks about what Miles said, about Nicole throwing the rabbit against the fence, and decides that Nicole probably wasn't actually very nice at all.

'Is Ren able to speak to me?' Oli presses.

'Not right now, he's not here, but he said he's happy to talk to you. He called this morning from a mate's. He doesn't have a phone at the moment—there was another problem with the payment not going through. His dole money didn't come when it was supposed to. It's terrible how they just cut you off like that.'

'I understand,' Oli says kindly.

'But you can go see him if you want. Like I said, he's happy to talk to you. I'll give you his address?'

'Yes, please, Mrs Neroli, that would be very helpful.'

Oli scrawls it down: Bulleen. About a half-hour drive in weekday traffic. 'I won't be able to get out there today, but hopefully I can make it first thing tomorrow.'

'He doesn't go out much,' Marion says. 'He doesn't have a job at the moment. He likes playing all those online games. I'd say he'll be home.'

They hang up, and Oli leans back in her chair. This is good: another angle from the night should help validate some of the things

Miles told them, and if Ren's willing to talk, maybe they can get him to be interviewed for the podcast.

She grabs her things and gets the lift to the fifth floor, makes her way down the silent corridor to the studio. Cooper is there, headphones on. He doesn't look up when she walks in, but he tugs them off his ears.

'I've tracked down Ren Neroli.'

'Cool.' Cooper moves the mouse to the left, presses some buttons on the keyboard.

'I have to head off now, but I'm going to meet with him tomorrow morning, see if he wants to be on the podcast. We should start lining up interviews for the next few episodes. We need to present a range of perspectives from that night—people who knew the girls in different ways.'

'Obviously.' He finally looks at her. 'Mitchell has agreed to an interview. I'm thinking I can go to him. He's got a private hospital room, so it should be okay to record there.'

Oli cocks her head. 'You contacted Mitchell Stanley after I spoke to him?'

'Yep.'

She crosses her arms and curses in frustration. 'We should talk about how we approach it. We need to think about how we want to tell this story. It can't just be a series of interviews that we serve up. There needs to be a narrative.'

'You didn't ask him about the podcast yesterday, which seemed like a missed opportunity.' Cooper shifts his arm and accidentally pulls the headphones' cord out from the computer. A blast of haunting music fills the room before he cuts it off. 'For now, I'm focused on getting this edit done,' he says formally. 'I'll send it to you in the next few hours. Even though you're out of the office, do you think you'll be able to listen to it this afternoon and give me the green light to send it to Dawn?'

Oli's chest feels tight. 'Yes, of course, it's a priority.'

He gives a curt nod and slips his headphones back on, his fingers flying across the keyboard.

She stands there watching him for a minute. 'Right, well, see you later.'

He lifts his hand, his eyes fixed on the computer monitor.

In the lift, Oli glowers. Cooper's the one who is out of line. In fact, she wouldn't have to worry about him at all if he hadn't bluffed his way into working with her. She wrestles with the resentment that burns through her. Maybe he'll come around once the first episode is done. No matter what he says, she knows he's nervous about it; perhaps that's why he's acting so childishly. It's a shame, because they were getting into a rhythm. But they can hardly keep working together if they're not talking, and this first episode is the easy one. She feels another flutter of her own nerves at the thought of her voice being blasted out into the world. Publishing articles never feels this confronting, and a big part of her wants to head back upstairs and tell Cooper she wants out.

Compared to the quiet of his studio, the newsroom is a madhouse. Her colleagues are still hostages to the bank of screens, typing with one eye fixed on the news reports. An intern in a tie-dyed boilersuit stands at the printer, stapling sheets of paper together before they even have a chance to hit the tray.

'We're running it with or without your quote,' Brent says firmly into his mobile as she walks past. 'I'll give you until four pm to come back to me.' He hangs up with the wild-eyed look of a spooked kitten. Pia's cheeks are flushed as she types a message on her phone, her foot tapping against the floor.

Remnants of a birthday cake sit on the corner of TJ's empty desk, a knife lying across the crumby carcass. Oli's insides clench at the memory of his strange intervention in the car park. They should talk properly, cut the bullshit, but the whole thing just feels so tedious. She really hates the politics, she always has, and she's aware that her refusal to aggressively play the game might mean she loses. TJ, however, is clearly in his element.

The TV footage cuts to Bowman stepping out from police headquarters. Mics and phones are thrust into his face. He ushers the media away, not bothering to hide his irritation. The entire newsroom quietens; people freeze mid-task or hastily end phone calls.

'I'll make this easy for you all.' Bowman's voice is gruff but clear. 'I have no comment regarding the recent accusations against John O'Brien, but they will be dealt with through the appropriate channels. If an arrest is made, I'm sure you will all follow the necessary reporting rules. In relation to Alexandra Riboni's death, there is growing evidence Ms Riboni's mental health deteriorated over the past few weeks, and we believe she may have gone to the property with the intention of causing harm to a former acquaintance before deciding to end her life. We believe this incident triggered a chain of events that has led to the disappearance of a young woman.' He brings his stocky fingers together and looks around with a sense of non-negotiable finality. 'That's it, folks, I have a meeting to get to.'

A few feeble cries follow his hunched figure up the footpath. The live cross cuts back to the studio with graphics behind the anchor reading, ANOTHER O'BRIEN VICTIM? The same tired montage fills the screen, ending with the earlier footage of the accuser's walrus-like lawyer holding court with the pack of journalists.

Oli almost goes straight back up to the studio to discuss Bowman's theory with Cooper. Is he right? Did a mentally unstable Alex Riboni track her old friend down in Crystalbrook and attempt to finish the job she started all those years ago? Did she hold Nicole responsible for what happened to Evelyn, blame her for the time she spent in gaol? But then, why did Alex end her own life? Maybe she wanted Nicole to find her body as some kind of punishment. And what about the fire? Was it intentional?

Oli blinks several times, trying to rally her tired eyes. There's no point interrupting Cooper again today, but tomorrow they're going to have to call a truce. She checks the time: just over two hours until the swimming carnival. She heads to the lift and down to the car park, her long hair flying behind her.

—

Oli hangs her bag on a kitchen chair. A pigeon parades along the window ledge, stopping every few steps to peer down its beak at her. The appliances gleam, and the marble bench is spotless. Thursday, of course: cleaning day. How odd to have a stranger come here, touching their things and judging their lives. Her father was always yelling at her mother about the state of the house, not that he was ever motivated enough to clean it himself.

Oli removes a glass from the dishwasher, fills it with water and drinks slowly. Sometimes when she thinks about how different her life is compared to twelve months ago, it's overwhelming. She often feels like she doesn't quite measure up to her new surrounds. Only her work is the same, and even that seems to be slipping out from under her.

Just after she moved in, she invited her mother and stepfather over. She hated the way Sally Groves's eyes widened as she entered each room; the way her head bobbed stupidly as she took it all in. 'Well, Olive,' she said, perched on the couch next to Max, her lipsticked mouth pulling into a squishy pout as she sipped the expensive champagne Dean had insisted on opening, 'aren't you lucky. This is certainly quite a house. And Dean's girls are lovely.'

Oli couldn't wait for them to leave. For Sally to stop looking at everything—to stop being so *obvious.*

She puts her glass down too quickly, and its rattle against the marble echoes around the house. Through the archway, the gauzy curtains in the lounge flare out from the window. Resettle.

The house was renovated right before the twins were born; Dean mentioned once that the last lick of paint was applied just in time. A new kitchen and bathroom, the entire upstairs remodelled. State-of-the-art technology in every room, security systems and surround sound. Oli can imagine the petite detective stalking through the sunlit rooms, gliding down the staircase like a cat. Dean mentioned a while ago that Oli should suggest some changes, make sure it feels like her home too, but she can't see how her relaxed bohemian style will work with the sleek lines and monochrome colour scheme.

The grandfather clock starts to chime. An uneasy feeling takes hold. The high ceilings and abundance of space make her feel vulnerable. Even though she was often alone in her old apartment, she always felt safe. The old couple next door bickered constantly, the dog on level one yapped at people walking past, and the three young guys in number five often had friends over. The flat was hardly big enough for a kitchen table yet it was all she needed.

Oddly, her favourite room in this house is Isabelle's old study.

Oli straightens, her ears tuning in to the silence. She quickly texts Dean. *Hey, are you still at work?*

Dots appear on her screen, followed by a message. *Sure am, why? You're at home?*

She pictures the wedding dress in the cupboard upstairs. *Just wrapping up a few things at the office. I'll leave to pick up the girls soon.*

Her thighs burning, she takes the stairs two at a time. The second-last step creaks loudly, and her throat tightens. She reaches out to hold the bannister. From the ceiling above the staircase, Alex Riboni swings, lifeless and limp. Oli folds forward, dizzy. She's barely eaten today. There's a dark shape on the floor a little further down the dark corridor. What is that? Music fills the house. Kate playing the piano? The sound triggers a flood of memories. Sneaking into the house to grab some things, she didn't want to see her mother, didn't want to endure another draining exchange. Music was playing that day too. She slips past the photo of Isabelle, her reflection a white blur on the detective's perfect face.

Oli stumbles into the bedroom. She changes her clothes, out of breath. *Stop, Oli, breathe.*

Still the music plays. She knows she must be imagining it, but she can hear it, *feel* it, vibrating through the floorboards. She lurches forward, her hands braced against the bed as the old shock knifes her, fresh and real. Sunlight pushes in around the closed curtains. The pill bottle, the upended bottle of gin. The stench of vomit and perfume. Music playing from somewhere. Her mother's limp hand, fingers curled toward the ceiling. The glistening white crescents of her eyes. The cluster of melting candles crammed onto the bedside table, billowing smoke from the tips of their flames.

Oli falls to her knees, lurching toward Sally Groves. 'Mum? Mum! No. No.' Eyes shut and gripping the bedhead, seventeen-year-old Oli gathers her mother's limp body into her lap, pushing dirty blonde hair from Sally's cold face. 'Mum!' A sob erupts from Oli, and she gasps for air. Sally moans, and Oli almost chokes on a surge of hope. She shakes her mother gently at first, then more frantically. 'Mum, please. Come on. I'm going to get help, I promise.'

Oli grabs the phone from the other side of the bed, her father's side, empty for years now. She is surprised to see a couple of books and a pen. No one ever got rid of his things. He's still here, still hurting them.

She calls triple zero. 'Ambulance!' she tells the emergency services after giving the address. 'Please hurry. It's my mum.'

Oli drops the phone on the floor and returns to Sally. As she shakes her, talks to her, begs her to live, she notices an open notebook on the carpet. One of Oli's old journals, with lines and lines of her neat handwriting detailing her deepest secrets. 'Oh god, Mum, no. What have you done?' Tears drip down Oli's face as she gropes Sally's neck for a pulse. 'Mum, please.' Oli flips the notebook shut and kicks it under the bed.

She can't feel anything. She lies Sally on the ground and starts CPR. *One, two, three, four. In, out. Pray. One, two, three, four. In, out. Pray.*

Oli stands up, the horror slowly fading. The candlelight disappears, but her hand still grips her throat. A sob escapes her mouth, and she wipes at her eyes impatiently. What has got into her? There's no point reliving that awful moment.

Disoriented, she heads to Isabelle's study, where the glaring sunlight showcases flecks of dust that float across the room. Oli wants to try on the dresses, but that would be crazy. They won't fit her, anyway.

A message pings on her phone, the blast of sound almost causing her to drop it.

I hope work has been okay. Tell the girls good luck from me. It's looking pretty doubtful I'll get to the pool but I'll try. Have fun x

Oli expels a lungful of breath. *Relax*, she orders herself. Dean is still at work, and he thinks she's at the office. She places her phone on the sofa and opens the cupboard. Pauses. Zips open the third clothing bag and fingers the delicate material.

She lets out a laugh. She's being ridiculous.

After zipping the bag closed with a flourish, she scans the neat stacks of boxes. Her eyes climb higher to more boxes and several fabric bags. More of Dean and Isabelle's shared history. How often does Dean think about his old life? He must compare her with Isabelle all the time; it would be impossible not to.

Oli stands on the arm of the sofa, carefully reaches up, and manoeuvres down the closest box on the upper shelf and two of the bags. The box is full of cards and school reports. Oli reads a few of the cards, most from Isabelle's twenty-first birthday. The first bag contains postcards, folded pieces of paper and hundreds of loose photos. She reads a postcard Dean sent to Isabelle from Thailand in 2003, his loopy font exactly as it is today. There are photos of them at a wedding, and of them skiing somewhere, Isabelle's pretty face split in half by a smile.

The last bag contains a few more photos and several notebooks. The photos are of Isabelle as a little girl taken at some kind of gymnastics competition. She looks eerily like the twins. Oli puts them aside and flicks through the first one, A5 with a flecked gold cover. It's full of to-do and shopping lists.

The other three notebooks have navy covers. One is from 2005, the others from 2006 and 2011. The Victoria Police insignia is embossed in the lower right corners.

Oli gasps. When Isabelle died, these diaries should have been tagged and processed, sent off to the police archives. They shouldn't be here.

Shaking, she opens the 2005 diary and fans through the pages. It's full of Isabelle's distinctive handwriting. Appointments are recorded in the daily planner, followed by several pages of notes. Inexplicably, a tear runs down Oli's cheek, and she hastily wipes it away. This feels like the ultimate betrayal, like she is breaking an unspoken code, but she also feels an intense connection. Maybe

Isabelle sat in this room, on this very couch, with Dean sleeping down the hall, writing in these books.

Flipping to the start of the notes pages, Oli skims over Isabelle's words. There are shorthand references to cases. A few names are familiar from old news stories, but most have no context, just pages of half thoughts. Isabelle has a tendency to summarise each page with a series of questions: *Link between tram and Willis? Is the script relevant to the doctor appointment? Gun licence in 1992. Son lives on a farm. Connected?*

Oli glances at her watch—she has to leave. She places the diaries on the desk, then returns the box and bags to the cupboard. A frenzied feeling takes over, and she rushes to the bedroom, grabbing a calico shopping bag from the hook on the back of the door and sliding the diaries inside. She wraps the excess material around the bulk before forcing the bag into her satchel. Heart hammering, she hurries downstairs to pick up the twins.

CHAPTER TWENTY-TWO

CHLORINE STINGS HER EYES, NEEDLES HER PORES AND CLINGS TO her hair. There's the piercing screech of a whistle followed by splashing, the rumble of cheering. Oli loses track of Amy and Kate in the milieu of sleek black swimming costumes, pale limbs and disturbed water. Most people in the stands are on their feet, whooping and pumping their fists. One father is yelling at such volume, his face such an alarming shade of red, that she worries he might induce a heart attack. The swimmers reach the other end and disappear under the water in tumble turns, reappearing a few metres from the wall. Mouths gulp for air, light bouncing off goggles.

After her strange episode at the house and discovery of the diaries, Oli feels completely off kilter. She rolls her shoulders and feigns interest as she looks down at the pool. Remnants of adrenaline are still circulating in her bloodstream, and her heart rate picks up as she thinks about the pages and pages of Isabelle's diaries waiting for her to devour.

Her phone beeps. The audio file Cooper sent when they arrived at the pool finally loads. He sent the link with no message, just a password. He's obviously still pissed. Oli eases in her earbuds, and presses the play icon, her deep voice merging with the steady hum of the carnival.

She listens for a few minutes. It sounds good. Really good. It builds well, and she's delivered a nice balance of emotion and fact. The way Cooper has edited the old news grabs around her narration is masterful. Their back-and-forth format sings, and there's an undeniable chemistry. It feels original but familiar, his gentle questions leaving plenty of room for her husky answers. The recording only goes for twenty-eight minutes; the other episodes will probably be longer, but Oli can already tell that people will like it. The strangeness of that morning on Paradise Street is conveyed perfectly.

For the first time, Oli wonders what will happen if it really takes off—what it will mean for her status at the office. Uncharacteristic spite churns in her gut: TJ might not be so quick to assume she'll follow him off a cliff. She thinks back to what he said in the car park. He must have sussed out that Dawn is on the nose with the exec, and now he's angling for her editor-in-chief role. It makes sense, and if Oli's honest he would be a good candidate. But she doesn't want to report to TJ. On the other hand, maybe he was testing her loyalty and reporting back to Joosten—checking to see if she'd throw Dawn under the bus. Or maybe she's being completely paranoid.

When Oli yanks out her earbuds, she's slightly startled by the sudden onslaught of noise. All of the school parents look like they're under a spell, their attention fixed on the pool. She flicks an email to Cooper letting him know she's happy for the podcast to go to Dawn for final approval.

Breathing slowly in and out, she lets her gaze drift to her satchel. In the car earlier, Amy asked for a drink of water, and Oli muttered that there was a bottle in her bag. 'I'll get it!' she cried hastily, snatching the bag from Amy and throwing it into the passenger seat before Isabelle's police diaries were exposed. Ridiculous, as if the girls would even know what they are.

Now Oli bends forward and eases out the diary that she'd looked at in the house. She quickly pulls it into her lap and opens it, a pen poised in her hand, then flips to October. Scans words hoping for a clue from the grave.

About a metre away one of the school mums—Belinda? Linda?—is on the phone, excitedly relaying the action in the pool, probably to her high-flying husband. Oli vaguely remembers meeting him, a self-important guy who delighted in telling her that no one would be reading newspapers by 2020. Belinda-Linda gives Oli a funny look, then smiles and looks pointedly at the water. The cheering intensifies, and Oli gets to her feet, squinting at the finish line. Two girls hit the side of the pool in unison, pulling their goggles off as they turn around, faces hopeful. One of the twins reaches out, clutching the tiled ledge. Third place? Oli is surprised to register a surge of pride as she watches Kate—she's pretty sure it's Kate—accept congratulations from her teammates before hoisting herself out of the pool. Oli waves to her, but she doesn't notice, shuffling over to the bench wrapped in a towel, still wearing her cap. Amy remains in the pool, holding on to a lane rope and staring at the scoreboard.

Oli sits back down, looking from twin to twin. All of the other swimmers are out of the pool now except Amy. Oli tries to read the situation. Is she upset? Should Oli go down and talk to her? On the way here, the swimming competition didn't seem that important to her, and both girls were fairly subdued, but perhaps Amy's embarrassed that Kate swam so much better. Oli doesn't pretend to understand the dynamics of life as a twin, but for the first time she wonders how it might feel to have your identical sister outshine you. It was bad enough for Oli with Lily being so popular.

One of the teachers crouches at the edge of the pool and speaks to Amy. She gets out of the water, joins her sister on the bench. Belinda-Linda throws Oli a sympathetic smile before waving madly at one of her kids, mouthing something even though he has no chance of comprehending from this distance.

It's like interval at the theatre. Oli hears snippets: problems with builders, problems at work, a new environmentally friendly laundry detergent, someone's husband has left them for someone else's wife. She recognises some faces from her sporadic morning drop-offs but has no desire to chime in. She's very aware that as the fiancée of a widow, she unintentionally brings an awkwardness to situations like this. No doubt these people all loved Isabelle. Her insides twist. She hates that she can't work out how much of this paranoia is driven by her own insecurities and how much of it is real.

The twins make their way up the stairs of the stands, joining the throng of other kids who aren't in the next race and are returning to their parents for praise and food. Oli tenses, closes the diary and shoves it back in her bag. Fixes a smile on her face. 'Hi, girls! That was great.'

'Kate came third,' Amy says.

'I saw! Well done.' Oli places a hand on Kate's wet shoulder.

'Do you have food?' Kate is dripping in front of her, red marks on her face from her goggles.

'I have muesli bars, but do you think you should eat before you swim again?'

Both twins dive for her satchel.

'Girls!' It comes out more sharply than she intends, and they pull away. 'Here.' She hands a muesli bar to each of them. Wipes her clammy hands on the thighs of her jeans. 'I used to swim all the time,' she says as they chew. 'I love swimming. Maybe we should come here sometime, just the three of us. What do you think?'

Two sets of pale-blue eyes stare at her from beneath long black hair drying in loose waves. No one is ever going to mistake them for her children.

'Did your mum like swimming?'

Amy and Kate look slightly alarmed, and Oli is flustered. Where did that come from?

'I think she did,' Kate says uncertainly. 'But only at the beach.'

'Well, that's so nice,' babbles Oli. 'Swimming in the ocean is great.' She's suddenly tempted to ask them everything, find out what kind of mother Isabelle was, what she was like in the mornings and at Christmas. Ask them if Dean is different with her. Is he less affectionate or more? Their imaginary answers rattle around in her head, torturing her. Would it be better to know? 'What else did your mum like?' she says, trying to keep her voice even.

'Can we get a dog?' Kate says abruptly, looking expectantly at Oli.

'Oh, well, I'm not sure. We'll have to see.'

'We were going to get a dog before you lived with us,' adds Amy. 'Or a cat. Dad said.'

'I didn't know that,' stammers Oli.

'It's true,' Amy says, shrugging her narrow shoulders. She looks down at the pool and steps closer to her sister until the backs of their hands touch. 'We need to go.'

'Of course, of course.' Oli gestures toward the pool. 'Well, off you go. Good luck!'

The girls walk away, their shoulder blades flaring grotesquely.

Oli sits, the tension leaving her body. Checks her phone. She retrieves the diary and flips back to October. Isabelle wasn't supposed to be working on the Saturday that Evelyn died, the words *day off* printed along the top of that weekend. Dean must have hated the randomness of her job, even more unpredictable than Oli's and a hell of a lot more demanding. Rusty used to joke about bringing home the smell of death with him some days, but it was true—sometimes tragedy and evil hovered around him like a fog, turning the air in the house or his car to an unpleasant fleshy odour like spoiled meat. Isabelle must have been the same, or worse.

Quickly, Oli checks the poolside area for the girls. Kate is on the bench waiting for her next heat, while Amy is sitting with a group of girls to the left of the pool.

Oli turns the pages to 12 October, just over a week after Evelyn died. Several familiar names are listed, including Evelyn's parents and Miles Wu, and Julian and Diana McCrae. Oli recognises references from other high-profile stories. There are two court appearances the following week, and an appointment with Michael and April Carter, the couple whose little girl was taken.

A whistle cuts through the buzz. Kate and her competitors launch into the water, and she instantly falls behind three girls who are very strong swimmers. Oli shifts her weight on the wooden slats; her arse isn't used to the hard surface, and she didn't think to bring a cushion like the other parents.

She thumbs through the rest of the 2005 planner. She assumes *AR* is Alex, as there are several references to this in the weeks after Evelyn's death. There are a few questions at the bottom of some pages, and a few notes about tests for Nicole's DNA at the scene and Miles's bank statements, but nothing stands out.

Frustrated, Oli turns her attention back to the pool. The race is over, and Kate is climbing out of the water. Oli watches as she falls into step with another girl and sits with a group of families who are set up in the front row of the stands. Oli has no idea if Kate placed or not; her face gives nothing away. A woman in a bright-pink hoodie offers her a giant smile and something to eat.

Oli flips to the notes section of the diary. She scans a few paragraphs of fine handwriting. Some sections are more organised, grouped into themes, while some are shorthand summaries of interviews. She forces herself to start again and read every word. It's not until the third page that there's any reference to the Housemate case. Oli's breath catches. There are a few neat lines of notes from a conversation with Mitchell Stanley, but they're just details about Evelyn as a teenager, such as her high school boyfriend and her part-time job at Coles. There's a list of phone numbers with initials that don't seem related to the case. Oli's eyes burn as she reads without blinking, desperate not to miss anything. On the next two pages, Isabelle put together a timeline of the evening before Evelyn died. Oli conjures an image of Isabelle writing out the sequence, her elegant hand moving across the page. There are a few comments about evidence, all of it pointing to Alex. And then there are pages of notes on Evelyn: her movements on the day she died, recent phone calls, her babysitting jobs, university grades. The word 'rabbit' is question-marked and circled further down the page, next to a question: *never let out in the yard, where is it?* Oli wonders about this. Had Isabelle known about the rabbit? Had Nicole got rid of it before she left the house?

On the next page Oli traces some notes about Louise Carter with her finger. She'd forgotten that the little girl's uncle, Jason Carter, a telecommunications technician, was charged with a violent date rape several weeks after his young niece went missing. The media collectively bared their teeth and seized on this fact, publishing pages of copy with the word 'allegedly' scattered throughout. But nothing came of it. Jason served a few years in gaol and slithered back into the general population, never to be heard of again.

Oli becomes aware of the crowd around her, the noisy chorus blaring into her eardrums as the past fades into the present. She gets the feeling someone is watching her.

When she looks up, she gasps, clutching her throat. 'Dean!' He's looking down at Isabelle's diary, which Oli slams shut and thrusts into her bag. Bringing her hands to her thighs, she jumps awkwardly to her feet. 'What are you doing here?'

He gazes into her eyes for an impossibly long moment before slowly lifting her chin with his index finger. He kisses her hard. In her peripheral vision, she sees Linda-Belinda and another couple watching them.

'We wrapped earlier than I expected,' he says, 'so I thought I'd come and see my girls.' He squeezes her hand and smiles down at the pool. 'Are they still racing?'

'Um.' Oli's face grows hot. 'Amy didn't get through to the next heat. Kate came third and I'm not sure if she . . . I lost track of where they're up to.'

Dean waves at someone over her shoulder, smiles at someone else. Gives someone else a thumbs-up. With his top button undone and his sleeves rolled up, his transition from corporate hotshot to down-to-earth, hands-on father is seamless. In both roles he exudes an easy, comfortable charm. Standing next to him, Oli feels even more exposed, her shapeless jumper somehow making her more mumsy than the actual parents around her, who are almost universally clad in branded activewear.

'I think that's Kate,' Oli says desperately. 'Down there.' She points to a huddle of girls wrapped in towels near the end of the pool. 'See?'

Dean gives her a strange look. 'I'll head down, make sure they know I'm here.'

'Okay. Yes, of course. I'll stay here with all this stuff.'

He nods and squeezes her hand again, then jerks his head toward her phone, which has started to ring on the wooden bench, slowly vibrating its way toward the edge. Cooper's name flashes up on the screen. 'Looks like your boyfriend's calling you,' Dean says lightly, heading off to find his daughters.

CHAPTER TWENTY-THREE

DEAN IS TAKING HER OUT FOR DINNER. HE ANNOUNCES THIS AS THE night air hits their faces, freezing after the warmth of the leisure centre. The twins walk in front of them, exclaiming at the cold.

'I got a cab here,' Dean says, 'so I'll come with you guys. I'll drive.' He gives Oli's hand a suggestive squeeze. 'Nina's at the house, so we can just drop the girls off and go somewhere local.'

'Okay.' Oli can't shake the feeling she is in trouble. Isabelle's diaries are like a lead weight in her bag, and all she wants to do is go somewhere on her own to read them. She's working on different theories, running them through her mind until something catches.

The podcast is going live in the morning, sometime between nine and ten—as long as the paper can set up the technology quickly enough. The advertising is on standby along with the brand new bespoke social media accounts. Cooper is still angry; he was all business on the phone, only calling to let her know everyone had approved the edit. But there was a definite hint of pride when he told her that Samsung had signed on as a major sponsor.

The car comes to a stop, and Oli looks up, confused. Blinks into the light of a neon sign.

Dean stretches across the console and whispers, 'Special treat for the girls.' He turns to the twins. 'Dumplings for my star swimmers?'

Kate and Amy squeal, throwing themselves against the seat with uncharacteristic physicality. Dean grins and jumps out of the car, then disappears into the restaurant.

'My hair is still wet,' Amy says. 'Mum used to say that you can get a cold if you have wet hair for too long.'

Oli squeezes her eyes shut briefly. 'I think that's just an old wives' tale. I'm pretty sure it's not true.' In the rear-view mirror, she sees the girls exchange a glance. 'I'm serious,' she says, turning around. 'It's just one of those things people say, but it's not scientific.'

Amy and Kate exchange another look. 'Okay,' Kate says.

'The swimming carnival was fun, wasn't it?' Oli says enthusiastically. 'I can't believe it's the last day of term tomorrow! Are you excited about going away?'

'We won't be able to visit Mum when we're in Lakes Entrance,' Kate says solemnly.

Oli looks at her blankly. 'What?'

'We can't visit her at the cemetery,' Amy clarifies. 'Sometimes we go on Sundays.'

'You do?' Sundays are when Oli meets up with friends or catches up on work, and Dean usually takes the girls out. He's never mentioned visiting Isabelle's grave. Oli glances up at the restaurant—no sign of him. 'Do you go with your dad?'

Amy nods. 'And Grandma Mary goes too, every Sunday at lunchtime.'

'Well, that's nice,' Oli manages to say.

'Why is Nina coming over tonight?' Kate asks abruptly.

'Um, your dad and I are going out for dinner.'

'He'll probably take you to Liane's.' Amy's pale eyes glow in the half-light.

Dean returns, cold air flooding into the car as he gets in. He passes a brown paper bag to Oli. 'Can you please keep these safe from the barbarians?' He winks at the girls and rubs his hands together. 'Right. Let's get you two home and into the bath before you catch a cold.'

—

Liane's is small and cosy, and less than five minutes away. Animated waitstaff in crisp white shirts and red aprons dash around madly, delivering wine and food to tables with aplomb.

'Smells delicious,' Oli says, realising how hungry she is. 'Have you been here before?'

But Dean is chatting to the heavily made-up maître d', who nods enthusiastically and gestures to one of the staff. Her eyes rake over Oli with interest.

'This way, this way,' calls the beaming waiter, leading them to a corner table. He takes their coats, and they slide into their seats. Dean orders a bottle of champagne, which arrives almost immediately.

'What's the occasion?' Oli says, smothering a yawn with a smile.

They clink glasses. She keeps her eyes on him as he takes a sip.

'Do we need one?' He slides his hand over hers, and she feels a rush of pleasure. Against all odds she has Dean, the thing that was impossible, the thing she barely dared to hope for. He traces his fingers across her palm, sending shivers up her arm. 'We need to do this more.'

She nods. The stress of the day is slowly receding, along with the tension she feels around the twins, the strangeness of finding Isabelle's diaries. 'Just like old times.'

Dean removes his hand and flips open the menu. He clears his throat softly. 'Were you at the house today?'

'What?' Her hand goes to her necklace, which she toys with nervously. 'Not since first thing this morning. Why?'

'The front door was unlocked when I dropped the car off, that's all.'

Shaking her head, she swallows a mouthful of champagne. She definitely locked the door—she remembers doing it. 'It wasn't me, I was at work. Maybe it was the cleaner?'

'Maybe.' His eyes burn into hers. 'The girls loved you picking them up today.'

Oli deflates, releasing the breath she was holding.

'And having you there to watch them swim,' he adds. 'They really did. So did I. And now we can have this special time.' He grins at her again.

She very much doubts the twins could care less about her taking them to the carnival, but regardless she finds Dean's tone a little condescending. Like she's a well-behaved dog that he's rewarding with a treat. 'Let's order,' she says.

Dean chooses salmon, Oli chooses steak. They sip more champagne.

'Did your meeting go okay?' she asks.

'Yes, it was fine. Nath and his team need a lot of hand-holding at the moment, but I think the kid is going to drop the charges against the uni and move back overseas, so that will help.' Dean looks over at the table next to them, where a trio of couples are laughing at something on a phone screen. 'How is your story going?'

'I'm not sure,' Oli admits. 'I want it to be more than just a rehash of the old facts, but there's not a lot of new material to go on. The cops are keeping pretty quiet about what they found up in Crystalbrook. And the abandoned car in Warrandyte seems to be a dead end. There's no trace of Nicole or the child.'

Their meals arrive. 'Enjoy!' declares the waiter, looking delighted.

'I just don't get why Alex Riboni would suicide now—it doesn't make sense,' Oli says after a few mouthfuls. 'I keep going over it. She was about to do an exclusive with our paper, come clean about the past. Then what, she just decides to top herself?' Oli shakes her head. 'It's weird.'

Dean shrugs, cutting his fish into tiny pieces. 'She clearly had issues.'

'I spoke to Evelyn Stanley's father yesterday, and he told me his daughter lent him a large amount of money a few months before she died.' Oli puts her fork down and drinks the rest of her champagne. 'I think the girls were involved in something serious.'

Dean laughs. 'Mitchell Stanley? Come on, Oli, he's a total hack. He copped too many knocks to the head. He was a mess ten years ago, and I've heard he's been in and out of rehab for the past couple of years. He probably barely remembers half of what was going on back then.'

'I still think he's right that something strange was going on in that house,' says Oli, as she skewers a piece of steak with her fork. 'I want to push it as far as I can. If cash was coming into that house, chances are it was from drugs, prostitution or both, and I'm convinced it's linked to Alex killing Evelyn.'

Dean casually gestures for the waiter and orders a bottle of red. Oli is surprised—he rarely drinks this much, and neither does she. He has seemed stressed lately; maybe it's getting on top of him.

'This is a big deal for me,' she says quietly.

'Hey, I know.' He takes her hand and kisses it. 'No matter what, you'll write a great piece, you always do. And I'll get to brag about my clever fiancée.'

'There's a thing coming out tomorrow,' she blurts. She needs to go easy on the wine, she's already feeling light-headed. 'A podcast about cold cases, starting with the Housemate case. We're doing a bunch of interviews with people who knew the girls, and I'm in the first episode. It's totally different from print, but I think it sounds okay.'

'Huh.' His eyes glitter in the candlelight. 'I don't know how I feel about the world listening to your sexy voice. It's supposed to be just for me.'

She waves his comment away. 'I'm really not sure that many people will listen to it anyway.'

'I'm sure it will be very popular.'

'TJ reckons the sale of the paper is imminent,' she finds herself saying. 'He tried to talk to me about leaving and doing something else, a start-up, but I don't really understand what he was getting at. He said the paper will sell out and turn into a tabloid.'

Dean dabs at his mouth with a napkin. 'I've heard the rumours about a sale, but it's not confirmed. I think most companies can smell a bad investment.'

Oli looks at him. Doesn't know what to say.

'TJ doesn't have a family,' Dean continues. 'It's easier for him. He's got lots of options—TV, or he can go overseas. But there's no way you want to get involved in a start-up. Take it from someone who knows, it's a shit ton of work. Way too stressful.'

'I guess so.' Heat creeps up her neck, spreading along the side of her face.

Dean puts the last of his fish in his mouth, oblivious to her frustration. 'God, this is good.'

Oli speaks before she can change her mind. The wine has weakened her usual filter. 'Did Isabelle have any theories about the Housemate case that she told you about?'

Dean frowns mid-chew. 'No. She didn't talk about it. We always kept work pretty separate.'

'Surely you talked about the big cases she worked on?' Oli pushes.

'We really didn't.' He clasps his hands, seems to consider whether to say something or not.

'What?'

He looks pained. 'Isabelle . . . She was going to quit. Just before the accident she told me she planned to quit the force and focus on the girls—work until that Christmas, then pull the pin.'

'Really?'

'She wasn't enjoying the strain it put us all under. I think she'd become disillusioned.'

Oli feels uneasy. This revelation doesn't fit with her impression of Isabelle Yardley, who always seemed so ambitious and in control. 'And how did you feel about it?'

'I was supportive of her taking a step back. I thought she worked too hard, and it was affecting her mental health. She was acting oddly at times. The cases were getting to her. I'm actually not sure she was doing a great job, and things were falling over at home too.'

Oli's jaw clenches. 'Maybe you should have helped more,' she says stiffly. 'It can't have been easy with the twins.'

His mouth twitches. 'I did help.'

The adjacent table erupts with laughter again. Oli and Dean sip their wine in silence.

Isabelle was going to quit? Trade being a detective for being a housewife? Oli feels inexplicably annoyed at the dead woman.

'Anyway, it's all in the past,' Dean says. 'But it is a reminder to keep things in perspective. Work wise. She never got the chance to enjoy the downtime she was craving.'

'I guess,' Oli says, feeling distinctly uncomfortable.

The waiter returns, deftly clearing their plates. 'Dessert?'

'Absolutely,' Dean says firmly. He takes the menu and scans the back page. 'Do you want to share some chocolate cake?'

'You'll have some?'

'Sure, why not.' He laughs.

'Are you still taking the girls to Lakes Entrance tomorrow?'

'Yep, I can't wait to get out of town for a bit.' He rubs his hands together. 'The weather is actually looking pretty good too.'

'I'm sure they will love it,' Oli says.

'Are you sure you can't come?'

'I really don't think I can. I need to get this feature written, and we need to lock down the next few podcast episodes.'

'You and Cooper?'

Oli doesn't rise to the bait. 'Plus, I've got interviews scheduled. Bowman's agreed to talk to me about the case.'

Dean's eyes widen, then narrow. 'Greg Bowman's a prick,' he snaps.

'Okay. Care to elaborate?'

'I just don't trust the guy. Don't be fooled by his ridding-the-streets-of-evil bullshit, he's all politics and game playing.' Dean smirks meanly. 'His head's so far up his own arse, he probably believes it.'

'I'll take that on board, but I really just want him to spill the beans on the Housemate case. It's weird how he seems to want it swept under—'

'Oli, listen to me.' Dean grabs her wrist, his fingers pressing into her skin. 'I love you, okay? *You* are my priority. You know that, right?'

She's startled. 'Yes, I know.'

'I realise we agreed no children, that the twins were enough, but if it's what you really want then let's try, let's do it. I just want you to be happy.'

Energy charges between them. The other patrons smile and talk, cutlery scraping against plates. After a moment Dean loosens his grip and sits back against his chair, eyes not leaving hers, even when shrieks of laughter erupt from the adjacent table as the maître d' approaches with a birthday cake and a playful smile.

'I am happy,' she says, tears brimming in her eyes. 'It's just a lot to get used to at once.'

'But this is what you always wanted, right?' he insists. 'To be with me?'

Her tongue feels too big for her mouth. 'Yes,' she whispers. 'It is.'

CHAPTER TWENTY-FOUR

FRIDAY, 11 SEPTEMBER 2015

OLI IS TALKING TO ISABELLE. IT'S SUNNY, HOT. OLI IS VAGUELY aware they're at a picnic. She's drinking something lemony. Gin and tonic? She can't see the others. Not that she remembers exactly who else is there. Maybe they are alone? Yes, that's it, Isabelle wants to tell her something. Oli needs to concentrate. Listen. They stand next to a bright-green hedge, so close their shoulders almost touch. Then there's a confusing moment when Oli's vision tilts like a knocked video recorder, and Isabelle's light honeyed voice darts in and out of her ears—angry? urgent?—before a dark whip of hair hits Oli's cheek and she's gone.

Oli lies on her back, staring at the ceiling. She smells her own body odour mixed with last night's perfume. Another night of sleep that has left her more tired than rested. She blinks several times, her fingers settling into the soft dip of her wrist as they feel for the pulsing blood. *One, two, three, four. One, two, three, four.*

The dream fog fades, and she hears the shower running in the ensuite. She reaches her arm across the bed. The sheets are still warm. How strange to lie next to Dean, dreaming about his former wife.

She glances at the clock. More sleep than she's had in ages, but more alcohol too.

Pulling herself up, she sits on the side of the bed and stretches her hands to the ceiling. She can still feel Isabelle's hair hitting her face. What Dean said about Isabelle wanting to quit her job aches like an old bruise. It's lodged in Oli's head, but it jars, a square peg that refuses to be jammed into a round hole.

Faint music penetrates the closed bedroom door. The shower has stopped. It's not her imagination this time: Kate is playing the piano.

Oli quickly checks her phone. There's a text from Lily. *Come on, Oli. Call Mum. Today.* She gets to her feet. She should call her mother, and about five of her old friends too. Mim's baby must not be far off now, and Oli hasn't seen Shonnie for months. Between work and Dean and the twins, there's never any time.

Dean steps out of the bathroom wrapped in a towel, sees her and grins. He kneels on the floor next to the bed and kisses her, running his hands up and down her chest and torso. Oli's body sings without her permission, the strange intensity of last night and her bizarre dream giving into a flirty lightness. He pulls away, throwing her a regretful look as he starts to get dressed.

She puts on her robe and settles back on the bed, watching him. He bends forward to rub the towel through his wet hair. He's in a good mood, and standing there in suit pants, shirtless, he is perfect.

'Did you sleep well?' he asks. 'You were dead to the world before.'

She nods. Near Dean's feet is her satchel, Isabelle's diaries tucked safely inside. Once again, panic rises at the thought of him discovering she has them. What would she say? At the pool he surely wasn't close enough to see anything but a standard diary, and it isn't unusual for her to be hunched over a notebook. He probably doesn't even know that they were in the cupboard. She imagines him in a fog of grief, blindly stashing Isabelle's things away after she died.

'So you're out tonight, right?'

'What?'

He's bounding around, fetching socks and underwear then putting them in his gym bag. 'Girls!' he calls suddenly. 'I hope you're all packed and ready to go.'

Affirmative replies come from downstairs.

'I asked Nina to sort out breakfast.' He sniffs the air and looks doubtful. 'Maybe she made cereal.'

Oli's thoughts are drifting. *Everyone said the housemates were close, but something had shifted in the months leading up to that night.*

Dean frees a suit jacket from a coathanger, slips it on. 'We'll probably leave straight after school finishes. I'm keen to get up to Phil's before dark.'

'Makes sense,' Oli says, nodding. 'I'll miss you guys.' Her voice sounds flat, distracted. 'I wish that . . .' She pauses, her thoughts oily. For some reason, she feels like she might say the wrong thing.

'It's probably good we're getting out of your way. Seeing as you're so busy.' He stands back, looking around as if he's forgotten something. 'Towels, we need beach towels.'

'In the laundry.'

He nods. Swings the bag onto his shoulder. 'Alright, we'll head off then. I've got a new business meeting this morning, and a few last-minute things to sort out with Nath and his comms team.'

'Okay.' Oli gets to her feet and stands in front of him. 'I'll come down and say goodbye to the girls.'

He pulls her close, his arms wrapped around her tightly as he kisses her forehead. 'Just make sure you check in,' he says lightly. 'I like knowing what you're up to.'

—

The first podcast episode drops just as the sky opens. The already dull day turns a blurry, hopeless grey, and Oli lifts her foot off the accelerator to avoid running up the back of an oversize truck that has slowed on the highway. The windscreen-wipers efficiently push the rain away, only to have the windows instantly turn to liquid again.

Oli reloads the home page at the lights. *Introducing our true crime podcast series,* The Housemate. *Download episode one now.* The graphics look good, the girls' faces superimposed on a black strip, floating in the darkness.

The driver behind beeps their horn, and Oli switches her foot from brake to accelerator. Feels jittery even though she's only had one coffee. She listens to the news then flicks the radio off. The traffic thickens, and the rain comes down harder. She hates driving in the rain. Her mother hated it too. Oli recalls watching Sally from the back seat, her small hands clutching the steering wheel as she scolded her daughters, shoulders hunched as she peered through the sweeping arms of the windscreen-wipers, looking like an old lady rather than a young woman in her late thirties. Oli's father always drove when they went on family trips. He used to take his hands off the wheel and drive with his knees. Pretend to swerve into oncoming cars. Oli's fingers would go to her wrist, count the beats, while her mother closed her eyes and whimpered.

Oli edges along Nicholson Street, trying to stay calm. Ren Neroli might not even be home; this whole trip might be a massive waste of time. Her thoughts drift to the diaries. She's barely going to get a chance to keep reading them today. It's clear that Isabelle thought the girls were involved in something—she was investigating their lives, not trying to hunt down a random stranger. Frustration courses through Oli. If only she could ask Isabelle.

A spark of memory ignites, flickering like a weak signal. Isabelle walking away. Oli calling out her name. Dark hair flaring in the wind as she spun around, lips plump in a soft pout. A slight crease between her eyebrows as she crossed her arms and looked Oli up and down. 'Can I help you?' Her voice was wary and perhaps a touch amused. She was so fearless. So goddamn *assured*.

'I think you can.' Straight away, Oli knew the words had come out wrong, less cocky and more awkward. Emphasised in the wrong places.

Old humiliation creeps back now, a tightness in her ribs. This woman was the reason she didn't have what she wanted. She could sense Dean slipping away; their impulsiveness had become more planned, their kisses slightly less hungry. She could only assume that for Dean, the pull of obligation, temporarily forgotten these past few months, was strengthening. And so Oli had orchestrated this moment, sought Isabelle out, because . . . why? Because she wanted to see for herself what Dean found so impossible to leave? To see if Isabelle really was so much better than her? It was all and none of these reasons. It was a mistake; Oli had known that before she opened her mouth, but she couldn't just turn around and run despite the desire to do so charging through her limbs.

Standing in front of Isabelle was confusing. Like gazing in a mirror even though they looked nothing alike.

'Yes?' said Isabelle, clearly growing impatient.

'How do you feel? About Alex's conviction.'

She looked annoyed. 'We've already made comments to the press.'

'There's been a lot of criticism about the way your investigation was managed. Do you have a comment?'

A soft tic started to pulse below Isabelle's left eye. 'I'm sorry, what is this about?'

'Nothing,' Oli muttered, fast losing confidence.

In that moment Oli got the sense that Isabelle knew about her relationship with Dean, and she also knew Dean would never leave her, and her knowing this made her powerful.

'I think it's time for you to go,' said Isabelle, her beautiful voice as clear as a bell. 'Do you understand?'

The final look Isabelle gave her was the strangest mix of pity and triumph, and Oli retreated like a wounded dog, one that had barrelled into a fight before realising its opponent was a bull terrier.

A text from Pia appears on her phone, followed by a steady flow of calls and messages. The public have listened to the podcast and have opinions. Oli senses the tweets and comments loading. A swirling mass of feedback.

She wishes Cooper was with her. Rain lashes the windows. She breathes in, then out, forcing her mind to count the beats. Grips the steering wheel. Drives.

—

Ren's house looks like it's about to be demolished. A faded yellow building permit is strung across the front fence, which is missing several pickets. Weeds have grown through the gaps, twisting around the rotted beam at the base and embedding themselves in the cracked concrete. The house rises up from the scant lawn like a toilet block made of bright-orange bricks. Dark blinds hang in every window.

Oli twists the key out of the ignition, grabs her bag. Walks through the drizzle and unlatches the gate, pushes it open. It groans in response. Shoes, bags, sports equipment and cans of food line the porch, as if the insides of the house are on the outside. Oli's considering whether to text a photo to Cooper, but the front door swings open before she has a chance.

'Hello!' A man with greasy shoulder-length hair bounces on the spot and holds out his hand. 'Welcome, and good morning!'

She reaches out her hand to shake his. 'Ren?'

'Yes!' He beams. He's tall and he wears a faded blue T-shirt and baggy grey tracksuit pants that have split at the seams so the cuffs flap over his bare feet. 'Mum said she would give you my address. Olivia, right?'

'Oli.'

'Cool, yep, cool. Wow, it's freezing out here, hey?' Ren looks at the sky, confused. 'Come in, come in.' Old cigarette smoke stirs as she enters the house. He pulls the door shut. 'This way,' he calls cheerfully, bounding down the hallway like a golden retriever.

The house seems to consist of six rooms, three on either side of the dim corridor. She and Ren walk past an unfamiliar movie poster—two angry-looking men in a stand-off—that's stuck over the wallpaper, blobs of Blu-Tack obvious in the corners. An empty picture frame is propped on the floor further down. Oli peers into one of the dark rooms: a bed with a rumpled sheet and not much else.

'In here.' Ren gestures to the last doorway on the right. An old-fashioned gas heater glows like lava in the far-right corner. It looks dangerously close to an armchair, the foamy guts of which are escaping from a large hole near one of the buttons. A lamp with an exposed bulb sits on a narrow side table. The wooden grain is cloudy with the remnants of something—milk, maybe?—that's been half wiped off.

Ren commandeers the armchair and points to a grotty two-seater opposite. Oli lowers herself onto it as he unashamedly brushes crumbs from his armrests onto the floor. 'Shit!' he exclaims.

She jumps a mile. 'What?'

'Do you want a drink?' He leaps back to his feet and sways alarmingly. 'I think I have some Coke.' He looks around, uncertain. 'Somewhere. I'm always forgetting my manners.'

'No, no, I'm absolutely fine,' Oli insists. 'Honestly.'

'Okay.' He sinks back into the chair, rocking forward and clasping his hands together. His eyes flit around the room before fixing on her again. 'So, you're what? A journo?'

'Yes, that's right,' she says, pulling out her notebook and a pen.

'On TV?' He squints at her doubtfully.

'No, print. Newspapers.'

'Newspapers,' he echoes, as if he's never heard the word before.

'Ren, I really appreciate you speaking with me. I'm working on a story about what happened to Evelyn Stanley.'

'Sure, yep.' Lines furrow Ren's wide forehead, and he sits up a little straighter. 'Man, I was just thinking about that, I dunno, it must have been last week. What a trip. Feels like yesterday.' His unfocused gaze fixes on the heater.

Oli hesitates. 'Ren, you know that Alex Riboni was found dead earlier this week, right?'

'Oh, yep.' He laces his bony fingers. He's still staring at the heater. 'Mum told me. Alex, man. I liked her a lot.'

Oli can't tell whether Ren is stoned or simply operates at a slower pace, or both, but she's determined to mine his brain for whatever old information might be floating around in there. 'Ren, can you tell me what you remember about the night Evelyn died?'

'Sure, yep, no problem.' He balances his bony elbows on his kneecaps. 'We had dinner together. The girls wanted to cook for everyone.'

'Did they often do that?' asks Oli. 'Cook for you guys?'

'Matt's dead,' Ren replies brightly. 'Did you know that? He fell off a roof when he was on a job a few years ago. I don't know what happened, but someone told me. Can't remember who. We went to his funeral together, me and Mum. Fuck it was sad.'

'Yes, I can imagine, and I'm sorry,' Oli says, meaning it.

Ren picks a scab on his elbow. 'It's just life.' He smiles ruefully. 'It sucks sometimes. And I hadn't seen him for years. It's weird how you're sometimes only friends with people for a short time, isn't it?'

She's finding this roundabout conversation vaguely therapeutic: his childlike manner is oddly charming. 'Did you speak to Evelyn on the night she died, at the party?'

'Yeah, a bit.' He narrows his eyes. 'When we came over, she was cooking in the kitchen. I remember because I tried to sneak a taste of sauce from the pot, and she flicked me with a tea towel. It really hurt, actually.' He rubs his arm as if the pain is still fresh.

Oli nods encouragingly.

'We mostly hung with Miles. All us guys got pretty wasted that night. I guess that's why I don't remember much.'

'How often did you see Miles?'

'Pretty often,' Ren says, scratching his head absently. 'But he wasn't, like, a mate. It was more like, if he was at the girls' place we'd go over, or he'd come around to ours. Miles was a smart guy. He was studying business at uni.'

'What about if he wasn't there? Were you friends with the girls?'

'Yeah, we were friends.'

'Were you more than that?'

'Nah, I wouldn't say that.' He looks sheepish.

'Really?' Oli presses. 'Three pretty girls living next door?'

He chortles. 'Well, yeah, I mean we talked about them a bit. You know, just mucking around. But we liked Miles, so we would never have touched Alex. And the others, I dunno. They were so busy, studying and working. Real go-getters. Not like us.'

Oli leans forward. 'What kind of work?'

Ren looks thoughtful. 'Just . . . working. I'm not sure. Evelyn worked in a cafe in St Kilda for a while. She used to sneak us free coffees sometimes, which was cool, but that was when we first met them. After that they all did babysitting.' He unhooks his gangly legs and rearranges them. 'But they were . . . what's the word? Ambitious. Like they had big plans.' He shrugs again. 'They went to auditions sometimes, well Evelyn did, but I think Nicole wanted to be an actress as well.'

'Miles remembers going to the shops that night. Do you remember that?'

'We went to the shops?' Ren's forehead furrows before smoothing again. 'Yeah, we did.'

'Can you remember walking back home? Did Miles say anything to you about the girls?'

'Yeah, he was going on and on about Alex. Matt and I said he should speak to her the next day—we wanted him to come back to ours for a smoke.'

'And that's all you did? None of you left the house after that?'

'I'm positive. We all fell asleep in the lounge room. Miles was totally cooked. He couldn't handle much booze, let alone weed, and he passed out.' Ren rubs his nose, which seems to trigger an itch on his elbow. 'We accidentally locked the cat out, and it started up its crying first thing. I was pissed 'cause it woke me up around five. I got up to let it in, and the guys were dead to the world on the couch, snoring their heads off.'

Oli sighs. She wants something else—not the same old story from a slightly different angle. 'What were the girls doing when you left the house?'

Ren thinks for a moment. 'I reckon Evelyn was in the lounge room. The other girls were in one of the bedrooms.' He looks up and squares his shoulders. 'I saw them down on the corner after that, though.'

Oli's fingers tighten around the pen she's holding. 'You saw Alex and Nicole after you left the house?'

Ren nods. 'Yeah. They were walking down toward the foreshore.'

'When you were at the shops?' Oli asks.

'Yeah. I didn't say anything to Miles, 'cause he was already upset about her. I didn't think they should talk for a bit.'

Oli's nerves are firing. 'Were Nicole and Alex talking? Arguing?'

Ren scrunches up his face. 'I dunno. They were just walking together. Alex was wearing a backpack, so I thought maybe they were going to the twenty-four-hour bottle shop.'

Oli knows that the cops asked shopkeepers to come forward if they saw the girls that night, but no one did. Neither of them had used their bank cards, and all of Nicole's things were at the house. With so little CCTV back then, the defence could never prove whether or not the walk Alex insisted had happened actually took place.

'You didn't mention this at the trial, Ren. Why not?'

He shrugs. 'I can't really remember what I said back then. I probably did mention it.'

She knows he didn't but lets it slide. She's trying to think what it all means. Did Alex and Nicole kill Evelyn together? And if so, why did Alex draw the short straw? 'A lot of people said the girls were fighting before Evelyn was killed. Did you notice that?'

'I saw them argue a lot, yeah. Like when Evelyn put the paint all over Alex's car.' Ren is clearly impressed at this memory. 'That was pretty weird.'

Oli blinks. 'Do you know why she did that?'

'No. They were yelling—me and Matt were pissing ourselves listening to it, but we couldn't hear what they were saying. We went onto the balcony for a smoke, and we could see Evelyn painting a canvas in the carport. She was into art, always making something, paintings and sketches, that kind of thing. I think the others were inside, and Evelyn, she just suddenly put down her brush and threw a tin of paint all over Alex's car.'

'What did Alex do?'

Ren squeezes his eyes shut for moment. 'She just stood there staring at it. The paint was white, so it looked like bird shit on the red. After a second, she just, like, stomped back into the house. Alex washed it off, it wasn't permanent or anything.'

'Were they always fighting like that?'

'Nah, but they could all be pretty moody. Sometimes they would get pissed at me and Matt even though we were just mucking about. I think they got sick of us coming over all the time. One time I remember Alex went right off at me for no reason.'

'What were you doing?'

'I don't know. I just picked up her camera—you know, pretending to take photos or whatever—and she lost her mind. Told me to get out of the house.' A mobile phone starts buzzing on the mantelpiece, and Ren looks up, suddenly alert. 'Gotta get that.' He disappears into another room, talking in a surprisingly assertive voice.

Through the window the charcoal sky is bloated, set for another release. Time feels warped, sluggish. Oli thinks about the housemates, the tension brewing between them, pressure mounting until suddenly Alex exploded and it was all over. Or was it? Have the same forces resurfaced now?

'Sorry.' Ren returns, his face sporting more colour as he shifts his weight from one foot to another. 'Um. You might have to go soon.' His eyes dart around the room. 'Is that okay?'

Oli has zero interest in being there when his drug pals turn up. 'No worries. I just want to ask you a few more questions, but I'll be quick.'

'Sure.' He resettles on his chair but he's twitchier now, and Oli can't tell if it's in anticipation of a hit or a sale.

'You said the girls worked a lot, they had goals and wanted to do well in auditions and things, but what were they like? Were they wild? Did they drink a lot?'

Ren looks thoughtful. 'Sort of. I think they drank a normal amount. They didn't get stoned as much as we did. They used to sunbake topless in the yard, and if you opened the bathroom window you could see.' Oli doesn't say anything, and he rushes to fill the silence. 'But they had their shit together, you know? They had plans. They had this big diary on their kitchen wall, and they always wrote down their uni assignments, auditions, stuff like that. We used to give them shit about it. They had weird rules and little codes and numbers next to stuff they wrote. I don't know.' He bites his lip. 'When Evelyn died it totally fucked us. We couldn't believe it.'

'What sort of codes?' Oli is tempted to grab his head and shake it until the right answers fall out.

Ren stares at her like she's crazy. 'I don't know because they were codes. Like if one of the girls was babysitting, the others would block out the time on their calendars—probably because they all shared the car, I guess.' He fixes his gaze on the dirty carpet. 'There were stars on some of the days. And they had numbers at the end of the months.' He chews his fingernail. 'One time I asked if it was some kind of astrology shit, but they all just laughed at me.'

Oli's muscles are tense, her feet straining against the leather of her boots. 'What else do you remember?'

'Nothing, really. But that last night at the house, the calendar was gone, and a poster was stuck there instead. I asked them why they'd taken it down, but they all just acted like I hadn't said anything.'

CHAPTER TWENTY-FIVE

TWO MEN LOPE AROUND THE CORNER. ONE—DARK HAIR, ROUND features, bright-red baseball cap, and a foot taller than the other—kicks a discarded Coke can that rattles noisily into the gutter. The shorter one—skinny, shaved head—wears gravity-defying jeans, every move threatening to make them plummet to his ankles. Neither seems to notice the rain falling in thick sheets.

Across the road from Ren's, Oli is hunched in the driver's seat, trying to decide whether to wait until the rain stops before she heads back to the office.

Ren's sketchy account plays out in her mind. Was he right about the girls having a coded schedule? Were they doing drug drops and using babysitting jobs as a cover? And where did Alex and Nicole go that night? Were they meeting with someone?

Oli stretches her leg to fend off a cramp, thoughts still swirling. She hasn't heard from Cooper today, a sure-fire indication he's still angry with her, and she wonders what he's doing. He might be in the studio working on another episode, or out and about trying to bank an interview. Oli feels a frisson of guilt at her behaviour yesterday. She acted like Jo used to, using her position to pull rank. Plus, she doesn't have the energy to sustain it.

The two men reach Ren's house, and the tall one shoves a hand down the front of his tracksuit pants, giving Oli an unwelcome view of him adjusting his privates before he knocks on the door. Ren appears, greeting them with the same enthusiastic head movements that Oli was treated to earlier. They disappear inside the house, and she stares at the door for a few moments, wondering what's going on inside.

Sighing, she starts the car. It promptly begins to hail. She flinches as a particularly large hailstone ricochets off the windshield. Turning off the engine, she leaves the heater running. There's no way she's going to drive in this.

The nature strips turn white as she goes through her voicemails, with Isabelle's diaries on her lap. She scans the pages as she listens to an excited message from Joosten. Isabelle's neat notes run in parallel to Oli's questing thoughts. *Search the entire property for DNA proof she was there that night. The house and out house. Request was shut down, but why? Unexplained visit. Sexual relationship doesn't seem likely so something else.* Oli has no idea what thread the detective was pulling at.

There's a voicemail from Dawn twenty minutes earlier saying the podcast has hit over two thousand downloads already, and that traffic to the website has gone through the roof since it went live. A rush of pleasure rolls through Oli, followed by an intense hit of validation.

After she completed her degree as a mature-age student, her tutor encouraged her to consider TV. He set up a few meetings with industry contacts. One executive insisted on meeting her in a hotel lobby for an afternoon coffee, and suggested she stick around until he could return after work and get a room with her. Another, a large sweaty man who wore a cravat, talked about his knack for finding talent, then proceeded to talk about himself for over an hour without asking her a single question. The third and final meeting was lunch at an expensive restaurant on Collins Street.

'You're Scandinavian,' the high-profile executive stated knowingly, shoving another risotto ball into his mouth. 'Mm, yes, very nice,' he added, eyes on Oli as he licked his fingers, chewing sloppily.

'No, actually,' she said, her appetite vanishing. 'I don't have any Scandinavian heritage.'

'Doesn't matter. Between your looks and your voice, men will be wanking into their cereal all over the country.'

Oli looked at the tabletop, gripping her knife and doing her best to keep it pointed down even though she wanted to stab his giant beer gut.

The exec guffawed to himself. 'We might even need you to tone it down a bit so it's not too much. We could do some covert PR, get people to know who you are.' He looked at the hint of her cleavage appreciatively. A few minutes later his foot rubbed against her leg, and she faked a phone call and left.

Print was safest, she decided; better to hide behind the anonymity of a by-line, let her words do the talking.

Oddly, that was one of the only times her mother conveyed an opinion about her career. At a family dinner, when Oli reluctantly recounted the unfortunate interactions, Sally knotted her hands together and said it was a shame Oli was only pursuing print, because she'd always thought it would be nice to see her on TV. *Pretty Lily, jolly Oli.*

As suddenly as it started, the hail stops, replaced by tiny javelins of rain. Easing out of the cul-de-sac, Oli connects her phone to Bluetooth and calls her mother.

'Olive?' Sally Groves answers straight after the first ring, her voice ready for bad news.

'Hi, Mum.' Oli's organs tense one by one.

'Oh. Well.' Sally sounds both relieved and concerned. 'How are you?'

'I'm fine, Mum. Busy. There's a lot going on at work.'

'Yes. Lily said that.'

This is why I don't call, thinks Oli. *It's so excruciating.*

'How are you, Mum? How is Max?'

'Not too good,' Sally says glumly. 'Max has to get a mole removed next week.'

Oli stifles a sigh. 'What did the doctor say?'

'Just that he needs to have it removed.'

'But they don't think it's malignant or anything?'

'No,' Sally admits.

'Hopefully he'll be fine, then.'

'I suppose so.'

Oli finds it hard to remember whether Sally has been worse since that night at the house, the horrible night when she found Oli's diary, or whether she has always been like this. On a daily basis, life swallows Sally up and spits her out again. She finds simple tasks overwhelming and the concept of looking on the bright side unfathomable. Her melancholy is like a huge sinkhole, threatening to suck Oli in every time they talk. She can't get off the phone fast enough.

'How are the girls?' Sally asks.

'Good. Busy with their music and school.'

'They must be so sad. Poor things, losing their mother like that.'

For a brief moment Oli considers telling Sally about the swimming carnival, just to give her a peek into her life as a stepmother, but she fears Sally will sense her vulnerability, pounce on it and amplify her own doubts.

'It must be school holidays next week already? My word, it will be Christmas again before we know it. No doubt there will be more horrible hot weather.'

Disproportionally annoyed, Oli wonders if this is what every one of their conversations will be like until one of them dies: an awkward circling of the one thing they have never spoken about; Oli's anger and Sally's guilt, a dark filth that grows and festers between them.

'Yes, holidays start tomorrow. I'm actually just driving back to the office now, Mum, so I can't talk for long.' Oli's tone is firm.

'Of course not, no.' Oli knows Sally is sitting somewhere in the small unit she shares with Max, knees crossed, shoulders hunched, taking up as little space as possible.

'Okay. Well, take care, Mum.' Relief builds in anticipation of the call ending.

'One thing, Oli.'

'What is it, Mum?'

'I listened to your new radio show this morning. About that horrible murder.' Sally's words come out in a hasty tumble. 'It was very good.'

—

At the office Oli heads straight to the studio, hoping to find Cooper so they can call a truce, but he's not there. She tries his phone as she scans the dim room. Leaves a voice message. Since she was here yesterday, he has stuck two giant Post-it notes on the back wall and filled them with their movements since the morning Alex was found in Crystalbrook. On a third, *Ep 2* is scrawled along the top with a few notes in bullet points. *News headlines from Sun 7th/Mon 8th Oct. Mitchell Stanley and Miles i/views. Nicole's parents? Oli to recount the police presser? Talk about her theories and what the public sentiment was back then? Would the case be handled differently now?*

Along the bottom of the page, Cooper has written: *interesting enough??*

Oli smiles to herself and arranges her things on the desk. All she wants is to keep reading Isabelle's notebooks, but she needs to see if she can corroborate any of Ren's claims. She searches for mentions of a camera in the news articles and court records about the case, then checks her old notes. One of the party guests, Tanya Dukov, wrote a court statement in which she recalls Alex taking a photo in the kitchen early in the evening, but there is nothing else.

Frustrated, Oli gathers her hair into a ponytail. What happened to the camera? She thinks about Alex yelling at Ren, snatching it off him. Was she just sick of the guys coming over all the time, or was there something on there she didn't want him to see? Cara said the girls were arguing about a computer. Maybe both leads have dead ends.

The quiet of the studio becomes loud, and Alex Riboni's hanging corpse springs into Oli's mind. She fumbles for her phone, playing the podcast episode again, typing away to her own voice and trying to emulate the style as she crafts the script for the next episode. She makes sure it flows on from the foundations they've laid down, writing about Isabelle's press conference the day after Evelyn's murder, the heated calls into talkback radio, the facts and the rumours, building to the moment in the newsroom when the call came through: Alex Riboni had been arrested.

Pausing, Oli lets her weight fall against the chair, rotating her sore shoulders as she reads over her work. The first episode is still playing on loop, and she tunes in to catch the end: Cooper signs off with a custom email address and appeals for anyone with information about the case to get in touch. Oli gets back to work, making notes from various interviews Evelyn's mother has given over the years.

The studio, cushioned away from the world, has a strange effect on time. Hours slip by, and before she knows it, it's almost five. Where is Cooper? He hasn't called her back. Swallowing her pride, she texts him. She apologises and suggests that they meet in the morning. *I have updates,* she adds at the end. *And a script for ep 2.*

It does the trick. Pulsing dots appear, followed by a message. *Apology accepted. Sounds good. I have updates too. Also, podcast listeners over 6K already. Not bad!*

Oli smiles. He's a lot more stubborn than she gave him credit for. She gets to her feet, white spots appearing in her vision as the blood rushes from her head. It's almost time for her meeting with Bowman.

JULY 2005

'Fire!' Matt's head disappears from the top of the fence before it reappears as he hoists himself up and over, dropping down the other side. 'You made a fire.' He looks at it appreciatively. 'Fuck, you're crazy bitches.'

'You love us,' Nicole says sardonically. She's propped up, queen-like, on an old sunlounge that Evelyn bought at an op-shop last summer, wrapped in a mohair blanket.

Matt winks then runs at the homemade bonfire and starts doing a mock tribal dance around its perimeter. He's as high as a kite.

Alex laughs along with Nicole, but she can't shake the slightly uneasy feeling that has hovered over her for months. She lights another cigarette and pulls her coat around her. It's freezing, and she's not close enough to the flames to catch their warmth.

Nicole grabs a bottle of rum and sloshes some into her glass of Coke.

'Where's Evelyn?' Matt asks in a floaty monotone.

Alex wonders the same thing. Evelyn arrived home earlier, finished with her babysitting job, and dumped her things on the table. Headed straight into the shower. After that, she came into the yard wearing a new outfit: a coat with a fur collar, thigh-high boots. She had a cigarette and a drink but she was subdued, flatter than usual. She took a phone call then left a few minutes later.

Alex wriggles in the wooden deckchair as the gnawing sensation returns to her stomach. She braces her wrists and pushes herself up to sit a bit straighter. It's got dark, must be at least 9 pm.

'I think she went to the movies.' Nicole teases her long hair at the roots, throws the rum bottle onto the grass. 'She's probably gone out for a drink afterwards or something.'

Alex nods but looks away. She hasn't heard from Miles all day. He's annoyed with her, she can tell. Last week he accused her of being secretive.

If only he knew.

She wishes Evelyn would come home. She doesn't like it when they aren't all together. No matter the configuration, when she's only with either Evelyn or Nicole these days, it feels off kilter.

Abandoning his stupid dance, Matt sinks onto the ground and stares blankly at the fire.

Ren's scruffy head appears over the fence, and he treats them all to a clumsy salute. 'Shit, you guys made a fire!' he remarks, before repeating the same fence-jumping entrance as his housemate. 'Ladies, hello.' He bows to Alex then curtseys to Nicole. 'Hey, man.' He and Matt execute a complicated handshake with several fist bumps.

Nicole rolls her eyes, but Alex smiles. Ren is charming in his bumbling way, and she's happy to listen to his inane chatter. It's a good distraction.

Nicole is right: everything is going well. It's almost too easy—so far there hasn't been a hint of risk. And it's not like anyone is getting hurt.

Alex can almost convince herself that what they're doing is fine.

Ren sits on one of the plastic chairs with legs slightly buckled from the sun. 'You ladies need to get some nice furniture out here. Tart it up a bit. Get it party ready for summer.'

'Oh, we probably won't be here by summer,' Nicole says breezily.

'Really?' Ren says.

'Really?' Alex echoes.

'Oh well, you never know. We might move up in the world. Have a little upgrade.' Nicole winks at Alex. 'Right, Al?'

'You never know,' she says softly.

'Is there more beer inside?' Ren asks. 'Otherwise I can grab some from home.'

'We have beer in the fridge,' Alex says. 'Help yourself.'

Ren plods over to the back door, causing a cloud of bugs to vacate the grass visible in the low glow of the outdoor light. He disappears into the house.

'What's on for the weekend, ladies?' Matt asks. 'Apart from conquering the world.'

Nicole stretches her arms and her legs, yawns daintily. 'Bit of this, bit of that. Study. I'm babysitting.'

'Same,' Alex says. Her breath makes a little white swirl in the air. 'Fuck, it's cold.'

The wire door smacks noisily against the brick wall of the house. 'Say cheese to this fancy camera I found!' Ren stumbles outside holding the camera in one hand and a beer can in the other. 'Hey, how do you turn this on?' He frowns as he presses buttons. 'Oh, got it.'

Alex is moving before she registers it. Her chair almost flips over as she scrambles to her feet. 'Don't touch that, Ren! Give it to me!'

He dances on the spot like a jester, delighted at her reaction. 'What's it got on it, hey? Nudie shots?'

Nicole's voice is ice. 'Give it to her, Ren.'

He holds the camera in front of him, randomly pressing buttons.

Reaching him, Alex grabs it from his hands.

'Hey, come on, I was only kidding.'

She clutches the camera to her chest. Her skin is crawling, buzzing. She looks around. Matt is still sitting on the plastic chair near the fire, watching them with stoned interest. Nicole is standing a few metres away, her own chest rising and falling, fists clenched. Ren stands in front of her, opening his beer. A long lock of hair falls into his eyes and accentuates his goofiness.

'Just ask next time,' Alex mutters, trying not to cry as she storms into the house.

CHAPTER TWENTY-SIX

OLI DUCKS AND WEAVES THROUGH THE PARADE OF BUSINESSMEN on King Street. One catches her eye, unashamedly looking her up and down before walking with exaggerated nonchalance into a strip club. Two boxy bouncers flank the door with glassy-eyed stares.

As she nears the Lion & Ox, she feels sick with nerves. A man like Bowman rarely enjoys being the interviewee. On her way she briefly considered reinviting Cooper to join her, just to really drive home the peace-offering, but Bowman doesn't seem like the type to appreciate surprises. Plus, there's a chance he'll provide more insight into what Isabelle was like, and that's not something Oli's willing to share.

She pushes the heavy door open, and it closes behind her with a thud. Her pupils swell. The walls, bar, tables and chairs are all made from wood, and the clientele are, without exception, over sixty. Beer has soaked and sweated its way into both the carpet and the wooden panels, giving the whole place a stale, musky smell. A giant stag head protrudes from the only section of the back wall that isn't covered in framed photos of vintage cars. The dead beast stares at its own reflection in the long mirror hanging opposite.

Bowman doesn't appear to be here yet. Oli commandeers a small table in the corner away from the communal benches, faces the door, arranges her satchel on the floor and makes sure there's no way Isabelle's diaries can fall out. When the door swings open, she jerks to attention. Just a pair of elderly men, one with a patch over his left eye. She's about to venture to the bar for a beer when the door opens again.

Bowman heads straight to her table without scanning the room. He nods and holds out his hand. 'Ms Groves.'

'Chief Inspector.'

They shake, her fingers like jelly in his firm grip. He sits down, flicking his hand at a barman who plucks a glass from the drying rack and starts pouring a beer.

'You having a drink?' Bowman asks her gruffly, shrugging off his coat.

'Just a beer, please.'

He nods. 'Henno will sort you out in a minute.'

Bowman's face is a map of peaks and dips. The lines seem to rest across a complicated grid system, not symmetrical exactly, but pleasing all the same, as if a sculptor has deliberated over every flick of their scalpel. In the buttery light, his thick hair is so white it almost looks fake. His distinctive voice cuts cleanly through the buzz of nearby revellers.

Henno arrives with a beer, and Oli orders. Bowman curls a paw-like hand around the glass and takes a practised gulp. Oli licks her lips, swallows. She wants to start strong, establish her authority early, but Bowman beats her to it. 'Have you noticed how everyone's always hammering on about technology changing things?' He doesn't wait for a response. 'Well, that's utter bullshit. The tools and platforms might change, but people don't.'

Disarmed, Oli tries to think how to respond.

He watches her and drinks more beer, clearly enjoying her discomfort. 'It's the same in your industry, Ms Groves. I'm sure there are one hundred superficial ways that your job is different now than it was when you were a fresh-faced cadet, but it's fundamentally the same. People are still gobbling up lie after lie.' His grey gaze is like a drill.

'People do consume an incredible amount of content these days,' she says lightly, in an attempt to conceal her irritation. 'But we don't lie—or at least I don't.'

'A journalist claiming integrity,' Bowman says sarcastically. 'How novel.'

'A detective using intimidation tactics,' she quips. 'How unimaginative.'

He tips his head back and guffaws, rubbing a watery eye with a pudgy finger. 'Alright, Ms Groves,' he says, still smiling, 'you lured me here with the promise of a theory. Let's have it, then.'

'Do you think Alex Riboni killed Evelyn Stanley?' Oli asks firmly. Henno places a beer in front of her.

'That's a question, not a theory,' he says, eyes twinkling. 'But yes, I do. The evidence always suggested she did. Even without her confession, we were certain.' He leans forward. 'I'm not going to lie to you, though—we were under a lot of pressure back then. We wanted it to be her. We were still in the throes of the gangland killings, and our track record was poor. We needed a conviction. That wasn't a secret, so I'm not surprised there was a bit of speculation about Alex being our only real suspect. But I was never concerned we put the wrong person away, not for a moment.'

Oli falters at this unexpected revelation. 'Why would she take her life now?'

'Guilt?' he suggests gruffly. 'Her life wasn't much fun after she left gaol. According to her colleagues, she was depressed and self-medicating.'

'Can I report that?'

He lifts his boxy shoulders. 'As long as I'm not the source.'

Oli nods.

'Suicide doesn't discriminate, especially when you lot get involved. It's the shame that does it—shame can eat away at a person even years later. Hard to move on from something like that once it's been splashed across the front pages. Just look at Julie O'Brien.'

A loud posse of older men file into the pub, red-faced and jeering, football scarfs hooked around their thick necks. Oli raises her voice to be heard over the din. 'I hardly think you can blame the media for Julie O'Brien's death.'

'We can debate that another time, but all I'm saying is no one is immune. An individual dealing with remorse and mental health issues is hardly a surprise suicide statistic.'

'Okay, what about Nicole Horrowitz, then? Did you know she was still alive?'

'Your voice really is something, isn't it? Very unusual.' Bowman's eyes glitter, but there's no malice. He sighs, nods to himself. 'Look, what I think is that those girls got in over their heads. Both back then and probably now as well.'

'In what way?' Oli says.

He sniffs loudly, an old-man sound. 'Drugs. And we're almost certain they were dabbling in prostitution.'

'But that angle never went anywhere. We were all running around for days trying to validate the rumours about Evelyn working at Calamity Jane's, but only one woman claimed to remember her. No paper trail, nothing.'

He shrugs. 'Doesn't mean she wasn't there. I know for a fact she was at the brothel more than once. And you have to remember, by that stage the sex industry was on edge. There'd been the two murders a few months before, which we never solved, and multiple assaults on working girls. I think everyone had decided to keep their mouths shut.'

Oli considers this; maybe the calendar Ren saw was mapping appointments the girls had with clients. 'Do you think the housemates were all involved in prostitution?'

'It's likely. After they moved out of home they worked up quite the debt. We had some solid leads—they were mixing with some pretty unpleasant characters. They were young and foolish, and it's a shame they didn't have the chance to grow out of it.'

'Young and foolish doesn't often lead to murder.'

'No, not often. But sometimes.'

'I still don't get why Alex would kill Evelyn?'

Bowman folds his arms and rests his forearms on the table, making his chair squeak against the wooden floor. One of his elbows sits in a ring of moisture, but he doesn't seem to notice. 'I think Alex was high, off her head on drugs, and I think she was angry. They had been fighting for weeks, probably over money or drugs, or both, then I think she got it in her head that her boyfriend was fooling around with the Stanley girl and that their little world was about to be blown apart.' He pushes his weight away from the table again. 'These things are not always as exciting as everyone wants them to be.'

'You don't buy the self-defence claim?'

'Depends on how far you want to stretch the definition. I think Evelyn fought back, but in my book what happened at that house was murder.'

'I have a witness who saw Nicole and Alex heading toward the foreshore that night. I think Alex was telling the truth about that part of the night.' Oli rocks back against her chair and folds her arms.

Bowman looks doubtful. 'Really? We could never find anyone to confirm it. But regardless, I don't think it changes anything.'

'Well, it would mean that Alex was telling the truth. Which might mean she was also telling the truth about Nicole suddenly running off.' Oli pauses. 'But why would she disappear *before* Evelyn's murder?'

Bowman seems to think about this. Oli imagines she's Isabelle, sitting across from him, her long slender fingers gripping a dewy beer, or perhaps a wine, her diary open in front of her as they debate the case. She wonders if Bowman is finding her dull in comparison to his former protégée.

'I tend to focus on motive, capability and opportunity, Ms Groves. We had all three in Alex Riboni, plus her confession.'

'There are a lot of bogus confessions. Especially right after a crime.'

'Sure.' He nods. 'But like I said, we had the other things. Plus DNA evidence. Despite the public interest it was fairly open and shut from my perspective, although I do understand the fascination of a female killer.'

'Okay,' Oli says. 'Okay, so say you're right. Didn't you think Nicole being missing was a pretty serious loose end?'

'Yardley always thought Alex killed her,' Bowman says matter-of-factly. 'I figured she shot through so she could start over. I assumed she woke up during the attack, witnessed the death of her friend, or the aftermath, realised how messed up her life had become, and ran. I suspect she was terrified of having to drag her family through a trial that would not have painted her in a very complimentary light. From what we've pieced together so far, it seems she made her way interstate, lived rough for a few years. Changed her name. We're not sure about the child who's evidently in her care, but for several reasons we don't believe she was pregnant at the time of her disappearance. She clearly never wanted to return to her former life.' He shakes his head slightly, as if to reiterate how crazy the whole scenario is. 'I'm aware of all the rumours,' he continues, sounding weary. 'But unfortunately for your mob, this is no Joanne Lees situation. There's no evidence anyone else was there that night, no random killer. And I didn't think Alex killed Nicole, or we would have gone after her for it. But with no body we had Buckley's in any case.' He flicks the end of his nose with his finger. 'I think this was a crime of passion, fuelled by drugs. Something Alex Riboni should have served a lot more gaol time for.'

Oli baulks at his harsh tone. Thinks about the photo Cooper took. 'I would say she paid her dues.'

'You didn't have to deal with Evelyn Stanley's mother after she lost her daughter,' Bowman says softly. 'I'm not sure Alex paid nearly enough.'

Oli changes the subject. 'Evelyn lent her father thousands of dollars before she died. If she was pulling in that much money, she must have been dealing.'

Bowman's eyes flicker upwards. 'Mitchell Stanley certainly was. That man wasted so much of our time, I had to tell him we'd serve him with a warrant if he didn't stop coming into the station. His story changed every five minutes, and I got the feeling he was just trying to earn a dime out of the whole thing. He's not someone I have a lot of time for, and I suggest you don't waste yours on him either.'

'What about the rabbit?' Oli says, frustrated.

'The rabbit?' Bowman's expression is blank. 'You mean the pet? No idea. Someone let it out. The cage was empty by the time we got there, and it was long gone.'

'We've linked it to what happened to Evelyn.'

'Linked what?'

'It died.'

'Really?' He makes an amused grunt. 'How so?' He turns his hands into a teepee and peers at her. 'We never found a rabbit, dead or otherwise.'

Heat rises in her cheeks. 'What about their computers?'

'I checked the files after we spoke the other day. There was a shared computer we seized from the house, but nothing turned up on it.'

'And Alex never said anything about a camera?'

'Did you know that having a beer with a reporter kind of takes the fun out of the beer?' Bowman says wryly, stifling a yawn. 'I wasn't in all of the interviews, but it doesn't ring a bell.' He pushes his lips together. 'Although admittedly, getting anything out of Alex Riboni was like squeezing blood from a stone. She wasn't exactly forthcoming.'

Oli doesn't reply. Bowman's dogged rebuttal has been like a millstone to her flighty theories, and she's starting to feel both stupid and frustrated.

'Listen.' He glances over at Henno and shakes his head, declining another drink. 'Like I said, I think they were naive girls who got caught up in the freedom of having a bit of money and being out of home for the first time. We see it a lot. Middle-class kids who have a bit of a wobble, maybe one of them comes from a troubled background and leads the others astray. That was Alex's story. Perhaps it wasn't her fault she didn't know which way was up, but she dragged her mates down a nasty path in a pretty spectacular way. And that parting stunt she pulled off at the house this week could have been a lot worse.'

'The fire in Crystalbrook? You're sure that was her?'

'Forensics thinks it was a bomb she rigged up. We're not sure if she was trying to harm Nicole or just thought the cops would set it off. We're lucky it didn't go off when someone was in the joint.'

Oli thinks of Rusty. Thank god he wasn't injured.

Sensing the conversation is running out of steam, she blurts, 'We spoke to her last week.'

Bowman's furry eyebrows shoot up. 'You spoke to Alex Riboni?'

'Yes,' Oli says, her heart thrumming. 'Well, my colleague Cooper did. We're working on a podcast. She was going to be a guest.'

'I know all about your podcast,' Bowman says, looking unimpressed. 'Well? Don't keep me in suspense. Was there a deathbed confession? A dramatic accusation?'

'Not exactly. But she definitely didn't seem suicidal.'

He polishes off his beer and rests his hands on his slightly round belly. 'They often don't.'

'I think it's possible the girls were selling explicit photos of themselves online,' she says, revealing her trump card.

Bowman pushes his empty glass back and forth. 'Yardley had a hunch about that too, but she could never make it fly. She got lost down some deep rabbit hole.'

'What do you mean?'

He looks fraught before the gruffness returns to his face. 'Yardley fell in with some cops who were bad news. Ones who promised her the world in regard to her career. They've since been cleaned out of the force, but she was fed some bogus information here and there, and may have got a bit confused.' He looks Oli straight in the eye; clearly this information isn't common knowledge, and he's trusting her with it. 'But like I said to Yardley back then, even if the girls were selling nude photographs of themselves, I doubt it's relevant to what happened.'

Oli considers this. Maybe it explains why Isabelle hid her diaries at the house. Maybe she didn't know who to trust at work. But all she says to Bowman is, 'What if it was linked to the prostitution?'

He seems to consider this. 'Bring me anything you find. I'm always happy to chat.' He checks his watch. 'I hate to tell you this, Ms Groves, but it's getting close to my bedtime. Old bastards like me need our rest.'

He insists on paying, and she waits at the door like a child.

Outside the cold air is shocking. Oli is surprised to discover it's almost ten.

They face each other in the circle of light formed by the street lamp.

'You're a good journalist,' Bowman says. 'I wouldn't have met with you if you weren't. I'm not in the habit of wasting my time.'

'Neither am I.'

He shoves his hands deep into his coat pockets and rocks on his feet. His white hair glows like a halo. 'And also, I was curious,' he admits.

Oli blinks, not sure if she heard correctly. 'Excuse me?'

'You're nothing like her. Nothing like her at all.' Bowman scans the street, his breath sending a thread of white steam skyward. 'My wife died almost exactly twelve months before Yardley did. It was the worst year of my life. It's stupid, really. I'm used to death. But, well, my wife, her sickness was very cruel. And then Yardley on top of that. It was, gah.' He waves a hand as if he's sick of himself talking, then forces a cough. 'The guilt really knocked me for six. I used to think about it all the time, how she must have felt that morning. I always wonder if I could have done more to protect her.'

Oli observes the telltale face tics, the pull of his jaw. Watery eyes. She speaks hastily. 'I'm sure that—'

'Does he ever talk about her?' Bowman's grey eyes shine like marbles. 'Has he told you what she'd decided?'

'I'm sorry?' Oli feels the world tilt. Her eyelids are heavy, and the sound of the cars sliding past on the wet asphalt makes her skin crawl.

'Hey!' A security guard at the club next door steps away from his post. 'Do you want a taxi?' He gestures to a cab idling near the kerb.

She turns back to Bowman, who clasps her shoulders briefly. 'My gut says this story is a dead end, Ms Groves. But at my age, perhaps they all are.' He laughs, though he seems sad. 'Look after those little girls.' He dips his head, looks her hard in the eye, and walks off into the night.

CHAPTER TWENTY-SEVEN

SATURDAY, 12 SEPTEMBER 2015

OLI SLEEPS LONG AND DEEP. WAKES TO A SILENT HOUSE. SHE FELL asleep reading Isabelle's diaries, and they lie on Dean's side of the bed next to her. She's almost gone through every page now, but it's impossible to know which details matter, which clues had kept Isabelle up at night as she tried to make sense of the housemates. Oli gets up and slides the diaries into her satchel and flicks on the radio in the bathroom, ducking her head in and out of the water to listen as she showers. Charges are going to be laid against O'Brien: his latest accuser allegedly told a family member about the incident all those years ago, and they are willing to back his claims. Oli rubs the mirror with her hand, staring at her cloudy reflection as she combs her hair and applies moisturiser. She dresses and heads to the garage before remembering her car is at the office.

She waits out the front for her cab. Kicks a few stones from the driveway back into the garden bed with the tip of her boot. Her insides feel mushy, as if she's about to get on a plane.

In the cab she texts Dean, who calls her immediately. 'You didn't sleep at the office, did you?' he says, teasing.

'What? No, why?'

'I just know how hard you work.'

'I actually slept pretty well last night,' she says. Dean's voice has triggered the uncertainty she felt after she left Bowman outside the pub. *Has he told you what she'd decided?*

'Maybe I should go away more often, then,' he jokes.

They fall into a brief silence. A couple in the adjacent car are arguing. Oli asks about the girls.

'They're loving it here,' replies Dean. 'We'll probably go to the beach today. It's not hot but it's warm enough.'

Oli looks up at the grey sky. 'Sounds nice.'

'How was Bowman?'

'Not particularly helpful in the end,' she says.

'I've always thought he was a fraud. And what's on for today? More work?'

'Just a bit. I'm heading in now. I left the car there anyway, but I'll probably be in the studio for a few hours sorting out the next podcast episode. And I need to get petrol. Go to the shops.'

'The studio sounds cosy.'

The cab jerks to a stop outside the office, and Oli fishes around in her bag for her wallet. 'More stuffy than cosy.' She hands over her credit card.

There's an awkward pause.

'Anyway, I better let you go,' Dean says eventually. 'I love you. Call me later.'

'Love you too.'

The cab drives off. The weight of Isabelle's notebooks makes her bag strap dig painfully into her shoulder. Her gaze drifts to the office, then over to Breakers. Food first.

'It's not an olive branch, but it does have a lot of vitamins in it.' She places a bottle of juice on the desk in front of Cooper and hands him a paper bag bulging with freshly baked muffins.

He peeks inside. 'For me?'

'One for you, one for me.'

'So, we're good?' He fiddles with his watch. His shirt. The cuff of his jacket.

'We're good,' she confirms. 'Let's break bread. Or apple muffin.' She tears off a piece with her teeth.

'You eat a lot,' Cooper says tentatively. 'I completely forgot to eat all day yesterday without you around to remind me.'

Their eyes lock, and Oli bursts out laughing. She drinks her coffee, more relaxed than she's felt in days.

'People are going crazy over your voice on the podcast,' he says. 'There's a Facebook group dedicated to it and everything. Twelve fan emails so far. One marriage proposal.'

'I don't want to know,' she says, shaking her head. She gestures at the wall. 'I wrote up a script for episode two based on your outline.'

He looks pleased. 'Can I see?'

'Sure.' She gets her computer from her bag, loads her email and sends it to him. 'In your inbox.'

'Got it,' he says, dark eyes darting around as his fingers fly across the keyboard.

He plays her the grabs he's edited from his conversation with Mitchell Stanley yesterday, then proudly reveals an interview he recorded with Amber Halcon, one of the other party guests. The one Oli couldn't track down. As Oli listens, she can see how it will all weave together—the news snippets, her script. It's the same way her mind locks down the pieces of her stories before she starts to write. 'It's going to be good,' she says, eyes gleaming.

'I know.' Cooper is unable to keep the excitement from his voice.

She tells him about her meeting with Bowman.

'I had to stop myself from texting you to ask how it went,' Cooper admits. 'I even put my phone in a drawer so I wouldn't be tempted. What did you think overall?'

Oli laces her fingers and pushes her hands away from her body until her knuckles crack. 'He seems pretty sure about Alex's guilt. But he did say if we turn anything up about the girls selling pornography to let him know.'

Cooper looks at her. 'Funny how he said Detective Yardley thought the girls might have been involved in porn.'

Oli's phone rings from the depths of her bag, making them both jump. It's Dawn. Oli answers on speaker.

'There's been a sighting of Nicole Horrowitz and her kid,' Dawn yells. 'In Bendigo. Channel Nine are running with it right now.'

'What exactly are they running with?' replies Oli.

'Melissa bloody Warren is shoving a microphone in the face of some convenience-store worker who claims she saw Nicole and her kid last night.'

'Do you want me to head out there?' Oli says reluctantly. 'I can.'

'It's fine. TJ's going.'

'TJ?'

'He got word from a source that something was brewing, so he's already on his way. There's nothing new on O'Brien today, and he was happy to step in on this. I just wanted you to know in case it blows up.' In a slightly gentler tone, Dawn adds, 'The podcast is going well. The sales guys have been inundated with advertising interest, so just focus on that, okay?'

'We're on it.' Oli hangs up with a flourish. 'Fuck,' she mutters.

'She gave TJ the scoop?' Cooper asks.

'I think he gave himself the scoop.'

He shrugs good-naturedly. 'All the more reason to make this second episode incredible. You ready?'

'Now?' she says, wiping coffee off her lip.

'Why not? Now we've created the hunger, we need to feed the beast!'

She attempts to put aside her bruised ego, clears her throat and fixes headphones over her ears.

It takes longer this time. They re-record several sections as Oli loses her way a few times and Cooper stumbles over some questions.

Three hours later, she pulls off her headphones. The hair around her ears is damp, and she rubs her eyes. 'No chance of forgetting lunch today. I'm starving.'

They pack up and head downstairs, walking in silence to a Vietnamese restaurant around the corner. The city is different on the weekend, full of tourists who have their eyes trained to the sky, exclaiming over buildings and landmarks that Oli barely ever notices.

After the steaming food is placed in front of them, she raises her chopsticks and eats while Cooper babbles away, laying out various ideas for the third episode. She welcomes the chance to sit and listen, to block the nagging worry about work and Dean.

Cooper pauses for breath and water. 'We need more,' he says, wiping his mouth. 'We don't have much that's new. Miles will be interesting, but we need more.'

'Ren will add some flavour, but you're right, it's not enough. Maybe I really should ask Bowman. He knows about the podcast.'

'As long as he keeps an open mind,' Cooper says earnestly.

They eat in silence for a few minutes, Oli watching Cooper navigate his way around a plate of dumplings. 'I found something,' she blurts out. 'Some old notebooks.' She imagines Isabelle's words escaping from the pages and sprawled across the table, and she immediately wants to collect them up and cram them back in. 'They might help us with the story.'

'You found them at work?' Cooper wrinkles his nose.

'No. At my house.'

His eyes widen. 'Isabelle Yardley's?'

Oli doesn't reply, letting her eyes provide confirmation.

'Police diaries,' he whispers, jumping as a waiter appears behind him to clear his plate. Cooper's Adam's apple punches in and out of his throat.

Oli nods. 'Three of them.'

'Holy shit, are you kidding? Oli, this is nuts!' His voice drops. 'Is it legal?'

'I found them in my house,' she says, dodging the question.

He moistens his lips. 'Have you read them?'

'Some.' She zips open her bag, hands him the 2006 diary. 'I haven't looked at this one yet. I've barely had a chance to look through them at all.'

He sticks out his neck, gaze shifting all over the restaurant. 'You want to do this here? Are you crazy?'

'I don't think Chilli Town is under police surveillance,' she says drily. 'We'll order some green tea, read some old diaries. No big deal. Bowman might be right, this whole case might be a fizzer, but what if he's wrong?' Isabelle's face hovers in her mind. 'Because the thing is, I don't think Alex killed her friend over drugs, and I don't think Isabelle Yardley thought she did either.'

'This is *incredible*.' Cooper holds the diary in front of him like a Holy Grail.

'I'll order some more tea.'

The afternoon sun redirects off the venetian blinds, and swords of light hit their table as they read. They make notes and occasional comments, but mostly they read in silence, side by side, tracing over Isabelle's version of the past.

'Look at this,' Oli says. 'Isabelle thought that Melanie from Calamity Jane's was full of shit.' She points to the notes where Isabelle has written: *Melanie can't confirm claims. Who was the original source? No evidence E was ever there.*

'But why would she lie?' Cooper asks.

'To make the girls seem like trouble,' Oli replies. 'And maybe to suggest that Evelyn's death was linked to the prostitute murders from the year before.'

'If that's true, it might mean there really is more to this whole thing. That type of cover-up seems pretty sophisticated.'

'That's what I'm starting to think. Although Bowman was pretty sure that Evelyn had been linked to the club.' She looks down at the notes. 'Isabelle might have been totally off base. I guess we need to keep that in mind. These are just her theories.'

Cooper nods. 'It's hard not to see it as a flashing arrow pointing to a clue though, huh?'

Oli smiles. 'Yep.' Her smile turns to a frown when she remembers what Bowman said. 'We also need to consider that Isabelle wasn't entirely above board.'

Cooper looks shocked. 'You think she was corrupt?'

'Not necessarily corrupt. But she might have been influenced or pressured by the wrong people. We just don't have context is all I mean.'

They fall into silence. Oli can tell Cooper is worried that he might be reading the musings of a dirty cop.

There are bank account balances and phone numbers. Isabelle made notes about a website called stkildasitters.com.au, which Oli types into her phone. All she gets is an error message. Next she tries the archive site but has no luck there either.

'I know some guys who might be able to trace the old site,' Cooper murmurs.

Two pages later, Isabelle has written: *BS jobs. Link between quitting other jobs and increase in their spending. New bed (N) and new computer (A). Nothing in bank accounts + still collecting gov money. McCrae?*

Oli sits up straight, neurons firing. These scrawled notes are only half the story—she'd give anything to know what Isabelle was thinking.

'How long was this before she died?' Cooper asks.

'Six years.'

'God, I remember some of these other cases. It's weird to think we know what ended up happening in a few of them, but she never did.'

Oli feels a stab of guilt at sharing this private part of Isabelle. *She would understand—she would trust Cooper. And she would want the truth to come out.* The thought arrives from nowhere, but somehow Oli knows it's true.

She refocuses and reads a page of notes about a web platform and file transfers. Then there's a list of names she doesn't recognise relating to the suspicious death of a man in St Albans.

Her eyelids start to droop. She needs a coffee. She shifts position and has more tea. She pulls out the 2011 diary and opens it.

'Holy shit!' exclaims Cooper, a few moments later. He jabs at the page and grabs her forearm. 'There's a note here, look. *ES babysat in Malvern area. LC?* Holy shit, do you think she means Louise Carter?'

Oli's heart starts hammering as she looks to where he's pointing, but her mind is fixed on what she just read: something she missed when she read this page last night, battling to keep her eyes open, in dark-blue ink on the Friday afternoon after Isabelle died are the words *1 pm, Noel & Young Lawyers.*

CHAPTER TWENTY-EIGHT

SUNDAY, 13 SEPTEMBER 2015

OLI DRIVES AROUND THE METICULOUSLY MANICURED BOULEVARDS of Brighton Cemetery for almost twenty minutes, craning her neck to read the custom street signs: Breeze Lane, Ocean Road, but no Saltwater Drive. Giving up, she parks outside a building with Information written across the wall. She really should just leave, but the ferocious urge to be here has been gnawing at her ever since the idea speared into her consciousness while she sat with Cooper in Chili Town yesterday.

Noel & Young Lawyers specialise in divorce. Oli knows this because Lily has frequently raged about how much money Shaun has paid them to settle things with Rebecca. Lying awake in the early hours, Oli conjured up reasons for Isabelle to have an appointment there—reasons that weren't related to ending her marriage. A case she was working on? Or was she going to support a friend? But none of those possibilities seemed right. Oli had known the truth the moment she saw those words: just before she died, Isabelle was planning to divorce Dean or vice versa.

It's hot inside the building, stale air buzzing noisily from a vent in the ceiling. Oli approaches the information desk and gives Isabelle's name to a kid in a suit who has a bleeding pimple on his chin. With an orange highlighter he draws a few lines on an A4 map and hands it to her without uttering a word.

A little further along there's a cafe packed full of people—most of whom, Oli notes absently, aren't wearing black. She glances outside at the drizzle and decides to order a coffee. *More caffeine, just what I need*, she thinks wryly, smiling at an older lady who is sitting by herself and eating a large cupcake topped with pink icing.

Back in the car, Oli holds the map in one hand. Left, right, right, left until she arrives at the base of a green hill dotted with graves. Double-checks the map. This is it, with the impossibly perfect lawns and the relentless chirping of birds. She plods up the knoll, clutching her oat slice and coffee, half expecting to find that there's been some mistake, that Isabelle is not here after all, that she never was. But then Oli sees it, the bed of quartz under a giant weeping willow.

ISABELLE ANNE YARDLEY

1970—2011

Beloved wife, mother and daughter.

No mention of her being a detective. At the head of the slab there's a posy of blue flowers and a huge bouquet of dying tulips, identical to the ones Dean often buys for Oli.

She looks around. The girls said Mary comes here every Sunday at lunchtime. It's midday.

Light-headed, Oli takes a seat on a nearby bench, eats and waits. As she stares at Isabelle's grave, memories roll through her mind of the day Dean's wife died, how confusing it was. She swallows a sob, trying to quell unexpected emotion.

'I certainly didn't expect to see you here.'

Oli whirls around.

Mary Masterton is staring at her daughter's grave, lips pursed. She is dressed for another era, or perhaps another setting. The collar of her ivory blouse is high under a navy blazer; jodhpurs grip her slender legs, and tiny gold buckles sit on each side of her leather boots. Sharp cheekbones stand to attention, her thick dark hair glossy and curling obediently against her neck.

Oli wipes coffee from her sleeve and wrist, her pulse racing.

'Or maybe it makes perfect sense.' Mary marches over to the bench and sits down with such force that it shakes.

'I'm sorry.' Oli doesn't know what else to say. How can she explain the urge that brought her here? 'The twins told me you come here on Sundays.'

Mary clenches her jaw and doesn't say anything.

Oli falters. 'Should I go?'

'Stay.' It feels like an order.

'I don't really know why I'm here,' Oli admits.

'That, at least, is obvious.' Mary's tone is droll. 'I suspect it has something to do with confronting the ghosts in your life.'

Oli feels disoriented, as if she's on the verge of waking from a vivid dream.

'Do you smoke?' Mary pulls a packet from her jacket pocket, lights one and raises a groomed eyebrow.

Oli stutters. 'I used to, a long time ago.'

'It's like riding a bike. You'll remember.' Mary holds out a cigarette.

Oli accepts it and tilts forward so Mary can light the tip. Their eyes lock; hers are the same pale blue as her daughter's and granddaughters'. The cigarettes are strong, and Oli retches slightly as the smoke hits her lungs. 'God, this takes me back,' she says in an attempt to keep up the façade of being a non-smoker.

'To happier times?' inquires Mary.

Oli shrugs awkwardly.

'I found marijuana in her schoolbag when she was fifteen,' says Mary, squinting at Isabelle's grave. 'I was so angry, I grounded her for a month.' Mary sucks hard on the cigarette, her carefully lipsticked mouth puckering like that of a fish. 'Of course, I couldn't care less what she smoked now, as long as she was here.'

'I can't imagine,' Oli says feebly, struggling to align this knowledge with the pure mental image she has of Isabelle.

Mary snorts politely, dropping the butt onto the dirt and smothering it with her heel. 'I didn't want her to be a cop either. Problem was, she was too old to be grounded by then.'

A raindrop hits the tip of Oli's cigarette, which fizzes softly.

'Bloody hell.' Mary hisses at the sky.

'Wait here.' Oli runs to the car, grabs a golf umbrella from the boot and holds it above the two of them. She finishes her cigarette and drops it on the ground next to Mary's. Extinguishes it with her shoe.

Mary asks, 'How do you think my grandchildren are?'

Oli blows out the last of the smoke, adjusting her grip on the umbrella. 'They seem okay.'

'Strange little girls.'

Oli shifts her eyes sideways. Mary looks like she's in a trance. A sparrow drops from a nearby tree and hops madly along the grass to Isabelle's grave, where it dances in tiny circles.

'They miss her,' blurts Oli, tears welling in her eyes. 'They really miss their mother.'

Mary turns to look at her.

Oli wipes her eyes, mortified. 'I'm sorry. I don't know why I'm getting upset.'

Looking back at the grave, Mary says, 'Well, if you're going to cry, this is the place, Olivia.'

Oli doesn't bother to correct her. 'I guess so.'

'And it can't be easy for you. My Isabelle was quite the package.'

Oli's tongue is thick in her mouth. 'Was she happy?' she asks quietly. 'With Dean?'

Mary makes an odd snorting sound and leans back against the wooden slats. 'Was she happy? No, no, I don't think she was. But she was very private, even with me.'

'Did she ever say she was going to leave him?'

'No.' Mary shakes her head. 'Not explicitly, but I'm sure she thought about it. Deep down they were really quite different. And things had been strained ever since the IVF.'

Oli blinks.

'Probably before that, really,' Mary muses. 'Dean worried about her police work. It was one of the only things he and I agreed on.'

'He said she was thinking of quitting,' Oli manages to say.

'I doubt that,' Mary says dismissively. She crosses her legs. 'Anyway, I suppose you'll want to have your own children. How old are you anyway, thirty-five?'

'Thirty-nine,' Oli murmurs.

Mary makes a sympathetic sound. 'Will you try IVF?'

A man, woman and teenage girl walk across the grass a few metres away, heads bent, faces grim. The man is holding a bunch of daffodils.

'I don't, I'm not . . .' Oli stops, suddenly conscious of how bizarre this conversation is.

The man places the flowers on top of a grave, and the teenage girl wraps an arm around him.

'Well,' sniffs Mary, 'I must admit infertility is not a topic I'm very familiar with. I got pregnant just looking at William.' She points past Isabelle's grave. 'He's over there. Been dead for almost twenty years now.' With another sniff, she adds, 'Both my older girls were the same, pregnant at the drop of a hat. And I'm sure Isabelle would have been like that too.'

The man is crying now, his shoulders shaking as he kneels on the grave in front of the daffodils.

'But she wasn't.' Oli's blood is ice.

'No, and it was hard on her. She never complained, but I could tell. She had the girls in the end, of course, so it was obviously worth it, but she had to manage Dean's feelings of inadequacy on top of it all.' Mary recrosses her legs and smooths the material of her jodhpurs. 'Something you should be prepared to navigate.'

'What do you mean?' Oli asks, needing Mary to spell it out.

She pats her hair, even though every strand is perfect. 'It's supposed to be the woman's issue if children don't miraculously appear, so when the man is infertile, his ego takes a beating.'

CHAPTER TWENTY-NINE

LOUISE CARTER VANISHED WITHOUT A TRACE. ONCE MICHAEL Carter's brother was cleared, the cops had no suspects and no leads. The little girl had been taken from her bedroom, through a window widely reported to have been left open but which was eventually shown to have most likely been tampered with. In the wake of her disappearance, every aspect of the lives of Michael and April Carter was scrutinised. Why had they moved from South Africa to Australia in the first place? Why hadn't they been back since? Why had Michael Carter taken up a board position with a children's charity? Had April really swallowed a sleeping tablet that night? But in the end, it all amounted to nothing. The vicious swell of judgement eventually fell away, leaving the bereft family alone to deal with the unfathomable loss of their little girl.

Until now, at no point has Oli come across a suggestion that the case could be linked to the Housemate Homicide.

'I spoke to her!' Cooper exclaims when Oli answers the phone on Bluetooth as she turns out of the cemetery to head home. 'April Carter. I contacted her through the Missing Person's Facebook Group last night. She called me about an hour ago.'

Oli tries to focus on what he's saying, even though her stomach feels hollowed out. Mary's words haunt her.

'Does April remember Evelyn?' Oli manages to say.

'No,' Cooper says, slightly less exuberant. 'But she said they used new babysitters just before Louise went missing. Their nanny had fallen through, and they got a flier in their letterbox advertising local sitters, so they decided to give them a go. It was all through email apparently, a Hotmail address. Before you ask, yes, I checked if they still have any of the correspondence. They don't but they seem pretty sure.'

'But none of them were Evelyn?'

'April only remembers one babysitter they used, and she was Japanese. But it was April's *mother* who met the other one. April and her husband were away that weekend, and her mother was staying with the kids. She had plans on the Sunday, so April arranged a sitter.'

'Is her mother still around? Maybe she can ID Evelyn?'

'I already asked her,' Cooper trills. 'She thinks it's possible, says the girl she met definitely looked similar, but it was only a brief meeting. She wasn't using the name Evelyn, though.'

'Does April's mum remember the name she gave?'

'She thinks it might have been Jacqui.'

Oli thoughts rattle painfully. 'Alright. What are you thinking?' She indicates to switch lanes, dropping her arm to the right before pulling back when an elfin blonde in a white ute beeps her horn and gives Oli a filthy look as she sails past.

'Me?'

'Yes. What are your next steps?'

'I was going to see if I can find anything else about the girls' babysitting jobs. There must be people out there who know something. Pia's going to help me.' He pauses. 'Unless you think I should be doing something else?'

'No, that sounds good,' Oli says absently. Should she confront Dean? Maybe Mary doesn't know what she's talking about or is trying to cause trouble. But Oli recalls her conversation with Dean at Liane's, and her stomach twists uncomfortably. She's pretty sure Mary isn't lying.

'Episode two is sounding great,' Cooper adds. 'It was a bit hard to wrangle, but it's almost there. And we've received a whole bunch of emails to the podcast address. Most are rubbish, but one or two might be worth following up. I'll forward them to you.'

'Okay, sure,' Oli murmurs.

'You have another guy who wants to take you out for dinner. Shame you're taken, or this could be quite the dating strategy.'

Oli's face crumples. Her future with Dean is uncertain, something she hasn't wanted to admit until now.

'Oli? Are you still there?'

'I'm here,' she says, her voice shaking.

'Are you okay?'

'Yes, I'm fine. I'm just tired.'

'Oh my god, same. I guess it's just all the thinking.'

Oli can tell he's talking quickly to cover up the awkwardness of her crying. 'Great work, Cooper,' she says firmly. 'Something obviously made Isabelle draw a link between Evelyn and Louise, so hopefully we can find out what it is.'

'That's the plan,' he says cheerfully. 'Leave it with me—I'm not going to let this lead die, Oli. I'll see you back at base later on. How does a six o'clock wrap-up sound? I'll aim to have the edit ready by then.'

'Sounds like a plan,' she says, defeated. She realises she's happy for him to call the shots. Plus, he's doing a good job.

'Take care of yourself, okay?' He hangs up, and the road blurs in front of her.

—

At the house Oli showers again, washing the smell of Mary's cigarettes away. Dean calls, and she lets it go to voicemail, not ready to speak to him yet. Clad in the bathrobe he bought her for Christmas, she wanders around the house. She finds a photo album on the bookshelf in the lounge and spends almost an hour poring over the pictures of Isabelle, Dean and the twins. The perfect family. Closing the album, Oli sits still, letting the sharp corner of the cover dig into her thigh.

Maybe they were going to see the lawyers together; perhaps they had mutually decided to call it quits. The twins must have been hard to manage when they were little, and Dean and Isabelle had busy, stressful jobs. It's not unusual. And Dean wasn't the perfect husband—Oli knows that first hand. But even if this is true, he's still lying to her. Keeping things from her.

Returning upstairs, she does her hair and gets dressed. Checks the news. The police have now completely dismissed Melissa Warren's scoop and confirmed there are no developments concerning the death of Alex Riboni. The ABC is reporting that her private funeral will be held on Wednesday.

Oli has eighty new emails, and a text from TJ: *You in the office today? We should chat.* She rolls her eyes—he still hasn't mentioned the podcast, which feels deliberately obtuse.

She grabs a jacket from her wardrobe. It's nestled next to one of Dean's blazers, and his aftershave hits her nostrils as she pushes it aside. She's dizzy, out of sorts, like it's a new day rather than three in the afternoon. Her engagement ring glitters in the soft light. She should call Dean back, but she can't, not yet. The tulips on Isabelle's grave surface in her mind. Did he put them there? And what if he did? He is allowed to mourn his murdered wife. But when she pictures him visiting Isabelle's grave in secret, the thought burns. Does he go there out of sadness? Or guilt?

Even if Dean and Isabelle were having problems, he didn't want Isabelle gone. He didn't want her dead. He didn't know what was about to happen.

But Mary's words push their way into Oli's consciousness until she lets out a little cry of frustration. Groping for her wrist, she counts the beats as the panic surges then subsides.

A cool breeze swirls around her, and she flinches. Glances around the bedroom. A draft? She looks outside, but the trees are completely still. After shoving her feet in her shoes, she bolts down the stairs.

CHAPTER THIRTY

FAT MARSHMALLOW CLOUDS CHASE AWAY THE LAST OF THE AFTERnoon sun. Teenagers fill bus stops and shopping strips, stalking around in ripped jeans and puffy jackets with the brazen confidence of hardened media moguls. Oli stops at the traffic lights under a new billboard on the corner of Flinders and Elizabeth streets, advertising the launch of a television series: three girls in nurse outfits are draped over an older man with a stethoscope around his neck. *Saving lives by day, turning tricks by night.*

Oli massages her neck before stopping abruptly, fingers mid-prod. What if McCrae wasn't there that night because of some pathetic crush on one of his students? What if he was there because he was pimping out the girls or selling their images online? Pia said that Diana McCrae was a photographer. Maybe the camera—the one that Alex was so protective of—was Diana's; Julian might have given it to Alex at some point that year, then taken it home with him that night. Feeling energised by this theory, Oli takes the fire-escape stairs from the car park all the way to level five.

The studio is empty, a discarded juice bottle suggesting that Cooper has been here recently. And there's a sticky note on her side of the table. *Emailed you the new ep. We sound awesome!* Followed by a smiley face.

Out of breath, Oli sinks into one of the seats. She finds the email and plays the recording while she reviews copy and replies to emails. Cooper's right: the podcast does sound good. The edit is clever, mixing snippets of Alex's phone call, the old press conferences and the one from earlier this week. The whole thing feels incredibly claustrophobic.

Oli smiles. Cooper must have got the paper's legal rep to give the go-ahead on Alex's audio. Good for him.

After a few more hours of work, she's inexplicably restless. It's six. Where's Cooper?

She flips open Isabelle's 2005 diary again, re-reads some of the passages. On one of the last pages, the detective wrote: *Went to see them, not happy. Worth looking into background more and see if there's a link to the internet site?*

Oli shuts the book, gets up and stretches. The second hand on the cheap wall clock clicks clumsily. She calls Cooper and listens to his voicemail greeting: 'Hi there. You've reached CNN central, aka Cooper Ng. Leave me a hot tip—or, failing that, a friendly personal message. Have a great day!' She doesn't bother leaving a message, just grabs her things and leaves.

In the elevator she jabs the ground-floor button with her fist. A chorus of ringing phones, office chatter and coughing greet her there. On the TV, the prime minister is wearing a hard hat and grinning like an idiot.

Oli nods a greeting to one of the weekend sports editors as they pass each other. He holds out a bright-green foil bag. 'Chip?'

'No, thanks.' She waves and rolls her eyes, suggesting there's a mountain of work she is about to get stuck into.

'Good work on that podcast,' he says, spraying chip crumbs in her direction. 'Really felt like being there.'

'Thanks.'

She plonks herself down at her desk and adjusts her chair so her knees don't hit its underside. The coffee cup from earlier in the week is still there, congealed milk caking the base.

Loading the University of Melbourne website, she curses the terrible navigation. After several dead ends, she finds what she's looking for. McCrae lectures twice a week, on Monday and Tuesday mornings.

Still no word from Cooper. Oli wonders if he's gone rogue again. Did something else he read in Isabelle's diaries give him a lead to pitch to Dawn? Surely not.

Clenching her teeth, Oli texts Dean, explaining she has a sore throat and will head to bed early in the hope of shaking it off, and that she'll call tomorrow.

An email arrives in her inbox, the name catching her eye: Richard Mann from *The Daily*. Frowning, she clicks on it and reads the short message.

Dear Olive, I've heard you're looking to move and I'd love to chat. Lots of exciting opportunities here in news, we're making some big investments. I don't want to get into too much detail over email but I suspect you could go a long way with a bit more autonomy. Give me a call. R

Oli throws her phone onto her desk, where it clatters noisily. TJ is really getting on her nerves now. He's clearly been in Richard's ear—she knows they're mates.

She grabs her bag and pulls on her jacket before wrestling it off again and stalking into Dawn's office. 'Where's TJ?'

'Good evening to you too, Oli.' Dawn arches an eyebrow. Over the course of the day her blusher has slid from her cheekbones, giving her a slightly clownish look.

'Where is he?'

'Working, I presume. He's been putting in some serious hours on O'Brien in the background, among other things. When he checked in earlier, he said he was meeting with a source who made contact with him. I mean, who knows if it will *amount* to anything, but—'

'What's going on around here, Dawn?' Oli interrupts.

'I'm sorry?'

'TJ said . . .' Oli stops. Her thoughts are all jumbled.

'TJ said what?' Dawn's freckles are almost completely hidden by her thick foundation. 'Oli, what are you talking about?'

'Have you seen Cooper?' Oli says stiffly.

'Cooper?' Dawn shakes her head, exasperated. 'I thought you wanted TJ?'

Oli glances back out at the newsroom. It's virtually empty. 'Have you seen him today?'

'No.' Dawn gestures for her to sit, looking concerned. 'What's gotten into you lately? Is everything alright at home?'

Oli wavers at the uncharacteristic kindness in Dawn's voice. Her arms and legs feel heavy, and her knees start to give.

'Don't get me wrong,' Dawn continues, 'the podcast is shaping up well, but you seem a bit off. Do you need to take some personal time?'

Noise builds in Oli's ears: a fine thread of sound, like the ground cracking before an earthquake. The memory of Mary's pitying look flares in her mind's eye.

'If you want to have a break, that's fine—we can cover it if we have to.'

Oli blinks. Her eyes feel hot, and she shakes her head.

'TJ's worried about you too, Oli.'

'I bet he bloody is.'

She stumbles out of Dawn's office and calls Cooper again. Gets voicemail.

At her desk, she punches in Kylie's extension without sitting down. It rings twice then clicks, diverting to her mobile. 'Kylie, hi. Do you know where Cooper is?'

'Who's this?' Kylie is somewhere noisy. 'Hang on, gimme a tick.' A series of sounds, like the phone is being thrown around in a wooden box.

'It's Oli.'

'Oh! Hey, Oli. You're after Cooper? Sorry, I left early today. I'm taking my mother-in-law out for her birthday. Honestly, I deserve all the medals.'

'You have no idea where he is?' Oli starts to feel hot and rolls up her sleeves. Lifts the edge of her jumper to fan her clammy stomach.

'Nope. I really haven't seen him much the past few days. He's loving working with you. He's in and out of the office like some kind of spy. Why? Is everything okay?'

'Yes, yes, I'm sure it's fine. We were supposed to meet, but maybe he got held up.'

'He's easily distracted! See you tomorrow.'

Oli pulls on her coat and heads outside. She has no particular destination in mind, but she needs to eat. The icy wind chills her teeth, making her jaw ache. Leaves and rubbish clog the gutters, haphazard obstacles for the rainwater to navigate. She falls into step alongside the throng of suit-clad workers, the beat of their steps matching the throb of her headache. A hearty roll of thunder erupts, and a few people look up and laugh nervously. Oli barely registers it. Faces merge into each other as she walks along Lonsdale Street. Smokers huddle in doorways, blocking lighters from the wind. She ducks into a tiny alcove outside a Commonwealth Bank and scans the street, spotting a wine bar on the other side. She darts across, sidestepping a lycra-clad man who flies past on a bike.

'Ciao.' An artificially suntanned barman greets her when she enters. 'We have hairdryers in the bathroom,' he says conspiratorially, after she orders a hot chocolate and apple pie.

The drink is on her table when she returns from the bathroom. She sips it slowly, the rosy glow of the restaurant washing over her. Her theory from earlier resurfaces, and she fumbles for her phone and calls Miles Wu. 'Miles? It's Oli Groves from *Melbourne Today*.'

'Oh, hi,' he stutters nervously.

'We're still piecing together our story, and I just wanted to ask whether you ever saw anything that made you think the girls might have been involved in creating or selling any kind of explicit content.' She's talking too quickly and tries to force herself to slow down.

'No,' stammers Miles. 'I never saw anything like that. And honestly I just can't see Alex doing that kind of stuff. She was quite a private person.'

'And McCrae never did or said anything that made you think he was trying to coerce the girls into doing something?'

'Like porn?'

'Sure, porn or anything, really.'

'I don't think so. Nicole was the one closest to him, but it didn't seem sexual. It was just weird.'

'I'm also wondering if perhaps they had the internet disconnected because they were concerned about explicit content being traced back to the house.'

'I think that's a bit of a leap,' Miles says doubtfully. 'I really don't think Alex could have been doing that without my knowledge. But Evelyn was really outgoing, and she was trying to crack into the acting scene, so maybe she would have been tempted.'

'But you said it was Nicole and Alex who justified cancelling their home internet,' Oli presses. 'Not Evelyn.'

Miles doesn't say anything for a few moments. 'Yeah, I think it was. Honestly, it's hard to remember, I just thought it was odd that they didn't want it at home. Once you've had internet it's not common to go backwards, right? But like I said, there were computers at the uni, and they had phones so it wasn't like they cut themselves off from the world or anything.' He pauses. 'Is this for the same article your workmate called me about earlier?'

'Cooper called you today?'

'Yes.' Miles sounds wary.

'When?'

'Around three, I think.'

'Why?'

'He was asking questions about that little kid who went missing around the time Evelyn died. He wanted to know whether the girls ever said anything about it.'

'Right, of course,' Oli says. 'Cooper and I keep missing each other today.'

'Okay.' Miles sounds downright uncomfortable now.

He doesn't say anything else, so Oli fills the silence. 'And *did* the housemates ever say anything about the Carter girl?'

'Not specifically,' Miles says slowly. 'Although Evelyn seemed quite upset about it. She was watching the news after it happened, and Nicole turned it off saying it was pointless seeing the same updates over and over, which seemed to really piss Evelyn off. I told Cooper this already.'

Oli ends the call, and the waiter clears the dishes.

A text flashes onto her phone. Cooper, she thinks. But it's Dean.

Why are you lying to me?

CHAPTER THIRTY-ONE

OLI FRANTICALLY PAYS THE WAITER AND RACES BACK TOWARD THE office, heart galloping. She reads Dean's message again, feeling an increasing sense of dread. It's so blunt, so unlike Dean. He rarely shows anger—'optics above emotion' is his mantra at work, and it's a philosophy he extends to his personal life. Hot chocolate sloshes in her stomach. *You can just pretend you were asleep*, she thinks, *that you didn't get the message until the morning. No need to do anything right now.*

The moon hangs low over the city, white and bright. Feeling horribly alone, Oli falls into step behind a group of women waiting to cross Spencer Street. Dean no longer feels like her safety net. She thinks of the twins, and an icy fear clutches her heart. Surely they're fine. Dean is their father; he adores them.

Oli triggers the sensors as she darts across the basement car park. Lights slam on in sequence, *boom, boom, boom*. Fumbling in her bag for her security pass, she takes the lift straight to level five again. It's pitch-black, silent. Breathing hard, she reaches the studio and flicks the light on. Blinks. Scans the room. Were those papers there before? She's not sure, but she thinks so.

Cooper never came back. What the hell is he up to?

She turns on the radio to break the silence and tries to steady her breathing. She needs to calm down and call Dean. Sort all this out. He'll be her husband soon. If she can reassure him, she can buy some time to work out what the hell to do. To work out how she feels. A hopeful thought niggles: maybe it's all a big misunderstanding. She turns down the radio volume and calls before she loses her nerve.

'Hi.' Dean's voice is clipped.

'Hi. Guess what? I got dragged back into work. I was literally in bed when I got the call but I did manage to get some sleep. I just drove back here. I feel terrible.' She knows she is babbling but can't seem to stop. 'I took some Cold & Flu, which helped a bit.'

'Are you at work now?' Dean says slowly, as if he has to think about each word.

'Yep, yep, I'm in the office.'

'At this hour?' His tone is unmistakable—he doesn't believe her.

'Developments on a story.' She coughs several times. 'I need to file something tonight. Dawn's in a state about it.'

'Really?

She laughs lightly. 'Yes, of course.'

He makes a soft grunt.

'Anyway, how are you? I was worried after you sent that message. How are the girls?'

'We're all fine,' he says. 'A few things have flared up with work, but I'm managing them.'

'Sounds like we're in the same boat.'

'I just want to be able to trust you,' he says finally. 'It's not easy, based on our history.'

She squeezes her eyes shut. She's suddenly angry, really angry. Is he trying to confuse things by making her feel guilty? How dare he use their past against her as if she's the only one to blame. He was the one with a wife. He was the one that lost nothing when they split all those years ago. 'Of course you can trust me.'

He sighs. 'I better leave you to it. Don't work too hard, okay?'

'I won't. Night.'

'Night.'

Shaking, she hangs up. Looks at the papers on the desk. Cooper's notes on the wall. Almost immediately, her phone rings. It's Rusty. The sound blares through the silent space, strumming her nerves. She glances around. It feels like a test. She answers.

'Oli!' A buzzing distorts his voice.

'Rusty?'

The buzz settles into a low hum. 'Oli, where are you?'

She shifts forward. The balls of her feet press into the carpet. 'At work.'

'I'm calling about that kid you were with.'

Oli shakes her head in frustration. 'What?'

'The kid who was with you in Crystalbrook. He's hurt, Oli. Bad. We've called his parents, but I thought you'd want to know.'

She slumps back against the chair. 'Cooper.'

'Yeah.' Rusty's voice sounds small, like it's trapped in his throat. 'He was attacked. He's on the way to the Alfred. It's not looking good.'

—

'There, there, just pull up there.' Oli points to the Emergency Department as the cab driver gives her a nervous sideways glance.

Random vignettes of Cooper's quips and expressions fill her thoughts. Those stupid purple headphones around his skinny neck. His ridiculous shoes. He's going to be okay. He has to be.

She tries to remember what Rusty said, but it's like the conversation never made it to the storage part of her brain. That Cooper had been in an accident? Rusty definitely said he was badly hurt. Her face crumples, and she hastily wipes her eyes.

The taxi accelerates up the driveway then comes to an abrupt stop. Her fingers dig into the sides of her wrists. Two ambulances are parked near the entrance; one has its back doors open, and a pair of paramedics are easing out a stretcher. An oxygen mask is clasped over the face of an elderly woman, and a worried-looking young woman in pyjamas runs after the trio as they rush into the hospital.

Oli throws a twenty-dollar note at the driver and yanks open the door. She stumbles as she runs.

This is where she came with her mother all those years ago. She was that girl in pyjamas hovering by Sally Groves's side.

'What did she take?'

'What?' Oli could still taste her mother's vomit on her lips.

'Do you know what she took?'

'I don't know.'

New faces appeared, and Sally disappeared into the bright lights.

'Do you have any idea what made her do this?' a doctor asked.

Dazed, Oli thought about the horrible secrets in her diary. The words that Sally had read. Things she must have known deep down but had somehow managed to ignore.

The paramedic squeezed Oli's arm. 'Hey, you did really well tonight. You saved her life.'

Oli went to the front desk to call Lily, trying not to think the awful thing. That if Sally didn't wake up, Oli wouldn't have to acknowledge what her dad had done to her, that they would never need to discuss it.

The hospital is different now, remodelled and sleek with creamy-white low lights and large potted plants. A crying woman hurtles past, clipping Oli's elbow. She reels sideways, increasingly panicked. But Sally had made it, surely Cooper will too.

Oli follows the signs, praying as she rushes into the crowded waiting room. Several children are crying. A little girl circles a toy train around an ancient wooden track, staring solemnly at all the adults in the room. A shocked-looking couple hold wads of tissues, their eyes leaking as they stare at the carpet.

Phones ring.

Oli feels like she's standing on air.

A blur of blue. Cops.

She staggers to a stop. Rusty is standing with two other officers, talking to a doctor. 'Rusty,' she breathes, hands on her hips.

The cops and the doctor exchange glances. Rusty steps away from the group, his arms out in front of him. The world blurs as she lets him hug her, her face pressed to his chest.

'I'm really sorry, Oli.' Rusty's heartbeat is strong and steady through his shirt, his breath hot on her scalp. 'Cooper didn't make it.'

CHAPTER THIRTY-TWO

COOPER LOOKS IMPOSSIBLY PALE AGAINST THE WHITE SHEETS. OLI stands at the end of the hospital bed and sobs. 'God!' she cries out. She covers her face with her hands. Brushes away the tears that drip down her face. The anger that burns through her is overwhelming. She wants to destroy something. Smash a window. Shake Cooper until he wakes up. She rounds the bed and moves closer to his face. His hair is still thick with wax and stands in a peak. The sheet sits across his neck. She imagines the damage underneath.

How could anyone hurt him?

'I'm sorry, I'm sorry,' she whispers, over and over. 'I'm so fucking sorry.'

He doesn't move, but she can almost hear his wry reply.

Eventually she retreats to the corridor, pulling the door shut even though every cell in her body hates leaving Cooper alone in that empty room. Her throat is sore; she can taste copper. She grips his mother's hands, trying to convey her utter grief and sorrow. His mum is just like him. His dad is short and overweight, with bloodshot eyes. There's a cartoon bandaid on his thumb. Their sadness is so much worse than her own, and their pain merges with hers until she feels she might faint.

'He was so excited to be working with you,' his mother whispers into a tissue. 'He was so happy.'

Oli forces herself to look into her eyes. 'I'm so sorry,' she chokes out. 'He was very special. I was lucky to know him.'

—

Oli holds the toilet bowl as her stomach expels the last of the hot chocolate. She tunes into the hospital sounds. The rattle of metal implements shifting on a trolley as it rolls past. Female voices talking about a physio appointment. The swell of approaching sirens. Oli slumps sideways, tipping her head against the worn porcelain. How can Cooper be dead? The thought hovers around her, refusing to land. Shock continues to slice through her body, and she rolls back onto her knees, dry-retching into the toilet. Cooper's face looms again, and her heaving turns to sobbing, sweat breaking out across her forehead.

Eventually she flushes the toilet and pulls the lid closed. She drops her head onto the surface and shuts her eyes, wishing everything would just go away.

But someone is calling her name. 'Oli? Oli, are you in there?'

With a huge effort, she lifts her head and scans the tiny room. Her satchel lies on the floor under the basin. Her phone is a few centimetres further away on the tiles.

'Oli?'

She staggers to her feet, her surrounds lurching like a sailboat on rough seas.

Rusty is standing outside the door, his face weighed down with worry. The tears come again. He doesn't say anything, just pulls her close, his shoulder propping the door open. He's taller than Dean, her head fitting into the curve of his chin. His shirt becomes wet against her face as his hand traces a comforting circle on her back. 'Come on, let's get you out of here.'

Oli stands in the doorway while he gathers her things. He pulls her satchel onto his shoulder and pats it. He looks ridiculous, and Oli tries to force a smile but it's impossible. 'What happened, Rusty?' she whispers. 'What happened to him?'

'Not here.' Rusty hustles her through the bright corridor, through the crowded waiting room and out into the night.

The tearstains on Oli's cheeks burn in the cool air, and the blue and red lights of an incoming ambulance hit the back of her eyeballs. She rushes to keep up with Rusty's long strides as they cross over a narrow road and a garden bed, entering the hospital car park.

'Get in.' He gestures to a dark sedan, and she does as she's told. 'Want water?' He hands her a bottle from the console, and she takes a few sips.

'I can't believe this,' she says. It feels like the longer she has known about Cooper being dead, the more unlikely it seems.

'Oli.' Rusty takes her hand. Her ring sparkles outrageously in the yellow glare of the streetlights.

She tries to separate herself from the story. Cooper needs her help, now more than ever. 'Tell me what happened.'

'We're not exactly sure yet. It got called in just as I was clocking off, but I went along for back up. We didn't know if it was a street fight or an attack, but when we got there it was just him. Someone stabbed him and ran, Ol. I knew he wasn't in good shape, but I thought he might pull through. I'm really sorry.'

Oli tries to block out the image of a blade cutting through Cooper's skinny body. He never stood a chance. She grips the edge of the car seat with her other hand. Squeezes her eyes shut. 'I don't understand. Was he mugged?'

Rusty grimaces. 'Maybe. His phone and wallet are gone.'

Oli's galloping thoughts come to a halt. 'How did you know it was him?'

'He had some business cards in his jacket pocket. That's when I realised I'd met him with you up in Crystalbrook.'

'Oh.' Oli has a vision of Cooper whipping out his business card to give to Rusty, an earnest look on his face.

'He was on his bike. We're not quite sure whether he stopped for some reason or someone attacked him while he was riding.'

Oli's throat feels like it's closing over. 'God, Rusty. He was just a kid.'

Rusty turns to face her. 'When did you last see him?'

'Yesterday. We had a late lunch in the city.' Her voice is so low, it's almost a hum. 'And we spoke earlier today. I tried to call him this afternoon, but he never got back to me. We were supposed to meet at the office.' She buries her face in her hands. 'I really can't believe this.'

'This is not your fault, Oli, you know that.'

She just shakes her head. The emptiness is taking hold, the utter hopelessness that sinks in when reality is unavoidable.

'I listened to your podcast.' Rusty watches an ambulance fly past.

Oli wipes her face even though tears are still streaming out. 'You did?'

'Yeah.' He rubs his eyes. 'Oli, I want you to be careful. That kind of thing can bring the crazies out. It's more personal than print—people hear a journo's voice, they might develop an unhealthy obsession. Especially with your voice.'

'Don't be silly.' She sniffs.

'I'm serious. People can easily google you, then once they see what you look like, well . . .' He seems annoyed with himself. 'You know I've always worried about you. It's one thing to do what I do, but you're out there asking questions and following people around with no authority and no protection. It's dangerous.'

'Do you think what happened to Cooper had something to do with the podcast?'

'I have no idea, but I still think you should be careful. Maybe he pissed someone off. Maybe he crossed paths with someone who didn't like him asking questions, or maybe it was completely random.'

Oli thinks about Cooper's excitement at the possible link between Evelyn and Louise Carter. His call to Miles. He was so determined to crack the case, to prove himself. Had someone worried he was inching too close to the truth?

'Oli? Ol?' Rusty has been trying to get her attention. 'Do you know what he was doing today?'

'I only met him last week.' A moment of incredulity at this realisation—it feels like so much longer. 'We were working together on the Housemate story.'

Rusty nods. 'Well, it might have just been a random attack. Or possibly racial. We need to check if anything similar has happened recently, or if he received any threats. That's what the guys will be doing now.'

'Where was he attacked?'

'North Melbourne. We'll pull his phone records and see if we can work out if he met with someone. Or was about to meet with someone.'

An ambulance charges into the hospital driveway, colouring the entire area red and blue. The scene from earlier is repeated. Stony-faced paramedics work with practised speed, efficiently ejecting the patient and holding various pieces of medical equipment above the body as they disappear into the hospital. Oli remembers the lactic acid that pumped through her limbs as she ran alongside her mother's stretcher. The cocktail of emotions that percolated as she watched Sally's face loll against the white material, traces of saliva still on her neck and in her hair.

Rusty rubs his eyes again. Yawns. Awkwardly stretches his long legs around the accelerator and brake pedals. 'You going to be okay, Ol?'

She looks at his profile, backlit by the moon. 'I'm glad you're here, Rusty.'

'Yeah, well.' He stares out the window. Doesn't glance at her. 'How did you get here?'

'Taxi.'

He nods. 'I should get you home.' When he turns the key in the ignition, it almost drowns out his next comment. 'Dean will be worried.'

CHAPTER THIRTY-THREE

MONDAY, 14 SEPTEMBER 2015

THE HORROR OF COOPER'S DEATH SEIZES OLI'S BODY THE MOMENT she wakes. She gasps for air in the middle of the king-sized bed, goose bumps rippling along her skin as she curls into the foetal position, hugging her legs and pushing her forehead into her knees. How can it be a new week and Cooper is dead? Yesterday he was alive and now he's dead. It is utterly unfathomable.

Underneath the devastation, persistent thoughts about Dean needle at her brain. She thinks back over the past eighteen months. When they first reconnected, she treated the relationship like a delicate bubble. She cleared her schedule for him, even took time off work to be with him. Their relationship was as addictive as ever. But the high faded more quickly this time. She threw herself back into work and tried to fit him into her world rather than the other way around. In turn, he pressured her to move in. He wanted more of her time. Made her feel guilty about the girls.

Her mind drifts to Dean pinning her down, his strength always teetering on the cusp of feeling dangerous; Dean demanding to know where she is. An uncomfortable medley of their recent conversations plays out in her mind, unease lodging in her gut. His quest for perfection is something she admires, but her inner voice insists there's an edge to it. His need for control always threatens to ruin a moment. The potential to disappoint him feels constant. But, she reassures herself, he's never shown a hint of aggression. He's possessive, yes, but that's not a crime. He might have high expectations and like things to be just so, but he is not violent. He's just not. As if to prove a point, she summons a series of moments: his quiet pride about the girls, the gentle encouragement he offers them. His relaxed teasing. The way he wants to look after her. His generosity. The way her body has always responded to him without hesitation.

Oli switches between dozing and crying. She closes her eyes and tries to think about nothing. After an hour or so, she feels wrung out. She flips onto her back and looks around the room. All of Dean's things are tucked out of sight. Even his nightstand is spotless; the water bottle that is usually there is gone, leaving only a photo of the twins. Oli has no idea what time it is, the block-out blinds doing an effective job. Her phone will be flat by now, and she feels a satisfying surge of rebellion at being uncontactable.

Without warning she's hot and clammy, sweat breaking out across her forehead and behind her knees. The plush pillows and satiny sheets feel revolting against her skin, and she desperately kicks them off, scrambling out of the bed and standing on the carpet in her underwear, breathing heavily, nerves jangling.

Last night, Rusty insisted on walking her to the door when she told him Dean and the girls were away. Rusty's eyes surreptitiously skimmed the house: the manicured front lawn, the standard rosebushes along the driveway. For a moment she thought he was going to offer to stay, but he mumbled something about needing sleep before his early start. Oli wonders if he's seeing anyone, maybe that female cop, but she dismisses the thought and sets about finding her bag. It's hanging on the end of the staircase. She takes out her laptop and phone, and connects them to the charger. Glances at the time: a quarter past nine.

In the shower she works the shampoo into foamy white peaks, lets the soft hum of the pipes massage her thoughts. What was Cooper doing yesterday before he was attacked?

Feeling sluggish, she dries herself and pulls her wet hair into a messy bun. Dresses quickly. Stuffs her laptop into her bag and grabs her phone. Messages fill the screen, and she instinctively goes to call Cooper. Then she pauses, determined not to let the grief paralyse her again.

As she heads down to the garage, the landline in the kitchen rings. She pauses. It's Dean. It has to be. He's tried her mobile and now he's trying to track her down at the house. The electronic trill snakes down the stairs and echoes into the shadowy room. Dust motes are caught in the half-light and swirl around the car like insects. Dean's wall of tools seems to watch her as she stands on the bottom step. She looks at the Audi.

Dean insisted on buying her a new car.

He always seems to know where she is. Where she's been.

Isabelle had an appointment with the lawyers. He knew she was at the gym that morning.

He's tracking her car, she knows he is.

Heart pounding, she heads back up the stairs, leaving the house on foot. She reaches the nearby shopping strip. Calls Pia.

'Oli? Oh my god, it's so awful about Cooper. I can't believe it. Are you okay?'

Oli feels herself cracking. 'I know, I'm okay. You spoke to him yesterday, right?'

'Um, yeah. I was helping him try to find info on the housemates' babysitting jobs. We were trying to access decommissioned websites and see if we could link them to their old mobiles. I spoke to the tech guys but didn't have any luck.'

'When he left the office, did Cooper say anything about what he was doing?'

'He mentioned he was going to the university. Something about a tip-off he got.'

Oli pauses. 'The university?'

'Yes.'

'Okay. Thanks, Pia.'

'Are you coming in, Oli? The cops have been here. Dawn is looking for you. So is TJ.'

'No, I'm sick,' she says. 'Listen, Pia, I'm about to send you episode two of the podcast. Can you get it through approvals? I want it published asap.'

'Even though—'

'Yes,' Oli snaps. 'Let's just get it online today.' She hangs up. Looks around. Spots a taxi rank outside the supermarket and jogs toward it. 'Melbourne uni, please, Parkville campus.'

As they pull into the morning traffic, her mind is trawling the possibilities. Did Cooper arrange to meet McCrae at the university, on a Sunday? Did they have a confrontation? Maybe McCrae followed him. Oli's knuckles are white as they bypass the city. She exits the cab and rushes onto the campus, realising she has no idea where to look for the professor. Students amble past, sunglasses on, earbuds in. She spies a map and hurries over to it, tugging her notebook out of her bag. McCrae's lecture should be starting in twenty-five minutes. She turns to look up at the buildings, shielding her eyes from the morning sun.

Someone grabs her shoulders, hard. She spins around.

'Oli, what are you doing here?'

It's Dean.

—

A basketball bounces past. Around them students talk, laugh, and drink takeaway coffees.

'What am *I* doing here? What are *you* doing here?' Oli's chest heaves as if she's been running. 'Why aren't you in Lakes Entrance with the girls?'

Dean's eyes dart around. 'I'm not supposed to be here. There's an issue. I can't discuss it, but it's going to cause us problems. It hasn't been made public yet, so we're trying to keep a lid on it.' He looks at her pointedly. 'I drove down this morning. I tried to call you,' he adds, reaching his hand out. 'Twice.'

'No.' She shuffles away.

'What do you mean, no?' He laughs nervously. 'Oli, are you alright?'

'No, I'm not.'

He drops his hand, his handsome face uncertain. 'What, because I'm here? Come on, Oli. Check your phone. I left you a message telling you what happened. I was worried about you because you said you were sick, and I figured you might be sleeping in because I knew you worked late.'

Oli tries to push the panic back inside of her, but it's like trying to catch smoke. 'Where were you last night? Were you here in Melbourne?'

He steps forward. 'No, I told you, I drove back early this morning.' He points to the cafeteria. 'Should we grab a coffee? I have a few minutes before I need to meet with Nath again.'

Oli's skin buzzes. Is he lying? Maybe he was in Melbourne yesterday. Last night. 'I don't want a coffee. I want to know what the fuck is going on.'

Dean's eyes narrow, his hands going to his hips. 'Likewise. I've told you why I'm here, but what are you doing here? Were you really sick last night? Are you sure there's nothing you want to tell me?'

Something inside Oli snaps. 'I can't do this right now. I have to go.'

People turn to stare at them, and she knows how it must look: a well-dressed couple arguing like teenagers. They probably think it's a lover's tiff, a wife jealous over a crush her husband has on a student. If only they knew the horrible thoughts crawling around in her head.

Dean grabs her arm, pulls her into a doorway.

She jerks out of his grip. 'Don't touch me!'

'Oli, stop! Stop it.' Dean bares his teeth, his voice rising. 'Just stop it.'

'No. I have to go. I don't want to talk to you right now.'

He deflates. 'I'm going to be sorting out this mess for the rest of the day. Do you want to talk later tonight when you've calmed down? I was planning on driving back, but I can stay.'

'No.' She sniffs, feeling like a child. 'Go back to the twins.'

'Oli, please.' His eyes are huge, bewildered. 'Why are you being like this?'

'Dean, enough. Just give me some space for a little while.'

She leaves him standing in the middle of the path staring after her, fists curled at his sides.

—

McCrae's not in today after all. A tall girl with tinted blue hair sitting up the back of the lecture hall tells Oli he must be sick.

'Or he might be caught up in some research thing. He's involved in lots of different studies.'

'Where's his office?' Oli asks.

Repeating the girls' directions under her breath Oli makes her way to the psychology building. McCrae's not in his office either. She doubles back the way she came and asks at the reception desk.

'He might be around here somewhere, but I doubt it.' A row of hoops line the left earlobe of the young woman behind the desk; a single stud glitters in her right. 'You can leave him a message, or otherwise he'll be back on, um,' she checks a complicated timetable, 'tomorrow.'

Oli exits the building and walks back along the main path, praying she won't see Dean. A young man wearing a vest covered in badges is playing a piano in a sheltered area of the quadrangle, and several students are sitting on the concrete in the sun, listening. It's almost lunchtime, Oli realises, noticing the line of students that snakes out of a cafe. She rounds a corner and almost walks headfirst into Nathan Farrow.

'Oli?'

'Nathan, hi.'

He looks distracted but smiles kindly. She's relieved to see that he has ditched the facial hair. 'Are you here to see Dean? I'm about to meet with him.'

'Um, sort of.'

'Come with me if you like?'

'No, that's okay.'

'Alright then, well, see you later.' He starts to walk off.

Oli blurts out, 'Nathan, did you ask Dean to come back? From Lakes Entrance?'

Nathan stops and turns around, giving her a funny look. 'No, but once he heard what was going on I think he wanted to handle things himself, and I certainly didn't oppose him being here in person. Ken's good, but he's not Dean.' Nathan smiles. 'Why, is everything okay?'

'When did he come back?'

Nathan swallows. 'I'm not sure. We spoke yesterday, so last night? This morning?' He pulls his head back, eyes sliding left then right. 'Ah, why do I feel like I'm saying the wrong thing?'

She bites her lip and tries to stop the tears coming. On the phone last night, Dean didn't say a word about coming back.

Nathan holds up his hands. 'I'm not sure what is going on, but I do know you can trust Dean. He's one of the most reliable people I've ever met.'

She inhales sharply. Nods. It's not like she can tell Nathan what she's thinking.

'I've got to go,' he says. 'Will you be okay?'

'Yes, of course.' She smiles weakly. 'Bye, Nathan.'

As she walks across the campus, she pushes thoughts of Dean aside and digs in her bag for her notebook. Locates the Post-it Pia gave her with the McCraes' phone number.

A woman answers. Diana.

'Hi, I have a courier delivery for a Professor McCrae.' Oli keeps her voice clipped, her tone slightly bored. 'It's from the university. I have East Melbourne as the postcode, but the number and street I have listed aren't showing up on Google. Is it 45 Orchid Road?'

'No, that's completely wrong,' Diana says. 'It's 68 George Street.'

'Typical,' Oli says. 'Okay, thanks. The courier will be around shortly.'

'You're welcome.'

Oli shoves her phone in her pocket, walks out to the street and hails another cab.

CHAPTER THIRTY-FOUR

DIANA AND JULIAN McCRAE LIVE IN A STUNNING DOUBLE-STOREY terrace just a few streets from the Melbourne Cricket Ground. Rich green ivy weaves between cast-iron railings on both balconies, and rows of iris fill the neat front garden. A small pond to the left of the brick path brims with lily pads, and Oli catches a flash of orange scales in the water. She steps onto the front porch and peers into the side window. Sees a large indoor palm. A pair of leather boots.

She presses the doorbell, and a low note sounds inside.

'Coming!' calls a male voice. Julian McCrae opens the door. 'Hello.' He's balding, the remaining hair a light grey. He wears a Reebok sweatshirt, jeans with socks, and holds a newspaper and a pen, midway through a crossword. 'Can I help you?' He smiles, brown eyes kind. He coughs. 'Sorry, I'm a bit under the weather actually.'

Oli notes that he does look unwell, his nostrils red as if he's been blowing his nose.

A woman appears behind him. Pearl-grey hair, an apron belted around her slender waist.

'Professor McCrae. I've been trying to talk to you. I'm a journalist. My name is Oli Groves.'

Diana makes eye contact with Oli, understanding straight away. Her mouth forms a little circle, and she looks nervously at her husband.

'I'm sorry, you're a journalist?' He looks Oli up and down.

'Yes. I'm from *Melbourne Today*. And I want to speak to you about the night Evelyn Stanley was murdered.'

His face drops. Hardens. 'No, I'm sorry. I have nothing to say about that. It's all in the past. And I don't appreciate you coming to my house.' He shakes his head. 'No.'

'Please!' Oli steps into the doorway. 'My colleague was killed last night, and I think it had something to do with what happened back then. Something that someone is trying to cover up.' Does she really think this, she wonders? She pulls out her wallet and fumbles with her business cards, then thrusts a handful at him, several falling to the ground. 'I just want your help. Maybe you need some time to think about it, but please talk to me. Please.'

'I'm sorry. I can't help you.' His voice is quiet but firm. He places his hand on the door, starts to close it. It hits her boot, and he pushes harder.

'Please!' Her throat constricts as she pulls her throbbing foot out of the gap.

'You need to leave, or I *will* call the police,' Julian hisses in the manner of someone not used to conflict. He looks horrified with himself and annoyed at Oli all over again.

The door clicks shut. She stands on the porch, staring at the pond through her tears. On the other side of the door Julian and Diana start to argue, their polite angry voices fading as they move into the bowels of the house.

After a few minutes Oli walks slowly back down the driveway. She's unsure what to do next. She wishes she could talk to Cooper, but he's dead in the morgue, his scrawny body enduring unthinkable examination.

As she wanders along George Street, tears stream down her face. All around her are signs of spring: flowers budding on the branches, bulbs pushing through the ground, birds collecting moss and lichen. But to Oli it feels like everything is falling apart. Cooper is dead, and TJ is waging some kind of war to ensure he's the last man standing at the paper.

And Dean—what is she going to do about Dean? The horrible doubt won't leave her alone: could he have told Theo Bouris where Isabelle was the morning she died? Oli bites her lip. Surely not. No. She's losing her mind. The attack on Cooper has made her paranoid, questioning everything she knows. Dean might have lied to her about his fertility, and about Isabelle's plans, but that doesn't make him a killer. *He lied to Isabelle too,* she reminds herself. *For almost two years he snuck around with you.*

She reaches the corner of Clarendon Street and Wellington Parade. Trams roll past, and the Fitzroy Gardens stretch out in front of her, pretty in the sunshine. She looks around and shivers. Every car that drives past is making her feel nervous. When her phone rings, she jumps. An unfamiliar mobile.

She answers tentatively, trying not to let her voice shake. 'Hello.'

'It's Diana. Diana McCrae.'

Oli's eyebrows shoot skyward. 'Diana, hi.'

'Yes. I'm sorry about before. Julian doesn't like to talk about what happened. That's why I was rude the other day when you called.'

'I understand.' Oli feels slightly hysterical.

'Yes, well. Oh, god, I'm not sure if I should be talking to you, but I think there's something very wrong. I'm not sure what to do.'

'Diana, do you want me to come back to the house? I can come right now.'

'No, no,' she says hastily. 'I'm walking the dog. Do you want to . . . ?'

'Where are you?'

'Let's meet at Yarra Park.' Diana sounds relieved. 'Near the playground.'

Oli is already jogging. 'I'll be there in five.'

—

Perched on a park bench next to a huge German shepherd, Diana is watching two small children play on the slide. Oli takes a seat next to her, and the dog swallows and sticks its neck out to give her a cursory sniff before resuming its position, huge tongue flapping in the breeze. The MCG towers behind them like a castle set against the mottled grey sky. Tall trees line the crisscrossing paths, their fresh new leaves stirring gently. The grass carpet is emerald green. An elderly man zaps by on a motorised scooter, and the children giggle, racing each other to the top of the slide. Oli notices their mother nearby on a picnic rug, arranging little containers of food as she talks on the phone.

Diana thrusts her hands into the thick mane around the dog's neck and gives it a vigorous rub, smiling sadly. 'This is Hugo. He's old and blind and generally out of sorts these days.'

Diana is younger than her husband, perhaps in her late forties. Fine-boned, her tiny frame swims in a long tartan coat. Her luminous skin spruiks the benefits of sunscreen and expensive treatments. Thin gold chains loop delicately around both wrists, and tiny pearls hang from her ears. She seems upset but determined, reminding Oli of an abuse victim ready to talk.

'Hi, Hugo.' Oli digs her fingers into the dog's fur. 'Does your husband know you're here?'

'No, he doesn't.' Diana looks back at the playground, loosens her hair from its clasp. It swings around her face, and Oli smells her perfume.

'Are you in danger?' Oli asks quietly.

'Ha!' The sound is bitter. 'Danger? No, I'm not in any danger. I just think I've been an idiot all this time.' She hesitates, glances at Oli. 'But I guess we are all the sum of the decisions we make.'

'None of this has to be on the record, Diana. Right now I just want to understand what really happened that night on Paradise Street. Because I think it's still happening.' Oli hopes she doesn't sound crazy; the last thing she wants is to scare Diana away.

The woman nods, her eyes glassy. 'I think you're right.'

'What was Julian really doing there?'

'We were going to pay her, you know,' Diana says. 'That's how desperate we were.'

Oli doesn't understand. 'Pay who?'

'We couldn't have children. Well, I couldn't anyway. We'd tried everything—IVF, natural remedies. Even adoption. But there were so many hoops to jump through, and in the end we decided we wanted a biological link to the child. It was tearing us apart. I was a mess, and Julian was beside himself. My husband is a fixer, you see, but he couldn't fix this. It is very strange to grieve something you never had, but that's what I did. I was in mourning.'

'I understand.'

Diana looks at Oli. 'Maybe you do. And in a way, maybe it was worse for Julian. The issue was mine, but he felt helpless.' She adjusts her wedding ring. 'I could actually hear a giant clock ticking. It followed me around, every waking minute.' With a laugh, she adds, 'Probably sounds completely insane.'

'No, it doesn't,' Oli murmurs. 'Not at all.'

'Anyway. Nicole and Evelyn were in Julian's classes that year. He liked them, and I guess they liked him. He met with them outside of class. They were all passionate about early twentieth-century cinema. It wasn't inappropriate or anything. Our situation came up.' Diana waves her hand as if Oli is about to protest. 'I was fine with him talking about it, I wasn't someone who wanted it to be a big secret. But about a week later, Nicole came to him with a proposition. She said she was willing to be our egg donor and surrogate. She had done some research—she wanted fifteen thousand dollars and all of the expenses paid.' Diana hesitates. 'I met her, and I liked her. It seemed too good to be true. Looking back, I can see how problematic it was, but she made it sound so easy, and she was so confident. Her positivity was contagious, and I was desperate.'

Oli thinks about what Cara said, about her sister being able to convince people to do anything. Then she thinks about Nicole throwing Billy against the fence. The more Oli knows about Nicole the more mysterious she seems. 'She was your silver bullet.'

Diana looks grateful. 'She was. I started to hope. She was so young and healthy.' Her jaw wobbles. 'I started to picture our child.'

'But then?'

'A few weeks later Nicole disappeared.'

'Right,' Oli says, trying to fit it all together. 'And this was before you had proceeded with anything?'

'Yes. We hadn't gone through with the insemination at that stage. We'd agreed to it in principle and made a few inquiries, but that was it. We thought it best to wait for her exams to be over.' Diana clears her throat elegantly. 'So she wasn't Julian's student anymore.'

Oli's heart is thumping in her chest. 'Right, so . . .'

Diana transfers Hugo's leash to her other hand, sighs and tucks stray hair behind her elfin ears. 'So suddenly Nicole was gone, and it seemed my dreams were dead in the water again. It was a hideous time. We knew how it looked, Julian being at the house that night with a bunch of young students, but I knew the truth. I had been planning to go with him that night. They were our friends. In a way, it was like Nicole was going to be a part of our family. But we decided not to say anything about it to anyone.' Diana looks pained. 'We didn't want the details of our lives splashed all over the papers, especially because we knew the facts would be twisted into something tacky. After the whole saga, Julian became very introverted. He would barely even talk to me. I knew he felt guilty, which I could understand, but . . . I don't know. Maybe I just didn't want to see what was right in front of me.'

'Which was what?'

Diana's hand drifts down to Hugo again. 'Julian sold some shares about two weeks after that night. A week after that, he withdrew ten thousand dollars from his account. He thinks I didn't notice, but I knew. I've known the whole time.'

'Why?'

She twists her mouth into a line. 'I don't know.'

'You think he paid Nicole? That they were still in contact?'

'That is my guess.'

Oli reels back against the bench. Evie, the little girl, is about ten years old. 'What are you saying?'

'I'm not sure!' Diana exclaims. 'I guess I just didn't want to believe it. For a long time, I didn't want to know. I don't want to believe it now either, but the facts are right there, aren't they?' Julian's betrayal seems to ooze out of her, veins bulging in her neck, in her temples.

'You think they slept together?'

'Yes.' Diana crosses her legs at the ankles. 'We had talked about a medical procedure, but I guess the plan changed unbeknown to me. Or maybe it just happened. I fell a little bit in love with her, maybe Julian did too.'

'Do you think that's why she disappeared?'

'I wondered. I thought maybe she felt guilty about what happened and fled.'

Could that be it? Could Nicole's disappearance and Evelyn's murder be unrelated?

'I'm not sure that would be enough to make her abandon her whole life,' Oli says. 'It must have had something to do with what happened to Evelyn.'

Diana shrugs and fondles Hugo's ear.

'We need to find Nicole,' Oli says. 'We need to find out what really happened that night.'

'But I don't understand the rest of it. Evelyn being attacked like that was awful. Julian was so upset—he might not be perfect, but he didn't have anything to do with that. He did come home early that night.' She sighs. 'Since the ten thousand dollars, he's withdrawn more money.'

'How much?'

'Around seventy thousand dollars, I think. His mother died a few years ago, and I'm not across all of the assets. It may be more.'

Oli's eyes bulge at the amount. 'I don't understand. Why wouldn't he just tell you?'

'I don't know,' says Diana, her jaw shaking. 'Guilt, I suppose. Fear that I'll leave, maybe?' She glances at Oli before looking back at the children, who are now picnicking with their mother. 'There's more. He took a phone call on Thursday. After he answered it, he went to the study and shut the door to continue the conversation. It was very out of character.'

'Did he say who it was?'

Diana purses her lips. 'He said it was someone from the university, but then on Friday he withdrew twelve thousand dollars from his savings account. That's his limit. He doesn't know I have his password.' Diana looks up, her blue eyes sparking with rage and something else: determination. 'Later that day I followed him. He said he was going in to work, but I knew he was lying. He went to a house in Carlton. I couldn't see very well, but I think a woman answered the door.' Diana tenses. 'I think she's there. I think Nicole is there with my baby.'

AUGUST 2004

Fuck, Alex thinks. *Fuck.* This is bad, really bad. She stares at the wooden panelling, allows her vision to fall out of focus.

Nicole looks pretty when she cries, not red and blotchy like most people. 'It was only the one time,' she says, wiping her eyes. 'I had to babysit, that's how we pay rent, it's what we all do for work. And then I got sick last week and just ran out of time.' She glances at Alex and Evelyn. 'We're all really struggling to get by. Our parents aren't wealthy, and my dad is paying for some expensive medical treatment so they've stopped paying for my textbooks.' Nicole breathes through a sob. 'This whole thing is totally my fault—it was my idea, and I guess I just didn't think it was going to do any real harm. We're housemates, we study together all the time. It's not like we're bad students. Alex was just doing me a favour.'

Alex looks at her friend, wondering if any of this is true. Nicole has never mentioned that her dad is unwell, but you can never be sure with her. She is the human equivalent of an onion, revealing new layers when you least expect it.

The professor folds his arms and reclines back in his chair. He has evenly tanned skin and good teeth, but he needs a haircut. Despite his neat clothes he often conveys a slightly flustered vibe, walking a little more quickly than is required. One of Alex's foster mothers told her that you should never hurry in public, that it makes you look stupid. Alex can't even remember the name of that foster mother. She runs through a few options, but nothing seems right. Danielle? Emily?

Unfortunately, the professor doesn't seem flustered now. He seems completely in control.

The three of them never talked about what would happen if they got caught. *Don't jinx it,* she remembers Nicole saying when Evelyn voiced her doubts. *If we keep it simple, it will be fine.*

Nicole is good at calming people down. She usually isn't scared of anything, and her conviction is contagious. But right now, even she looks rattled.

It made sense: they all agreed with that. There just wasn't time for them to do everything. Evelyn's auditions would pop up out of nowhere, clashing with her classes, and they needed to make time for babysitting and waitressing or they'd have no money. Study was always pushed to the bottom of the list. Alex had studied several of Nicole's subjects the previous year, Evelyn the others, and vice versa. It was easy to rework old essays and assignments.

It's smart, Nicole had insisted when it first came up. *We're using our initiative. This way we all play to our strengths. And there has to be a benefit to us all looking so similar—we're like sisters.* She'd grinned at Alex, holding her hand up. *And Evelyn's a weapon when it comes to essays. We all win.*

Alex had high-fived her back, but her stomach had rolled. And when she'd showed Nicole's ID at the exam entrance, trying to look as nonchalant as possible, she'd thought she might pass out.

It wasn't supposed to be all the time. They still went to tutorials, the occasional lecture. But it took the pressure off, and Nicole was right, it was smart. For the past twelve months they'd all averaged distinctions. They'd worked more and finally earned some decent cash. And it was never as bad as that first time. It got easier.

There was tension, though. The loose rules they had all agreed to slipped a little. Evelyn started complaining that she was doing more than her fair share. They got sloppy. The essay that Alex and Nicole handed in for their psychology class was too similar, with short sections copied and pasted. They'd argued about it, but there hadn't been time to change it.

Alex wrinkles her nose. The professor's office smells of body odour, damp boots and old coffee. Someone should open a window.

A few weeks ago, Alex was in her bedroom, and Nicole was in the backyard smoking a cigarette while talking on her phone. Alex overheard her mention a deadline and that she could pay two hundred dollars. She'd gone outside the group, and now they're here, probably about to get expelled. Blacklisted from every university in the country. Everything Alex has ever worked for is about to go up in smoke.

'Nice try,' the professor says eventually. 'But I'm well aware this isn't the first time, Ms Horrowitz. I have proof.'

Nicole's eyes narrow momentarily before widening in protest. She opens her mouth, but he holds up his hand.

'I understand how challenging it is when you come into financial hardship.' He takes off his glasses to rub at his eyes. 'How it can lead to poor decisions.' Returns the glasses to the bridge of his nose. 'Decisions that have long-term implications.'

Nicole nods slightly. Alex holds her breath as the energy shifts in the stuffy room.

'But perhaps you are willing to make this all go away. And earn the money you need to build a wonderful future.' His hands make the shape of a triangle, neat fingernails meeting at the top. He looks at Alex, then at Evelyn. 'I must say, the alternative is not good, not good at all.'

Alex closes her eyes, fear gripping her heart. She doesn't want to touch him, doesn't want to let him touch her. She thinks back to some of her foster brothers, the things they made her do.

'Yes, of course.' Nicole wipes her eyes. 'Of course we are.'

The professor puts his elbows on the desk. 'I'm glad to hear that. It's really very simple. And it's important to remember that no one gets hurt, that's the beauty of it.'

CHAPTER THIRTY-FIVE

OLI LEAVES DIANA ON THE PARK BENCH, HER PETITE FRAME HUNCHED over as she pets Hugo. She's finally free of her secret, but Oli's not sure it will bring her any peace. She heads back toward Nicholson Street, turning the whole thing over in her head. It makes sense that Julian went to the house that night if he thought he had a chance of sleeping with Nicole, but why did he invite Diana to come with him? He couldn't have predicted she would get sick. It must not have been planned at all; maybe Diana has it wrong and Julian is giving money to Nicole for some other reason—or giving money to someone else altogether.

Oli peels off her coat, flushed from walking. She crosses at the lights and heads along Hoddle Street. A man holding a toolkit passes by and whistles under his breath. 'Hey, blondie.'

She ignores him, keeps walking. Even if Diana is right about her husband, none of it explains why Evelyn was murdered. McCrae might be guilty of infidelity, but everyone agrees he left the house by ten. He's not a killer, but maybe he set off a chain of events that led to her death. Perhaps Evelyn found out about Nicole and Julian, and threatened to tell Diana. Or Alex found out, and somehow Evelyn got caught in the fray, trying to break up the argument? But that doesn't seem to fit either. Surely Alex wouldn't be that upset about Nicole sleeping with one of her professors, at least not enough to grab a kitchen knife and stab Evelyn four times. Unless she was in love with him? The housemates taunt Oli, their faces trading places in her mind. She desperately wants to speak to Cooper, even TJ, but neither is an option. Her feet sweat in her boots.

She'll have to go to the house in Carlton where Diana followed her husband on Friday. But before that, Oli's going to prison. It's time to talk to Theo Bouris.

—

Oli has been in close proximity to murderers during her time as a crime reporter—mostly in court, once at a crime scene, and twice when she conducted interviews in prison. Only one, Jackson Roy, completely unnerved her, eagerly recounting his gruesome crimes in explicit detail, and repeatedly commenting on how much Oli reminded him of his third victim, a budding poet called Sienna Forrest with whom Oli shared more than a passing resemblance. Roy got under her skin, which crawled for days, but she knows evil exists on a scale just like everything else. Thankfully Roy is a rare breed of human. Most murderers made a terrible mistake, a poor decision. Drinking too much, driving too fast. Like most things in life, murder isn't as black and white as people would like it to be.

Oli isn't sure what kind of murderer Theo Bouris is. He's from a crime dynasty of sorts: generations of people intent on colouring outside the lines, offspring resolutely groomed for the family business. Hardwired to feel hard done by, men like Bouris don't tend to embrace self-reflection, but perhaps some of his hubris has faded now that he's in his forties and facing up to another twenty years in prison. Regardless, he was the person who killed Isabelle. He cut her life short and ultimately changed the trajectory of Oli's. The thought of being in his presence is both horrifying and magnetic.

Oli pulls her newly rented Toyota into the visitor car park and enters the prison. She presents ID, goes through security. She tugs at the hem of her shirt and tries to get some air against her skin as she waits. After thirty excruciating minutes, a guard who looks well past retirement age leads her to a closed door at the end of a short corridor. He stops and turns to her, his fingers on the doorhandle. 'Any problems, you just yell out, but you should be fine. He's restrained and generally pretty even-tempered. He can be a funny prick, to tell you the truth. Anyway, I'll be right outside.'

Oli nods. Swallows and wipes her palms on her jeans. Steps inside the windowless room. There are three tables, and Theo Bouris sits at the one furthest from the door. Five chairs are arranged in a messy circle to his left as if the occupants exited the room in haste. Scuff marks from the rubber tips of the chair legs cover the grey lino.

The door closes behind her. Bouris looks at her expectantly, smiling. He has dimples. She takes a step backwards. What the hell is she doing here?

'Hello,' he says. 'Today is clearly my lucky day. Please sit down.' As he reaches out his hand, the chains around his wrists clink together. 'Already regret coming to visit me?' He shrugs good-naturedly. 'Fair enough.'

'Sorry.' Immediately cursing herself for apologising, she sits in the chair opposite Isabelle's killer. She has seen footage and photos of him—the truth is, she devoured everything she could find about him online when he was arrested—but in person he looks younger than she expected. He's attractive, his features symmetrical except for his nose, which bends roguishly to the left. A small bruise blossoms on his temple, but other than that his tawny skin is clear.

She has a strange urge to ask how he is, but he gets in first. 'How are you, Miss Journalist?' He looks amused. 'No, don't tell me. You're trying to get inside the mind of a killer? Grappling with good old nature and nurture?' He laughs, revealing straight beige teeth. 'Am I on the right track?'

'No.' Her hair swings forward as she rests her elbows on the table. 'I want to know how you knew where Isabelle Yardley was going to be the morning you killed her.'

Bouris cocks his head. 'Righto, we're playing that game, are we? Right, right.' He strokes his stubble, his gaze piercing. 'We had a special bond, Yardley and me. I could sense she was going to be there.'

Fury bursts like a dam inside Oli. 'Bullshit.'

'Okay, fine.' He traces his finger across the table. 'I followed her. You haven't done your homework, you naughty girl.'

'I know what you said in court—I just don't believe you. I think she would have noticed if an amateur like you was following her, especially that early in the morning.'

He throws his weight back against his chair, his face sullen.

They sit in silence for a few moments. Tingles run up and down Oli's limbs. 'I think someone told you Isabelle was going to be there.' She almost chokes on the words. 'And I want to know who it was.'

He eyes her with renewed curiosity. 'She was a friend of yours?'

'Just tell me,' Oli says through gritted teeth. 'What have you got to lose now?'

'I'm a man of my word.' He crosses his arms.

She stands, pushing back her chair, her legs shaky. She can't tell if he's messing with her or not.

'Your perfect detective friend wasn't so perfect, you know.'

'What do you mean?'

He shrugs. 'Just that. Perhaps you didn't know her as well as you think you did.'

Oli has an urge to laugh before her hands start to shudder uncontrollably. 'If you're not going to tell me, there's no point me being here.' She takes a few steps backwards, wanting to keep her eyes on him.

'I might have got a call.' His voice snakes through the air between them.

She stops. 'A call.'

'Yeah.' He holds out his thumb and little finger then puts them against his head, miming a phone, and grins. 'You know, a call.'

'From who?' Her jaw feels like it's going to come off its hinges, it aches so badly. She can't bear for him to say the words, but she has to know even if it breaks her heart.

Bouris clicks his tongue. 'I can't say. That would be completely unprofessional.'

To Oli's horror, a tear slides down her cheek. Her mind glitches. She is Isabelle, standing in front of the man who mowed her down. Fine-boned, with long black hair, her ice-blue eyes pleading to know who wanted her dead.

Oli chokes on a dry sob, threads of saliva caught between her lips. 'Please.'

Bouris makes a sad face. 'Oh, honey, I want to, but I can't. I made a deal with the devil himself. All I can say is that someone hated that smug bitch even more than I did.'

CHAPTER THIRTY-SIX

THE GUARD UNBOLTS THE DOOR. IT SCRAPES HORRIBLY AS HE PUSHES it open. Oli rushes down the corridor, avoiding eye contact with the other guards before bursting through the double doors and into the late afternoon sun. A horn blares, and she stumbles backwards, narrowly avoiding being hit by a spluttering Mitsubishi. It burps a cloud of smoke from its exhaust, and Oli stands frozen on the kerb, her stomach clenching.

She thinks of Dean's huge empty house and wonders if she should call Lily, ask if she can stay with her and Shaun. But it feels too dramatic, like a kid running home to its mother.

The last of the adrenaline leaves her system, and her teeth start to chatter. She rubs her arms through her jacket sleeves and gets back into the rental car. Cranks the heater. She stares straight ahead, her brain numb. A woman in a bright-yellow jumper with a long braid down her back bursts from the prison entrance, her face streaked with tears. She runs off down the street, her handbag slapping against her leg.

Shuddering through a deep breath, Oli calls Rusty.

'Oli?' His voice almost has her in pieces.

'Rusty.'

'Ol. Are you okay?'

'Is there any news on Cooper's attack?' she chokes out.

'No, I'm sorry. We've got nothing yet.'

'Right.' She feels a crushing hopelessness.

'We're still going through everything, though—CCTV and phone records. We went to your office this morning and took his computer and some other items. If there's anything to find, we'll find it.'

'He also works—' Oli cuts herself off. The cops don't know about the studio, and all of a sudden she wants to keep it that way.

He mistakes her hesitation for emotion. 'Ol, I promise to let you know the moment we find anything, okay?'

She sniffs.

'Are you sure you're alright?'

'Rusty, I think something's going on.'

'What do you mean?'

'I don't know.' She begins to cry. 'I think it's all linked.'

'Hey. Oli, talk to me. What's linked?'

She bites one of her fingers. It hurts. 'I've just been with Theo Bouris.'

There are a few beats of silence. Rusty's breathing intensifies. 'What? Why would you do that?'

The words come out in a rush. 'I think someone tipped Bouris off about Isabelle that morning. He wasn't acting alone.'

'Oli.' Rusty sounds wary.

'I'm serious!'

He breathes out in a whoosh. 'Where are you now?'

'At the prison.'

'You're driving?'

'Yes.'

'Right,' he says. 'I'm at home. Come past, we'll go and get some food. Talk. I don't think you should be alone right now.'

She bites her lip. Decides. 'Okay. I'll be there soon.'

—

The sky darkens as Oli drives back toward the city. She pulls up at a set of lights, keeping her gaze fixed forward. Feels the person in the next car staring at her. She shifts lower in her seat. Exhales as the traffic gives way and starts to flow.

Twenty minutes later, she arrives at Rusty's townhouse in Kensington. Flashes the headlights into the front window a few times. His front door swings open, and he steps out and saunters down the path. He gets into the Toyota and looks at her doubtfully. 'Oli,' he says simply.

Her shock has given away to a grim determination. She throws the car into drive. 'I don't care if this all sounds crazy. I think there's more to Isabelle's murder than everyone thought.'

He flicks at the plastic sign hanging off the rear-view mirror and glances sideways at her. 'Not your car?'

'It's a rental.'

'Okay.' He looks out the window then back at her. 'Want to tell me why you're driving a rental?'

She doesn't take her eyes off the road. 'Not really.'

Pulling at his jaw, he shifts in the seat. She can tell he's tired. He's wearing a baseball cap, and his freckles glow against his pale skin. 'Want to tell me where this theory on Bouris came from?'

'Still no.'

He expels air from his nostrils. 'I understand Isabelle's death must hold a strange fascination for you.' He holds up his hands as if Oli has protested, before adding, 'But I'm not sure that digging around, meeting with scum like Bouris, is a good idea.'

She indicates and speeds up to overtake a station wagon. 'But if someone else was involved in her death and was working with Bouris, then surely the police would want to know, right?'

'Of course! But you don't need to get involved.'

'Really? 'Cause it doesn't seem like you guys did a very good job the first time around.'

'Oli.'

She hovers on the brink of tears, desperately trying to keep them at bay. 'She was going for a run, and someone set that . . . monster on her.' Her face spasms. 'I mean, fuck, Rusty, her kids were waiting for her at home.'

He rests a hand lightly on hers. 'Your stepdaughters.'

'That's not why it matters!'

He removes his hand. Gazes out the window. 'I'll look into Bouris. Dig around and see if something turns up. If anything feels off, I'll put in a request to reopen the investigation.'

'Thank you,' she whispers.

Shadows crisscross their faces as they pass under streetlights.

Rusty shifts in his seat, turns to face her. 'Ol, I want to be here for you, I really do, but it's hard for me to be around you. Surely you must know that?'

Oli's stomach lurches. She pulls over outside a pizza parlour, turns off the car. Through the window a couple is having dinner, and the woman laughs then rolls her eyes. Oli tips her head forward and rests it on the steering wheel. 'Rusty.'

'It's fine. I know you're upset about your colleague, and about what Bouris said. And of course I care about you, but that doesn't mean it's easy.'

'Do you remember that day we went to Siglo? On the rooftop?'

'Yes,' he says, looking puzzled. 'We were celebrating that series you wrote on domestic violence. Why?'

'Remember how you announced to the whole bar how amazing I was and how proud you were of me?'

He smiles. 'I was a bit tipsy. But I *was* proud of you. You worked so hard on that story, and it was really important.'

'It was sweet when you did that,' she says quietly. 'I always felt like I could do anything when I was with you.'

'Huh.' He slumps back against the seat. 'Come on, Ol, that's clearly not true.'

'It is true! It's just that things got really confusing, and I got scared.'

He snorts. 'What, of commitment? I'm sorry, Oli, but you ditched me and shacked up with a widower and his two children six months later, so if you want to talk about confusing I think you win.' Rusty lightly cuffs the window with his fist.

'I was with Dean before.' Her voice sounds hollow.

'Before what?'

'Before I was with you. A long time ago.' Saying it aloud is bizarre, years of deceit purged in an instant.

Rusty is shaking his head, clearly trying to understand. 'Hang on, but he was with—'

'I was with him when he was with Isabelle,' she interjects.

'When?'

'Ten years ago.'

'Jesus, Oli, for how long?'

'Long enough.' She glances at him. 'It really screwed me up.'

'You should have told me.'

She manages a laugh. 'I didn't think it was much of a selling point.'

'I guess not.' His face relaxes, and she can tell that he is thinking. 'Were you with him when you were with me?'

'No, I wasn't. Never. I hope you believe that. I didn't see or speak to Dean until weeks after we broke up.'

He releases a breath. Clasps his hands together, then takes Oli's. 'Well, I'm glad about that. I don't know why it matters, but it does.'

She grips his hand back. They watch the couple in the restaurant for a few moments.

'After Isabelle died you were different.' A statement.

'Yes,' she replies. 'I was.'

He nods. Swallows noisily. 'Should we get some food?'

Oli pulls her hand away and starts the car. 'Maybe later. First there's something we need to do.'

—

Oli's admission hovers in the car like a fog, but Rusty doesn't ask any more questions, for which she is grateful. She guides the car past the sweeping grounds of the museum. Despite the cold, diners spill out onto Faraday Street, cheerful groups talking and laughing as waiters rush back and forth from the kitchen to the tables. People in gym gear jog along the footpath, snaking from side to side to avoid a collision. A rider flies past on his bike, almost clipping the side mirror.

Oli's resolve crumbles. 'Can you get my phone? The address is in the notes.'

He finds it in her bag and looks at the screen. 'Dean has called you three times.'

'It's fine.' She tells him her password, and he plugs the address into the GPS.

Just before the Johnston Street intersection she turns left, then left and right down a few streets until they reach 19 Flockheart Lane. She turns off the GPS and checks her phone. Dean has sent a text. *I've gone back to Lakes Entrance. I'll give you some space but we need to talk later this week. I love you.*

Rusty looks at the house. 'Are you going to tell me who lives here?'

She yanks the handbrake, trying to push Dean from her mind. 'I don't know who lives here.'

'Oli,' he says.

'Julian McCrae came here a few days ago, and there's a chance that Nicole Horrowitz is here with her daughter.'

'Are you serious?'

Oli gets out of the car. 'Come on.'

'Oli, if that's what you really think, then I need to call in backup.'

'I thought that's what you were,' she quips, already halfway up the narrow path. She rings the doorbell.

Rusty stops a few steps behind on her right, primed to go into cop mode if it's required.

Movement behind the door. A key turns in the lock. A face appears in the narrow gap. Oli blinks as a baby wails from somewhere in the house. 'Cara?'

Oli remembers what Cara said about her sister when they met at the cafe. *I wasn't immune to her. Plus, she was my sister. It was just the two of us.*

'What the hell are you doing here?' Cara's eyes drift to Rusty. 'And who is he?'

'It doesn't matter.' Oli's mind is whirling.

'It matters to me.' Cara's bright-pink nails curl around the edges of the door. 'How dare you turn up to my house late at night with no warning and bring some strange man with you.' She glances backwards, and Oli wonders if Nicole is inside. 'I don't even *know* you.'

'It's okay, I'm a cop,' Rusty says.

'That doesn't make me feel better. You need to leave. I already told you everything I know.'

'I don't think that's true,' Oli says. 'Please, Cara, let us in. I know you want to do the right thing.'

'No, I just want you to go.' She pushes the door closed, and for the second time today Oli jams her boot in the gap, although this time she shoulders it wider too.

Rusty steps forward. Cara pushes back, but she's not quick enough, and the door swings open. Oli falls into the hallway. Gets her bearings as quickly as possible and rushes forward. The baby is still crying, but she can't tell from which direction the sound is coming. Rusty yells out, 'Stop!' and Cara grabs her from behind, tugs at her coat, but she makes it to the end of the hallway. Cara pushes past her then reels around, her dark eyes full of fire. Rusty is behind her, his breathing heavy.

'Get out now.' Cara's collarbones are like knives pointing out of her heaving chest.

'Cara, let us help you,' says Oli.

The baby isn't crying now, and the house is silent apart from their breathing.

'Help me what?' Cara seethes, her face distorted with fury.

Oli's eyes jump around the room. A messy bookshelf. A colourful rug. Photos of Cara with a baby.

'Who lives here with you, Cara?' Oli's husky voice rumbles.

'It's just me. Just me and my kid. And I want you to leave now.'

'I don't believe you. I think she's here. I think Nicole is here.'

The women lock eyes, both burning with intensity.

'Maybe we can sit down,' suggests Rusty.

Oli senses movement in the hallway behind them. She shifts sideways, her gaze still on Cara as she slowly turns. In her peripheral vision she sees a figure coming up the hallway.

Rusty murmurs something under his breath.

'No.' Cara lifts her arms in pointless protest.

A little girl stands at the mouth of the hallway. She has clearly just woken up, her blonde hair flaring messily around her face.

A long T-shirt skims her knees, an AC/DC logo splashed across the front of it.

'Go back to bed,' Cara says.

'No!' Oli says. 'We want to talk to you. Is your name Evie?'

The little girl nods.

'What's going on, Oli?' Rusty is holding his phone.

Oli puts her hands on her knees. 'Where's your mum, Evie?'

Evie looks at Cara then back at Oli. She takes a step away.

'Please leave us alone,' Cara says hopelessly.

Oli ignores her and tries to remain calm. 'Can you tell me where she is, Evie?'

'Oli,' Rusty cautions.

The baby begins to cry again, in long screeching wails that dance up Oli's spine. She moves toward Evie and kneels on the floor, knees cracking. 'Evie, I'm looking for your mum. Is she here?'

Evie shakes her head.

Oli's stomach drops as an anvil of realisation ploughs through her, the past few days streaming by in fast forward. She looks at Evie's face: her wideset eyes, snub nose, ivory skin. Wavy blonde hair.

'My mum's gone,' Evie says, as Oli scrambles to her feet.

It can't be true, but she knows it is. She backs away from Evie and collides with Rusty, who grips her shoulders. 'Rusty,' she breathes.

'I'm calling Bowman,' he says firmly.

Cara is crying. Her sobs merge with the baby's cries. 'Please, let me explain.'

'Rusty.' Oli's voice catches. 'Oh god.'

He's already on the phone, giving someone the address. After he hangs up, Oli pulls him into the corner of the room, still staring at Cara and Evie.

'What is it, Oli?' he says, looking into her eyes. 'What?'

'It's her,' she whispers. 'I think we've found Louise Carter.'

CHAPTER THIRTY-SEVEN

RUSTY TALKS TO EVIE IN THE KITCHEN WHILE CARA TELLS OLI THAT Nicole is gone. She had called Cara out of the blue on Tuesday morning, pleading for her sister to come pick up her and her daughter from Warrandyte. She needed a place to stay. She'd finally escaped an abusive relationship that had essentially seen her a prisoner for years, and asked if Cara could find it in her heart to forgive her, to let them stay. She wanted to protect her daughter, the one good thing in her life. Cara insists that Nicole refused to talk much about the past, but said Alex had threatened her that night at Paradise Street, screaming at her after acting oddly for weeks. Nicole said she had no idea what set her off. 'When Nicole told Alex she would call the cops if she didn't calm down, Alex threatened her with a knife,' says Cara. 'Apparently, Alex just kept saying she had got herself mixed up with some bad people, and that the same people now wanted her dead. She accused Nicole of being a snitch and said they were all in real danger,' Cara says. 'That's why Nicole left. She was absolutely terrified.'

'Where was Evelyn when this happened?'

'Asleep, I think. Alex must have killed her just after Nicole left. It sounds like she was having a full paranoid episode.'

'She didn't have a history of mental illness,' Oli says.

'Well, perhaps whatever drugs she was taking messed her up.'

'Did you believe Nicole?' Oli asks, trying to decide how she feels about this version of events. It's basically the same story that Alex told everyone in court about Evelyn. It's clear one of the girls lied, but with Alex and Evelyn both dead it's impossible to know which scenario is bogus.

'She seemed pretty upset. She wouldn't talk about Alex's suicide except to say that the guilt of killing Evelyn must have got to her. I asked her if she saw Alex when she came to Crystalbrook, but Nicole just shut down and said she didn't want to talk about it.'

Rusty's voice drifts in and out of Oli's consciousness as he talks gently to Evie.

'When did Nicole leave here?' Oli says quietly.

'Friday. She left a note on the bench asking me to look after Evie for a few days while she sorts some things out.' Cara's eyes brim with tears. 'I didn't know what to do. And I was so fucking angry. I kept telling myself she was coming back, that she would come back for Evie, but she's not, is she?'

Oli senses that Cara was initially flattered by Nicole seeking her out, but now she feels betrayed—and taken advantage of. She should have known better.

'Did she say anything about her ex-partner?' Oli asks just as a pair of cops arrive.

Oli and Cara remain opposite each other in the lounge. The baby suckles noisily at Cara's breast, his tiny hand sporadically smacking against her shoulder or reaching out to grab her shirt. Cara's either forgotten her question or is ignoring it. She stares straight ahead looking stunned but also resigned, as if part of her expected something like this to happen.

'A man came here on Friday,' Oli says, as Cara rearranges her clothes and burps the baby, his head bobbling atop his neck while she holds him over her shoulder. 'Do you know who he was?'

Cara shakes her head. 'I don't know anything about that. But I went out to do some shopping in the afternoon, so maybe he came then? I took the kids with me. Nicole was gone when we got home.' Cara is completely deflated now, it's clear there is zero fight remaining in her.

'Why did you meet with me last week?'

'Nicole wanted me to. She wanted to know what you knew.'

From the other side of the room, Oli can hear snippets of Rusty's account of the situation. He explains his relationship to Oli, the words 'journalist' and 'ex-girlfriend' breaking through the multiple conversations buzzing around the room. There's something wrong with his tone. Ever since Oli told him she thinks Evie might be Louise Carter, he's been distant.

Another detective squats in front of Evie, the little girl listening solemnly to whatever he's saying. Cooper would be losing his mind at the turn of events. Oli tries not to think about him. Her jaw starts shaking just as the kid looks over at her. She stares back at Evie, and her grief turns to rage. She clenches her fists and drags one of them across her face, flicking the tear away.

She stands up and walks to the back door. Slides it open and steps outside. Shuts it behind her. Rusty calls out to her from the other side of the glass. She ignores him and tries to get a handle on the emotions bouncing around in her skull.

It's cool out. The white light of a plane flashes intermittently as it glides through the navy sky. After a few minutes, the door swooshes open. Oli tenses but keeps her eyes on the plane, anticipating Rusty's gentle coaxing to come inside.

'Ms Groves. It seems you are trying to promote yourself from writing the news to *being* the news.'

She whirls around. Bowman. He's wearing the tan trench again but with corduroy pants and a black jumper instead of a suit. He's clearly come straight from bed, with grey stubble peppering his fleshy cheeks.

'I think that might be Louise Carter in there,' Oli cries, stabbing her finger toward the house. 'I think Nicole Horrowitz has been hiding her away for ten years!'

'Well, we'll have to see about that.' Bowman's baritone is authoritative as always, but Oli senses he's unsure. His normally stony face has softened, and he glances from her to the house.

'You need to find Nicole.' Oli's chest heaves, her cheeks burn. She fights an urge to scream into the night.

Bowman nods slowly. He eases his hands into his coat pockets and looks up at the stars. 'I appreciate your urgency, Ms Groves, but this is a criminal investigation and we need to take things slowly.'

'Fuck that,' mutters Oli.

He doesn't reply, just looks at her.

She explodes. 'I mean, come on! What are you waiting for? How can you stand it, not knowing the answers? It's *unbearable.*' She reels around blindly, almost losing her balance on the edge of the small porch. Her sadness is heavy, both rising up and bearing down.

'I'm sorry about your colleague,' Bowman says bluntly. 'I know what that's like.'

Against her will, Oli's face twists.

'Were you at home with your family last night?'

She shakes her head. 'No,' she murmurs. 'They're away. I was at work until Rusty called to tell me about Cooper.'

Bowman clears his throat.

'What?' she asks.

'This is bigger than you know.'

She turns slowly to face him again. 'What's that supposed to mean?'

He sighs. 'I think you should head home.'

'Cooper thought there was a link between the housemates and Louise Carter, you know.'

Bowman's expression doesn't change. 'Do you know what made him think that?'

Oli pictures Isabelle's handwriting in the diaries. 'I don't know.'

Bowman lifts his head and looks back at the sky. 'Good intentions aside, it's not helpful when people who have no information try to connect dots that aren't there. There is a lot of information you don't have.'

'I don't care what Nicole told her sister. Those girls, they were all involved in something bad. It wasn't just Alex.' She pauses, catches her breath. 'Did *you* think there was a link between the housemates and Louise Carter?'

He glances inside. Scratches his head. 'I'll give you an exclusive, give you a quote, but I want you to hold off for a few hours. Let us have a chance to work through this mess.'

'Until when?' she counters. She can't get anything in print tomorrow now anyway—a few hours exclusive online is probably the best she can expect at this point.

'How does midday sound?' He coughs.

A possum rustles the leaves of a nearby tree, and they both look in its direction.

'No, earlier,' says Oli. 'How about 9 am?'

'You've had a busy day, Ms Groves. And a difficult week.' Bowman seems to hesitate. 'Constable Frost tells me you're under a lot of pressure, and with what happened to your colleague, well,' he holds up his hands, 'you really should get some rest. We can talk in the morning. I'm sure I can work with your deadline if required.'

His tone is patronising, but when she meets his gaze she only sees concern. Has Rusty told him about her visit to Bouris? She crosses her arms to try to keep warm. 'I want everything you have,' she says, forcing herself to look him straight in the eye. 'Everything.' Oli catches Rusty staring at them from the kitchen window. 'And you should know, I'm not scared to run a story on how you failed to draw a link between the cases ten years ago.'

A white puff of air bursts from Bowman's mouth. 'No point standing around in the cold, then. I'd best get to it.' He turns on his heel and stalks back into the house.

CHAPTER THIRTY-EIGHT

TUESDAY, 15 SEPTEMBER 2015

OLI DRIVES STRAIGHT TO THE OFFICE. BOTH HER HUNGER AND exhaustion have vanished, no match for the fiery charge of a story. The streets are almost empty, giving the world a strange apocalyptic feel. Nineties hits play on the radio, the graveyard shift DJ recounting stories from his youth in between songs. Oli taps her fingers along to Green Day, Nirvana, No Doubt.

At the office she pauses briefly at the news desk to speak to Kay, a plump redhead who has been working nights for over a decade. Oli tells her she will file copy for editorial to review by 8 am. Suggests she get the legal team on standby. Without a word, Kay plonks her romance novel on the desk, moves her hands to her keyboard and starts to type.

As Oli takes the stairs to the studio, she fishes out the keys Cooper gave her. She flicks on the light and blinks as her pupils adjust. Cooper's juice is still on the table alongside his pens and notebook. She ignores it all and sits facing the door, opens her laptop. Flexes her fingers.

Oli writes hard and fast, her typing like gunfire. Her eyes sting and her back aches, but she doesn't stop until she's done. She re-reads the piece, replacing some words here and there, then emails it to Kay. Slumping back in her seat, she feels stunned; blood pounds through her head as if she's been running, and her arms and legs are floppy and weak.

She left Rusty at Cara's house with Bowman, barely saying goodbye. Shame at her earlier confession has crept in, paired with guilt at dragging him into her mess. He makes her feel safe, but he can't be her saviour. She feels caught between the past and the future. The perfect life with Dean that she had been sailing toward now seems completely out of reach. Maybe it always was.

Her encounter with Theo Bouris plays over in her mind. Someone must have tipped him off about Isabelle, cut him a deal to hunt her down. He wouldn't have needed much convincing—he was on parole, hours from being hauled in for a spate of fresh crimes, and he surely revelled in the idea of going down in flames. Killing Isabelle was his grand finale, and an act that quite possibly secured him some kind of financial future for his wife and kids while he was in gaol.

Oli's thoughts go to Dean again, her emotions running in opposite directions. She wants to be with him, back when it was just the two of them lost in their bubble. Not with the Dean who has appeared these past few days, the one she can't trust. The one she worries has done something truly evil.

On a whim, she turns on the sound system and moves to Cooper's chair. She puts on the headphones and speaks into the mic, her deep voice extra gritty from the lack of sleep. She provides some background on Isabelle, then on Bouris, explaining how they came to meet, before detailing Isabelle's final moments. Oli pauses before switching to the present. She lays out the questions that have plagued her during the past few days, then describes her visit to the prison.

Blood thrumming, she ends with an appeal for information before pressing stop. She pushes the equipment to the side and rests her arms on the table, tips her head forward and sleeps.

—

Oli wakes with a jolt. No concept of time. Checks her phone: almost 6 am. Ignoring a voicemail from Kay, she finds some gum in her bag and brushes her hair. She feels supercharged, as if she's drunk a dozen coffees. She plugs the recorder into her laptop, downloads the file she recorded about Isabelle's murder and attaches it to an email for Dawn, typing *Idea for a new podcast episode* into the subject line. Next she reads over the piece she wrote about Nicole and Evie, the babysitting link, and the possibility that Evie is Louise. The words are unfamiliar, as if written by a ghost. She sends it off to Kay and copies Dawn, explaining that Bowman agreed to revert to her by 9 am.

Sitting back against the chair, she looks over at Cooper's scrawled notes. Doubt grips her. If Nicole took Louise in 2005, where did she hide the little girl the month before she disappeared? Not the Paradise Street house—even if Alex and Evelyn were involved, it would have been impossible to conceal a one-year-old from Miles and the neighbours for over three weeks. Unless Louise was drugged, perhaps. But why would Nicole take her?

Oli presses her fingertips into the arches of her eyebrows. Julian McCrae went to Cara's house last Friday, that much is certain.

Just before Oli shuts her laptop, she notices the *Melbourne Today* home page is advertising a new episode of the Housemate podcast. The second episode is live. The last thing she and Cooper worked on together. She bolts from the room before the tears take hold.

—

The McCraes' double-storey terrace looks enchanted in the early morning light. Insects create a pretty haze across the small square of lawn, and ivy ripples gently at the eaves. Oli presses hard on the doorbell and glances nervously behind her. She's hedging her bets that the cops won't come calling here until later this morning, once changeover has happened and Bowman has had some sleep. A rustle inside makes it clear that she has woken the McCraes, and she braces herself for a confrontation.

Julian opens the door, Diana behind him. A repeat of the scene from yesterday—god, was it only yesterday?—but this time the couple are bleary-eyed, hair matted, dressing-gowns thrown over flannel pyjamas.

'Oh.' Julian looks both surprised and defeated.

Diana's small face puckers with nerves.

'Sorry,' Oli says. 'I'm sorry, but can I please come in? It's important.'

A beat goes by, but she can tell they will acquiesce. It seems they don't have the energy to turn her away, perhaps sensing the inevitability of what is to come.

Diana ushers Hugo ahead of her into an airy kitchen. 'Coffee?'

'Yes, please,' Oli says.

The house is stunning, a perfect alchemy of glossy textures. Tasteful art adorns the walls, flowers bursting from perfectly positioned vases. The kitchen looks out across a light-grey courtyard to a garden studio weighed down by ivy. A sparrow dips in and out of a sculpted bird bath, framed perfectly in the window.

Oli runs a finger under each eye, adjusts her coat. She must look awful.

Diana busies herself in the kitchen, and Julian watches her before his gaze drifts to Oli. 'Have a seat,' he says formally.

They sit opposite each other, waiting for Diana. She places a steaming mug down in front of Oli, hands her husband an espresso cup. They sip their drinks in unison. Oli puts hers on the coffee table, while Diana and Julian cling to theirs, eyes huge.

'Nicole Horrowitz has been in Melbourne this past week,' Oli says. 'But you both already know that.'

Diana's mouth falls open. Julian doesn't move.

Oli fixes her gaze on him. 'I know you met with her. You gave her money. Why?'

He puts the cup on the table and takes his wife's hand. Looks at his feet, clad in dark-green slippers.

'Professor McCrae?'

'Yes, yes. I mean, Christ, what do you want me to say?'

'How about the truth,' Diana says firmly.

They lock eyes. A long look.

'Yes, I gave her money.' Head in his hands.

'You've been giving her money for years,' says Oli. 'Why?'

'Because I was trying to do the right thing!' Flecks of saliva fly from his mouth. 'I didn't know what else to do.'

'Tell me what happened,' Oli says.

He moans quietly. 'She, Nicole . . . She was impossible.' He looks to Diana for confirmation, turns back to Oli. 'She was. In the beginning she was going to help us. We'd become close.' He holds up his hands. 'Nothing inappropriate, she was my student, but I guess I admired her. She had spunk. Evelyn did too, although she was more introverted. I enjoyed their company. One night we went to a student play in the city and got a drink afterwards. I told them that Diana and I were having trouble conceiving, that she'd been told she couldn't have a baby.'

Next to him Diana uncrosses her legs, recrosses them.

'It felt like it all happened quite quickly.' Julian looks confused. 'Nicole did some research and proposed how it might work, what we would pay her and such.' He glances at Diana again, who nods absently. 'It felt right. She was so sure of it all. It was as if we'd met her at the perfect moment.' His forehead crinkles. 'But then it all went horribly wrong. We became friends. All of us.' He squeezes Diana's hand again. 'Nicole was a real intellectual, wise beyond her years, and I liked talking to her. We discussed waiting until November to go ahead with the procedure—after exams. She came here for dinner once, then she invited us to dinner.'

'At her house.'

Julian moistens his lips. 'Yes.'

'But you didn't go,' Oli says to Diana.

'Diana came down with a migraine,' Julian answers for her. 'But I felt like I should still go.' He pauses. 'Nicole was very friendly, but the others were clearly uncomfortable that I was there. Even Evelyn seemed a bit frosty. I could tell something odd was going on between the three girls, although it was only the second time I met Alex.' He hangs his head. 'Even now I can't really explain it. It was the most reckless thing I've ever done. I was drunk, but I realise that's no excuse.'

'What happened?' Oli presses.

'After I'd been there a couple of hours, Nicole made it clear she wanted to sleep with me.'

Diana flinches.

'I came back from the bathroom, and she pulled me into her room. She said she'd had a terrible few weeks, that things weren't going her way and that I could make her feel better. She said we had a connection and that if she had our child it was essentially the same thing anyway. It was almost November. I was aroused, yes, but I also felt compelled. I don't know how else to explain it. Basically

I wasn't thinking, and what she was saying about the baby made sense in my muddled mind. She was so insistent, very determined. She locked the door and that was that.'

The house is silent. The McCraes' expensive appliances don't even hum.

'Afterwards I was mortified—I barely spoke to her, just said goodbye to the others and left.' He brings his hands together. 'I think for days I was in shock, not just about what had happened to Evelyn but also what I'd done. And once we learned Nicole had disappeared, I suppose I assumed it was my fault. That she was upset about what happened between us. I didn't know what to do. All I wanted was for it not to have happened.'

'You didn't tell anyone?'

'Not a soul. Diana was very upset about Nicole's disappearance. Not only were we worried about her, but she had been our source of hope. I have to admit, however, that a part of me was glad. I wanted to forget what had happened, and that would have been easier if she was gone.'

'But she wasn't,' Oli says.

'Well, not exactly. She contacted me, maybe eight weeks later.'

'Where from?'

'I don't know.'

'What did she say?'

'She said I had to give her money. That she was pregnant and that if I didn't give her money she would tell everyone I raped her that night and that's why she disappeared.'

Diana looks stricken. 'Oh, Julian.'

'So you sent her the money?' Oli asks.

'Yes.' He nods miserably. 'To a PO box in New South Wales.'

'And you've been doing that ever since?'

'Yes.' His voice is barely audible. 'She said that if I didn't, she would tell the child that I'd refused to provide support for her. It seemed like the least I could do. Over the years I sent money wherever Nicole asked me to.'

His sadness is contagious, and Oli feels it deep in her bones. 'What happened last week?'

'My mobile was playing up, and Nicole called me at the house. Said she was in Melbourne. I'd obviously seen the news and I was worried. She sounded desperate and asked me to bring her money in person.' His eyes snake to his wife. 'A large amount of money. She said I could meet the child.'

Diana flinches again.

'And I wanted to,' he says. 'I wanted to. In case it was my only chance.' As he looks at Diana, his expression is full of pain. 'I met her, the girl. Spoke to her. I barely talked to Nicole.'

'Did Nicole say anything about her plans?'

'No, not a word. I didn't ask any questions, not even about Alex's suicide. I just wanted to make sure the girl was okay.'

A truck shudders by in the street, causing a minor tremor.

'What happens now?' Diana asks quietly.

'Well—'

Oli's phone starts ringing, and they all jump.

'Good morning, Ms Groves. I hope I didn't wake you.' Bowman's voice is jarring in the sunny room.

'No. I'm up.' Oli glances at the McCraes, who look like they've been pulled from the wreckage of a car.

'Good. This is just a courtesy call based on our conversation last night. I thought you'd be interested to know that the child you saw last night is not Louise Carter, so I would strongly advise your organisation against making any references to this theory.'

Bowman adds, 'That's not all. She's not Nicole Horrowitz's daughter either.'

—

Oli gets into the Toyota and calls Bowman back. 'How do you know it's not her child?'

'Nicole has a condition that prevents her from having children. She had surgery as a very young child. Only her parents knew. Apparently, it caused her a great amount of distress as a teenager.'

Oli stares up at the McCraes' house. After Bowman called she made hurried excuses and left. Now she feels like her head is about to explode. 'But Nicole promised the McCraes.'

'What's that?' Bowman says.

She closes her eyes and tries to focus. 'Are you sure Nicole can't have children?'

'Based on what I've been told, I'm one hundred per cent certain.'

'And you're sure the kid isn't Louise Carter?' Oli almost screams.

'Yes. The forensics don't match. The investigation into Louise Carter's disappearance remains open.'

Oli's voice cracks as she says, 'Well, who is the child, then?'

'We don't know. Perhaps she belongs to a friend or an ex-partner. But we may never know.'

She kicks her leg out in frustration. 'This is bullshit.'

Bowman sighs. 'Ms Groves, I suggest you update your story and do your radio show, then get some rest. Take some time off. I'm still happy to provide a quote. Finding this child is still good work—you should be proud.'

A strange energy takes over Oli, a desperate feeling. Like everything is slipping away. 'What did you mean the other night when you asked me about Isabelle? About Dean telling me what she'd decided. Was it about not wanting to be a detective anymore?'

Bowman sounds confused. 'No, as far as I know she was still passionate about being a detective. But I do know she was finding other aspects of her life challenging.'

Oli swallows. 'Do you think Bouris acted alone?'

'I have never had a prouder moment than when we put that piece of shit away,' Bowman says with frightening intensity.

'Did he follow her from the house that morning?'

'We think he was following her for days.'

'But—'

'He is a monster. Pure evil.'

'Do you think it's possible he was tipped off? I've been wondering—'

'Get some sleep, Ms Groves.' Bowman hangs up.

Oli throws the phone in the console and starts the car. Nicole's manipulation is starting to become clear. She fooled everyone. She connects to Bluetooth and calls Dawn.

'I need to change the piece I sent you,' she says in greeting. 'Apparently it's not the Carter girl. But I've found out more about Nicole that I think is worth digging into. I think she might be involved in some kind of fraud—'

'We're not running them, Oli.' Dawn interrupts. She is in the office; phones bleat in the background, and a familiar voice is reading a news report. 'We're not running either of them.'

'What?' Oli asks, accelerating into the morning traffic.

'Oli, I appreciate that you've been working around the clock, but this isn't right. You need to slow down.'

'My piece needs to be re-worked, I get that, but why can't we run the podcast? I deliberately avoided hard claims. I know it needs editing, but I don't know how to do that.' Her voice cracks. 'I'm sure someone in Kylie's team does.'

'We can't risk it with the cops. And as far as I can tell, it's just your opinion. I think you're too close to it.'

'You mean *you* don't want to risk it.'

'Oli.'

'What? When did we lose the last of our spine?' She drops her voice. 'Come on, Dawn, this is important. This might prompt someone to come forward. People were sending Cooper emails after the first Housemate episode.'

Dawn sighs. 'Oli. I know you're upset about Cooper, but this isn't good. You're acting erratically. Update your piece if you can, and I'll review it, but the podcast episode you recorded is not going to happen. I'm not about to start an all-out war with the cops over a hunch.'

'But I'm on their side! Surely, everyone will want Isabelle's death re-examined if it turns out there's more to it.'

'Just focus on the piece.' Dawn's tone teeters on the edges of being patronising. 'We need to have a broader conversation about the podcast anyway and how we manage it going forward. I don't think it works with one person. I'll set up a meeting next week.'

'Hang on, wait. What do you mean?'

'We'll talk about it next week,' Dawn says firmly. 'File your piece if you want, then have a rest. Take the time.'

She hangs up, and Oli cries out in frustration. She's past tired now, somewhere in between furious and hopeless.

Outside Breakers there's a one-hour park that she eases the Toyota into. She orders a coffee, barely acknowledging Col, and stares moodily out the window while she waits. If the little girl isn't Louise and isn't Nicole's, then who is she? And why did Nicole offer the McCraes the chance to have a baby if she knew she was infertile? Why did she seduce Julian that night? Was it just to have the upper hand, a reason to blackmail him?

Oli's focus blurs as she stares at Col frothing the milk. She jumps when he calls her name.

'Looks like you need this today,' he says with a wink.

—

Back in the studio, Oli dumps her bag on the desk and looks at Cooper's timeline on the wall. His things on the desk. 'I'm so sorry,' she says to the empty room.

She sits and opens her laptop. She tries to edit the piece, massage it into a different shape, but without the Louise Carter revelation it loses its structure. And Nicole is still missing.

Giving up, Oli finishes her cold coffee and throws the cup in the bin. Amid the maddening churn of theories about Nicole, the conversation she needs to have with Dean is like a vice around her brain. Restless, she scrolls through her emails until she comes across several Cooper sent on Sunday morning. Her heart jolts as she remembers what Pia said about him chasing down something at the university after he received a tip-off.

All the emails were forwarded from the podcast address he set up. Two are from people spruiking theories about the housemates, claiming to have known the girls. Another Cooper has forwarded with a note: *I'm going to call her and see if she's legit.* Oli reads quickly: a woman who went to Melbourne uni at the same time as the girls believes they might have been involved in selling child pornography. She was approached to do the same thing.

Oli almost falls off her chair as she reaches across the table to grab her phone. She calls the number at the end of the email.

'Hello?' A woman's voice.

'Hello . . .' Oli frantically checks the name. 'Zoe? This is Oli Groves, I work at *Melbourne Today.* I've read your email. The one you sent in after we published the podcast.'

Her voice turns solemn. 'I saw the news about Cooper. I'm not sure I want to talk to you.'

Oli swallows. 'Why not?'

'I just . . . I don't know. As soon as I sent the email I regretted it, then I spoke to him the other day and look what happened.'

Oli's eyebrows knit together. 'Hang on, you think what happened to Cooper is linked to you contacting him?'

'I don't know,' Zoe says. 'Maybe. It's the reason why I didn't say anything for so long.'

'Please talk to me. I need to understand what's going on.'

'I want to, I'm so sick of not saying anything, but I'm not sure it's safe.'

'Please, Zoe,' Oli says. 'It's so important that if you know something you tell me. You know that, right?'

'Okay, look, I don't want to be linked to this at all. I mean it.'

'That's fine. Just talk to me, please. Tell me what you told Cooper.'

Zoe smothers a sob. 'I was a messed-up kid, okay? Drugs and whatever. But I was smart and I did alright at school. I got into uni and I was doing my best, but I was still struggling. I had no money, and my parents kicked me out, so I was doing whatever I could to earn cash—selling weed, stripping, the usual. Anyway, I got into some trouble with drug possession, stealing and stuff, and things weren't great for me. I met this girl and I was telling her how fucked things were, and she said there was an easy way I could make some cash.' Zoe pauses. 'It was so weird, but I was desperate, and she said there was this group of people who, like, sourced photos of kids.'

All the air seems to leave the room. 'You mean pornography.'

'Yeah, I guess. But not like, explicit or doing sex stuff. Just shots of them in the bath or getting dressed or whatever. She said it could be kids you knew or kids you babysat. The whole conversation was pretty bizarre.'

'Was it one of the housemates?' Oli can barely breathe.

'No, I'm sure it wasn't. It was a blonde girl. She had a tattoo on her neck under her hair. I don't know who she was.'

'Did she say how it would work?'

'Just that you would upload photos to this website. I think it was untraceable somehow.'

'Like a hidden Dropbox.' Oli remembers covering a story a few years ago where files and images were traded on the dark web.

'I guess so. She said you could do it at the uni library through a dummy account.'

Oli's eyebrows shoot up. 'At the library?'

'Yep. She said the whole thing went all the way to the top, and that's why it was safe—that no one involved had ever got in any trouble.'

'What did she mean by "the top"?'

'I dunno. Like, people with influence, I guess. She said that you could earn thousands of dollars, but that if you screwed it up or went to the cops or whatever then the guys running it could set you up for another crime and land you in gaol. That's how much power they had.'

'Zoe, when was this?'

'2004.'

A horrible thought anchors in Oli's gut.

'I didn't do it, by the way,' Zoe says. 'I kind of flipped out over it and ended up dropping out of uni and moving to Queensland.'

Oli's thoughts swarm around each other. 'And you told Cooper all this the other day?'

'Yeah. He asked lots of questions too. He asked if the girl I spoke to back then ever mentioned the premier.'

'John O'Brien?'

'Yeah. I said no, but he still seemed pretty fired up about it.'

Oli is struggling to concentrate. 'Thanks, Zoe, I really appreciate you talking to me.'

'Just be careful. Back then I could tell this was big and now, well, people are dying. I just don't know how far this goes.'

Oli hangs up, completely overwhelmed. Isabelle knew about this, she is sure of it. She glances at Cooper's notebook. Remembers writing Rusty's number on the front page. Did Cooper call Rusty and tell him what Zoe said? Did Rusty know where he went that day?

She starts pacing around the room, ignoring her ballooning bladder as it strains against her stomach. Clearly Cooper thought that O'Brien was involved or he wouldn't have asked Zoe about him. That line of thinking would have led him straight to TJ, seeing as it is his story. So Oli calls him.

'Oli! I've been worried about you. Are you okay?'

'TJ, did Cooper call you the other day?' She's practically yelling.

'I'm so sorry about what happened to him, Ol, it's just awful. They think it was a mugging, right?'

'Did he call you, TJ? About O'Brien?'

'We had a conversation.' TJ sounds perplexed. 'Downstairs in the newsroom. He asked a bunch of questions about whether I'd ever come across any suggestion that O'Brien was linked to a porn ring or whether any of his ministers and senior staffers had been. Cooper asked if I could get him a list of staff names from a few years back. Why?'

The anchor drops deeper in Oli's gut. 'Did you? Did you get him the list?'

'I didn't have a chance, but he said he had a few names to run with already. He, ah, he said not to mention it to you. Oli, what's going on? Is this porn thing legit? Please let me help, I feel terrible about the past few weeks. I've acted like a total wanker.'

Suddenly all her irritation toward TJ fades away. She's known him for so long, and despite his ego and the office politics there is genuine care and respect between them. Plus, she desperately needs an ally. She gathers her things, feeling short of breath. 'Okay, look, I know it sounds crazy but I think the housemates were selling pornography. Photos of kids they were babysitting. My source claims high-profile people were involved, but I don't know how far it goes. Find out whatever you can. Dawn's blocking me, but we can meet up later. Away from the office.'

'But, Oli—'

'I've got to go.'

AUGUST 2004

Funny how you can suddenly become someone you never thought you'd be. Do things you never thought you'd do, good and bad. Like that time Alex slapped her foster sister across the face when she told everyone Alex stole the biscuits from the kitchen. Or that time in high school when she realised she actually understood how to do the equations Mr Ayles was writing on the board.

Progress, thinks Alex, it's all progress. New things.

The professor explains what he wants them to do. The terms are clear: refuse, and they can kiss their future at the university goodbye. He has more than enough evidence to get them expelled. He also hinted at his ability to get them in trouble with the police, mentioning another student that found herself facing unexpected drug charges. Do what he asks, and there is serious money to be made. They stand in his office, breathing in the stale air, listening to him describe how it works. How it is foolproof.

The three of them leave his office in silence. Everything feels different. The air, the light.

'See you at the house, I've got class,' says Evelyn, fleeing to the bathroom. Alex can tell she's upset.

Alex and Nicole walk side by side down the scuffed corridor.

'Fucking hell,' Alex says.

'I know,' Nicole says. 'It's insane.'

'Do you think he's serious?'

'Absolutely. We do it, or we're screwed. I think he could stitch us up way beyond just being kicked out of uni. You heard him.'

Alex laughs, the sound hollow and wrong. She laughs again.

'I think we have to,' Nicole says. 'I mean, he's right, it's not like anyone gets hurt.'

Alex recognises her pragmatic tone. She's always explaining why certain things make sense.

They push through the doors and step outside. Everything looks the same. Strangers file past. A couple lie on the grass, kissing.

'We don't want to get kicked out.' Nicole slides her sunglasses on. 'Or worse.'

Alex's nostrils flare as she inhales. Thinks about what the professor said.

'We don't have a choice,' Nicole adds, with a resolute nod. 'You can tell he's not the kind of guy to mess around. I'll sort out Evelyn, don't worry.' Nicole veers off toward the cafeteria. 'Coming?'

Alex stands still, a thousand thoughts passing through her brain in one beat. As though for a second, she is more than just Alex. Tectonic plates shift deep in the ground. Lava churns. 'Yep.' She follows her friend across campus, the professor's camera heavy in her backpack.

CHAPTER THIRTY-NINE

TUESDAY, 15 SEPTEMBER 2015

OLI NEEDS TO LEAVE. NEEDS TO PACK HER THINGS AND LEAVE. ON some level she knows that she will need to confront Dean, that she can't just disappear, but the primal pulsing urge is to get out. She does her best to ignore Amy and Kate's pale faces lurking behind Dean's in her mind. She momentarily wonders if they will care if she leaves, but this thought morphs into a more pressing question: *Are they safe?*

The Toyota roars beneath her as she overtakes a delivery van on Swan Street. Its driver leers at her as she passes, a cigarette wobbling on his lip as he yells obscenities.

Jesus, she needs to calm down. Is it really possible? Could Dean be involved in all this? And if he is, how could she not have known? She thinks about Amy's night terrors. Could they be a result of abuse? Anxiety grips her like ice. What if Isabelle found out that Dean was harming the girls. He would have done anything to cover that up.

God, she wishes she could talk to Cooper. She calls Lily.

'Oli. Hello.' Lily drawls. 'This is a nice surprise. What's been going on?'

Her sister's voice triggers something, a disorienting sensation, like the road beneath her is water. 'Lily,' she manages to choke out.

'Ol?' Lily's voice loses all its sarcasm. 'You okay?'

'Not really.'

'Okay.' Oli can tell Lily is nodding. 'Where are you?'

'Driving.'

'You safe?'

Oli is flooded with nostalgia. That used to be their thing. *You safe?* they would text each other when one got home to find the other still out. *Yep, safe,* the other would reply.

It started after their mother was released from hospital, hollowed out and broken with guilt about what had been going on under her roof for all those years. About what had been done to Oli.

Well, it had actually started before that, when Oli would wake up in the morning with a migraine and refuse to go to school, and Lily would wait for Sally to leave for work then sneak into Oli's room, her eyes asking the question. Oli always nodded, even though she wasn't.

'I'm safe,' she says now.

'Are you working?'

'No, I just left.'

'Want to come over?'

'Can I stay with you for a while, Lil?' Oli wipes her nose, which has started to run. Sniffs. Tries to hold it together. Fails.

'You want to come stay at our place?' Lily asks, unable to hide her surprise.

'Yes,' Oli whispers.

Lily talks so fast her words tumble over each other. 'Of course, that is totally, absolutely fine. Yes, definitely.' She takes a breath. Pauses. 'You can stay with us for as long as you want.'

'Are you sure Shaun won't mind?'

'I don't give a shit if he does mind.'

Oli laughs through her tears. 'Thank you,' she whispers. She reaches the familiar curve of the road. She's almost at Dean's house. Her house. A muffled whimper escapes her mouth, and she bites the side of her knuckle.

'Oli, what is it? Please talk to me.'

She gulps in some air and forces herself to focus. 'I'm okay. I just need time to think, and there're a few things I need to do. I'll be at yours later.'

The sisters hang up. Oli pulls into Survey Drive and presses the button on the front-gate remote. 'Come on, come on,' she whispers. God, it's so slow. She puts her foot down and jerks the Toyota through the narrow gap while the doors are still opening, parking on an angle in front of the garage. The house looms over her, the cream façade looking dirty in the fading light.

The moment she gets out of the car, it starts to rain. Giant drops fall from the sky and splatter messily on the driveway. She stands smoking on the front porch as she stares into the downpour. The light is on upstairs at Toni's house, and Oli wonders what she's doing. She allows herself to admit that something probably happened between Toni and Dean after Isabelle died. Oli sucks hard on the cigarette, smoke filling her lungs. Maybe something happened between them when Isabelle was alive. Hell, maybe it's still happening.

'Evidence,' Oli murmurs, wiping her nose and eyes. 'There's no actual evidence.' Even in her own mind she is circling around the clues, not quite letting thoughts bind together. She's aware of the desperate way her brain is trying to counteract the possibility that Dean is far from the person she thought he was. Surely, *surely*, the police examined every aspect of Isabelle's death until they were satisfied he had nothing to do with it. The husband is usually under suspicion, but Dean was never a suspect, never linked to Bouris. Pages of Isabelle's diaries roll through her thoughts. Is John O'Brien behind all this? Did he somehow recruit Dean when they used to work together? Amy and Kate appear in her mind again, and she shakes her head. *No, no.* She just can't see it. He's not capable of this kind of evil. Even if O'Brien is involved, she's sure Dean isn't.

Another thought slams in: the twins might not be his biological children. Maybe Isabelle used donor sperm. If the girls aren't his, does that change things? Probably not. It certainly hadn't stopped Oli's father.

More tears come. Since the moment she met Dean, their connection has been intense and primal. Although muted over time, dulled by domesticity and proximity, it is still undeniable. But what if it's a trick? What if she's somehow drawn to danger because of what happened to her?

She sways, her knees threatening to buckle. Smoke hits her lungs, and she holds it there for a moment. The rosebushes along the front garden bed are perfectly spaced, giant white buds on the brink of bursting open. Dean loves those roses. Last year, when she was still living in her apartment, he would bring her one every week and present it to her when she opened the door. A sweet, small gesture that drove her crazy. They are probably Isabelle's roses.

When they first started seeing each other again, Dean never mentioned Isabelle. After a few weeks of bliss, of Oli pinching herself, she got up the courage to ask him about his dead wife.

I need to move on from Isabelle. I want to build a future with you, Oli.

And she lapped it up. She didn't want to press it, didn't want to ruin the magic. But he has lied to her—not once, but over and over. And she was so desperate to believe him. How pathetic.

She tries to remember the conversation they had when he asked her to move in. The scene flickers in her mind's eye, and it's hard to grab on to the exact words, but she remembers one sentence clearly: *If you decide you do want a baby, I'm in. I'd do that for you.* Discomfort squeezes her insides as she remembers the rush of pleasure that bloomed in her chest.

Oli knows how this ends. She's judged women in this very situation, women so blinded by love that they refuse to see what's right in front of them. Worse, she has pitied them. Even now, she's looking for excuses, ways that she might be wrong about Dean. Trying to reason around his lies, justify his actions. *Stop it*, she admonishes herself. *Stop trying to fix this for him. Just get your things and get to Lily's. You can work the rest out later.*

She extinguishes her cigarette against the concrete pillar, leaving a black smudge on the white paint. The scent of fresh rain mixes with the dirty smoke, and she takes a few deep breaths. Pulls out her keys.

Rusty calls, and she doesn't answer. She sends him a text saying she's resting and will call later. The thought of talking to him right now makes her claustrophobic.

She slides the key into the door. A flash of light behind her is followed by thunder, cracking like a whip through the darkness. She spins around, hand at her throat. The sky opens. Sheets of water fall, turning the front yard a hazy white. Her hand slips down to feel the mad fluttering of her heart. *It's just a storm*, she tells herself. *They've been predicting it all week.* But she has always hated storms. Hated what they help to conceal.

She enters the house, pulling the heavy door shut behind her, sealing out the chaos.

A text from Rusty: *Can you talk? Just found out that Bouris's missus bought a new house a few months after he was put away. It's a big place. I'm trying to trace the cash but it gives some credit to your theory.*

Another wave of tiredness hits. She was right: Bouris was paid to make the hit on Isabelle. *Please find out what you can,* she types back.

Nerves dance across her skin as she ignores the chiming grandfather clock, ignores her reflection in the huge round mirror on the wall. She heads straight upstairs to the bedroom, her thighs aching as she skips every second step. After flicking on the bedroom light, she sets about reversing her steps from months earlier, pulling clothes from hangers and bundling them into her suitcase, shoving in shoes and underwear. In the ensuite, she grabs her make-up bag and toiletries from the cupboard shelf. Lightning slices the sky. The rain keeps tumbling down. Returning to the bedroom, she piles the armful of things into the suitcase, remembers the pair of runners under the bed and jams them down each side, zips it shut. She yanks it upright and surveys the room. Like the rest of the house, it's glossy and plush, luxurious textures blending perfectly with modern technology. Nothing in the house creates friction; every room flows into the next. Not like Lily's ramshackle bungalow with its rabbit-warren layout, or their childhood home, Oli's bedroom an afterthought tacked onto the end of a long corridor separated from the rest of the house.

She props the bulging case against the door and sits on it. Watches tree branches lift and jerk in the wind. She squints, and Isabelle appears. Lying on the dark bed, faint at first then clearer, silencing her alarm and staring at the ceiling for a minute before she slips out of bed. She stands next to her sleeping husband, her bare feet on the creamy carpet as she reaches her hands into the darkness, arching her back, her long wavy hair spilling down. She moves like a cat, careful not to wake Dean or the girls. Applies deodorant in the bathroom, sits on the side of the bath and pulls on socks. Isabelle glances at Dean, still asleep in the bed, then skips right past Oli, heading down the stairs. She will be dead in less than two hours.

What was she thinking? Had she told Dean it was over, or was she still working through her plan? What did she think he was capable of? Did she have any inkling she was in danger?

Oli stands, weary. She follows Isabelle down the stairs, the suitcase slamming painfully into her thigh. Rusty sends her another text. *I just want to make sure you're okay. Are you alone?* She hauls the suitcase from the bottom step onto the smooth white entrance tiles. The dying tulips Dean gave her shudder slightly in the crystal vase on the side table. Puffing from the effort, she quickly types a reply. *Please don't worry. I'm just having an early night. Speak tomorrow.*

Oli takes a final look around. So little in this house is hers. Isabelle has always been here, a silent housemate, the rightful owner. Once Oli walks out the door it will be like she was never here. She flicks off the light and pulls open the door. Freezing air swirls inside. The buzz of the rain. She's forgotten to set the security alarm again. Behind her the grandfather clock starts to chime. Fuck the alarm, she thinks, stepping onto the porch. She just wants to get out of here. Away from the house.

A hand clamps across her mouth, snapping her head back. An arm slams across her stomach, winding her. She writhes against her assailant, trying to scream, eyes bulging as she is dragged back into the house.

—

Oli comes to before she opens her eyes. Everything is red and black. She's woozy, like when she used to drink spirits. Legs heavy, she tries to get up but she's too tired. The clock chimes signal a new hour, but the sound is coming from behind her. Is she in the lounge? How many times did the clock chime? One? Four? Twelve? The sound reverberates in her head, and she can't tell the notes apart. It might as well have been a hundred. Why can't she open her eyes? And what is wrong with her hands? She realises they're tied together at the same moment she realises she's been drugged. Her wrists barely strain against the soft ribbon. Is it the belt from her dressing-gown?

Someone is here. She can feel footsteps. She must be lying on the rug next to the sofa.

Her eyes flutter open. Through the dark she sees the entrance hall lit by soft moonlight, the tulips in the vase. The muted green glow of the panic button next to the light switch.

A boot steps into her vision. Her core seizes as she kicks her legs out, tries to get up, but she is so tired. Everything fades again.

—

Oli blinks awake again. She's still on the floor, but she's less woozy. Everything hurts. She rolls onto her back, sharp pains shooting down her arms and legs. Her eyes move in an arc: the front door, the tulips, the ceiling. Rain streaks down the side window. No one will hear her scream if it's raining. No one ever did. All those nights as a kid, trapped in her room. The nights he didn't come were almost as bad as the ones he did; her eyes would burn as she lay waiting in the dark, her stomach twisting in knots as she made deals with god. If he doesn't come tonight she will never fight with Lily again. If he doesn't come to her room for the rest of the week she will stop biting her fingernails until her skin bleeds.

Winter was always the worst. The piercing silence of balmy summer nights kept her safe. Especially after the night she called out for Lily. Oli can still remember the sting across her cheek, her neck snapping to the side. She never screamed again, not out loud anyway.

Rain swirls away from the window, lifted by the wind, before it spatters back against the glass like blood. Oli whimpers. A searing pain surges near her temple. She closes her eyes briefly but senses light and opens them again. Headlights. A car turning into the driveway?

Pushing her bound hands against the rug, she lifts her head and torso, curls upwards. She looks around for her satchel but can't see it. There's no way she can get to the panic button—it's all the way across the room, and she can barely get up. Instead she wriggles sideways, trying to reach the gap between the couch and the side table. Part of her knows it's pointless: the moment the lights are turned on she will be seen, hunched over on the floor in her white coat, her blonde hair like a neon sign, but the desire to hide is overwhelming. With great effort she propels herself forward. Her body is flush against the wooden frame, and she pauses to catch her breath. Through the steady hum of rain is the distinctive crunch of gravel: footsteps. She flattens herself against the ground. Tears needle her eyes. God, she wishes Lily were here. She feels the scratch of her old blankets, smells her old bedroom. Footsteps are coming down the hall. Her heart catches in her throat. The doorknob twists, the door opens. Moonlight cuts across the tiles, and a hazy plume of rain billows in. A shadowy figure steps inside.

Time freezes. Fear is the only thing that moves, snaking along her body. The horrible familiarity of someone she loves acting like a stranger.

Dean slowly closes the door behind him. He's wearing sweats, an oversized black hoodie and sneakers. Oli's thoughts fly every which way. Where has he been? Did he attack her then go somewhere to change, to get rid of evidence, before . . . before what?

He goes to the base of the stairs. Cranes his neck and looks up. He stage whispers her name. 'Oli?' He turns to walk across the tiles and into the dining room. More alert now, she wriggles her way to the armchair. She peers around the side, watching as Dean turns on the kitchen lights. 'Oli?'

Every nerve is registering panic. She starts doing desperate, pleading deals with the universe.

Dean returns to the lounge, flicks on the light. She recoils, the glare causing her to moan softly. Her head throbs.

'Oli!' He rushes over. He takes her face in his hands, stares into her eyes. 'Are you alright? What's happened?' He looks at her hands, pulls the knot undone. 'Oli, what the hell?'

Her body freezes. She swallows, her throat aching, and ducks out of his grip, inching away.

'Are you hurt?'

She meets his gaze. 'Someone attacked me.'

'What?' He looks around, muscles tensing. 'Are you sure?'

'Yes.' Her deep voice is especially flat.

'Where?'

'Here. On the doorstep.'

He looks confused. Tilts his head. 'I don't understand.'

A strange sense of calm washes over her. Dean is lying, just like he always does.

'Oli, hey, tell me what happened.' A soft dent appears on his tan forehead. 'Who did this?'

'It doesn't matter,' she mutters. She just needs to get away from him. Where the hell is her phone?

He rocks backwards onto his feet, towering over her. 'Jesus, Oli, let me help you. I know I fucked up, okay? I'm so sorry, but I'm also worried about you. You're not yourself.'

'I know about the IVF.'

'What?'

'I know that the twins weren't conceived naturally.'

He crosses his arms, face reddening. 'You don't know what you're talking about.'

'I think you should go,' she says.

'What?' He seems incredulous. 'There's no way I'm leaving you here if someone attacked you.'

Oli stares at him. Maybe he doesn't know what he's doing. Could he be having episodes? Blackouts?

'Why are you even here?' she spits back. 'Why aren't you with the girls?'

Now he just looks perplexed. 'Because of your message.'

'What message?'

'The one you sent me.'

Her gut clenching, she staggers to her feet. 'I haven't been in touch with you since yesterday.'

'Oli, come on, this is crazy.' He reaches out his hand.

She yanks it away. 'Don't call me crazy!'

'Fine.' He pulls his phone from his pocket and thrusts it toward her. 'Look.'

She does, still slightly dizzy, and reads a text from her phone sent at 4.17 pm: *We need to talk. Please come home asap.*

She shakes her head vigorously, ignoring the pain. 'I didn't send that.'

His nostrils flare. 'Oli, come on.'

'I didn't!' Her voice catches as she backs away from him. 'You sent it to yourself, you must have.'

'What the fuck are you talking about? I only just drove here. Stop doing this.' Dean lurches toward her, and she screams. He grabs her arm, pulling her elbow so hard that it almost slips from the socket.

'You're hurting me!'

When he lets her go she reels back, falling hard against the floor. He scrambles after her. She kicks at his face, and he twists his head to avoid the heel of her boot. 'Oli, stop it.'

'No!' Still kicking at him, she half crawls toward the tiles, then turns and backs into the wall, holding her hands out in front of her. 'No. No. Stay right there. Get out of here or I'll call the cops.'

'Oli, this is insane.'

She bares her teeth, eyes wild. 'You need to leave.'

'Oli.'

'Jesus, what have you done?'

'What are you talking about?'

'Isabelle. You knew she was going to leave you, didn't you?'

'What?' His mouth twists into an ugly shape.

'You knew. And there was other stuff as well—things she suspected you of doing. I know, Dean, I know about O'Brien.'

'What?'

Oli slides her eyes to the panic button. Could he have disabled it? Surely if the light is on, that means it's still working. 'Just leave. Please.'

Dean runs his hand through his hair. 'No way, no way, Oli. You don't get to say stuff like that. You don't know anything.' He steps closer, his whole body shaking. 'We had our problems, but she was my *wife*. The mother of my *children*.'

Chills zap up her spine. Dean's eyes blaze. Behind him the rain rages against the panel of glass next to the front door.

'Sure, but maybe when you thought she didn't want to be your wife anymore, you, you—'

'Fucking say it!' he roars. 'Come on, say it!'

Oli gasps around her sobs. She can't get the air to her lungs.

'Say it!'

She lurches sideways as he comes at her, throwing her weight hard against the side table before losing her balance altogether. The table slides a good metre over the floor before the oriental vase teeters and crashes spectacularly across the tiles, white and blue fragments scattering everywhere. Oli lies face down on the floor, the noise ringing in her ears.

'You think I wanted her dead. Say it! Jesus *Christ*, Oli!' Dean lets out a howl. Throws both hands around the back of his neck, his veins like ropes, and pulls his head forward. A gesture of defeat? Of guilt? Or is he dreading what he is about to do to her? What he thinks he needs to do to protect himself.

The night turns white before plummeting back into darkness.

A figure stands in the doorway near the stairs to the garage.

Thunder shudders through the sky. Oli blinks. Looks back. No one's there.

Dean's expression is unreadable in the dim light. His footsteps crunch against the rubble of the vase as he makes his way toward her. 'Oli.' His face is grotesque; he might be begging, he might be apologising.

'I trusted you,' she chokes. 'But you—'

She feels it before she hears it. A muffled gunshot.

Oli doesn't move. There's nowhere to go. She waits for the pain.

There is total silence. A screeching, deafening silence. She locks eyes with Dean, trying to understand. His mouth lolls open. He jerks upwards as if pulled to the ceiling by an invisible thread before he falls forward.

Outside the rain comes down even harder.

All Oli sees is the blood.

SEPTEMBER 2005

Alex looks at her housemates. 'I think we all need to calm down.'

Evelyn is still crying. Nicole is sitting at the kitchen table, the fingers of her left hand splayed across the wood. 'Alex is right.' Nicole stares at her hand. 'We need to calm down. This has nothing to do with us.'

Evelyn looks desperately back and forth between the two of them. 'How can you say that? This is all our fault. *My* fault.' She glances at the TV again. The same images play over and over. 'It has to be.'

'Evelyn, stop it.' Nicole steps toward her and enfolds her into a hug. 'It's not your fault.'

Evelyn ducks away. Her hand pulls at her hair. She wipes her eyes. 'I think we should go to the cops.'

Alex is suddenly floating above her body, looking down at herself and her friends. 'We can't,' she whispers. 'We can't do that.'

'Alex, please.' Evelyn is crying now, her pretty face mottled, the skin pulled tight over her skull. 'This isn't okay, none of it. You know it isn't.'

Alex is tempted to put her fingers in her ears. Yell like a child. 'Nicole's right.' She gestures at the TV. 'I know this is awful, but it has nothing to do with us.'

'You're both crazy,' whispers Evelyn. She goes to the sink. Pours a glass of water, drinks it, then cries as she swallows, water dribbling down her chin.

'Hey, hey.' Nicole walks over to her. Takes the water glass and holds her.

Alex watches her friends. They are like strangers.

Evelyn pulls away. 'I just keep thinking about it, you know? Taking the photos. And I'm pretty sure one of them had the house number in it. We were in the front yard with the sprinkler, even though it was freezing.' Her pupils are so large that her eyes look black. 'I think someone must have recognised the house. That's how they knew where to find her.'

'You don't know that,' soothes Nicole. 'It's just a horrible coincidence.'

'It can't be.'

Nicole tucks a strand of Evelyn's hair behind her ear. 'Horrible things happen all the time.'

'I can't do this anymore,' whispers Evelyn. 'Before I could separate it from everything else, you know? It felt harmless. But now I can't. I'm out.'

Nicole pulls Evelyn to her again as she crumples, rubs her back and stares at Alex over her shoulder. 'Let's just see how we all feel in the morning.'

CHAPTER FORTY

TUESDAY, 15 SEPTEMBER 2015

SUDDEN PRESSURE ON THE SIDE OF HER TEMPLE, COLD AND HARD.

Dean is on the floor next to the upturned table, his face twisted in pain. He clutches at his leg. A whoosh of air leaves Oli's body.

'Don't move.' A low voice, like the rumble of a train.

She doesn't. She barely breathes.

The pressure relents slightly. She slides her eyes sideways.

A gun. Aimed at her head.

Her body changes gear, and she starts to hyperventilate. Dean really is involved in this network of evil. Someone has come here and shot him.

It sinks in. Someone has shot Dean. They will probably shoot her. She cries out, but the sound is lost in the storm.

'Not a good idea.' The voice is calm. Familiar.

Dean whimpers, and Oli glances at him. Blood is smeared on the white tiles around him. He's taken off one of his socks and wrapped it around his leg, breathing through clenched teeth as he grips it.

The gunman steps backward, gun still on Oli but his eyes on Dean.

'What the fuck, mate?' Dean huffs.

Oli lifts her gaze. It's Nathan. He looks bizarre wearing a beanie. He looks bizarre holding a gun. 'Hi, Oli,' he says.

Fury flashes across Dean's face. He moans and drops his head.

'You were teaching back then,' Oli whispers. 'You were a professor at the uni.'

'Yes,' Nathan says.

'They sold photos of little kids,' Oli says. 'The housemates. You knew.'

Dean's eyes widen. He doesn't know, Oli realises. He doesn't know about any of this.

Nathan looks annoyed. 'It was just a transaction. No one got hurt. That's what most people don't understand about all this—it exists on a scale, and for most individuals it's very manageable. It's completely natural, no harm done. I'm sure you'll agree it's a lot better than individuals acting on their feelings.'

Oli shifts slightly, inching closer to the panic button. Now that the table is lying sideways on the floor, the tiny green light seems so much more obvious on the white wall.

Nathan senses her movement, trains the gun at her head again.

'What about Louise Carter?' Oli spits. 'You're saying no harm was done to her?'

'That was different,' admits Nathan. 'One member of our group crossed the line.'

She still can't quite see how it all fits together. 'And the girls found out?'

He sighs. 'Evelyn was the problem. Nicole raised the red flag—she knew Evelyn was a risk.'

Oli is trying to follow. 'So you killed her?'

Nathan blinks. 'That's enough.'

'Nicole helped you that night, helped you set up Alex.'

Nathan stretches his neck. The barrel of the gun shifts between Oli and Dean. 'I don't know what you're talking about.'

'You killed Evelyn, and you set Alex up. Then you helped Nicole escape.'

'*I* didn't kill anyone,' he says primly.

Oli's brain feels like mush. 'But why would—?'

'It doesn't matter.' His voice rises a few notches. 'We sorted it. And now we need to sort this.'

The front door flies open. A man walks in.

Bowman. Wearing his trench coat and dark gloves. He's holding a gun, his jaw set.

Oli almost weeps with relief. Her muscles spasm.

Dean cries out in pain. She pictures the twins at the cemetery with Mary laying flowers on two graves. *Hold on, Dean,* she pleads. *Hold on.*

The front door closes with a thud, and Nathan smiles.

Bowman nods. 'We don't have much time.'

CHAPTER FORTY-ONE

BOWMAN LEVELS THE GUN AT OLI. HE LOOKS TIRED AND DISHEVELLED, but there's a disconcerting hardness to his gaze. A grim determination. Oli pictures him arriving at the Paradise Street house. Sitting at the back of the ambulance after the fire up in Crystalbrook. Walking away from her after they met at the pub. Crying at Isabelle's funeral.

They lock eyes. 'I did tell you to drop it,' he says reasonably. 'You and your friend. He was very keen to alert the uni about the pornography ring that he thought was being run under their noses. He had a very vivid imagination—and, I suspect, a little too much to prove to his new colleague.'

'Cooper,' Oli murmurs.

'I told your boss involving him in all this was a bad idea weeks ago. It's a damn shame that a violent meth-head liked the look of his jacket.'

Boss? Is Bowman talking about Dawn or Joosten, or someone else? All of Oli's senses are in overdrive—she can smell the slightly foul odour of stale water from the vase, while the white of the tiles burns her eyes, her heartbeat shuddering through her limbs. The storm has settled into steady, relentless rain. Her brain shuffles the facts like a deck of cards. Bowman knew how to kill Evelyn and make it look like Alex did it. He knew how to make someone disappear. He knows how to get away with killing Oli. With killing Dean.

'Isabelle,' Oli says slowly. 'She told you her theory about the housemates generating child pornography. She linked it to the uni. You knew she wouldn't rest until she brought the whole thing crashing down.'

Dean flinches but doesn't look up. His face has turned a disturbing grey.

She edges slightly closer to the wall. Bowman adjusts his hold on the gun, and she freezes. *Lily,* Oli thinks suddenly, *Lily is expecting me. She will know something is wrong, and she will . . . what? Call? Come over?* A slow sinking feeling takes over. Lily will just figure that Oli has worked things out with Dean, not believing that she will actually leave. Oli pleads silently, just like she used to. *Please, Lily, please. Help me.*

'I had a huge amount of respect for Isabelle,' Bowman says bluntly. 'She was smart and she deserved better.' He glares at Dean, who glowers at him through his agony. 'It was clear she was throwing herself into work to avoid problems in her marriage.'

'How far does this go?' Oli asks weakly.

'Quite far,' replies Nathan. He could be talking about the weather.

'Send the message, Nathan,' Bowman orders. 'We've only got about thirty minutes till I'm supposed to arrive here.'

Nathan fetches Oli's phone from the sofa and awkwardly types a message with his gloved hand. 'What else do you need?' he asks, throwing the phone to Bowman.

'Her over here.' Bowman points to the floor in front of him.

Nathan grabs Oli's coat and pulls her roughly along the floor, closer to the wall. Pieces of broken porcelain pierce her hands. 'Here?' he asks Bowman.

'Yep.'

'Do I need to stand anywhere in particular?'

'You were here earlier this week, right?' Bowman replies.

Nathan nods. 'Twice.'

'Just avoid the blood, then. You've sent all the texts?'

'Yep. All sorted.'

'You should go. I'll sort this out. Leave the gun and head home, have a shower. Watch a movie.'

'Right.' Nathan looks at Oli then briefly at Dean. 'Right then.'

Oli rocks up onto her knees. Dean lifts his head but it falls back against the wall with a thud.

Nathan stares at him.

'Go.' Bowman flicks his head at the door. 'Get out of here.'

After placing the gun on the floor with his gloved hand, Nathan nods politely at Oli and leaves.

'You're a piece of shit,' Dean says weakly.

'Shut up,' growls Bowman. 'Now listen. You two have a terrible relationship.' He turns to Oli. 'I know you thought Dean was involved in Isabelle's death and, conveniently, my boy Bouris is going to corroborate this. He's very obedient—especially after my little reminder yesterday.'

Through his pain, Dean looks at Bowman with pure hatred.

'I also had a good chat with your boss this morning. I filled her in on your fragile mental state and your theories about your fiancé. We're both quite worried about you.'

'You spoke to Dawn?' Oli whispers, tilting herself backwards. The button is now only a few centimetres from her head. She hopes she is blocking it from Bowman's view.

He ignores her but says, 'She knows you've been spinning further and further into a manic episode, wrongly identifying a young girl as a missing toddler. Clearly you are grieving for your murdered colleague. You even hired a car because you were so scared of your fiancé following you. Classic paranoia.'

'Evie *is* Louise Carter, isn't she? Isn't she?!' Oli cries out, throwing her head against the wall. The button digs into her scalp. She feels it depress. A soft click. *Please, please.*

'Louise Carter is dead.' Bowman sneers. 'Everyone except you thinks so, and you're crazy.'

'How are you going to hide the truth from her family?'

He shrugs, trains the gun on Dean, and looks back and forth at the distance between them. 'Easy enough to misplace test results. Honestly, forensics has made everyone so lazy.'

Oli feels Dean's eyes on her. She lifts her chin to Bowman. Even if help comes, it'll probably be too late. She glares at Bowman, and a sharp rage courses through her body, a boldness born from hopelessness. 'Isabelle trusted you, and you fucking murdered her. You're paedophile scum.'

He steps forward and cuffs her on the side of the head with the gun. She sees stars. Icy pain burns her skull. 'Who do you think you are?'

She is too shocked to cry.

'I warned her. I fucking warned her.' He spits. 'She knew how deep in she was.'

Oli looks over at Dean, whose eyes are closing. 'Dean!' she whispers.

'Shut up or you'll cop another one.' Bowman stalks into the kitchen.

Choking on her sobs, Oli turns to press the panic button several times with her nose. Chest heaving, she faces forward again and wills Dean to stay awake. To stay alive.

Bowman returns holding a knife. Oli's stomach tightens. It must be for her.

He places her phone on the floor near her foot. 'There's a real art to this, you know, like doing a puzzle backwards. You almost dialled triple zero.' He shows her the screen with the number. 'Unfortunately, you didn't quite manage to place the call.'

Dean stirs as if he's having a bad dream.

Oli senses an energy, tension in the air before an explosion. Her breath catches. Stays deep in her lungs.

Everything happens at once. All the doors swing open as if possessed. Icy air floods the house. Cops stream in, weapons raised.

Oli slides to the floor. Stares through the navy-clad ankles at Dean. She can't tell if he's still breathing.

CHAPTER FORTY-TWO

BOWMAN STRAIGHTENS, SNIFFS CASUALLY AND GESTURES AT OLI. 'Ah, thank goodness. I was just about to ring this in. A nasty domestic, I'm afraid. This woman is very confused, but I've removed her weapon.'

The cops don't even look at Oli.

'I'm not sure if he's going to make it, but I'd say it's self-defence.' Bowman jerks a thumb at Dean.

One of them steps forward. 'I think you'd better come to the station with us, Chief.' His gun is steady, aimed at Bowman's chest.

He scowls. 'I think you'll find she called me earlier, making all kinds of outrageous claims.'

A pair of paramedics enter the house. Heads down, they make a beeline for Dean.

Handcuffs are fixed around Bowman's wrists. 'This is ridiculous!' he splutters. 'She shot him. And he's implicated in the death of his ex-wife, DS Isabelle Yardley. One of our own.'

Someone grabs Oli's wrist, checks her pulse. *One, two, three, four. One, two, three, four.*

Bowman is led away, his protests fading into the night.

It's stopped raining.

'Where do you feel pain?' The paramedic peers at her, pulls her eyes open and shines a torch in them.

Her mind struggles with the question. 'Please help my fiancé, he's injured.'

'He's being looked after, don't worry.'

'Is he going to be alright? He was shot.'

'Let's just worry about you for now,' the paramedic says kindly, examining her temple.

Rusty appears. 'Oli.' He smiles tentatively at her, fear lurking in his eyes. 'Are you okay?'

She's trying to think. 'Why are you here?'

'TJ called me.'

'TJ? I don't understand.'

'He said you talked earlier—that you told him a whole lot of stuff, then hung up. Then you didn't return his calls, and he was worried. He got Dean's address from HR and turned up just as Bowman arrived. TJ saw him go inside, thought it was weird. He already had suspicions about Bowman feeding information to Dawn but assumed him being here was something to do with Cooper and didn't want to interrupt, so he got back in his car and waited. He called me, wanted to see if I knew anything. But by then the lady next door had already called the cops.'

'Toni?'

'Yeah. She didn't recognise the Toyota in the driveway, and she knew Dean was supposed to be away, so she couldn't work out why his car was there. She couldn't get on to him, then she saw TJ waiting in his car and was worried that someone was planning to rob the house. Apparently there've been some break-ins around here lately?'

Oli remembers Toni talking about the break-ins the evening she came over. 'Apparently.'

'Anyway, the cops arrived just as Nathan was leaving. He said he was on his way to call for help. Babbled some excuse about Dean losing the plot and wanting to kill you like he killed his first wife. It all sounded off, then TJ told us Bowman was inside.' Rusty pauses. 'And then a call came through that the panic alarm had been triggered in the house.'

'Jesus.'

Rusty nods. 'I voiced some doubts about Bowman. We spoke earlier today, and he told me you were . . .'

'That I was what?'

'Losing it. Said you'd been calling him day and night about a bunch of old cases. And when I asked him about the girl, he fobbed me off, said he had proof she wasn't Louise Carter. He said I should avoid talking to you for a while.' Rusty balls his fists. 'It just didn't sit right with me, not with what happened to Cooper. I called in backup.' He looks around the room. 'Thank Christ.'

'You know he's been doing this for years, Rusty. Decades. He and Nathan. And who knows who else.'

Rusty doesn't reply, just clenches his jaw and squeezes her hand.

The paramedic slides a pillow under Oli's head. 'You'll need to go to the hospital. That's a nasty knock.'

Oli ignores her. 'Rusty, the girl *is* Louise Carter. I know she is. You have to tell her parents, you have to call them. And we have to find the twins. Dean said they're with his mother—we need to call her.' She knows she's babbling, but the thoughts won't stop. Her head feels like it's about to explode.

'Oli, don't worry, it's all under control. You just need to relax, okay?'

'Where is Dean? How is he?'

Rusty looks over his shoulder. His Adam's apple jerks. 'He's going to be fine, Oli.'

She nods, wondering if Rusty's lying. If Dean is going to die. She thinks about Cooper in the hospital bed and closes her eyes. 'Is TJ still here?'

'Yeah, out front. Your neighbour has taken quite a shine to him.'

Despite everything, Oli pictures Toni in her expensive designer coat flirting with TJ.

'God,' Oli says as she starts shaking uncontrollably.

'I can't believe it about Bowman,' Rusty says quietly. 'I liked him, Ol. I really did. How could he do this? How did he hide in plain sight like this, and no one figured it out?'

'I don't know,' she says, her teeth chattering.

'Oli!' Lily is at the front door, her wet hair hanging in strands, eyes bloodshot.

'I called her.' Rusty smiles tentatively. 'I hope that's okay.'

Oli's face collapses. Lily edges around the room, behind the circle of cops, and makes her way over. She exchanges a look with the paramedic, who nods reluctantly.

Lily drops dramatically to her knees. 'Oh, Oli.'

Oli lets her sister hold her, debris from the vase prickling the backs of her thighs. Over Lily's shoulder she sees Dean lifted onto a stretcher. His clothes have been cut off and pieces of material hang from his body.

'It's okay, Ol.' Lily smooths her hair, kisses her forehead. 'It's going to be okay.'

Oli buries her face in Lily's chest. Breathes in her familiar scent.

Something that has been bothering Oli finally clicks. *I met her, the girl.*

Through the archway, Isabelle watches from the mantelpiece, gazing down at the blood and broken glass.

Hiding in plain sight.

Oli lifts her head. 'I think I know where Nicole Horrowitz is.'

HOUSEMATE HOMICIDE ARREST

Wednesday, 16 September 2015

By Cooper Ng and Oli Groves

Almost ten years after the death of Melbourne University student Evelyn Stanley, detectives swarmed the East Melbourne property of Professor Julian McCrae and his wife Diana to arrest 31-year-old Nicole Horrowitz, who was discovered in a studio at the rear of the house. Ms Horrowitz has been charged with several offences including child abduction, abuse of a minor, and the production, publication and circulation of child pornography, and will appear in court later today. *Melbourne Today* understands the McCraes have also been taken into custody and are expected to be charged with similar offences shortly.

Ms Horrowitz's arrest followed an evening of stunning revelations that senior police officials and high-profile individuals in the higher education sector, including Nathan Farrow, the Dean of Melbourne University, are embroiled in a decades-old child pornography ring, which is believed to be linked to the October 2005 murder of Evelyn Stanley in her St Kilda home and the concurrent disappearance of then-housemate Ms Horrowitz. In 2006 a third housemate, Alexandra Riboni, was convicted of murdering Ms Stanley and served three years in gaol before she was released under a ruling of self-defence. Ms Riboni's body was discovered in Crystalbrook last week after a suspected suicide.

Melbourne Today understands that Horrowitz and the McCraes are alleged to have been commissioning and circulating child pornography via illegal internet sites, and that these platforms may also have been used to target and locate specific children for the purposes of kidnapping and trafficking.

The child recently in Ms Horrowitz's custody is unharmed and was not at the property at the time of the arrest. Her identity and suspected long-term abuse is currently being investigated. Detectives are remaining tight-lipped regarding the rumours she is missing toddler Louise Carter.

The alleged involvement of law-enforcement officials in this investigation has reopened the debate about systemic corruption in the force and the protection of whistle-blowers. It is understood that several police officers have been targeted after lodging complaints, with various tactics used to silence them.

Melbourne Today believes the murder of a homicide detective several years ago may be linked to police cover-ups. A major taskforce has been established to investigate, and the chief commissioner is due to provide an update at a press conference later today.

CHAPTER FORTY-THREE

THURSDAY, 17 SEPTEMBER 2015

A FOOD CART RATTLES DOWN THE CORRIDOR OUTSIDE OLI'S ROOM. A nurse with hair curled tight like tiny springs noses it into the doorway. 'Orange or apple juice, love?'

'Orange, please.'

Oli's head still throbs but perhaps slightly less than it did yesterday. She presses the button to elevate the top section of the bed. Drinks her juice and listens to the nurse push the trolley around the ward.

Yesterday morning, TJ came straight from the McCraes' house to the hospital and persuaded a nurse to let him in even though it was well before visiting hours. He charmed the same nurse into bringing him a latte. Looking more haggard than Oli had ever seen him, he drank the coffee and told her about Nicole's arrest. Then he set up his laptop on a side table. He typed while Oli dictated the exclusive. He corrected the facts and helped her fill in the details, and she closed her eyes while he read it back to her.

She was asleep before he filed the story. Dawn was missing in action so he sent the piece straight to Joosten. When Oli woke a few hours later, TJ was curled in the hospital chair, snoring lightly, his neck bent to the left, legs stretched awkwardly out in front of him.

Lily and Shaun visited in the afternoon, and they all watched the news together.

Diana McCrae had taken a chance with Oli, concocting a story that placed her and her husband squarely in the centre of the story, hoping this would explain away their link to Nicole and any evidence that surfaced.

Wrapped in Lily's arms after Bowman was taken away, Oli remembered Julian saying he'd met the girl he thought was his daughter when he went to the house in Carlton, but Cara had told Oli she'd taken Evie shopping with her. Suddenly, Diana's willingness to share her horrible secret felt sinister. Opportunistic. The notes in Isabelle's diary made sense: she'd wanted the McCraes' house searched for signs Louise had been there, but the request was rejected. Oli is sure Nicole went to the McCraes after Evelyn died and took Louise from them rather than going through with their original plan of selling her to someone in the network. That wouldn't have been safe if either the McCraes or Bowman were worried Evelyn had said something about Louise before she died. Probably Bowman helped. Clearly they'd all been working together, then and now. Oli tries not to think about what had been in store for Louise before the plan changed. And she tries not to think about what Nicole has subjected her to since.

Oli drinks her juice and eats one of the muffins Lily left for her. Chewing slowly, she watches the news on TV and scrolls through Twitter on her phone. Graphics flash up behind Manny Cho's bald head: photos of the McCraes on holiday, smiling with their arms around each other. Next there's a photo of Nathan. *Respected couple and university leader revealed to be at the centre of child pornography ring* reads the ticker along the bottom of the screen.

Manny's face is even more serious as he covers the next story. CHIEF INSPECTOR LINKED TO HOUSEMATE HOMICIDE. A photo of Bowman in full uniform shaking the former premier's hand appears, followed by a statement from the Chief Commissioner of Police, who is stony-faced and simmering with rage. She abhors Bowman's alleged actions and vows to stamp out every single hint of corruption in the force.

Oli dozes for a while. When she wakes she calls TJ, and he tells her things that aren't yet public. The paedophile ring is far-reaching: two priests, a high school teacher, a sports star and two high-profile businessmen have been implicated so far, but it's suspected there are many more. Several of them met at university, including Bowman and McCrae. Three women have come forward, admitting their role in the operation; all of them were from troubled homes, needing money or desperate to avoid a low-level conviction. They sold photos of their siblings or cousins, guilt chewing away at them like a tumour.

A significant amount of pornographic content featuring Louise has been found online. The photographs range from her as a toddler to now. Presumably, taken and distributed by Nicole in exchange for money.

Oli pushes the food away, closes her eyes and imagines the torrid virtual rubble her peers are trawling through—the relentless leads and fact checking, the cautious lawyers stamping their feet. No one in the media is going to get much sleep over the next few days.

She falls into a restless nap. Oli's dreams and memories mix with the news updates, forming a strange montage of fact and fiction.

She emerges from the fog when the afternoon news anchor says Isabelle's name. Her case is officially being reopened. Links to organised crime and police force corruption are being explored. Tears run down Oli's face.

By evening the news sites have exploded with think pieces pondering how the housemates could have committed the ultimate betrayal. The *Sun* is launching a podcast called *Evil Women: Why They Do It.*

Overall, there's more outrage about the women involved than the male instigators.

Feeling a little stronger, Oli eats her dinner. Afterwards, she stares out the window at the city. Time feels slippery. Out of order. The scene at the house with Bowman and Nathan seems like it happened weeks ago. Before she fell asleep last night, one of the nurses told her that Dean's surgery went well, that he's been asking for her. She flicks her phone to silent and slides it across the bedside table. A nub of apprehension is forming in her gut. Dean's mother is bringing the girls in to visit him tomorrow; they want to see her too.

Oli changes the channel and tries to focus on a cooking show, but now all she can think about is Dean.

CHAPTER FORTY-FOUR

FRIDAY, 18 SEPTEMBER 2015

OLI ZIPS UP THE BAG THAT LILY BROUGHT HER AND SQUARES HER shoulders. The doctor has given her the all clear, but she's still a little fragile, as if she can't rely on her reflexes.

'I really think we should just go home,' says Lily, wringing her hands.

'No, I want to see him. Will you wait for me?'

'Of course.' Lily nods several times. 'I'll have some more terrible coffee in the cafe downstairs. Do you know how much parking is here per day? Honestly, it's outrageous. It's not like people are coming here to gamble.' She complains all the way to the lift. 'I saw on Facebook that all these fan pages have popped up for Nicole. People who reckon she's innocent.'

'People are strange,' Oli replies. If Cooper were here, he'd be obsessing over the different factions, planning out the next podcast episode with her. There's still no update on his killer—no doubt someone from Bowman's extensive network of evil. Oli hates the thought they might never know; his parents deserve the tiny shred of closure a name will provide.

Lily heads down to the ground floor, and Oli makes her way to the third level and asks for directions to room seventeen.

The doctor explained Dean's injuries to her this morning. The bullet missed his major arteries but lodged deep in his thigh. Despite the life-saving tourniquet he made, he lost a lot of blood. He also hit the back of his skull and needed seventeen stitches. Infection is still a risk, but he should make a full recovery.

Oli steps into the room. Dean is awake, sitting upright in the bed. She stifles a gasp. His head is shaved, his scalp alien-white. The left side of his face is dark with a bruise that stretches from his temple to the curve of his cheekbone.

Oli sits gingerly in the seat next to the bed. Takes his hand.

'Jesus Christ, I hate what they did to you, Oli.' Anger ripples across Dean's face, and he winces. He squeezes her hands gently.

She knows she looks terrible, with a ferocious black eye and a bulky dressing that covers the stitches along her hairline. 'I'm okay,' she says. 'How do you feel?'

'Like shit.'

'How do you think the girls are going?' Oli asks. She endured their awkward visit earlier, Mary hovering in the doorway.

He rolls his eyes to the ceiling. 'I don't know. They seem okay, but this must be bringing up some bad memories.' Tears shimmer in his eyes, and he grips her hands. 'I love you, Oli.'

A familiar feeling erupts in her chest: desire, and the heat of being wanted. It's so tempting to surrender to it, to let it take over and relinquish all responsibility for what happens next. 'I know you do,' she whispers.

'I can't wait to get out of here and have everything go back to normal.'

She forces herself to look at him. 'I don't think that's possible.'

He blinks. 'I had no idea about Nath, Oli, no idea. About any of it. I still can't believe it. I'm pretty sure the emergency he asked me to come back for was completely bogus. He was trying to create trouble between us.'

'I know.'

'I'll be home in a couple of days. Not as agile, obviously, but I'm fit so I should recover pretty quickly.' He gestures to the laptop on the side table. 'I've been reading up on gunshot wounds. Hopefully by our holiday I'll be close to full strength.'

'Dean, stop.' Oli doesn't drop his hand, but she looks away—at the window, the door. Anywhere but his beautiful eyes.

'Oli,' his upbeat tone shifts swiftly to pleading, 'help me out here. I don't know what to do. I feel so lost and sick about everything.'

'I'm sorry you're hurt, I really am, but you lied to me. You never told me you can't have kids.'

He stops moving and closes his eyes. 'I know, but I was worried it would make you change your mind about being with me. I wanted everything to be perfect. Plus you did say you weren't sure you wanted to have a baby anyway.'

'Not being sure and not being able to is quite different.'

'I really am sorry,' he says.

Oli swallows past the giant lump in her throat. 'It's not just that.'

Tension ripples down his arms, and he pulls his hands away. 'You're the one who thought I was capable of god knows what, Oli.'

They face off angrily, both taking deep breaths.

'I was wrong,' she says finally. 'But what does it say about our relationship that I could even think it? We don't trust each other.'

He bites his lip. 'I'll do anything to fix this. Anything.'

He's a little boy in a man's body who thinks that with enough money and enough spin, anything is fixable. She's been addicted to him for over a decade, never quite able to put the possibility of being with him to rest. And when his perfect life imploded all those years later, he sucked her back in. She was no match for the pull of the past; all those feelings simply thawed, strong as ever. She landed right back where she'd started, and Dean—confident, self-assured Dean—wasn't about to let the one thing that stood in their way be a problem. In Dean's world, problems are just things you throw money at until they go away.

Isabelle's death had rocked him, no doubt, but even that was a helpful twist of fate. He avoided a messy, reputation-damaging divorce and got to play the heroic solo father, eventually enticing Oli to replace a troublesome wife with one he thought would be far more obedient.

'I'm sorry, Dean, but it's not fixable with us.'

'Because you want to have a baby.'

She suppresses a surge of anger. 'No, that's not why.' She presses her fingers gently to her aching head, wanting to explain properly. 'I don't want to be *yours*.' His brow furrows. 'I don't want to be your *thing*. I don't want you tracking my every move, telling me what to do.'

'I don't want that either.'

'I know you've been tracking the car, Dean.'

He lifts his chin, slightly defiant, but says, 'I shouldn't have done that. I just felt safer knowing where you were. Especially after what happened to Isabelle. Surely you can understand that?'

Despite the earnest look on his face, Oli knows that her safety isn't the reason he wants to know her every move.

'You want a woman who does what she's told and is happy to turn a blind eye to whatever takes your fancy,' she says softly. 'It wasn't Isabelle, and it's not me.'

'Oli, it's always been you. Come on, you must know that by now.'

The years of longing flare. 'Except when it wasn't. Which was a really long time. No, Dean, I'm sorry, but it's not what I want.'

He looks stunned. 'Are you sure you're thinking straight right now? This feels like something we should talk about when I'm home.'

'I'm sure.' She holds his gaze.

He swallows and sniffs, pulling at the end of his nose. 'I have no idea what I'll tell the girls.'

Oli tucks her hair behind her ears. 'You should tell them the truth.' She feels the question in her mouth, uncomfortable like cotton wool. But in the end, it stays there. Whether the girls are Dean's biological children or not doesn't change anything. She doesn't need to know.

'I can give you everything you want, Oli.' His deep voice is firm, certain; the voice he uses for work calls, or when he's at a restaurant ordering wine. The trademark conviction that she found so magnetic. 'Everything,' he adds.

'You need to look after the girls,' she says, her voice firm. 'And yourself.'

His eyes turn red. 'I can't believe this.'

'I wish things were different,' she offers. 'I'm sorry this has to happen now, but it does.'

'Oli, please.'

'I've got to get going.'

'Home?'

She shakes her head. 'To Lily's. I was going to leave before all this.'

He visibly deflates. 'What about your things?'

'We'll sort all that out later.' She thinks of the ring wrapped in a tissue down the side of her suitcase which is probably still somewhere at Dean's. Or perhaps the cops have it.

Dean looks bewildered. She kisses his hand, places it on the bed. Looks back at him as she leaves. He's staring straight ahead, eyes wide, mouth slightly open.

As Oli walks to the lift, she doesn't feel sad, just numb. Like her insides have been scooped out.

Lily jumps up the second she sees her. 'How'd you go? Quick, let's go before we tick into another hour. It's already going to cost me sixteen bucks.'

They walk side by side.

Lily jabs at the button to the downstairs car park. She looks sideways at Oli before saying quietly, 'I just saw a news report confirming the girl is Louise Carter. They've done tests.'

Oli nods. Doesn't trust herself to speak.

Cooper's funeral is tomorrow. She needs to get through that, then decide what happens next.

CHAPTER FORTY-FIVE

FIVE WEEKS LATER

OLI FINISHES HER COFFEE, SIGHS AND RE-READS THE PARAGRAPH she just typed. She hasn't been crippled by this type of palpable anxiety about her writing for years. In some ways it feels good to care so much, for the stakes to be so high. On the other hand, it feels like jumping out of a plane without a parachute.

She and TJ have gone around the grounds on everything from the name of their new business to whether they should bother to set up a landline number. And now it's less than twenty-four hours until the launch.

'We're a modern newsroom, and for a while at least there's only the three of us,' TJ said last week, his eyes virtually falling out of his head after another lengthy planning session. 'I think we just list our mobile numbers and be done with it.'

'I agree,' Chelsea mumbled from her spot on the couch at TJ's place, where she was coding their website.

'We will grow, though,' Oli countered.

'So we'll sort out a different phone number, then.' TJ yawned.

'We need to settle on some target numbers,' she reminded him. 'What do you think, two thousand subscribers in the first two weeks? We've already hit over three hundred.'

'No way—two thousand subscribers on day one,' he replied, grinning.

'*Serial* had over a million downloads in the first week,' Chelsea said. She shrugged her tattooed shoulders. 'Just saying.'

Dawn was stood down from *Melbourne Today* a week after Bowman's arrest. It was ostensibly due to the restructure but no doubt hurried along by the fact he was blackmailing her to bury certain stories, as well as feeding her convenient leads now and then. A few years ago he'd learned she had recently accepted a bribe from a senior figure in the Catholic Church to pull a story on alleged abuse at a suburban church, and Bowman had agreed to keep quiet if she did him a favour from time to time.

Neither TJ nor Oli wanted Dawn's role. They handed in their resignation to Joosten together. He wished them the best of luck, confirming that the paper would be sold within months and that its future was uncertain. The poor man looked close to tears.

Thirty people were let go from the paper a week later, and Chelsea Waters, Cooper's colleague and film club friend, was one of them. Within forty-eight hours she was talking Oli and TJ through an unsolicited twenty-slide PowerPoint presentation and a social media strategy for their new business. Her contagious energy was the kick they needed.

And now the three of them are partners in a media company. It's a subscription model that charges members a few dollars a week and offers comprehensive investigations, researched pieces and in-depth interviews, plus a daily news podcast that will drop at midday. They have no idea if it will work but have assembled a small team of freelancers and committed to a year: twelve months of praying they can make a living from doing things their way.

The bell on the door chimes, signalling new customers. Oli glances at the clock above the counter. She has a childish desire to pull the pin on the meeting she arranged, but she wants to get this done, and she wants it done before their first edition goes live. As she pushes back her chair it scrapes noisily on the polished concrete floor, jarring with the pop song that blares from the tiny speaker system on the counter. She looks around in apology, but the cafe owner grins and holds her hand up in a friendly wave. 'See you soon!'

Oli smiles and waves back. Looping her scarf around her neck, she crosses the road to enter the Fitzroy Gardens.

Just over a week ago, she moved out of Lily's and into her new place just around the corner. It's small, with a private balcony and a communal garden. She has started swimming at the local pool again; she does fewer laps than she used to, but enjoys the meditative effect. It feels like a small part of her former self reclaimed, and she likes the numbing effect it has on her brain. Her mother and Max are coming to her place for dinner tomorrow night, along with Shaun and Lily, to celebrate the launch of the business. Oli has decided to make an effort with Sally—to try, anyway.

'All you can do is try,' Lily said, blinking back tears, when Oli spoke to her about it late one night after Shaun went to bed. 'It was horrible for you, unforgiveable, Oli, but she's a victim too. We all are.'

Oli doesn't react to Lily's well-meaning words. Her sister will never really understand what she went through but that's not her fault and she's just trying to help.

A trio of teenage girls walk past, giggling at something on a phone. One says, 'I cannot believe you wrote that! You're the *worst*.' The tallest girl smacks her friend's arm playfully then grabs her, pulling her into a hug. An electronic beep is followed by a shriek, hands clapped over mouths in exaggerated shock.

Oli glances at her watch, brushes invisible lint from her coat. Licks her finger and bends to wipe dirt from her boot. She knows she looks perfectly fine on the outside, but on the inside she's a mess. She thinks about all the times she waited for Dean, tarted up like a doll, her face painted in the way she thought he would like. Perched in tiny wine bars she'd never heard of, hidden in dark corners of expensive restaurants. Instructed to wait in hotel bars, something she'd endlessly misread as an entrée to a main meal that never came. Or didn't come for a long time, anyway.

She sits on the edge of the fountain. Moss is embedded in the concrete surface, giving it a marbled appearance. She dips her hand in the freezing water and plucks a few leaves out one by one, arranging them in a row.

'Hey.' Rusty sits next to her.

'Hi.'

He squints into the sun. 'Weather's still a bit all over the place isn't it.'

'Rusty.'

'It's okay, Ol, I get it.'

She turns to look at him.

He smiles. 'I sort of figured when you wanted to meet outside in the middle of the day that you were doing everything possible to avoid giving me the wrong impression.'

'Well, I guess I just feel a bit confused right now.'

'That's understandable.'

She bats him with her fist. 'Stop being so nice.'

'Okay, fine. I don't think you're confused.'

'I'm sorry?'

'I think you're just not that into me.'

'Rusty, I—'

He holds up his hands. 'It's okay, I know you care about me. I care about you too, but I'm not sure I can go there again. Not unless we're both sure, and we're not.'

They sit in silence for a few moments.

'You're excited about tomorrow?'

'I really am,' she says.

'It's going to be great.' He pauses, weighing something up.

'What?'

'I've just been at the prison.'

Her spine straightens. 'Tell me.'

'We are now sure it was Nicole who originally kidnapped Louise and took her to the McCraes. Someone in the network had offered over a hundred thousand dollars for her, and Nicole and the McCraes did a deal. Nicole took her, and the McCraes planned to keep her at their house for a few months before they offloaded her to the buyer. We think Evelyn found out, or that she suspected Nicole was involved somehow. When she threatened to go to the cops, the plan had to change. We think that's why McCrae went to Paradise Street that night. He was trying to intimidate Evelyn and make it clear that if she spoke about any of it, they'd come after her.'

'Jesus.'

'Yeah, and that's not all. Two inmates have made statements about killings they claim Bowman orchestrated—a priest who got wind of the paedophile ring in 2001 and was about to blow the whistle on his colleague, and a gang member who was causing Bowman grief.'

'So he was paying people off all the way back then?'

'Ol, it looks like this has been going on since the eighties. Yesterday, a retired cop came in who reckons Bowman planted drugs at the house of a constable he had an issue with. That was in 1989.'

'Is he still refusing to say anything?'

'He hasn't said a word. But we have Bouris's statement about Yardley's death, and Nathan is talking, so we've got more than enough to make sure Bowman's going to die in prison. We just might not ever know the full extent of what he's done.'

'He told me he was going to conceal Louise's identity, that he could falsify test results.'

Rusty shakes his head in disgust. Oli knows how much he hates the police force being compromised in this way.

'What about the fire at Crystalbrook?'

'We're sure he lit it, we're just not sure why. We assume he realised there was something that would link Evie to Louise or implicate him in some way. Or maybe it was just another way to make Nicole seem unstable and dangerous.'

'Thank god you weren't injured,' she says, shuddering. Then, 'I still don't get why Bouris humoured me the day I went to see him. Surely that was risky?'

'Apparently his missus shacked up with a cop a few months ago. I think he decided the deal he made with Bowman to protect his family was expiring. Apparently, he's been mouthing off to other inmates recently too. I suspect if all this hadn't happened, Bouris may have had an unfortunate accident.'

'It's all so precarious,' Oli murmurs. 'I still can't believe they thought they'd get away with it forever.'

'I know.' Rusty clears his throat. 'A detective has confirmed Isabelle suspected something was off with Bowman, that she lodged a complaint with internal affairs that was squashed. We're trying to connect the dots.'

'Holy shit. So this goes further than Bowman in the force? Higher?'

Rusty winces. 'You didn't hear it from me.'

''Course not.'

He coughs. 'Anyway, we're not making a statement until tomorrow afternoon, so I guess there's that.'

'Thanks, Rusty. It means a lot.' Birds dart past, and she watches them until they're out of sight. 'Is there still nothing to connect O'Brien to any of this?'

'Not yet. We're honestly not sure there's a link. There's still nothing concrete on Cooper's attack either, but we'll keep looking. We know Bowman was behind it, we just don't know who he called on to do it.' Rusty drops his head into his hands. His hair glints gold in the sun, and she stops herself from reaching out to run her fingers through it. She pats his back instead.

'Alex Riboni didn't kill herself, did she?' Oli asks quietly.

'I doubt it.' Rusty clears his throat. 'We think Bowman was in Crystalbrook the day before her body was discovered. We think he followed her there and warned Nicole away.'

Oli shakes her head. 'Jesus.'

'Nicole refuses to say a word about it. She will only talk about the night at Paradise Street and insists she ran away because Alex threatened to kill her too. She keeps saying both of the housemates had developed a serious drug problem and that both girls had become increasingly erratic and violent. She says she was scared.'

'I don't think Nicole Horrowitz is scared of anything,' muses Oli.

'I know.'

'Maybe the little girl knows something.' Oli still struggles to think of her as Louise.

'I'm sure she does, but we're being really careful in terms of interviewing her. She's been through a lot.' Rusty gulps a breath and lifts his head. 'I've got to go. Good luck for tomorrow, Oli.'

They hug. Oli thinks how easy life would be if she liked him more.

He smiles at her ruefully. 'I'll call you.'

For a few minutes, she watches people walk past. She traces the soft scar in her hairline as she turns the story over in her mind.

Two little boys and their mother sit next to her. Their father moves to take a photo.

Oli asks, 'Would you like me to take one of all of you?'

The man hands her the camera and slots in next to his wife. Hoists one of the boys onto his lap. Oli takes several shots.

'Thank you!' the man beams as he flicks through the images. 'These are great.'

'No problem,' she murmurs, before setting off toward her apartment. She plugs her earbuds into her phone, then FaceTimes TJ and Chelsea. 'I hope you're both ready for a long night. We've got a new launch story.'

MONDAY, 7 SEPTEMBER 2015

Nicole is living less than an hour away. With a child. It makes Alex sick to think about it. She always used to assume she would have kids herself one day, in that faraway adult life that she occasionally thought about. She and Miles even talked about it a few times, but after Evelyn died she could never picture it. Monsters don't have children.

At work she is Allie. A few months ago, a guy from marketing asked her out for a drink, but she just stuttered an excuse and pretended to answer her phone. She's avoided him ever since, waiting for him to finish in the kitchen before she gets her lunch from the fridge. He tried to talk to her again about two weeks later, but that was the day Laney, her co-worker, emailed her the photo of Nicole. Alex almost vomited all over her keyboard. It was Nicole, but she was going by the name Natalie. And there was a little girl in another picture, a girl called Evie with the same last name: Maslan. Alex remembered Nicole talking about an author she liked with that surname.

In the office bathroom a few hours later, Alex vomited for real. After wiping her face with a wet paper towel she returned to her desk, head exploding with the past. She reopened the email attachment and read an article about the environmental program in Crystalbrook. Alex's workplace is connecting the Crystalbrook community with an inner-city workplace and arranging for a group of staff to go to the Dandenongs for a sustainability excursion. Alex will be the project lead.

Nicole looks different in the photo, but Alex has no doubt it's her. Her eyes are the giveaway.

Alex copied the photos to her desktop, printed them out after hours and took them home to her tiny apartment. She stuck them on the bedroom wall next to the photo of herself with Evelyn and Nicole at the Paradise Street house. In the weeks since, she has spent hours lying on her bed, staring at them.

Knowing where Nicole is has done something to her mind. A crack has appeared in its darkest corner, and it's slowly splitting open. Memories are fluttering out like bats. They invade her dreams and have started to appear everywhere—on the bus, at work. She is remembering. Finally, the black hole is being filled with colour: she was pulled out of bed, the knife pressed into her hand. Heavy footsteps on the floorboards. The man's whispers. The threats.

And once she started to remember, it unlocked something in the universe. A reporter found her on Twitter and asked her to do an interview for a newspaper radio show. For the first time, the urge to talk is stronger than the urge to stay silent.

The following day Miles crossed the road in front of her in the city last week, just walked right past talking into his phone. His voice sounded exactly the same. She tracked him down at work. Called him and told him she's finally going to speak. That she wants to speak to him first.

Then the death threats came: one to her work, two to her Twitter account. Alex is used to being hated, but this isn't crazed vitriol. It isn't preachy or accusatory. Someone wants her to stay silent; someone knows she's planning to talk.

They are coming after her. She doesn't have long. But this time she's not scared. She has nothing to lose.

In the end, it's easy to track down Nicole. A few phone calls, some pretending to be Natalie Maslan, and she has Nicole's address: the cottage house on Laker Drive, Crystalbrook.

Alex gets on the bus in the city and sits near the driver, clutching her handbag. Her mouth is dry, but there's heat under her arms. Nicole's old ID is in there; it was in Alex's purse the night of the murder, and it was still there along with her belongings when she got out of gaol. She brought the death threats too, tucked inside her bag.

She looks at the other people on the bus. Teenagers, the elderly. A young mother with two little kids. Probably on their way to friends' houses, appointments. Going on adventures. Alex looks out the window as the bus groans slowly up the mountain. Admires all the green. It's so pretty out here, unlike the grey shades of her life in the city. Maybe one day she'll move to a place like this. Live among the trees.

Alex hesitates. Maybe Nicole has found peace in the hills. Maybe she doesn't want what Alex wants. She might be happy to let the past be, for justice to remain out of reach.

For the first time in years, Alex marvels at how it all happened. How fast things got out of control. Coaxing the kids into the bath, stripping them to their underwear, hands shaking as she took the photos. Heading into the library, eyes down as she logged on to the network using the fake account. Staring at the door while the files uploaded. Deleting the images. Doing it all over again. The money, though, the money had come, and that had felt good.

They had some rules. Never the same house twice. Never talk about it. They would stop as soon as uni finished.

But once Louise Carter went missing, it all fell apart. Evelyn was convinced the photos she'd taken of the toddler had led to her kidnapping. She wanted out, but she didn't want to go quietly; she wanted to scream it from the rooftops, burn it all to the ground.

Alex gets off the bus. She slides on her cheap sunglasses and looks both ways up the street. A short row of shops on either side, like in a country town. She gets out her phone, orientates herself. Walks toward Laker Drive. She barely notices the older man a few metres behind her, his white hair stuffed into a baseball cap.

She needs her old friend now more than ever. They were far from innocent, but they were still victims. They were threatened and Nicole was driven into hiding. They had their voices taken away. But Alex has found hers. It's time to admit what they did. It's time to expose everyone involved in the dark, twisted mess. With Nicole's help she is going to blow it all up.

She reaches the end of the dirt driveway. The trees whisper.

Alex hopes her friend is ready to be brave.

ACKNOWLEDGEMENTS

ONCE AGAIN, HUGE THANKS GO TO MY AGENT LYN TRANTER, PUBLISHER Jane Palfreyman and editor Kate Goldsworthy. I know I am very fortunate to partner with such a formidable trio of writerly women.

Thanks also to Deanne Sheldon-Collins for her helpful advice on the draft and the wonderful team of editors, proofreaders and book-birthing experts at Allen & Unwin. I am eternally grateful to have so many talented people cheering for my books.

David Hurley deserves a shout out for letting me tag along with him to court and answering questions about being a journo, as do several experts who provided invaluable insight into their professional worlds. The maddening reality checks and attention to detail is much appreciated.

My 'non-professional team' continue to provide endless support, distraction and encouragement throughout the writing process. Firstly, to my amazing children, Oxford and Linus, who I am so glad are genuinely interested in ideas and stories, and love asking how many words I'm up to. It's like living with two mini personal trainers. Thanks also to my parents, who once again were early readers of this manuscript, and provided positive and useful feedback, and to my sister, my family and my brilliant group of friends. I get so much from all of you.

Much of this book was written during a strict COVID-induced lock-down, and while it undoubtedly helped me meet my deadline, it also made me appreciate all the wonderful people in my life and the oxygen I get from them. I hope we will always lift each other up and do life together.

The idea for *The Housemate* lodged in my brain several years before I put pen to paper. It rattled around for a while, taking various forms, until eventually becoming clearer. Oli appeared and with her came Dean, Cooper, the housemates, and of course Isabelle. I liked the idea of Oli navigating the ghostly force of Isabelle while trying to build a life with Dean, and simultaneously cracking one of the biggest stories of her career. I was excited to write it but found attempting a standalone story nerve-racking after focusing on another leading lady for so long. But Oli proved herself to have as much determination as Gemma. After several months and a few false starts, I found Oli's (husky) voice and set about bringing her world to life. Cooper in particular was a joy to write.

Of course, I still can't believe it turned into a book. I hope you enjoyed reading it.